'Riveting and all too realistic. Cleave is a writer to watch.'

Tess Gerritsen

'Cleave lea⟨…⟩ ⟨…⟩ ⟨…⟩atering spectre of horror, never
knowir⟨…⟩ ⟨…⟩ ar⟨…⟩ ⟨…⟩orner, or turning of a
page.'

Suspense Magazine

'Dark, bloody, and gripping, *Blood Men* is classic noir fiction. In Paul
Cleave, Jim Thompson has another worthy heir to his throne.'

John Connolly

'An intense and bloody noir thriller, one often descending into a violent
abyss reminiscent of Thomas Harris, creator of Hannibal Lecter.'

Kirkus Reviews

'Anyone who likes their crime fiction on the black and bloody side should
move Paul Cleave straight to the top of their must-read list.'

Mark Billingham

'A pulse-pounding serial killer thriller . . . The city of Christchurch
becomes a modern equivalent of James Ellroy's Los Angeles of the 1950s.'
Publishers Weekly (starred)

'Paul Cleave writes the kind of dark, intense thrillers that I never want to
end. Do yourself a favour and check him out.'

Simon Kernick

'Gripping and darkly funny.'

Globe and Mail

'An intense adrenalin rush from start to finish, I read *The Laughterhouse* in
one sitting. It'll have you up all night. Fantastic!'

S.J. Watson

Praise for PAUL CLEAVE

ALSO BY PAUL CLEAVE

The Cleaner
The Killing Hour
Cemetery Lake
Blood Men
Collecting Cooper
The Laughterhouse
Joe Victim
Five Minutes Alone
Trust No One

A KILLER HARVEST

PAUL CLEAVE

MULHOLLAND
BOOKS
HODDER

First published in New Zealand by Upstart Press Ltd in 2017

First published in Great Britain in 2019 by Mulholland Books
An imprint of Hodder & Stoughton
An Hachette UK company

1

Copyright © Paul Cleave 2017

A CIP catalogue record for this title is available from the British Library

Paperback ISBN 978 1 473 69028 8
eBook ISBN 978 1 473 69029 5

Printed and bound in Great Britain by Clays Ltd, Elcograf S.p.A.

Hodder & Stoughton policy is to use papers that are natural,
renewable and recyclable products and made from wood grown in sustainable
forests. The logging and manufacturing processes are expected to conform
to the environmental regulations of the country of origin.

Hodder & Stoughton Ltd
Carmelite House
50 Victoria Embankment
London EC4Y 0DZ

www.hodder.co.uk

To Tim Müller and Craig Sisterson—
the next few G&Ts are on me . . .

ONE

The office used to be an old shipping container, its walls scratched and dinged and pitted with rust, now painted gray. These days the only traveling it does is on the back of a truck as it rolls its way up and down the country—a journey it makes once, sometimes twice a year. One of its two long walls has been removed to make way for a door and for a window that over the years has looked out over empty lots as they've become apartment complexes and office blocks. Its current view is of a seven-story building. A few of the floors haven't evolved much beyond steel beams and slabs of concrete, all of it is surrounded by scaffolding stained with dirt and paint and sweat.

The inside of the office has found a way to attract cobwebs, and at the same time repel any warmth, both of these things making Detective Inspector Mitchell Logan shiver as he stands inside it on what so far has been a perfect Christchurch summer morning. The walls have been plastered over, and pinned to them are survey maps and design sketches and blueprints and photographs. There's a rack holding half a dozen hard hats by the door, with a sticker beneath it that says A HARD HAT A DAY KEEPS THE CONCUSSIONS AWAY. The dust on the window is thick enough to double the thickness of the glass. There's a desk full of papers, and on the other side of that desk an annoyed-looking foreman by the name of Simon Bower. Bower has slicked-back brown hair and what, up until recently, Mitchell would have called a Unabomber beard, but what his wife has recently pointed out is now called a hipster beard. Bower is a good-looking guy approaching his midthirties, tanned, athletic, and, by the way he keeps looking at his watch, impatient too.

Mitchell glances at his partner—Detective Inspector Ben Kirk—and looks for any sign his friend is cold, but Ben doesn't show any.

"What kind of questions?" Bower asks, looking at his watch again, as if to make sure it hasn't been lying to him.

"It's all fairly routine," Mitchell says—only it isn't. None of this is. Mitchell is forty years old, and is fast approaching the date when he will have spent exactly half his life on the force, and in that time he's learned that the bigger the lie, the bigger the secret. Today the lie is going to be massive. The man they are here to see is going to tell them he was on the other side of the planet visiting his sick mother in hospital. He was on a boat in the middle of the Pacific Ocean rescuing dolphins. He was orbiting the moon. He was anywhere except for the one place they know he had been—Andrea Walsh's car. And where is Andrea Walsh? They don't know. But the bloody power saw found near her car suggests she could be discovered in a variety of places—all at the same time. Not only was there blood on the saw, but hair and bone and pieces of flesh, some no bigger than a splinter, others the size of a knuckle, including, what the medical examiner told them, was an actual knuckle. The car was found abandoned two nights ago, pulled up off the motorway, out of petrol. A motorist who had almost run into it reported it. The police had not been able to contact the owner and, the following day, had begun to search the area. The bloody saw was found in a ditch fifty yards off the side of the road with the knuckle lodged under the retractable guard.

It was a mistake for the saw to be dumped so close to the car—but Mitchell is sure whoever dumped it felt it was the better alternative than walking down the motorway with it. The power saw had a serial number. The serial number told them it belonged to a construction company. That is what has led them on a path to this very shipping-container office to talk to this very foreman.

"So why do you need to know who the saw belongs to?" Bower asks. "Somebody steal it?"

"Something like that," Ben says.

"Don't you . . . like, you know, don't you like need a warrant or something?" Bower asks.

"We'd need one, if we were here to search the premises," Ben says.

"And we'll get one, if we need to," Mitchell says.

"Only we know there's no need," Ben says, "because we're not here to look around, we're here to talk to who uses the power saw that matches that serial number, and you're going to tell us who that is."

"All this for a stolen saw?" Bower asks.

"Just give us a name," Mitchell says.

"Fine, don't tell me then." Bower breathes heavily and does his best to sound put out as he moves his coffee cup to the side and slides some papers off his computer keyboard so he can tap at the keys. After a few seconds of typing and clicking, he starts to nod. "Oh," he says.

"Oh?" Mitchell says.

"The saw belongs to Boris McKenzie," Bower says.

"And?" Mitchell asks.

"And Boris is . . . well . . . a bit of a hothead. He's a good guy, a hard worker, but . . . just a suggestion, if you're here to hassle him for something, you might want to bring reinforcements. He can fire up pretty quick."

Okay, so it's not the biggest lie Mitchell has ever heard. It's not up there with him saying he was busy saving kids from a burning orphanage, but it's definitely a lie. Mitchell looks at Ben, and Ben gives him a slight nod. It's what they had expected.

"And where do we find this . . . ?" Mitchell asks.

"Boris McKenzie," Bower says. "He's on the fourth floor."

"What's it like up there?" Ben asks.

"It's easy to find."

"That's not what I asked."

Bower shrugs. "A mess, I guess. Some half-completed offices, some open planning."

"A bit of a maze then?" Ben asks.

"I wouldn't put it like that, but yeah, maybe."

"How about you show us the way?" Mitchell asks.

"I got a lot of work to do," Bower says, and proves this by looking again at his watch, and wincing while doing so, as if every passing second is hurting him. "We're behind schedule as it is, and to be honest, I don't really want Boris knowing it was me who sent you to him."

"A place like this, with all these materials and tools and open walls with big heights, it's better we know exactly who we're looking for and where we're going," Mitchell says.

"Plus, it's a hazardous area," Ben says. "Neither of us wants to end up getting electrocuted or having a steel beam dropped on us."

"Which means you're coming with us," Mitchell says.

"I really have to—"

"What?" Ben asks. "Impede an investigation? Or be a good citizen and do your best for the community?"

Bower exhales loudly again, then moves around the desk and grabs a hard hat. He hands one each to Mitchell and Ben. "You go where I go," he says. "And you do what I say. It's a danger zone up there if you don't know what you're doing."

"Exactly why you're coming with us," Ben reminds him.

They follow him outside. The warmth of the morning masked by the office comes back. They cover the twenty yards to the building, passing electricians' vans and plumbers' vans and glaziers' vans. There's the *beep-beep* of a cement truck backing onto the site. There's activity from every direction as things are measured and cut and poured and connected. They reach the elevators, which, Bower tells them, were installed four weeks ago. "Otherwise right now we'd be climbing a hell of a lot of ladders," he says.

Mitchell thinks the constant sound of power tools firing up and winding down would make him go crazy. Workers are yelling and arguing and laughing and Mitchell keeps waiting for somebody to shout *look out* as something heavy falls towards him. It's a relief to get inside the elevator, where there is no elevator music and no elevator small talk as they take the ride. The doors open. The building is as much a shell inside as it is out. There are internal walls with cables hanging out of them. Cables hang from the ceiling too. Nothing has been painted. No flooring has been put down—there's just concrete sprawling out in front of them, covered in sawdust and metal filings and the occasional nail. There are some windows, but there are also areas where windows haven't been put in yet, those gaps covered by polythene that flaps in the slight breeze.

"Watch your step," Bower says.

"How many people are on this floor?" Ben asks.

"Only Boris. And now us. Most of the crew are putting in big efforts on the ground floor today, but Boris is replacing some drywall that got damaged."

"I can still hear other people," Ben says.

"Once the windows and insulation are all in you won't hear a thing outside of this floor," Bower says.

Ben reaches inside his jacket and pulls out a gun. He points it at the floor.

"Bloody hell, is that necessary?" Bower asks.

"It is if Boris is as big a hothead as you suggest."

"This isn't just about a stolen power saw, is it?" Bower says.

"I think it's best we separate," Ben says.

"I agree," Mitchell says, pulling out his own gun.

"Maybe I should go," Bower says.

"Just stay behind us," Mitchell says. "You want left or right?" he asks Ben.

"Left."

"You're with me," Mitchell says, glancing back at Bower.

Ben goes left. Mitchell and the foreman go right. A sparrow flies down the corridor towards them, looking for an exit, and a moment later another one follows it. Mitchell can smell plaster. He keeps his gun pointing at the floor. Bower never strays any farther than a few footsteps. They reach the end of the corridor, where one of the windows has been installed, a six-foot-square view looking out over the office below. The glass dulls the sound from outside. Mitchell can see a truck dropping off more supplies and the cement truck still backing into position.

The next corridor isn't much different from the one they step out of. Drywall that's been plastered but still needs painting. Cables everywhere. Hand tools and sawhorses and two- and three-gallon pails of paint stacked along the walls, lengths of architrave next to boxes of nails and screws and soon-to-be-installed light switches, a nail gun and a tile cutter and bags of grout. Mitchell checks the rooms they pass and sees more of the same, some with windows, some with polythene. At the end is a six-foot window identical to that in the previous corridor, only this time instead of glass, a thick piece of polythene covers it. It's clear enough that he can make out the mounds of dirt and a few vehicles below, but not in any detail. All in all, not much of a view.

He turns back to check on Bower. "We should—"

He stops talking. Bower has picked up the nail gun they passed earlier and is now pointing it at him.

"Wait," Mitchell says.

Bower doesn't wait. He squeezes the trigger. Detective Mitchell feels no pain, just a tugging at his body, a tightness in his arm, then his chest, like his muscles are being squeezed. He tries to raise his gun, but his arm won't move. The nail gun makes a popping sound, another and another. There are four, five, now six nails in his chest. The gun falls out of his hand. He raises his other hand to pull at the nails, but before he can manage it one punctures his palm and goes right through it, sticking his hand to his shoulder. Still there is no pain, only numb pressure points across his body, acupuncture on a giant scale. There is a thud as a nail skims off the side of his hard hat.

"You've ruined everything," Bower says.

"Don't," he says, but he knows that isn't going to stop Bower. This is the moment when his nightmares come true. He can see the police visiting his wife. He can see her collapsing at the news. He can see the police looking into his past and uncovering all the bad shit he's been doing for the last five years, bad shit he wanted to take to his grave—which he guesses is what's about to happen. He drops to his knees. The smell of plaster is weaker. The concrete mixer isn't as noisy. He can no longer hear the cement truck backing up. He can taste blood. There are more popping sounds. Pressure in his neck. In the side of his face. Bower moves in closer. He places his foot against Mitchell's chest and there's nothing he can do to stay balanced as the foreman pushes him backwards.

The polythene separating the inside world from the outside holds his weight for a second, and then another. Then it stretches. It sags in the middle, then stretches some more.

Then it tears.

Mitchell looks up at the building as he falls. He slams into the outer railing of the scaffolding and instead of bouncing inwards, he bounces out, and he thinks, *Just typical* as he passes the third floor, the second floor, the first floor, gaining speed as he drops.

He doesn't hear his bones shatter when he hits the ground.

Doesn't feel his spine or his neck snap.

He doesn't feel anything.

TWO

When Ben Kirk moves into the corridor, his view is of his partner's feet as they disappear from view. Standing next to the torn polythene staring outwards is Simon Bower. The rage is immediate. Ben points his gun at the foreman and his hand is shaking and the urge to squeeze the trigger is immense.

"Don't move."

Bower doesn't move. He keeps looking outside.

"Put the nail gun down," Ben yells, "then slowly turn around to face me."

Bower doesn't put the nail gun down. He turns around holding it. "I don't know what you think happened," Bower says, "but it's not how it looks. Boris ran at him. They both went through the plastic. They're both down there. We need to help them."

"You've got two seconds to put the nail gun down before I open fire."

Bower puts down the nail gun.

"Face the wall," Ben yells.

"Your partner is down there," Bower says. "You're wasting time here."

"You put him down there."

Bower shakes his head. "I tried to warn you what Boris was like. I tried to stop it from happening. We need to hurry. Your partner is going to die if we don't do something."

Ben knows that unless Mitchell is hanging on to the scaffolding, he's already dead. The idea of that . . . it hurts, it breaks his heart, and it's going to break a lot of other hearts too. There has to be some way to take it all back, a big reset button, only there isn't—there's just death and pain. The only thing holding him together right now is the anger, and he has to hang on to it. If he lets it go, he's going to collapse.

"Face the wall and put your hands on it above you."

Bower complies. Ben moves over to the gaping hole in the polythene and looks out at the scaffolding where his partner isn't. People are yelling from the ground and moving towards something he can't see from this angle, but he knows what it is. He can feel something tearing in his chest. He can feel something inside him starting to snap. A certain kind of rage that needs a certain kind of release.

He's tempted to throw Bower through the window.

He takes a deep breath. He has to get himself under control. He reminds himself why he came here. "What do you weigh?"

"What?"

"You look like you take care of yourself. You run?"

Bower starts to turn back.

"Keep facing the wall and answer the question."

"What question?"

"You look like you run. You look like you hit the gym a little too. What about smoking? Are you a smoker?"

"What? No, no, I don't smoke. But what are—"

"You drink?"

"What the hell are you getting at?" Bower asks.

"Answer the question. Do you drink?"

Bower tries to turn again, but stops when Ben pushes his gun into the back of his neck. "I . . . I guess, on occasion, yeah, I drink. But not much. I run a little, but not much."

"You got cancer? You sick at all?"

"I want my lawyer."

Ben pushes the gun in harder. "I asked are you sick?"

"No. I'm not sick."

Ben pulls the trigger.

The bullet goes through the back of Bower's neck and out the front of his throat, making a mess of the wall ahead of him, but nothing some plaster and paint won't fix. Bower wraps his hands around the wound while falling to his knees. He twists towards Ben. The confused look on his face disappears as his body relaxes. His mouth opens and closes as he tries to say something, but the only sound he can make is a thud as he falls forward and hits the floor. His hands slip away from his throat. There's a pool of blood spreading beneath him.

Ben uses a handkerchief to pick up the nail gun. He fires it in the direction he came from earlier, shooting half a dozen shots into the walls and down the corridor. The seventh shot he fires into his arm. It doesn't hurt as bad as he thought it would, and for the moment there's hardly any blood. He drops the nail gun onto the floor. None of his colleagues are going to go out of their way to disprove his version of events—that Bower shot at him first, and he returned fire in self-defense.

He crouches down in front of Bower. The man is still alive and watching everything Ben is doing, and most likely figuring out what it all means.

"We knew it was you before we even came here," Ben says.

Bower says nothing.

"We were in your house before we came here this morning. We found your bloody clothes and her necklace, and my advice to you is you shouldn't cut out newspaper clippings of people you've killed and leave them on the coffee table. We knew you were bullshitting us about Boris, but you still got one over on us, you son of a bitch."

He reaches out and pinches Bower's nostrils shut, and Bower squirms a little but doesn't have the energy to do anything more than that. His eyes widen and blood starts drooling from the side of his mouth. Ben lets go.

"You're probably curious as to why we brought you up here, and didn't arrest you downstairs. Tell you what, if you tell me where Andrea Walsh's body is, I won't let you die wondering."

Bower manages to raise his hand. He turns his palm upwards and gives Ben the finger. Then he smiles.

"You tell me where her body is, or I'm going to hold a press conference and say we found a hidden directory on your computer that was full of child porn. That's going to be your legacy."

Bower lifts his other hand, and uses it to point at the hand that's giving Ben the finger. His smile widens, and he coughs, and blood comes out his mouth and his nose.

"So be it," Ben says, and he reaches forward to pinch Bower's nostrils shut again, but realizes there's no point. The man is already dead.

He pulls out his cell phone and makes a call.

"Two minutes," he says, then hangs up.

He wraps polythene around Bower's neck to contain the blood so he doesn't get it all over himself. He pulls the nail out of his arm and the blood starts to flow. He hauls Bower up into a fireman's lift and gets him to the elevator. He calls the station when he's on the ground floor and tells them what's happened. He tells them both Mitchell and his killer are being rushed to the hospital. He removes the plastic from around Bower's neck.

When the ambulance arrives, the paramedics look at the two dead men and don't try to save them. There's no point. They don't make any conversation as they get the bodies loaded into the back. Ben takes Mitchell's hand and tells him he'll honor the promise he made him if something like this ever happened, then the ambulance tears out of the parking lot, and a few minutes later police cars tear their way in. A second ambulance shows up. Police officers are ushering back the construction workers and setting up a cordon. A paramedic who smells and sounds like he spends a lot of time hanging out with cigarettes takes Ben into the back of the ambulance. He sounds miffed when Ben tells him he doesn't want to go to the hospital to have his arm checked out, that all he wants right now is to have it patched as best as he can. Police tape starts going up. There are so many people moving around, dirt and dust is getting kicked into the air.

Detectives start arriving. They have questions for him, and he promises them he will explain everything soon, but right now he has to leave. There's a clock ticking and a lot that needs to be done. He ducks under the tape, and his arm is throbbing and the paramedic warned him it would only get worse, but for now he wants it to hurt. He wants to suffer. He gets to his car. An hour ago there were two of them, now it's only him. He sits and stares at the passenger seat, remembering the conversation they had on the way here, remembering other conversations, other times, other close calls and near misses and the adrenaline rushes and the heartbreaks.

It's always been the heartbreaks that made him and Mitchell try to improve the world.

"I'm sorry," he says to the partner who is no longer there, and he clenches his jaw and swallows down his anger and his sorrow, because there'll be plenty of time for that later. Now he needs to stay calm and keep it together. The drive to see Michelle Logan is the hardest he's ever had to make. *Mitchell and Michelle—cute names for a cute couple*, he thinks. The kind of meant-to-be names. And they were meant to be. Everybody who knew them knew that. High school sweethearts who have been together for twenty-five years. Ben has known them that entire time—there were four of them who were best friends through high school, Mitchell, Michelle, Ben, and Ben's brother, Jesse. They were all in the same classes together, they had the same circle of friends, went to the same concerts and drank the same beer at the same parties, they smoked weed and swam at the beach and queued up outside nightclubs and did a million other things together as they grew up.

The partying stopped when Mitchell applied to police college—he went from smoking a little bit of weed to arresting those doing the same thing. Michelle went to university and spent five years studying to become a veterinarian, while Jesse went to teachers' college for three years, then started teaching. Ben broke up with his girlfriend to go and see the world, working behind bars and doing the minimum to scrape by. He did that for five years, coming back when Jesse got sick, which was around the same time Mitchell's sister died, sixteen, almost seventeen years ago now. Ben came back unemployed and with no direction. Mitchell convinced him to apply for the police force, and now . . . now he's turning a ten-minute drive into twenty because that will give Michelle a little extra time of not knowing.

The veterinary clinic she co-owns is in the north of the city. It shares its parking lot with a hairdresser and a pharmacy and a clothing outlet store. He parks next to a red BMW in which a woman is having a conversation with something in a cage that he can't see. He gets out and leans against his car and considers how he's going to break the news. He's done it before, but never to anybody he knows. A guy in a shirt and tie walks out of the front entrance of the clinic carrying a cat's cage at arm's length. His sleeves are rolled up and there are fresh claw marks up and down his arms. The man notices Ben's bandaged arm and nods at him, sharing a *cats, huh?* look, and Ben finds himself nodding back.

He can't put this off any longer.

He's most of the way to the door when it opens again. Michelle comes outside. At five feet nine, and with wavy red hair that reaches below her shoulders, Michelle always drew a lot of attention back in their school days, and is more beautiful now at forty than she was at twenty. This is going to destroy her. It already is. She's already crying, and he knows she must have seen him through the window with the blood on his shirt and the bandage on his arm and that's all it takes for the partner of somebody in law enforcement to know that her deepest fear has caught up with her.

"How bad?" she asks.

"I'm so sorry," he says, which tells her everything she needs to know. He wraps his arms around her and tries to hang on tight, but it's not tight enough and her legs go out from under her and she sits on the step and he sits next to her. He can see people staring out the windows at them, some with hands to their mouths. She sobs into his chest. He can feel his own tears on their way but he hangs on. He has to.

"How did . . ." she whispers, and the words get stuck and nothing else will follow.

He tells her how it happened, all the while looking down at the hot, gray asphalt.

He wipes a finger at his eyes. "There's something else."

"What kind of something?" she says.

He tells her about the promise Mitchell asked him to keep, with the hope she will agree to it.

THREE

Joshua doesn't know why he's cursed, he just knows that he is. He doesn't know how many generations back it goes, but he does know he's inherited it. Inherited it from parents he never knew. His dad jumped in front of a bus a few months before Joshua was born. He did it to save a small girl he'd never met who had slipped away from her mother's grasp and had stumbled into the street. This selfless act made his dad a hero, but he was a hero who wasn't around because of it. His mother, on the other hand, was in his life for five months before meeting a bus of her own, in the form of a brain embolism. Joshua was in a bouncy harness hanging from a doorframe when it happened, his feet barely touching the floor. Not that he remembers it. She strapped him in, and somewhere between Joshua and the hallway, everything in her head switched off. She was dead before she hit the floor. It was one of those things that the curse had placed on their road map. He bounced and cried and filled his nappy and went hungry as the afternoon turned to night turned to morning, and that's when a neighbor came over to see why the baby wouldn't stop screaming.

Predestination. It's been a long time since his mind has churned up those chestnuts, but right now his mind is playing an automatic form of word association because of what Mr. Fox, his science teacher, is lecturing about. He's talking about eye color. He's talking about genetics, which is a word that always makes Joshua think of the curse, because family curses are in the DNA too—Mr. Fox may not agree, but Joshua sure knows it's true. Mr. Fox is talking about how eye color is passed down from parent to child, what the combinations are, but really, it's a hard topic to care much about when you don't know what *blue* or *green* or *brown* even means. Joshua's eyes are blue. So he's been told. He knows the ocean is blue. He's been to the ocean, but he's never seen it. He's played in the sun and sand, and sometimes the water is warm and sometimes it's cold, sometimes he'll stand on a stick or a seashell and it'll hurt like crazy, sometimes he'll lie on the sand and feel the sun on his face, but none of that tells him what blue is. The sky is blue. Smurfs are blue. When people are sad, they feel blue. But Joshua's world is black. It has been his entire sixteen years. The curse made sure of that.

He shifts his legs and straightens himself behind his desk. His back is getting sore, and his legs are becoming numb and this lesson has slipped beyond boring and into the realm of pointless. Others in the classroom are repositioning themselves too. It's not unheard of for students to fall asleep in Mr. Fox's classes. Rumor has it a kid even wet his pants while taking a nap a few years back. Joshua stifles a yawn. He stayed up late listening to a horror novel about a guy who could put his fingers into his victims' eye sockets and see everything they have ever seen. It made Josh wonder what he would see if he could do the same thing, only he wouldn't know what he was seeing. It would be like learning a new language.

There's a knock at the classroom door, and Joshua is grateful because the sound stops him from falling asleep. Hopefully it will be somebody coming to say that school is finishing early for the day. "Excuse me for the interruption," a woman says, and it's the school secretary, Mrs. Templeton. "I need to borrow Mr. Fox for a moment."

There's the sound of shifting chairs and turning bodies as all fifteen students follow the sound of footsteps across the room. She says something else then, something too low for Joshua to make out, but then the door closes, and when there are no more footsteps he figures that Mr. Fox and Mrs. Templeton are out in the corridor discussing something. He's always wondered what she looks like. Mr. Fox too.

All at once, different conversations in the classroom start up. His friend next to him, William, says that Mr. Fox is probably being fired for being too fat. Pete says he bets they're out in the corridor with their hands all over each other. Others laugh and agree, then they all go quiet when the door opens back up.

"Joshua?" Mr. Fox says. "I'm going to need you to get your bag and go with Mrs. Templeton."

At first it doesn't register that he's the one being spoken to. Why would Mrs. Templeton want him?

"Joshua?"

The others make a collective *ooh* sound. Mr. Fox tells them to be quiet. Joshua grabs his bag and uses his cane to guide his way to the front of the class. "Have I done something?"

"Everything will be explained," Mr. Fox says. "Please go with Jenny . . . I mean, Mrs. Templeton."

He makes his way out of the classroom.

"This way," Mrs. Templeton says.

"Can I ask what it is I've done?"

"You haven't done anything," she says. "Principal Anderson needs to talk to you."

"About what?"

She doesn't answer. She starts walking. He follows her. With the hallway empty of students, the sound of his cane echoes as it taps against the ground. Whatever it is they think he did, it's all a big misunderstanding. A school of blind kids also means a school full of mistaken identities. Sometimes you can't know who pushed you over or stole your lunch. Yesterday somebody pulled the fire alarm, which always gets a laugh in hindsight, but isn't funny when you can't see the flames that may or may not be coming for you, flames that you might not hear over the sound of the alarm and stomping feet, smoke you might not smell until it's too late. Is that what this is? They think he's the one who pulled the alarm?

He has to use his cane more when they go up a flight of steps. This is new territory for him. This is bad-kid territory. He's never been to the principal's office before. It smells of books and old cigars, and the door makes a creaking sound when it closes behind him. It reminds him of his dad's study—though he's not technically his dad. Technically his mom and dad are his aunt and uncle—they took him in after his parents died, and his last name was changed to their last name. His biological mom was his dad's sister.

"Please, take a seat, Joshua," Principal Anderson says. His voice is deep and slow, and Joshua can tell from its direction that he's standing. It's the first time the principal has ever addressed him.

"Is this about the alarm?" Joshua asks, then immediately wishes he hadn't. Asking about it makes him look guilty.

"If you take a seat I can explain everything to you."

"It's going to be okay," Mrs. Templeton says, which doesn't feel like a good thing to hear. It seems the kind of thing one would say when the opposite is true. He finds the chair. He sits down. He holds the cane tightly. Something is wrong here. None of this . . . none of this feels right.

"I'm not sure how to . . . This . . . this is going to be hard," Principal Anderson says, "but I'm afraid . . . I'm afraid I have to give you some bad news, Joshua."

Joshua says nothing. How ironic, he thinks, that five minutes ago he was thinking about the family curse. Is that what has happened here? His memory reached out and woke it up?

"It's about your father," Principal Anderson says, and of course it is. The principal puts his hand on Joshua's shoulder. He crouches down so he can face him. "There's been an incident."

"No," he says. "Please, don't tell me. Don't—"

But Principal Anderson does tell him. All Joshua can do is sit silently and listen, his hands shaking as he cries.

"It's going to be okay," Mrs. Templeton tells him, only it isn't going to be okay.

How can it be?

FOUR

Joshua can't process the words. He can hear them well enough, but there's something about them that don't add up. Despite having accepted that the curse is real, despite knowing that his dad's job is dangerous, he can't believe that what he's hearing is true.

"I'm so sorry," Principal Anderson says. Some of the students here call Principal Anderson *Pineapple Andawoman*. There's no way somebody with such a stupid nickname can be telling him that his dad—his second dad—is dead. Something inside Joshua's body is getting smaller, a piece of him shrinking up and dying.

"Everything is going to be okay," Mrs. Templeton says.

Joshua stares in her direction. He's trying to put what she's saying into a narrative that reverses everything Principal Anderson has told him. Everything is going to be okay? How? In what way?

"We're here for you, Joshua," Principal Anderson says. "In any way you need us."

"I don't . . . I don't . . ." Joshua says, and he doesn't. He doesn't know what to do. Doesn't know what to say. Doesn't understand how this can be real. He is, he realizes, halfway to becoming an orphan again, and if the past is anything to go by, his mom now has a clock hanging over her. "He can't be dead," he says. "I was with him this morning. How can he be dead when he dropped me off at school? How can—"

"Joshua—"

He shrugs the principal's hand off his shoulder. "He can't be, that's how," he says, which is as true as everything else that is going on, and, when you boil down the facts, a curse is nothing more than paranoia and ignorance and superstition mixed into one.

"It's going to be okay," Mrs. Templeton says.

"Stop saying that," Joshua says. He stands up. He has to get out of here. Has to get some air. He moves towards the door and bumps into the side of the chair and drops his cane and keeps moving forward without it. He puts his hands out to guide the way, to where he isn't sure, and he trips over something, hits the ground and gets right back up. That's the trick to this—keep moving forward fast enough to stop the bad news from catching up.

"Joshua," Principal Anderson says.

"I have to go."

"Joshua . . ."

He gets his hands against the wall. The door should be to his right . . . but it's not, and then it is, and he's getting it open and a hand falls on his shoulder but he breaks free of it. He has to get downstairs. Needs to get outside. Once he finds his dad he can prove these people wrong. The hand he shrugged off grips him around the arm. Tight. He's turned around, fingers crushing into him, a grip he can't break.

"Joshua, please, please, I know this is difficult, but you have to try and calm yourself down," Principal Anderson says.

"I am calm."

"We'll help you through this."

"I don't need your help. I just want my dad."

"Your dad . . . your dad died," Mrs. Templeton says. "I'm so sorry, Joshua, but that's what we're trying to tell you."

No. His dad didn't die. If it were true, it wouldn't be Pineapple Andawoman telling him. It wouldn't be the school secretary trying to comfort him. "I don't want to talk to you anymore," Joshua says. "Either of you."

"We're going down the stairs now," Principal Anderson says, and a moment later that's what they do, the arm around him guiding the way.

The grip is still strong on Joshua's arm, and now it's starting to hurt. He knows it's going to bruise—he doesn't know what a bruise looks like, but he sure knows how one feels. All blind people do. The truth of what is happening is starting to set in. He could run as fast as humanly possible, and it wouldn't change what's happened.

"I know it doesn't seem like it right now, but you will get through this," Principal Anderson says.

Joshua says nothing.

"You can't fully acknowledge what's going on, but you will, and soon, and it's going to hurt. It's really going to hurt."

Joshua still says nothing. It already hurts. How can it get worse? They reach the bottom of the stairs.

Principal Anderson carries on talking. "It's going to be hard, and it won't make sense, and you're going to feel numb and lost, but you still have your mom. She'll be there for you, I'll be here for you, and all the teachers and students will be here for you."

"Not if the curse takes all of them."

"What curse?"

All of a sudden he needs to know what this man looks like. Until now, he's never cared, but in this moment it's important—especially if the man is going to give him such bad news. Black hair? Brown? He knows what black is, because black is all he sees. Brown is a lighter shade of that, a warmer shade. What does Principal Anderson have? Is he bald? Does he look like the kind of person who gets things wrong?

They continue to walk with Principal Anderson's hand on his shoulder. Joshua realizes he hasn't asked the big questions, the *how* and the *why*, and he still doesn't ask them now. *How* and *why* can lead only to more hurt.

They get outside. He can hear Mrs. Templeton catching up. He can hear birds in the trees and the warm breeze rustling through the leaves. They come to a stop, and Mrs. Templeton hands him his cane and his bag. He turns his face to the sun. He will remember these moments, he thinks. Next week, next month, in ten years' time, each of these moments following his father's death he will remember.

"Your ride is here," Principal Anderson says.

He hears the car making its way down the extended drive leading to the Canterbury School for the Blind. It comes to a stop in front of him. The door opens. Footsteps as someone approaches.

"Hi, Joshua," a woman says. "My name is Audrey Vega, I'm a detective who works with your dad, and I want to say . . . I want to say I'm so sorry about your father. He was a good man. A great man. I liked him a lot. Everybody on the force did. He was well liked and incredibly respected and . . . and this . . . this is a great loss to all of us."

Joshua doesn't know what to say.

"I'm taking you to see your mom at the hospital," she says.

"I don't understand. I thought . . ." Then it hits him, a sense of hope so strong his legs threaten to collapse under the weight of it. "He's still alive. The doctors are—"

"I wish that was it," Detective Vega says, and she puts a hand on his shoulder, as Principal Anderson did earlier. "I really do, Joshua. But he's gone. I'm sorry. I'm here to take you to your mom."

His mom. What is she thinking right now? What is she doing? He lets Detective Vega guide him into the car. He sits in the passenger seat, and before the door is closed Mrs. Templeton reminds him once more that everything is going to be okay, and Principal Anderson reminds him they are all there for him. Somebody puts his bag into the backseat, then Detective Vega climbs in behind the wheel. The car smells like takeout food and feels like an oven. He reaches for the panel to his side and finds the button to lower the window.

"Seat belt," Vega says.

He clicks his seat belt into place. They start to drive. He can hear a helicopter overhead, moving across his part of the city on its way to another, and he imagines perhaps it's a news crew going to where his dad died. If he switched on a TV right now, there'd be a dozen voices all yammering away about his father's death. His dad once said that bad news for everybody else is big news for the media. He would often say, *It's human tragedy that keeps them employed.* They'll be asking the *how* and the *why.* As they drive, the need to understand what happened intensifies the closer they get to the hospital. Soon he can't not know.

He leads with the *what*. "What happened?"

"Your father and Detective Kirk were following a lead," she says.

"What kind of lead?"

"They went to interview a suspect. There was a confrontation and it went bad."

"So dad was . . . was murdered?"

"Yes."

"The person who killed him?"

"He's dead too."

Joshua is happy that guy is dead too, but then he changes his mind. He would rather face the man who had done this to his dad. Being blind means he can't look him in the eye, but being blind wouldn't prevent him from swinging a sledgehammer.

"How did Dad die?"

"He . . . he fell," she says. "It happened at a construction site. I don't know all the details, but your father fell from a great height. He would have died instantly. He wouldn't have felt a thing."

"Except he would have," Joshua says. "He would have felt fear all the way down, and the higher he fell from, the longer he got to feel it."

Detective Vega doesn't say anything. She slows down for something, indicates, and a few seconds later takes a corner.

"What about Uncle Ben? Is he okay?"

"He's fine. He's with your mother now."

A monstrous thought emerges. He wishes, and he can't deny it, but he wishes it'd been Uncle Ben who had fallen, and not his father. He knows he'll be having thoughts like this a lot over the next few days, the next few weeks, maybe forever. He can already feel himself obsessing over the what-ifs. Wishing like mad his dad had turned left instead of right, or called in sick that day, or gotten stuck at a red light when he had a green. Wishing away all the chain reactions that had brought them to this place.

He wipes at his eyes. Will the tears ever dry up?

"I know this may not mean much right now, but your dad died a hero," Detective Vega says. "Any cop who dies on the job dies a hero."

"My first father died a hero too," he says.

"I . . . I know," she says, and he's grateful when she doesn't add *everything is going to be okay*. They continue to drive. He doesn't ask any more questions. He can hear other cars and motorbikes and buses and trucks. Occasionally somebody yells out at another driver. Horns toot and walk signals beep and brakes squeal. "We're here," Detective Vega says a short while later, and the car slows down, then comes to a stop.

They get out, and Detective Vega hands him his cane and carries his bag. "This way," she says, and he takes her arm. He can hear traffic behind him and people around him; the hustle and bustle of the hospital nearly overwhelms him. "Doors are ahead," she says.

The doors open and they step into the lobby. Joshua can't tell how big the room is, but it sounds big. He can hear lots of voices, mostly soft murmuring, a desperate-sounding conversation perhaps between a patient at reception and a nurse.

"Joshua!"

Joshua turns towards Uncle Ben. Captain Kirk, as his dad always used to call him, not only because of his name, but because he looks like the original Captain Kirk too, according to his mom. A hand lands on his shoulder. It's warm and firm and Joshua can smell familiar aftershave.

"I'm really sorry, kiddo," Uncle Ben says, and he has always been Uncle Ben even though he's not really an uncle. They hug each other tight, and suddenly he thinks back to the last time they hugged. It was a year ago. His dad had fired up the barbecue and his uncle Ben had come around for some steaks and some beers and had brought his girlfriend with him. Everybody had hugged hello. Back then, Joshua came up only to Uncle Ben's chest, and now there's only a few inches separating them. Joshua has always been skinny, but the last year has seen him on the path to becoming tall and skinny. His dad had noticed that very thing just a few days ago and had acted like it was some sort of amazing phenomenon, a source of pride, as if Joshua himself had done something to make it happen.

How can it be his dad won't see him as an adult? Won't continue to get excited about each and every inch?

He realizes Uncle Ben is saying something.

"Sorry . . . what?"

"I'm saying it all just . . . just happened so quick, you know? And your dad, he . . . Ah, hell," he says, and Joshua knows Uncle Ben is close to tears too. They break the embrace and Uncle Ben puts both of his hands on his shoulders. "I wish . . ." Uncle Ben adds, but doesn't say what it is he's wishing for. Instead he says, "Thanks, Audrey, for getting him."

"Good-bye, Joshua," Vega says, and she gives him a hug before disappearing.

"Is he really dead?" Joshua asks.

"Yeah, buddy, he is. I'm really sorry. It wasn't his fault. I want you to know that the guy who did this . . . He got what he deserved, okay? I've made sure he's being put to good use. I mean . . . I mean—well, don't say that to anybody," he says, and his uncle sounds like his dad used to sometimes when he was wired on coffee, and he guesses his uncle is running on adrenaline. "I shouldn't have said that. In fact I didn't say that, okay? Do you understand what I'm saying?"

"Yes," Joshua says, but really he means no. His uncle isn't making any sense.

"Good. Good. The guy that killed your dad, he was a bad guy, and your dad died making sure that guy couldn't hurt anybody else."

Joshua isn't so sure. He thinks his dad didn't need to die. He thinks the thing Uncle Ben did that he can't talk about could have been done earlier. That way his dad would be coming home from work tonight the same as always, and Joshua would be napping in Mr. Fox's class.

"Where's Mom?"

Before Uncle Ben can answer, they are joined by someone else. "Hi, Joshua." A woman, warm and mature sounding, perhaps even as old as forty. "It's a real pleasure to meet you, I only wish it were under different circumstances."

"Joshua, this is Dr. Toni Coleman," Uncle Ben says, and he knows the name but can't figure out how.

"People prefer to call me Dr. Toni," she says, and then there is a hand on Joshua's elbow. A moment later a hand is in his, shaking it. He can sense her smiling and looking sympathetic at the same time.

"Did you try to save my dad?" Joshua asks.

"Dr. Toni is a different kind of doctor," Uncle Ben says.

"Different how?"

"I'm an ophthalmologist," she says.

Now he knows where he knows her name from. She's been in the news. "I don't understand," he says. "What's going on?"

"Your dad has died, Joshua," she says, "and I'm sorry for that, but his wish was that if something ever happened to him, he wanted to give you a gift. We're hoping to make you able to see the world the way your dad saw it. We're hoping to give you his eyes."

FIVE

—◉—

The technology is still in its infant stages. That's what Dr. Coleman will be telling the family right now, Dr. Tahana thinks, as he stands over the body of Detective Inspector Mitchell Logan. He imagines Dr. Coleman will tell them the procedure has been done no more than fifty times throughout the world, and all of those within the last two years. Giving sight to those who don't have it—it's hard only to thank medical science when it feels like a miracle. Twice it's been done in New Zealand, each time at Christchurch Hospital by Dr. Coleman and her team. Coleman is a brilliant doctor who, he believes, still hasn't reached the peak of her career—and one of only a dozen doctors on the world stage doing these procedures. She accepts the accolades and the respect that comes with that position, but he knows she doesn't really care about them. If she did, she certainly wouldn't be involved in what he was doing right now.

Tahana looks over the body of Detective Logan. His hand is nailed to his shoulder, more nails in his chest, one in his neck and another embedded into his gum via his cheek. It wasn't the nails that killed him—and if it hadn't been for the fall, Mitchell would have survived with minimal scarring.

Mitchell isn't the only dead man in the room, and Tahana walks over to the second body—cause of death, a gunshot to the throat. Unlike Mitchell, whose internal organs were crushed in the fall and cut into by broken bones, this man's organs are in perfect working order.

"At least you're finally good for something," he says to the dead man, which is something he has said to other dead men in similar circumstances. For twenty-eight years he has been harvesting organs and bones from the dead to save the living—and for the last five years, he's been harvesting them from the likes of Simon Bower. Those killed in the commission of a crime have had their names retroactively added to the database of organ donors whether they wanted to donate or not. Earlier this morning, Simon Bower's name was added. History has been rewritten so that, for all intents and purposes, when Bower applied for a driver's license at the age of sixteen, he checked the box that said yes to donating his organs. There are fourteen people walking the streets of Christchurch who would be in the grave by now if Tahana and the others hadn't been prepared to put their careers and their freedom on the line by illegally harvesting organs from these people who never wanted to be donors. However, he doesn't care what their wishes were. The way he sees it, those who took from the community were, in death, able to give a little back.

He moves back to Mitchell. Removing the dead man's eyeballs requires delicate work that cannot be rushed. One wrong cut, the tiniest of slips, and the eye becomes useless. He's looking at forty-five minutes, perhaps an hour, per eyeball. It would take longer in a living patient—removing Joshua's will be a far more delicate operation for Dr. Coleman, but even that will pale in comparison to the work required to attach the replacements.

As he makes the incisions to loosen the skin and muscle around the eye, he wonders how Dr. Coleman will describe the procedure to Joshua and his mother. It will be in simple enough terms, he thinks. A stem cell cocktail injected between the optic nerve and the new eyeball will help gel everything together after everything is attached, the eyeball carefully put into place and bandaged for it to heal, the biggest concern being the information from the eye to the brain traveling without corruption. Of course, it is more complicated than that—that's why the technology is still groundbreaking—but in ten years' time, hell, maybe even in five, it will be as common as a heart transplant.

A pair of surgeons enter the room. They acknowledge him with a nod before they begin working on the second body. Tahana listens to ribs being cut and bone being sawed as they open Bower to remove what can be saved. Neither of the surgeons knows Bower isn't really a donor. Nobody will ever question it, least of all Bower's family. The family never do—they're too busy wondering what turned their child into a monster.

Like Mitchell, Simon Bower is also having his eyes harvested, and the doctor doing the harvesting matches Tahana's pace. An hour later, each body has a single eyeball removed. Each eyeball is placed into a sterile bag full of saline, then each set placed into separate organ-transport containers filled with ice, each container carefully labeled. Other containers are filled with Bower's organs and whisked away by interns coming in to get them, a heart rushed into an operating room, a kidney put onto a helicopter and raced to another hospital. Stored correctly, the eyes will last up to twenty-four hours, which gives them more time than they need.

It's going to be a long day for Dr. Coleman and her team.

He goes to work around the second eye.

SIX

—◆—

It's hot in Dr. Toni's office. There's a fan in the corner of the room that blows air over Joshua's face as it turns one way, and ten seconds later blows air over his face as it turns the other. He can hear sounds coming from the waiting room and the corridor beyond. He can hear somebody revving a car loudly in the parking lot several stories below. The chair he is sitting in is comfortable. His mother sits in the chair next to him and holds his hand tightly as they listen to Dr. Toni explain the procedure. Occasionally he can hear his mom crying, and each time it happens she tries to hide it. Hearing her cry makes him want to cry.

He feels like something vital has been scooped out from inside him. If somebody were to cut him open, his stomach would be empty, his chest would be only a cavity, all that would be left would be some blood and bones and his empty thoughts. He listens to Dr. Toni's words. He wishes he knew what she looked like. Of course, after all of this, he might be granted that wish. Of course, if wishes came true, he'd be asking for his father back. He'd give up the chance of seeing in a heartbeat to have him here. He keeps expecting him to show up and apologize for being late to this appointment, before firing off questions about the operation.

The first thing Dr. Toni says is that they've met before, a long time ago, back when he was much smaller. She used to know his mom and dad a little, and Uncle Ben too, so she met Joshua back then as a friend of the family, not as his doctor. She tells him she's the only person in New Zealand who's performed these operations.

"I'm sure you've heard of them," she says, and she's right, he has.

He imagines blind people everywhere have been following the progress of the operations. The first one took place two and a half years ago in Japan and made the front pages of newspapers around the world. He spoke a lot about it with his parents, and then in class Mr. Fox spoke a lot about it too.

"It's an exciting time," Mr. Fox had said, "but it doesn't mean any of you can slacken off from your studies. You have to plan for how the world is now, not for how it might be. And of course you can hope. We can all hope."

Which is what Joshua and everybody else in the school was doing—they were hoping. The second procedure was performed four months later in the United States, then the third not long after that, also in the States. Now it no longer makes the news, but of course there are still stories online. Every week or two somebody somewhere gets the procedure done, and, other than a few cases, all the operations have been successful. When it was finally performed here in New Zealand two years ago, it made the news again. There is, of course, a downside—as there often is with transplants. They require something nasty to have happened to someone healthy. That's the price of admittance.

Shapes, colors, lights—they are waiting for him, according to Dr. Toni. Faces, movies, words on a page—hell, he'll even be able to drive. He'll be able to walk through parks and cities and sail the seas and look up into the stars. This permanent darkness of his will disappear. What will fill his dreams? Until now, his dreams have been of sounds and tastes and falling and floating. His whole sense of reality is going to change. And, of course, the Joshua who woke this morning isn't the same Joshua who will fall asleep tonight. This new Joshua Logan is going to be angry at the loss of his father. This new Joshua Logan is going to see for the first time, something he has wanted more than anything—just not at this price.

"If we had more time, I'd run through it again, but I'm afraid we don't have that," Dr. Toni says.

His mother asks about the risk of infection, the complications that can come from that, but Joshua tunes the conversation out. He closes his eyes and studies the darkness he's grown up with, aware of a different darkness in his life now. The words drift past him, the breeze from the fan scatters them around the room. His mother asks another question, and the conversation continues.

"Can we get started?" he asks, interrupting them.

"Only when your mom is ready," Dr. Toni says.

"I . . . I can't risk anything going badly," his mom says. "I can't . . . I can't . . . bear to think . . ."

"Joshua is going to be in good hands," Dr. Toni says.

"It's going to be okay, Mom," he says, then smiles at the irony of saying the one thing he's gotten sick of hearing. "I want to get started and . . . and to be honest, being asleep means I won't have to hurt so much, right? All I feel now is pain," he says—but more than pain, he feels empty inside. He's tired too. He doesn't want to talk anymore.

"I know, baby," his mom says, and she leans across and hugs him. He can feel her tears on his cheek.

"I'll leave you for a few minutes," Dr. Toni says, and Joshua hears her get up and leave. The door closes behind her.

"Did you see Dad?" he asks.

"Yes," she says, still holding him.

"How did he look?"

"He looked . . . peaceful," she says.

"Is that the truth?"

"Yes," she says, but he doesn't believe her. People who die in their sleep might look peaceful. He imagines people who have fallen to their death look the absolute opposite of peaceful.

"Is it going to be weird?" he asks. "When you look at me, you're going to see his eyes."

She holds on tighter then, and her body shakes as she cries.

"Because I think it might be weird," he adds, struggling to get the words out.

"I don't know," she says.

"Will you stay with me? During the operation?"

"I can't be in there with you."

"But you can be outside the room, right?"

"And I will be," she says, "for as much of it as I can. But I have other things to . . . to arrange."

"Things to do with Dad?"

"Yes."

"What will happen after?"

"After the funeral?"

"After I can see again. What will happen to me?"

"I don't know yet," she says, "but it will be an exciting time for you, despite what's happened."

"I doubt that."

"Joshua . . ." she says, and in the pause that follows he knows she's thinking carefully about what she wants to say. "What your father has given you is a miracle, and you need to honor him by using that miracle to the best of your abilities. You're only sixteen, but now you have a lot of growing up to do. You owe it to your father to be the best man you can be."

Dr. Toni comes back and tells them it's time. He's taken down the corridor in a wheelchair. He catches snippets of conversations, people talking about broken bones and cancers and the weather and how hard it is to find decent parking. They enter an elevator. His mother still has his hand in hers. Somebody slaps at a button and they begin to move. A few moments later he's being wheeled down a different corridor, this one quieter and cooler.

"Okay, Michelle, this is as far as you can go. I'm sorry," Dr. Toni says, and he can hear a familiarity in the way Dr. Toni uses his mom's first name and he wonders how well they used to know each other.

His mother crouches and puts her arms around him and hugs him tight again. He can smell her hair. Can feel her breath on his neck. He's scared. He doesn't want to let go. "I'll be right here for most of it. I promise," she says.

He can't speak. His throat feels blocked. His tongue feels fat. She lets him go.

"You're going to be okay," Dr. Toni says. "I have a great team."

"Is this going to hurt?" he asks.

"No."

"I mean . . . after. Will it hurt when I wake up?"

"There are drugs we can give you for the pain, but mostly it will just be uncomfortable. The thing you'll suffer from the most is the boredom of being kept in a hospital. Well, that and the food."

"I'm going to be different, right? When this is done? Not because I can see again, but . . . I mean . . . everything will be different."

"Life won't be the same anymore, Joshua, and I'm sorry we haven't had time to prepare you for the changes that are going to happen in your life."

"What do you mean?" his mom asks.

"Not only will he see the world differently," Dr. Toni says, "but the world he knows will see him differently. I'm sorry, but we really must get started."

He climbs out of the wheelchair and onto a bed. The bed is rolled into a room that sounds like it's the same size as his classroom. He wonders what his classmates are up to now. He imagines Mr. Fox telling them what happened. He wonders how his two best friends are reacting. He's known William and Pete since his first day at school. They've been to his house a million times, as he's been to theirs. He knows their parents, and they know his. Right now their shock will be the same as his, but not their pain.

"Are you ready?" Dr. Toni asks him.

He knows he's so empty inside that when Dr. Toni removes his eyes, she's going to see nothing behind them, only a cavity and the back of his skull.

"I'm ready," he says, and he falls into sleep.

SEVEN

Todd Wilkinson pushes open the door to the operating theater where the two bodies are being stripped for parts. Todd has always thought of it as an icky process, and the idea of having some other bloke's heart or kidney or whatever inside you has always creeped the bejesus out of him. He guesses desperate people will do anything.

He lets the door close behind him. The operating theater serves two purposes: first, it's a teaching theater, where has-been surgeons try to keep themselves relevant by sharing their knowledge; and second, it's to this theater where bodies are brought to have their organs harvested. Over the years the theater has become known as the Cutting Room to the students who come here.

Dr. Tahana is staring at him with a stupid look on his face. His default setting, Todd thinks. Tahana is a bit of a loser, truth be told, a guy who, for some reason, never works on the living. He thinks that *some reason* has something to do with the fact that cutting bits and pieces out of corpses is no more complicated than assembling a drive-through hamburger, and Tahana can't cope with complicated. In fact, in a few years when Todd is running this place, the first thing he's going to do is fire the balding hack. He'll do it publically too, really humiliate the guy.

He pops out his headphones to the sound of Dr. Tahana jabbering on at him that he shouldn't be listening to music during work hours, to which Todd wants to tell him that *he* shouldn't be so bald and gross during work hours, and that even though the guy is fifty years old, he may as well be five thousand, since all his techniques are Stone Age. Todd says nothing. He turns the music off and stands there listening to instructions exactly the same way any good intern would. It's not like it's complicated. Two sets of eyes. One set goes to operating theater B. One set goes to operating theater D. Both theaters are on the second floor, and both boxes are clearly labeled. The instructions are so simple, his thoughts start to drift. He wonders what Tahana would look like with a mustache, or if somebody cut off his ears.

"Are you even listening to me?" Dr. Tahana asks.

"Always."

"Good. Now don't make me remind you again, but stop listening to your MP3 player during work hours."

"Sure thing," Todd says, as he picks up the transplant boxes. Once he's in the corridor he puts the boxes down so he can put his headphones back in. Then he carries on, an organ-transplant box in each hand. Part of his job as an intern is to be underutilized and treated like a delivery boy. He hates it. The flip side is that he has been able to work with a few of the transplant teams. Two hearts and one kidney. Though *work* is a loose term, one he uses when he's telling stories over drinks at the bar. *Observed* would be more accurate, but *observed* doesn't impress the ladies.

He reaches the elevator and has to wait for it. The elevators in this place have always been too slow. It's empty when it arrives. He steps inside. The doors close. He sets the containers on the floor and takes out the small yellow plastic bottle from his pocket and pops the lid. Inside are methamphetamine pills. They're stronger than the caffeine tablets other doctors use to stay awake. They help make him feel sharper. More alive. They'll help get him through the day with enough energy to have a good time at the bar tonight. He takes one. Within seconds his body feels like it's getting warmer. The music is getting louder. He presses the button. The elevator goes up. The climb takes longer than it ought to, even taking the slow elevators into account, and when the doors open he realizes why—he's pressed the wrong button. He looks at the panel and sees that instead of pressing the 2, he's pressed the 4, though really he probably did press the 2 and the mistake lies with the elevator, not with him. He can't ride it back down to 2 either, because another doctor steps onto the elevator, and that doctor would think the mistake is Todd's. And Todd isn't a guy who makes mistakes.

He steps out and walks to the stairwell as if that were the plan all along, and when he gets there he decides what he really needs even more than a brisk walk down the stairs is another pill, and what he needs as much as that other pill is to crank his music up even louder. He gets into the stairwell and goes about fixing both of those problems. He turns up the volume, puts one container under his arm while still holding the other, then reaches into his pocket.

He has the pill halfway to his mouth when the song ends, and in the two seconds between tracks he hears the door on the floor beneath him close, then footsteps on the stairs. With the start of the new song already blasting in his ears, he shoves the pills back into his pocket—at least that's the plan, but the edge of the container gets caught on the side of his pocket, it tips, and, because the lid is still off, the pills rain down the stairs.

"Ah geez . . ."

He starts after them, knocking the transplant container in his left hand against the stair rail, causing it to fly from his grip. It hits the top step and, like the pills only a few seconds earlier, it heads downhill.

"Damn it," he says, and he reaches forward to grab it, and then he, like the pills and the organ box, begins an uncontrollable descent. His legs slip out from underneath him as he overreaches, and he has to let go of the second box he is holding to grab for the rail. Which he misses. He lands on his back, his shoulder hitting the second organ box and sending it to the landing with the first.

He switches off the music and listens for the footsteps he heard earlier, but whoever it is must have gone through another door. There is only silence. He is, he believes, alone.

If only he'd pushed the correct button in the elevator.

He wiggles his fingers and toes and nothing is broken, which goes to prove how awesome he is—no chance Tahana could fall down a flight of stairs completely unscathed. He imagines the doctor bouncing his way down, a cartoon version doing cartwheels, his head bouncing off one step, then his feet, like a starfish.

He is sitting on the floor surrounded by pills. It would be impossible for him to talk his way out of this situation if anyone saw him right now. He plucks the pills off the ground one by one, in the process discovering they are the least of his problems. Both organ containers are open. Ice and eyeballs have scattered across the landing. Three of the bags have come out of the containers, and two of those bags have survived the fall, the eyes resting undisturbed in the saline solution. But the other bag hasn't been so lucky. There's a tear down the side through which the eyeball has escaped. It's come to a stop against the wall.

He moves down the stairs, sweeping the pills into his hand. When they're all in his pocket he works with the ice, scooping it into the containers, not needing to be as thorough as with the pills, because any pieces he misses will melt. The bags are labeled left and right, but not which left goes with which right, but that's an easy fix. He picks up the one that didn't fall out of the container. It's labeled left. The eye is blue. He picks up one of the surviving bags. It's labeled right. The eye is also blue. Easy. He puts them into the container. He picks up the other bag. It's labeled left.

The eye is also blue.

Oh no . . .

That means the other eye is going to also be blue.

That means he could have gotten the other set wrong.

Or right . . .

He can see only one solution. He has to guess. If he tells Dr. Tahana, he'll be fired. This way he has a fifty-fifty chance of getting it right—more like seventy-five, twenty-five, really, when he factors in a 25 percent awesomeness bump for being so damn awesome all the time.

If there's a problem, and the patients reject their new eyeballs, and somebody figures it out, well . . . well, that's a long-term problem, and one that's unlikely to occur. There is only one way forward. Guess now, and if necessary, blame someone else later.

He is buzzing from the pills. If he had to choose one word to sum up how he feels right now, it'd be *excited* and *amused. Oops—that's two words*, he thinks, and he has to fight the urge to laugh. He is, he must admit, a little concerned that he's not actually freaking out. There's dirt and dust stuck to the eyeball that came out of the bag. He tries his best to blow it away, but it's too stubborn to move. He's about to wipe it across the front of his scrubs when he realizes the damage it will cause. That's when it comes to him—a simple solution. He licks the eye, knowing it's not ideal, but far better than being found out. His tongue has barely made contact with the clammy surface when he wonders what the hell he's doing. This is not what someone in his right mind would be doing, especially when he's got two containers full of ice.

It's the pills. The damn pills are messing with him.

He melts some ice in his hand, then drips it over the eye until it's clean. He puts the eyeball into the split bag and puts it next to its partner. He'll slip it into a fresh bag of saline once he gets to the operating theater—which, he then realizes, would have been the better way to clean it.

"No more pills," he murmurs, but he doesn't really mean it.

He carries on down the stairs. On the second floor, he straightens his clothes and wipes the sweat off his face. For the briefest moment he thinks Dr. Tahana might have had a point about not wearing his MP3 player at work, but then that moment passes and he remembers what a has-been that old guy is anyway. Outside the first operating theater he finds a fresh bag and some fresh saline, and a few minutes later hands the container off to one of Dr. Coleman's nurses. Nobody will ever know what happened. He takes the second container to the second theater. Aside from a little scare, all in all it's been a job well done.

EIGHT

Two hours in, and the surgery is going well. Some surgeons like to listen to classical music while they operate, but Toni isn't like other surgeons. Sometimes it's Pink Floyd, or Springsteen, or the Rolling Stones. She always operates to music, but never the radio. You don't want to be hands deep in somebody while listening to ads for whiteware and taxi companies, or when some DJ is making a joke.

Today she is listening to the Beatles, and the Beatles are keeping her calm. The two other times she's performed this operation have also been to the Beatles, and both of those patients came out of the surgery how she hoped, and she sees no reason to mess with a winning formula. There have been no slipups.

Six hours in, and the first eye is complete, and Joshua's second eye is in the process of being removed. Dr. Toni is happy—slightly fatigued, but happy. Her team is right on schedule. The Beatles are on their second go-around on her playlist, and magic is being made.

Outside the operating room and downstairs, Michelle Logan is sitting with Ben Kirk. There is a spot of blood on her palm that she notices for the first time, and a couple more on her sleeve, blood that must have come from Mitchell when she held his hand before the surgeon told her it was time. She wipes at them, getting rid of the one on her hand, but the one on her blouse only sets in deeper.

"You should be with family. I'll stay here and make sure everything is running smoothly," Ben says.

She turns to look at him and focuses on the bandaging around his arm. The same thing that happened to Mitchell could have easily happened to Ben. "Are you okay?" she asks him.

"It's only a flesh wound," he says. He looks down. "I'm sorry I couldn't have done more. If I could switch places with him I—"

"Don't say that," she says.

"He was more than a friend, he was like a brother to me."

"I know."

"I just wish . . . I wish, ah, hell . . ."

"I know," she says.

"I should have done more," he says.

"You did what you could, Benjamin," she says, but really she wants to shake him and tell him yes, he should have done more. He should have done whatever it took to keep her husband alive. "Why didn't you have backup?" she asks.

It takes him a few seconds to answer. "You know why," he tells her, looking down as he talks, and yes, she knows why.

Ben tells her that Mitchell will be given a full police funeral, and he tells her they will have people make all the arrangements, if she so wishes. She thinks that if the police take care of the arrangements it leaves her more time to lie in bed and cry her eyes out, so she nods and thanks him and tells him yes, she's happy for them to plan everything. Of course, as much as she wants to hide herself away, she knows she can't. She has Joshua to care for. Having somebody take care of the funeral arrangements will give her more time to spend with her son.

They sit in silence then, both in their own thoughts, Michelle thinking about what tomorrow will bring without her husband, the first day of her adult life in which he will no longer exist. Ben is thinking about how the morning unfolded. He's running through the events at the construction yard. He's thinking that if they had done things by the book, none of this would have happened, but they needed it done in secret. They had broken into Simon Bower's house without a warrant because the previous night they had unsealed his childhood court records and found that when he was thirteen, he killed a neighbor's dog, and when he was fourteen, he molested that same neighbor's daughter. They decided Simon Bower could be a perfect candidate, and after leaving his house they knew he was. They went to the construction site knowing he was their guy. They were going to get him alone upstairs and they were going to question him, and if there was no doubt he had killed Andrea Walsh, then Bower was going to have an accident. There was no place in the world for people who cut women into pieces. No place at all.

He can still smell the gunpowder. Can still hear the sound of the bullet as it entered Bower's neck. Pulling that trigger after Mitchell was dead gave him a brief moment of satisfaction in this nightmare—but they shouldn't have been so cocky. They should have known how Bower would react. They never should have split up.

On the other side of town is Vincent Archer. Vincent is the last person Simon Bower thought of before his death, and right now Vincent is sanding back the final edges on the rocking horse he has built for his niece. His niece is four years old, and her name is Matilda, and Matilda is good at turning any conversation back to the pony she's always wanted. Its name, she tells him, will be George. So he's been crafting the rocking horse from solid pieces of rimu that he's joined together, hoping it will be a good substitute for George, and this week the plan was to paint it, and next weekend give it to her for her fifth birthday. So far he's spent two months handcrafting it in his spare time, and he's been working on it since getting home from work an hour ago. Sawdust has gotten into his beer, but it doesn't stop him from drinking it. His garage is full of power and hand tools. In fact, it's been five years since he was able to fit his car in here, and he thinks he should leave some of the tools out in the cabin he's been renovating. He spends half his time there anyway, and his dog lives there, only makes sense his tools can live there too. He has a radio on for background noise, and he pauses when he hears his friend's name. He puts down the sanding block and moves over to the radio and turns up the volume, but the newsreader has moved on to the next story.

He grabs his beer and carries it upstairs. He doesn't have a TV, and hasn't had one for nearly ten years now—for which Matilda calls him Crazy Uncle Vinnie. He uses the computer in his study to go online. His friend is the lead story.

His dead friend.

Shit.

He reads the articles. Simon killed a policeman. Simon is accused of killing a woman and cutting her into pieces. What the hell? Would Simon do something like that? He probably would, yeah. As he reads the articles, he thinks about Ruby. No doubt that's where all of this started. Three months ago, out on the river. He and Simon had been fishing. He'd been standing while Simon had had the foresight to bring along a foldable camping chair. The nose of their boat was jammed up on the bank. They'd been drinking and fishing and watching the river crawl. They'd been swatting at sand flies and shooting the breeze and reapplying sunblock every hour because the week before they'd both gotten pretty burned. Simon was in a grumpy mood and the beer was only making it worse. The woman he'd been seeing for the previous month had decided not to see him anymore. Vincent wasn't sure why, but her being a complete bitch topped Simon's list of reasons. The other bitch was Simon's boss at work. He was already doing the impossible, but she still demanded more from him. Vincent was counting the minutes. His friend could get like this sometimes, and it never made for a fun afternoon.

All that changed with Ruby. She had come out of the woods behind them. She was carrying a mountain bike with a twisted-to-hell front wheel. There was blood and dirt on her elbows and knees in equal parts. She was limping. She smiled at them, and waved, and told them the car park was too far away to carry her bike. She said there was no cell phone reception. She asked if they could help her.

He can't believe that was three months ago.

He puts his beer down and grabs his keys and goes outside to the car. Simon lived only a few blocks away. He'd bought his house a few weeks after Vincent purchased his. They actually considered flatting together, but decided against it, both men being the kind who enjoy the other's company but who also enjoy their own company too. It's nearly dark outside, but still warm, the summer lingering into autumn, which suits Vincent fine because he hates autumn. He hates the way the leaves mess up his garden and how dirt sticks to his shoes and gets on the carpet. He makes it to the street Simon lives on but doesn't go down it. There are police cars and media vans parked everywhere. He thinks about the last time he saw Simon. It was three nights ago. They'd had a beer out on the porch of Simon's house, the same porch that police officers are now traipsing all over.

He turns his car around and drives back home. If the police connect Simon to what they did to Ruby . . . How would they? Through her DNA, if there's still some on Simon's clothes. He isn't sure how long it takes to run DNA samples, but he believes it takes a month, perhaps two. He could leave the country. Take advantage of those open borders in Europe and get himself lost somewhere. Get a job on a vineyard, or as a carpenter working on a run-down house. He could learn a language and never come back.

That's plan B. By the time he gets back home, he has plan A, and plan A is to not panic. He doesn't see how the police can connect the dots. They will come and see him, but their interest in him won't be any different from the interest they'll have in other friends and family and colleagues of Simon. They will want to piece together a narrative, but there's no way for them to know that narrative should include Ruby Carter. Even if they do match the DNA, they'll never figure out what truly happened to her. There's also no way they can know about the cabin. He and Simon made sure to leave no sign of it at their houses in town. No, the cabin is safe.

Back inside, he sits again in front of the computer. There's an article with a photograph of the detective who shot his friend. He clicks on it to make it bigger. He sips at his sawdust-tainted beer that's gotten warmer but hardly tastes it. He studies the photograph of Detective Inspector Ben Kirk.

"You're the one who should be dead," he says, tapping the screen.

All those power tools in his garage, well now, there are a thousand different ways he could torture Detective Ben Kirk out at the cabin. He could make it last for days. Maybe weeks. He'd even let the dog watch.

He carries the beer into the kitchen and tips it into the sink. The beer he brews and bottles himself, and he grabs the last one out of the fridge. He pops it open and stares out at the backyard. It will be dark in less than an hour. He thinks about all the ways he could kill Ben Kirk for what he has done.

After a while, it occurs to him that he's thinking about this all wrong.

He takes his beer to the garage and picks up the sanding block and gets back to work. Revenge for Simon isn't about killing Ben. It's about making him suffer. When he's done working, he will drive out to the cabin. It will be strange being there without Simon, but being there will help him get through this.

While Vincent finishes sanding the rocking horse, and while Mitchell Logan's body is driven away by an undertaker to be prepared for the funeral, and as Dr. Coleman begins to remove Joshua's second eye, Joshua Logan, for the first real time in his life, starts to dream.

To really dream.

NINE

— ◉ —

Joshua dreams of things he cannot understand. In the past he's only ever dreamed of shapes, and textures, and smells, but now those shapes are starting to come out of the dark, and they're taking on more texture than ever before and, for the first time, color too. There are people in these new dreams, and though he's dreamed of people before, they were avatars without any detail, a collection of blurry shapes. He's never actually seen a tree in his life, but he sees one now, a large giant on the landscape, then dozens and dozens of them side by side. He sees a river, the water flowing and reflecting light. There is a woman next to a bike. There are fishing rods and a cooler full of beer. The woman is crying. There is a boat. There is a cabin. He sees blood raining down, a storm of it splattering against plastic-lined walls. He sees a woman at a dinner table. She's laughing. A boy sits next to her. A man falls to his death. He sees all of it but makes sense of none of it as the anesthetic courses through his veins.

When he finally wakes, he doesn't know what's happening. School? He thinks so, and he thinks he's running late. Unless . . . Wait, is it a weekend? No . . . no, because yesterday was Monday and—

He's in a hospital.

His father. Is. Dead.

And the world. Is. Still. Dark.

A hand clutches at his.

"Mom?"

"No," somebody says. "I'm Sally. I'm your nurse," the woman says, and gives his hand a gentle squeeze. "It's okay, Joshua, you were dreaming."

"I . . . I don't remember," he says, and he doesn't. All those images have disappeared, but there's a sense the dreams were different from normal. But how? He reaches up. There is bandaging wrapped around his head, covering his eyes.

"The surgery went well," Nurse Sally says, and he doesn't know whether to believe her. She could just be saying that to keep him calm. He holds his breath, then tests the one thing he's worried about the most—and that's whether or not he can feel his eyes. He moves them left, and yes—they move! He moves them right, then left again. They hurt, for sure they hurt, but it's so incredibly comforting to know he can feel them.

"Dr. Coleman said try not to move your eyes around," Nurse Sally says.

"You can see me doing that?" he asks.

"No," she says. "I just know that you are. I know how impossible that's going to be, but do try your best."

"I will," he says. "Where is Dr. Toni?"

"She's with another patient," Nurse Sally says. "The same surgery she gave you, she's now performing on somebody else. Two people today are getting the gift of sight. It's a blessing."

He wonders if the other person's dad died as well. "What time is it?"

"One o'clock," she says.

"In the afternoon?" he asks.

"In the morning."

"Where's my mom?"

"At home," she says. "She's not allowed to be here. Not at this time."

"I'm really thirsty," he says.

"Here," she says, and she hands him a glass of water. He sips some, then hands it back.

"You should go back to sleep," she says. "You need it. Dr. Coleman will be here in the morning to check on you."

He doesn't think he'll be able to get back to sleep, but he's wrong.

He's asleep within a minute of Nurse Sally leaving, and soon he is dreaming again. There is a construction site. He looks down and sees nails sticking out of his chest. One has pinned his hand to his shoulder. Ahead of him an angry-looking man, then all of that shifts and changes, there is sunlight and the building is racing by and . . .

He wakes up. Somebody is squeezing his hand. This time it is his mom.

"You were having a nightmare," she says.

"I . . . I don't know," he says, and already it's fading . . . fading . . . gone.

"They tell me the operation went great," she says.

"What time is it?"

"It's nine," she says.

"In the morning?" he asks. He's disorientated. He feels light-headed.

"Yes."

"What's happening with dad?" he asks.

He senses her composing herself. "All of that . . . it's being taken care of."

"When's the funeral?"

"Thursday."

"What's today?"

"Tuesday."

"Will I be able to go?"

"I don't think so, honey. It won't be a good idea. We can't risk you getting any kind of infection."

"I want to be there," he says.

"I know, but your dad would want what's best for you. If something happened to your eyes . . . Can you imagine how that would make him feel?"

His dad doesn't feel anything, not anymore, Joshua thinks. He'll never feel anything again.

"How about I discuss it with Dr. Toni and see what she says," his mom says. "In fact, here she is now."

He can hear approaching footsteps.

"How are you feeling?" Dr. Toni asks.

He isn't sure where to begin. Tired. Sad. Sore. "I don't know. Okay, I guess."

"The operation went well," she says. "We'll know exactly how well in a few days when we can take the bandages off."

"So you don't know if I can see?"

"It's important we keep your expectations under control," she says. Her voice sounds different, less confident, than it did yesterday. "I'm optimistic," she says, "and we'll know more in a few days' time. Is there any pain?"

"Only when I move them."

"You need to try not to move them."

"And there's a lot of pressure on them."

"That's to be expected," she says. "That area of your face has experienced a lot of trauma. It'll take a week for the swelling to go down, and of course you've got the bandages pressing against them. Now, there is something I need to tell you again, because it's important. Your eyes are going to start itching and it's going to get bad. You might even be tempted to rip the bandages away to scratch at them, but you can't. You have to promise me that, okay? Because if you can't keep from scratching, we'll have to either sedate you or strap you down. Otherwise you're going to risk undoing all the good work we've done."

He isn't sure if she's joking about being strapped down. "I promise," he says, which is an easy promise to make because at the moment his eyes aren't itching.

"I'll get a nurse to bring in some breakfast for you, okay?"

"Will I be able to go to Dad's funeral?"

There's silence for a few seconds, in which he imagines Dr. Toni and his mom are exchanging looks. He's heard that's what people do. "I'm sorry, Joshua," Dr. Toni says. "I really have to advise against it. It's not a decision I make easily, but if something were to happen—"

"Nothing's going to happen," he says, and yesterday his dad would have been thinking the same thing.

"I'm going to need you to stay here. I'm sure your father would understand."

"How do you know?"

"Joshua," his mom says, her tone letting him know she's unhappy with the way he's talking.

"I used to know him, remember?" Dr. Toni says. She sits down on the edge of his bed, and his body weight shifts towards her. She puts her hand on his arm. "I first met him years ago, when I wasn't much older than you are now."

"How come I haven't met you before?" he asks.

"You have," she says, and he remembers her telling him she'd met him a long time ago, when he was small. "But the last few years I've only seen your dad around the hospital."

"You worked with him? How?"

"We didn't work together," she says, "but sometimes criminals get injured and he'd be in here. The point is I have a pretty good idea of what he would and wouldn't approve of, and you taking an unnecessary risk to leave the hospital to go to his funeral is one thing he wouldn't approve of."

"But—"

"Dr. Toni is right," his mom says. "It doesn't make you love him any less, and nobody there will question why you couldn't go. When you leave here next week we can go to the cemetery together to see him. By then you'll even be able to see."

He knows it's an argument he can't win.

Dr. Toni gives his arm a quick rub. "Now, you must be hungry, right? Let me get the nurse to bring you something to eat. We'll talk again later today."

She gets up off the bed, and her footsteps fade. His mom takes her place. He can hear footsteps and squeaking wheels and crutches padding the ground. His mom tells him how happy she is the operation went okay. She doesn't sound like she's crying. Soon he can smell food.

"I hope you're hungry," a nurse says to him. She sounds friendly, like all the nurses.

He pictures toast, not just the shape of toast, but what it looks like, golden in color, because he's been told that's how it looks. The sun, sand, the way light can play off a calm ocean at the end of the day—golden.

If the operation truly has been a success, he'll soon know what all of that means.

TEN

It arrives a couple of hours after his mother leaves. The itching. It's not only behind his eyes, but somewhere in his brain, deep within, like a splinter he can't get to, and every second that passes with him unable to dig into it, it grows.

He has a private hospital room. He knows most people in the hospital have to share large rooms with four or five other patients, and he's grateful that's not him. He doesn't want to make conversation with strangers he can't see. Sometimes he lies on the bed listening to the sounds of the hospital. There are always voices somewhere, there are often things being wheeled past his door. Sometimes he can hear crying, other times laughing.

When he's not listening to the hospital, he listens to his MP3 player, which his mom brought in for him. It's full of music and books. He is currently one-third of the way through a novel about a vegetarian vampire. The vampire's name is Frederick, who, before he was turned into the living dead, lived on a diet of fruit and vegetables, and now that he has fangs is forced to eat animals. Of course, his challenge is to not eat people—that's where the story is going—and Joshua likes Frederick and hopes the best for him. The itch behind his eyes is matching Frederick's increasing need for blood, and by chapter ten it's really getting its groove on. He tries to ignore it the same way Frederick ignores the itch to separate people from their blood. A couple of chapters later, neither of them are doing that great. Frederick drains a serial killer he thinks society can do without, while Joshua pushes his palms into the bandaging, twisting them back and forth. With enough pressure, he's able to make the itch disappear. He wins. This time.

Day two of his recovery, Wednesday, starts out with a breakfast he eats quickly, and a shower he's allowed to take as long as he keeps the bandages dry. Doctors and nurses come and go throughout the morning. His mom hugs him when she arrives, and hugs him again before leaving. He is lonely. He is bored. He is sad. He wants to go home. He wants to go back to school. He wants life to be how it was a week ago. He wonders what Mr. Fox is teaching right now, figuring he's probably moved past eye color and on to something else. He misses his friends. Misses Mr. Fox, for that matter. Misses learning. Most of all, he misses his dad. His hunger returns around lunchtime, as does the itch. The palm trick doesn't work. He forces his eyes closed as hard as he can, moves them around, then forces them closed even tighter. It's painful, but the itch fades.

It's the middle of the afternoon when William and Pete show up. He's so happy to hear their voices, he could cry. Having his mom around is one thing, but having his best friends around is another. They ask him how he is, and he tells them he's okay, which isn't true, and he asks how they are, and they tell him the same thing. He asks what happened after he left school, and they tell him Mr. Fox told them all what had happened. As they give him the details, he can hear the pity in their voices, and soon it becomes clear they're not really sure what to say, which is fine because he doesn't know what he wants to hear. They talk about his operation. There is something different in their voices, but he can't identify what it is, just that it's something he doesn't like. After twenty minutes William and Pete tell him they need to go. They sound like they would rather be somewhere else, perhaps anywhere else. He tells himself that hospitals are like that, because even he doesn't want to be here.

"I'll see you at school," Joshua says, trying to keep hidden his disappointment that they're leaving so soon. At least they came.

"Yeah, but that's the thing, right?" William says.

"What thing?"

"You'll be able to see us, but we won't be able to see you," William says.

"And anyway, you won't be going back there," Pete says.

"Of course I'll be going back to school."

"Not *our* school," William says, in a way that makes the school sound like it belongs to a lot of people, and Joshua isn't one of them. "A few days ago you were one of us. Now you're somebody who can see, and that means you'll be going to a school where everybody else can see too."

William is right, and Joshua feels like a fool for not having thought of this sooner.

"There's no place for you at our school anymore," Pete says.

"I . . . I hadn't thought about it like that."

"Yeah, well, we have," William says.

"We'll still hang out though," Joshua says.

"Will we? Will we really?" William asks.

"Of course."

"You'll make new friends. You won't need us anymore," William says.

"It's not about needing you for anything," he says. "You guys are my friends. My best friends."

"You'll have new best friends soon enough," Pete says. "Friends who can see."

Joshua doesn't get it. They sound annoyed. "Are you guys mad at me?"

Nobody answers, not for a few seconds. Then one of his friends sighs, but he can't tell which one, and then William talks. "No. Not mad," he says, "but things aren't the same anymore, Joshua, not for you and not for us."

"I'm sorry," Joshua says.

"No, you're not," William says, "because you don't even know what to be sorry for, and anyway, you don't need to be."

"I don't understand what's happening," Joshua says.

"We better go," Pete says. "My mom is waiting for us in the corridor."

"Please, please don't go."

"Good-bye, Josh," William says, and there is something final in that, as if he's never going to see them again.

"We'll see you around," Pete says, which is a joke they always used to say back in school, but this time it doesn't sound funny. Then they're gone, leaving him confused about their visit. Everybody is leaving him, the curse is making sure of that, taking them one by one.

The afternoon rolls on. Music. The itch. Frederick keeps fighting the desire to kill. A nurse catches him rubbing at the itch and tells him off, and another nurse catches him doing the same thing an hour later.

"You need to stay strong, Joshua," the second nurse tells him. "You have to fight it."

He fights it. Fights it while his grandparents on his mom's side come and visit, his grandmother patting his arm and his grandfather tussling his hair. His grandparents on his father's side visit too, and he thinks that as hard as it is for him, and for his mom, it could even be harder for them. They lost their daughter, who was his biological mother, sixteen years ago, and now they've lost their son. They do their best to sound upbeat, but he can hear the pain in their voices. He fights the itch while they talk to him, fights it while eating dinner that evening, fights it right through to the end of the day when a nurse catches him unwinding the bandaging to make way for his finger. He doesn't get far. She tells him off, he ignores her and keeps on trying. He can't fight it anymore. They sedate him.

Day three is the day of the funeral. Dr. Toni tells them that the previous night, while he was sedated, she checked his eyes and replaced the bandages. "It's all looking good," she tells him. "Your pupils responded to the light. There's no sign of infection and every reason to be positive."

His mum spends the morning with him. They talk about everything else other than the funeral, other than his father, and they do this until they can avoid the subject no longer.

"It's time," she tells him.

"Are you sure I can't come?"

"I wish you could." He can hear her fighting back her tears. "It would make it easier for me if you were there, but you can't, Joshua, I'm sorry," she says. "You can't."

She hugs him good-bye and then she's gone, and he's alone. He sits near the window so he can feel the sun on his face while eating lunch. He listens to his horror novel and he thinks about Frederick's lifestyle choice to eat only those who deserve it—and to Frederick, that involves feasting on murderers.

He wishes it had been Frederick who had gone to the construction site instead of his dad. He wishes . . .

"Joshua?"

He takes out his headphones. "Dr. Toni?"

"I wanted to come by and see how you were doing and answer any questions you might have. It's a good opportunity to discuss the changes that are going to happen in your life."

"You're here because my dad is being buried right now, and you want to make sure I'm okay."

"Joshua—"

"It's okay," he says. "I appreciate it, I really do. It's really nice of you."

She pulls a chair close to his and sits down. He tries to imagine what she looks like with the sun hitting her face.

"How come you didn't go to the funeral too? If you knew him?" he asks.

"I . . . I wanted to be here for you," she says.

He isn't sure whether to believe her, but either way, it doesn't matter. "I don't think my friends like me anymore."

"No, it's not that, Joshua. They don't know how to be around you, or what to say. You've lost your dad, and they're sad for you, but you're getting your sight back, and for that they're happy."

"They didn't sound happy."

"I want you to do something for me," she says. "I want you to imagine that right now you weren't getting your sight back. I want you to think about how you would feel if you got the news your friends were getting the gift of sight, and you were facing a life of blindness. Tell me, how do you think you would feel?"

"I don't know," he says.

"I think you do know."

He shrugs. "I guess I'd be happy for them."

"I'm sure you would be, in the same way your friends are happy for you."

"But?"

"But there's something else you'd be feeling."

He nods. She's right. He's annoyed at himself for not figuring it out earlier. "Jealousy."

"There would be something wrong with you if didn't feel it."

"Don't they get what the cost was?"

"I'm sure they do," she says, "but they don't get it as much as you get it. They don't feel it the same. Give them time," she says. "They'll come around."

"They said I'll have to go to a different school now. Is that true?"

"Yes."

"I don't know how to write, or read." He starts to laugh. "I don't even know what an alphabet looks like. How am I supposed to go to a school full of people who can do all of that?"

"You'll be able to go because people are going to support you, Joshua. Nobody expects you to be at their level on day one. It's going to take time, and this might sound funny, but you'll start on children's books."

"Like A is for apple?"

"Something like that," she says.

"I don't even know what an A looks like."

"No, but what you are doing is talking yourself into a panic. You have to give it time. Think of it this way," she says. "If a five-year-old can learn to read and write, I think you can learn too."

He laughs again, and she laughs with him. "You're focusing on small things that you're going to overcome so quickly, when what you should be doing is focusing on how the world is going to open up to you. You are going to see things that will take your breath away."

"What else?" he asks.

"You'll see things that—"

He shakes his head. "You said there are going to be changes in my life, and I know I've never seen the world, but I know enough about it to know not all the changes can be good."

"That's . . . that's showing a wisdom beyond your years," she says.

He wants to tell her it's not wisdom at all, but the curse. It's true his dad died, enabling him to see—but the curse isn't about balance. The curse takes and takes and takes.

"I've been doing this a long time," she says, "and I've helped countless patients with vision problems. I've performed enucleations, removed cataracts, transplanted corneas, I've done it all, and it changes people's lives for the better. But the surgery I gave you I've only ever performed twice before, and I can tell you that it doesn't change only your life, but the lives of those around you in fundamental ways. One of those recipients, her husband left her three months later, and she still doesn't quite know why. The thing is, what I've learned from my patients is there are going to be people who won't know what to say, there will be others who are jealous, and in this day and age of social media, there will be those who will call you a freak."

"Why would people do that?"

"Because people who don't like themselves are drawn to the idea of belittling others online." She takes his hand. "Look, Joshua, those are small trade-offs for what you're being given, and the reality is most people are going to be excited for you. I just think you should know not everybody will be."

When his mom shows up later in the day she's brought dinner with her. They go outside and sit on a bench in the sun. They eat burgers and fries and he drinks cola while she tells him about the funeral. It was held in a Catholic church even though his dad wasn't a Catholic. His dad wasn't an anything when it came to religion, but it was a police funeral and police funerals usually require big churches with lots of standing room.

"There were so many people, not all of them could fit inside," she says. "And the day, the day was so beautiful, so warm, it was the kind of day your father used to call 'good funeral weather' if he ever had to attend one."

The priest's name was Father Jacob, and she tells Joshua that he would have liked him. "Kind and considerate, he spoke incredibly well. Your father had met him, actually. They met at a police funeral last year that Father Jacob presided over. You remember the one? I went to it with him while you were at school."

"I remember."

"They met again a few months ago at"—and he hears her breath catch for a moment—"at another police funeral. It seems . . ." she says, and lets the words trail off. He knows what it seems like. It seems like lots of police officers are dying. It seems like the funeral business is a good business to be in.

She tells him who was there. All his grandparents, of course. Cousins and aunts and uncles from every branch of the family tree. Most of the seats were taken up by colleagues from the police force. "There had to be over a hundred of them," she says. His mom's work colleagues, friends from school, from life. People his dad had helped through the years came to pay their respects. William and Pete came with their parents. "Even Principal Anderson was there," she says. "So many people loved him. It was . . . it was a beautiful service, and so many people had stories to tell."

"I wish I had been there."

"I know you do, honey, I know you do. Reporters were there. It's going to be all over the news, so you'll be able to see footage of it when the bandages come off."

He doesn't know if he wants to. He wanted to be there, yes, but watching it replayed on television or on the Internet . . . he isn't sure. They finish their burgers. His father isn't just dead anymore, but dead and buried. Life is moving on. His eyes don't itch that night. Maybe the tears are helping.

Day four and it's Friday and it's the itch that wakes him. He claws at the bandages. He has to get them off. Has to. He pulls at them, then there are hands grabbing at him, he's being held down and they're treating him like a madman. He yells at them, and they tell him he's going to be okay. He's sedated. When he wakes up a few hours later the itch has gone and the bandages have been replaced once again. He wants to go home. He can't do this anymore.

He listens to his audiobooks when he's awake, or talks to his mother. He listens to music. He eats. Nurses flow in and out of his room. In eighteen hours the bandages will come off. In twelve hours. Nighttime comes. Nighttime goes. Saturday morning arrives. It's day five. It's early. His eyes are itching.

This time nobody has to hold him down.

Day five, and Dr. Toni Coleman tells him that it's time.

ELEVEN

—◉—

The day after Simon's death starts with a hangover and a call to his boss to report in sick. It's been years since he's had a hangover. Sure, he and Simon would drink when they were out at the cabin, but never enough to end up blacking out like he did last night and waking up feeling like he had fallen asleep in a desert. The worst thing is he didn't have any of his own beer left, and even though he had another batch fermenting out at the cabin, it wouldn't be ready for a few more days, so last night after he finished sanding down the rocking horse he went out and bought some. The bottle stores and supermarkets were closed, so he ended up buying it from a gas station. The stuff he bought had dragons on the label. It looked cheap, and that's exactly how it tasted. The dragons should have been a giveaway, but he didn't give a fuck, and he drank it anyway, and he drank it at home rather than driving out to the cabin as he had planned. He couldn't be bothered making the drive. Sure, he needed to go out there to feed the dog—she was cooped up inside, and he needed to walk her too—but she was used to being left alone for a day or two and never seemed to mind, as long as they left enough food and water out for her.

So far he's spent the morning massaging his hangover while reading news online about Simon. For the first time in years he misses having a TV. It would have been easier to relax on the couch and watch the media paint his friend as the worst human being to have ever lived rather than sitting upright at his computer having to Google it. People who worked with him or lived near him say Simon was quiet, Simon was a good neighbor, Simon was a good person to work for, Simon was quiet, was quiet, was quiet. He was a guy who dotted his *i*'s and crossed his *t*'s and took pride in his work, but he's also a guy who killed a woman and a policeman. The people interviewed are folks Vincent has never seen before. It's all six-degrees-of-separation bullshit by sad sacks wanting to get their faces in the news. Vincent doesn't have any social media accounts, but a quick check shows him that Simon is trending. The six-degrees folks didn't have much to say on camera, but online they can't keep their traps shut, calling him a hundred different kinds of pervert and a hundred different kinds of creep, and they're all wrong, because Simon wasn't like that. Part of Vincent still can't believe his best friend is dead. Part of him keeps holding out hope for his cell phone to ring, and for Simon to say, *Geez, buddy, have you heard about the guy with the same name as me being accused of all that weird shit?*

He closes his computer. He applies a primer to the rocking horse in the garage. It's oil based, so he opens the windows to help with the smell, but it still gives him a headache. He keeps waiting for the police to show up, or at least call, but they don't. That worries him. It makes him think maybe they're putting something together. Could be they're even following him. His mom calls, though. As does his brother. They ask him, *Is it true, what the police are saying?* They ask him, *Could Simon really have done these things?* They ask him, *How did we miss this? How did any of us miss this?*

He tells them it can't be true.

When the day turns to night, Vincent sits in the backyard in a deck chair he built last summer that is now covered in spiderwebs but no spiders, and he wonders where they've gone. He stares at the stars, at the half moon, and he drinks another dragon beer, knowing if he has enough of them he can stay calm.

He thinks about that day fishing. The girl with the mountain bike. Ruby.

She didn't tell them her last name, but they saw it all over the news in the days and weeks following her disappearance. The funny thing is that neither Simon nor Vincent had ever talked about doing anything like that before. It just happened.

Ruby was cute. She was in her midtwenties, which made her almost ten years younger than them. She biked a lot, so she said, and on this occasion she had mistimed a turn through the trail and hit a stump and the wheel was bent so badly it wouldn't turn. This far out into nowhere, of course there was no phone reception. Yes, they would help her. They had a cabin a few miles upstream. There was a phone there she was welcome to use. They could take the bike with them in the boat, or leave it there and pick it up later. It was up to her. She wanted to take it with her. She was slim. Athletic. They helped her into the boat. Ruby had a killer smile, and when she turned it on, it made him smile. Simon too. She had a way about her, no doubt about it, the kind of personality you wanted to bottle and store and break out on cold, dark days. If she hadn't have been those things, then it probably would have gone very differently.

But she had been all those things. And their intention to help her changed when they were halfway back to the cabin. It changed when Simon asked if she would be interested in going on a date with him. She smiled, and said thanks, but she wasn't looking for a boyfriend.

Why? I'm not good enough for you?

The words didn't match the real Simon he knew, but they did line up with the one who'd been getting steadily drunk over the previous two hours. The one whose girlfriend had dumped him. He did, however, deliver the words with a venom that didn't line up with any version of Simon that Vincent had ever known. The mood on the boat changed. It was sudden.

Ruby looked uncomfortable. *No, it's not that, I . . . I don't really date . . . maybe some other time.*

Some other time, huh? Simon said.

Cool it, Vincent said.

How about we help you some other time instead?

I didn't mean to upset you.

Yeah, you never do, Simon said, and in that moment Vincent knew *you* was for the woman who had broken up with him. It was for his boss. It was for every woman who had ever turned him down.

Simon . . . Vincent said, but his friend didn't hear. Instead he shoved Ruby hard.

You're a psychopath, she said.

Yeah? You really think that? Simon asked, and then he went about proving her point, and Vincent, well, he sat there and watched. There are ways you always think you will behave in life. Neighbor's house on fire? Vincent always knew he'd run inside to save who he could, even if it meant dying. Somebody got a flat tire on the side of the road? He'd pull over and help. Somebody outside a bar getting beaten up? Vincent would stop it. A woman being assaulted? He would never put up with that kind of shit. He would step in. Of course he would.

Only he didn't. He found himself standing back and watching. The truth is, he can't even say exactly what was running through his mind at that moment, and he's tried so many times to figure it out. His life changed then. The person he always thought he was wasn't there. That guy had moved out, and Vincent has no idea when exactly that happened. Maybe he was never there. He was a myth, because, after all, Vincent never had been forced to run into a burning building. He never had seen anybody beaten up outside a bar, and he'd never come across somebody on the road with a flat tire who looked like he or she needed help. It's possible that Vincent was nothing more than a hypothetical, and it took Ruby to make that hypothetical disappear.

So yes, his life changed in that moment—as did Simon's. Their lives became better. On that boat, once the shock of both his inability to act and Simon's ability to act left him, it washed over him—this sense of power like nothing he had ever felt.

Sitting out on his deck chair drinking his third beer, he thinks about what a good thing Ruby had been for them. A positive experience overall. She gave him something he never knew he had wanted until then and, according to the news, it was the same something Simon must have been searching for again with Andrea Walsh.

Day two, and the media are still all over the story like white on rice, like red on blood. He opens the curtains and windows and he calls in sick and leaves the cheap beer alone and considers taking a trip out to the cabin. There's still plenty of work to do out there. He and Simon have been working on it for the last nine years, turning the beaten-up old cabin into a thing of beauty—an ongoing project that he doesn't believe either of them really thought they'd ever finish. Not because they weren't able, and not because there were problems, but because they were always looking for more to do, and when it looked like things were getting done, one of them would float an idea to expand something, or convert something, or even add on a room. Hell, nine years ago the cabin was barely above ground, a single-story shithole handed down from his grandparents to his parents. When he was a kid, his folks used to take the family there for a few days every summer, and every time they showed up, he hoped the place had been hit by lightning or eaten by termites, and often it sure looked like it had been. Ten years ago he took Simon there to see if he thought it was worth salvaging so his family could sell the place. Simon said all the value was in the land, but also believed that together they could turn the cabin into something that would make them a huge profit. Vincent was doubtful—he'd never picked up a power tool in his life—but under Simon's guidance he quickly adapted to the point where he now considers himself just as good a builder as Simon ever was. The goal was always to renovate and then sell it, but soon they never spoke about selling it. It became a labor of love, one neither of them was willing to say good-bye to. Perhaps that's why the cabin grew. Some weekends they would drive out there and spend the days constructing, with the occasional weekend of fishing and drinking, but over the last few years, and especially after they bought the boat, the balance changed. Hell, they even got themselves a dog because it felt like they were living there—every second day, or sometimes every day, one of them goes out there and feeds it.

Which he's going to have to do. Soon.

Yesterday he was in no mood, but now that he's a single parent to her, if he doesn't go out there she's going to starve to death. He puts on his shoes and grabs his keys and steps outside. The sun is out, but it doesn't have the same heat in it that it did even a week ago. His car is in the driveway, and he has his hand on the door when another car comes to a stop outside his house. He turns and leans against his car and watches as a man in a dark suit and a woman in a red blouse and dark pants climb out. They walk over to him. The woman has a scar on her face and no wedding ring, and he suspects those two details are connected. The man has slicked-back hair and a pair of designer glasses that makes his eyes look small and is dressed better than any cop he's seen before—and he knows that's what they are before they introduce themselves, which they do a moment later. Detective Inspector Rebecca Kent and Detective Inspector Brian Travers. He wonders how much they know or think they know, and decides not that much. Otherwise it wouldn't be just these two cops, but a team with dogs and guns and bulletproof vests. They ask if they can have a few minutes of his time, and he tells them sure, no problem, and invites them inside.

"You're painting something?" Travers asks, sniffing the air.

"Sorry, I'd gotten used to the smell," Vincent says. "We can sit outside, if you like."

"In here is fine," Travers says, as they take a seat in the lounge.

"What are you painting?" Kent asks him.

"A rocking horse for my niece. It's her birthday."

"How old?" Travers asks.

He knows what they're doing. They're making small talk while evaluating him. It's a game, but a game easy to win once you know it's being played. Building a rocking horse for his niece, what could be better?

"She turns five next week. Okay, don't judge me, but I can't help myself," he says, and he pulls out his wallet and opens it to show them the photo of her. She's wearing a Spider-Man outfit that he bought her for Christmas ever since she fell in love with the crime fighter. Now she wears it all the time. "Her name is Matilda."

"Such a cute age," Travers says.

He closes up his wallet and puts it back into his pocket. Matilda has scored him some points. He offers them a drink to score some more, but they say no. He needs to be careful.

"So no doubt you're here to ask me about Simon," he says.

"You were expecting us?" Kent asks.

"Kind of, yeah. I figured you'd be wanting to talk to anybody who knew him."

"You two were close," she says. "Best friends, even."

They've been best friends since the day they met in high school, almost twenty years ago. Simon's family had lived in Auckland but moved to Christchurch because his dad was taking on a new job, and Simon joined his school halfway through the year. They were fifteen. Simon sat next to him in class that day, and during the first recess Vincent asked him where he was from. They started talking. Vincent didn't have any real friends back then, and Simon didn't know anybody, so they started hanging out. They became fast friends, but actually it felt like they were brothers. More than brothers. They grew up seeing the world the same way, a world that was unfair, so you had to take what you could, because nothing ever came for free. Neither of them excelled in school, neither of them went to university, both of them were concerned with current events but never willing to help make change. They didn't vote, because they didn't see a point, neither had had a relationship that lasted longer than a few months, and even then those relationships were few and far between. Often a skill one of them didn't have, the other would. In a way, their friendship was symbiotic. Vincent knows that through the years there have been some who thought they were more than friends. The truth is they loved each other, like brothers, and without each other they had nothing, and right now Vincent has nothing.

Well, nothing except his desperate need to burn Detective Inspector Ben Kirk's corner of the world.

"You could say that," he says.

"Everybody else seems to," she says. "In fact, I'm saying his death is the reason you've called in sick, because you sure look okay."

He shrugs. "Everything is so . . . so messed up. You're right, we were best friends, and that's why I know Simon didn't do whatever you think he's done. I know you think different, and I know you've come here with preconceived ideas to go along with the narrative you're creating about Simon, and I'm telling you now I'm not going to go along with it. Simon was a good guy. A really good guy. Whatever you think he did, he didn't do."

The detectives stare at him. He doesn't add anything.

"When was the last time you saw him?" Kent asks.

"Why? So you can tell me he killed somebody that night too?"

Both detectives frown at him. "Mr. Archer—"

He puts his hand up to stop Detective Kent from saying whatever it is she's about to say. "I'm sorry," he says. "I . . . I don't know. I mean . . . it's been a difficult few days. Not only is my best friend dead, but now people want me to believe he was a monster. Put yourself in my shoes. How'd you feel if you woke up tomorrow being told your best friend was dead and that they were a murderer?"

"It would be difficult," Kent says.

"Difficult doesn't even begin to sum it up."

"We appreciate how hard this is for you," Travers says, "but we need to piece together Simon's life and learn more about him. Can you remember the last time you saw him?"

He leans back into the couch. He puts his hand over his mouth and strokes his beard and acts like he's giving it some serious thought, even though he can remember exactly when it was. Only he doesn't want to tell them he was at Simon's house a few nights before he died. "I don't know. A week ago maybe. Monday last week I think it was. He came by on his way home from work. He does that sometimes and hangs out for a bit."

"And what do you normally chat about?" Travers asks.

"I don't know. Stuff. Just stuff. Life. Work."

"Women?" Kent asks.

"Everything," he says. "Just not . . . not the kind of things you think he did."

"What kind of places did you go with him? Bars? Strip joints?"

"Strip joints?" He laughs. "I don't know why you'd think that, but no. We were into fishing," he says, immediately regretting it.

"Fishing?" she asks. "Where would you go fishing?"

"Lots of places."

"Like where?" she asks.

"Wherever there's water. The beach, usually. Off the rocks out by the estuary," he says, even though he's never fished there before. He can't tell them where he really fishes. Can't lead them in that direction. "Places around there. It's peaceful. We'd go out there and fish and shoot the breeze, maybe have a beer or two." He smiles at Kent, who doesn't smile back, so he tries his luck with Travers. He's hoping the fishing-relaxing-drinking thing might help form a connection. It doesn't. Maybe he should get the photo of Matilda back out and show them.

"You met Simon in school, right?" Kent asks.

"High school, yeah."

"So you've known him for twenty years," Kent says.

"Something like that."

"How is it a guy you've known for so long, a guy you're best friends with, a guy you go fishing with to shoot the breeze, how is it you couldn't know what he was capable of?"

The question angers him, but he doesn't take the bait. Every day people get arrested for doing things their husbands and wives didn't know about it. Everybody has secrets. He knows they know this. He knows they've arrested people before whose partners and friends and family had no idea of the truth. This is no different from any of those times, no different from learning your next-door neighbor was beating up his wife or that the really lovely nurse at the care home was stealing from the old folks. He shrugs. "I don't know," he says. "It makes no sense. I keep thinking back on things we've spoken about, but he never said anything to ever make me suspect something like this. It's why I know you guys are wrong about him."

"We're not wrong," Kent says.

"And I'm telling you that you are," he says. "The Simon I knew, that's not him. You can say whatever you want about him, but eventually the truth will come out and you'll see he's innocent."

What else can he tell them about Simon? Well, he can tell them Simon is/was a quiet guy. Simon is/was a good guy. Simon isn't/wasn't possible of doing the kinds of things they're saying he did. He hammers on the point not because it's true, which it isn't, but because if he shows a steadfast belief in his friend's innocence then the police will see him as the unsuspecting friend rather than the eager enabler.

They spend thirty minutes with him. They ask him about their school days. They ask him if Simon ever spoke about his days before they met, which he had, and he tells them so. There wasn't much to tell, other than that Simon didn't have a lot of friends, and had to change schools when his dad got a new job and they all moved down from Auckland. They ask him if he'd ever heard of Andrea Walsh, which he hadn't, up until the news. They ask him a lot of things and they take notes and he doesn't think he's added anything to the narrative of Simon they're trying to piece together.

He walks them to the door when they're done. He shakes their hands, and Detective Kent holds on to his and stares at him, and says, "That was bullshit, what he told you, about his dad getting a new job."

"What?"

"When they moved down from Auckland. They moved for a fresh start. Simon tied up his fourteen-year-old neighbor and kept her in an empty neighboring house that was for sale. He kept her for six hours because he wanted to spend more time with her so he could convince her to be his girlfriend."

He doesn't know what to say. Simon never mentioned it.

"She escaped when she told him she needed to use the bathroom, and when he let her, she climbed through the window. Because of his age, he was given name suppression and the record of the crime was sealed. Nobody at the school was ever told, and the girl's family moved away within days of it happening, and then Simon's family moved too. You said before the Simon you knew wasn't capable of hurting anybody. The thing is, Vincent, that's the same Simon who kidnapped his neighbor, and before that he killed that same neighbor's dog. That's the Simon you've known for twenty years." She lets go of his hand and gives him her card. "If you think of anything else, give us a call."

He watches them as they walk down the path to their car. He's always thought that everything started with Ruby. If what Detective Kent told him is true, then it didn't.

He wonders if Ruby was even his second.

He waits a few minutes until they're gone. They have no reason to follow him, but even so, he takes an indirect way out to the motorway, checking his mirrors often. It adds thirty minutes to what is normally a forty-minute drive.

The cabin is at the end of an access road that takes a couple of minutes to traverse. Out here it's mostly beech trees, with the occasional pine tree too. It's not a rough road, but it is a dirt road that's been packed down hard, and not impervious to tree roots growing out of it or wildlife burrowing into it, and of course it's not impervious to the weather. This time of year it's at its best, but over the years there have been winters when the road has threatened to bog down anything moving over it.

The cabin overlooks the river; their boat is parked up on a trailer next to it. The cabin all those years ago was less than half the size it is now—and really, the most original thing left is the address. Bit by bit most pieces have been replaced, and it stopped being a cabin years ago and became a house—even though neither he nor Simon ever referred to it as such, and he isn't going to begin now. With two stories and four bedrooms and two lounges and three bathrooms, the cabin looks like a home stripped out of the heart of an expensive suburban neighborhood and planted into the forest. The top floor has floor-to-ceiling windows that face north, looking out over the river, where the sun streams in, and on the balcony up there they would talk about carpentry, about work, about their families, about their school days. They never ran out of stuff to talk about—though they often did talk about the same things. They'd have breakfast up there, and when he comes out here alone, he sits up there with a book and often falls asleep in the sun. Once they spent weeks trying to come up with a way to fish from the balcony, even though there were fifteen yards of dirt and stumps between the cabin and the river, and when they finally devised a way through a series of pulleys wrapped over tree branches, they thought it was cheating so never followed through.

The cabin has a smell that only homes in forests have, the scent of wood and the fresh air moving over the river, and the scent of the forest floor and fallen leaves rotting in the sun. It's the smell of nature, and it relaxes him. The cabin, at the moment, also has the smell of his fermenting beer. The dog hears him come inside, and she comes crawling out of the kennel in the utility room and sits in the doorway of the hallway. She's hungry and really thirsty. He should have come out here last night instead of drinking all the beer to take the edge off his grief.

"Hey there, girl," he says, and he strokes her behind her ear and she says nothing, just looks at him like he betrayed her for leaving her alone so long. "What's that on your leg?" He crouches down next to her. "Is that blood?"

Concerned, he goes into the utility room. It's the last room out here they modified. It used to be a boot room, but they extended it to become a combined boot room, laundry, and bathroom a few months back. The kennel is in there too.

There are drops of blood splashed around the entire room. There are pieces of tape on the walls, and torn bits of plastic. This is where Simon brought the woman he killed. He taped plastic up on the walls, and covered the floor, and he probably killed the woman in front of the dog, then cleaned up. What did he do with the body? He looks at the chest freezer and hopes she's not in there, but when he opens it up, his hopes are wasted. She's in there, cut up in pieces and wrapped tightly in plastic bags. He's going to have to get rid of her, and he's going to have to get rid of all the plastic that was taped to the walls that he guesses is jammed into the garbage bin out back. He has no idea what the hell Simon was planning. Was he keeping her as a souvenir? Was he planning on getting rid of the parts one at a time in dark corners of the city? Toss them into the river? He realizes he's never going to know.

He uses a towel to wipe down the dog. Then he fills one bowl with water and one with dog meat and watches her eat for a few minutes before spending the next hour cleaning up the mess Simon made. When he's done, he stands in the doorway staring at the dog, wondering what he's going to do with her. Getting the dog was Simon's idea, and now that he's gone he's not real sure he wants to keep her. Looking after her now will mean twice the work for him. He certainly feels a sense of contentment having her around—Simon felt the same—and so he decides her future will be a decision for another day.

He hits the bookshelves upstairs and finds the copy of *Of Mice and Men* that his brother gave him for his birthday nearly ten years ago. He's never read it. He reads it out in the sun, imagining that he's George from the book, and Simon was Lenny, but that doesn't work, because really they'd both be George—both willing to shoot somebody they loved if it came down to it. He closes out day two by falling asleep on the couch in the upstairs lounge.

On day three he leaves the cabin early and goes home and gets changed for work. For the last two years he's been a courier driver, hauling people's crap from one side of the city to the other. Before being a courier, he spent a year working in a coffee shop, and before that he spent six months cleaning cars at a car yard, and before that he spent a year stacking supermarket shelves at night. He's worked in shops, he's dug graves at cemeteries, he's landscaped, he's been a farmhand, he's spent summers picking fruit, he once worked for a phone company, and his first job out of school was working in a factory that built vacuum cleaners. Simon used to tell him to come and work for him, that with his building skills he'd fit right in, but Vincent never liked the idea of it. He loves building, he loves carpentry, but there's an intimacy to what he creates that he doesn't want to share with people he doesn't know. He's always been one of those guys who bounce from job to job with few ambitions, and he's always been okay with that. He doesn't want to be anything more than he is, because he doesn't like the responsibility that comes with it. Hell, even looking after a dog is more responsibility than he's ever wanted.

Every morning, the van is waiting for him full of packages at the depot. There's no end to his work, because there's no end to the amount of crap people ship and receive. The truth is that over the last few months he'd been thinking about taking the job Simon was offering. At least being a builder would give him a sense of completion. Now it's too late, but maybe it's time he started looking for something else— something that involves the skills he's developed.

He spends Thursday morning picking up and delivering packages with no sense of urgency. At one o'clock he decides that if people don't get what they ordered yesterday until tomorrow, their lives aren't going to end. He drives back to the depot, changes into the black suit he brought, and prepares himself to say good-bye to his best friend.

The cemetery is peaceful. He locks his car and sees there is no sea of people; in fact, the cemetery is so empty he's beginning to wonder if he got the right day. He walks among the gravestones, sweating in the sun with his hands in his pockets. Up ahead are Simon's parents and Simon's sister and her husband and the priest and nobody else. Did everybody else in Simon's life think so little of him that they actually believe he did those bad things? Of course, he did do them, but why aren't people doubting that? They can't know, not for sure, yet they're quick to believe the worst.

Simon's dad looks like an older version of Simon, he has the same beard, the same hair, only a little thinner, the same eyes, and he nods at Vincent in the way of a greeting but says nothing. Simon's mom, the only religious one in the family, won't even look at him, and nor will Simon's sister. Her husband gives him a shrug that Vincent can't decipher. Do they even want him here? Because it's starting to feel like they don't. Do they blame him somehow? Or are they embarrassed? He keeps a small distance from them in case they have the urge to throw him in with his best friend.

When the priest sees that nobody else is coming, he gets the proceedings under way. His name is Father Daniels, and Father Daniels is thin and gaunt and looks more like somebody you'd see on the other side of death. He appears to be in his fifties, with thick, dark hair that's losing its war against the grays. He doesn't really have a lot to say. What is there? *Simon was a quiet guy?* But Daniels does his best, summing up a man he never knew but who did bad things into a eulogy full of platitudes and clichés that avoids mentioning his skill with a power saw.

During the service other people start arriving, not for Simon, but for the story. The papers are starting to call him Simply Simon, because the police say he was simple to find, he simply died, and the case is simply over. Vincent thinks the name is a stretch and doesn't like it. Those who are now arriving are the people who gave him that name, and they stand thirty yards away speaking into microphones and TV cameras with the funeral as the backdrop. As soon as the service is over, Vincent takes a wide berth to get around them to get back to his car. By the time all of this is over, Simon will be so demonized he'll be blamed for everything from global warming to the struggling economy.

The parking lot is full now. His car is a dark-blue station wagon twenty years old with stickers on the back bumper and cobwebs in the corners. It creaks as he climbs into it, and things rattle behind the dashboard when he drives. He bought it ten years ago when he was selling cell phones and has never been able to afford anything better. Halfway home it breaks down. He pops the hood and doesn't know what he's looking at. When it comes to working with wood, or working on houses, he's become an artist, but he doesn't know much about cars. Simon did. Simon would simply . . .

Simply Simon.

Damn it, he has to make sure he doesn't think of his friend that way.

He pulls the caps off the spark plugs and pushes them back down, wiggles some cables, and whatever he does works because the car starts. He makes it home, promising himself that he'll go and see a mechanic next week. Or maybe the week after.

He fries up some bacon and some chicken and makes himself a Caesar salad for dinner that night that, reluctantly, he ends up pairing with the last of his dragon beer. He lets day three close out by falling asleep on the couch listening to the radio.

Day four, and the routine of life is kicking in. Breakfast. Work. Lunch. Work. He alters the routine after work and drives to the police station and waits outside. It's Friday, and Fridays always have twice as many cars on the road for some reason that's never been explained to him. He sits in his car munching away at a bag of chips and drinking from a can of soda until Detective Inspector Ben Kirk pulls out from the parking lot behind the police station. He's driving a white sports car that's low to the ground. Vincent stays a few cars behind. They get caught in traffic. Cars fail to indicate and busses cut people off, but he keeps Ben in sight. Fifteen minutes later, Ben pulls into the parking lot of a restaurant in town that would have been quicker to walk to in this traffic than drive. Vincent parks on the street opposite. The restaurant has large Asian symbols all over the side of the building, as well as pictures of dragons that remind him of the beer he wishes he hadn't bought the other night. Through the window of the restaurant he sees Ben hugging a blond woman. She's wearing a tight black dress that doesn't have any sleeves. She's attractive. She looks familiar, but he can't figure out from where.

He watches them talk. He watches them order. He watches them eat. He watches them stand and hug tightly during dessert while everybody else in the restaurant watches. He watches them pay the bill and watches them leave in separate cars.

They all head west, taking the road that cuts through the center of the biggest park in the city, Hagley Park. Every time he drives past it, he's reminded of the fact that his first kiss took place on the bank of the Avon River in Hagley Park. He was fourteen years old and had to pay the girl five dollars for it, but it was worth it because she charged the other kids in their class ten. They continue east into Riccarton and into a nicer neighborhood than the one Vincent lives in, with nicer-looking houses with nicer-looking cars parked out front and up driveways. The houses in the street they end up in are all less than twenty years old. Both cars pull into the driveway of a redbrick town-house with large windows and a well-kept garden, but not one as well kept as his own.

He writes the address down on the back of his hand and leaves.

Day four ends with him back out at the cabin with the dog tied to a tree while he digs a hole for the body parts being stored in the freezer. He's happier having her out of the cabin, as if the freezer were a gate through which she could haunt him, but later that evening he thinks that before winter arrives he will bury her farther away. He decides to spend the night at the cabin. Day five, and there will be more driving, more packages, more knocking on doors and getting people to sign for things because people want their shit on Saturdays, too. But day five is also the first day of the rest of his life.

Day five, he has decided, is the day Detective Ben Kirk starts to suffer.

TWELVE

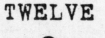

Joshua imagines the air in the room must be thinning out as everybody takes a deep breath in anticipation. All the sadness at what happened, all the fear and the excitement of what might happen, it's all lead to this moment. He sits on the edge of the bed with his mom next to him holding his hand. His other hand is shaking a little.

"I need you to stay still, okay?" Dr. Toni says.

"Okay," he says.

"You don't need to hold your breath."

"I can't help it."

"Here we go," Dr. Toni says.

There's a hand on the back of his head, then pressure as a blade goes between layers of the bandaging. It sounds incredibly loud as the scissors go through it. It's pulled away. The pressure on his eyes relaxes.

Slowly, he opens them.

Nothing but darkness.

He tightens his grip on his mom's hand so hard she cries out. "I can't see anything," he says.

"There's still padding on your eyes," Dr. Toni says.

"There is?"

"There is," she says, and then she starts to remove the tape that's been crisscrossed over the padding. It tugs at his skin but doesn't hurt and is as loud as the scissors were. "Almost there," she says, and then something wet is on his skin, it's touching the side of the padding, loosening it from his face.

"You're doing good, honey," his mom says.

"I want you to keep your eyes closed," Dr. Toni says. "Okay? It's important."

"Okay."

There is more tugging at his skin, it hurts but he says nothing, and then . . . then the darkness out to the left isn't as dark anymore. It's lighter, a shade of . . . he doesn't know. A shade of something he's never experienced. The same shade as the sun, maybe. It's warmth. It's a glow. He's smiling now. He has the urge to laugh. More tugging, and then a similar sensation in his other eye. Something wet is wiped in downward motions over each of them. Then something soft to dry them. He's holding his breath again.

"Okay, Joshua, I want you to try and open your eyes, slowly, okay? Really slowly."

"Okay," he says.

He opens his eyes.

He doesn't know what he's supposed to see, but there's light and color and there is so much of it he has to close them again, and when he opens them there's nothing more than what he previously saw. There are no sharp lines, no edges, no detail. Is this vision? Is this what everybody sees? Dr. Toni is standing in front of him.

"Give it a few moments," she says.

"For what?"

"For them to adjust."

"Adjust in what way?" he asks, and she doesn't answer, nor does she need to, because he sees in which way as the shapes in the room sharpen. Dr. Toni comes into focus, and within seconds he knows he can never go back to the dark from which he's emerged. He will fight tooth and nail to keep what he's been given.

He turns to face his mom. She's wearing a shirt the same color as Dr. Toni's jacket, which he thinks might be white, because that's what doctors wear. His mom is smiling so much her face looks like it's going to break, but perhaps that's how people always look when they're happy. He's always wondered what she looked like, and yet she looks like how he imagined. How he knew she would look. He can't explain it.

"I can see you," he says.

She tries to say something but can't. She wipes at her tears. He tightens his grip on her hand.

"Joshua?"

"I can see you," he says, louder this time.

He looks at Dr. Toni. She has long hair that comes to her shoulders. Her skin looks soft. He wonders if she's beautiful. To him she is. She's the most beautiful woman in the world because she's made it possible for him to see. He realizes he's smiling so much his face might break too. When was the last time he felt like laughing out of sheer happiness?

"Tell me what you can see," Dr. Toni says.

"Everything," he says, and he can't hold back the laughter. "I can see everything."

"That's good, Joshua, really good. Now I want you to tilt your head back for me so I can put in some drops. These will help with the itching."

He tilts his head back. She puts a thumb on his eyelids one at a time and lets a couple of drops fall in. They're cold and make him flinch. He blinks a few times. The itching is disappearing. He straightens himself up. He holds his right hand in front of his face. Four fingers and a thumb and the palm of his hand, life lines going across it, fingernails and hair, and he looks at his wrist, he's always thought he'd be able to see his pulse, but he can't see it moving. He's been able to see for barely a minute and he's learned something new. He lowers his hand and Dr. Toni raises hers.

"How many fingers am I holding up?" she asks.

He has to process that. He can count, but he's never counted visually before, so he has to figure it out. "Three. Now one. Now four."

She backs away until she's in the doorway. "And now?"

"Four. Two. Four."

"Good," Dr. Toni says, coming back towards him, and already he's sick of this. Yes, he can count fingers, yes, he can see the inside of this room, but he wants to see more. He lets go of his mother and scoots to the edge of the bed. "Wait," Dr. Toni says.

But he doesn't wait. He gets to his feet and the next thing he knows, both Dr. Toni and his mom are holding on to him and he can't stand straight.

"What's happening?" his mom asks, sounding concerned.

"Joshua's brain is being overloaded with new stimuli," Dr. Toni says, as they prop him back up on the bed. "Joshua, I know this sounds crazy, but you're going to have to get used to walking. Your balance is going to be off."

"I feel dizzy."

"Give it a few hours. By the end of the day you'll be fine. How about I go and get you a wheelchair, and your mom can show you around a little."

His mom hugs him when Dr. Toni has gone. His mother with red hair tied into a ponytail because he's been told that's what color it is and how she wears it, and now he knows what that means. Smooth skin and a big smile, green eyes, warm and friendly and loving and familiar. Now that he's sitting, the dizziness has gone. She pulls away from him and looks into his eyes and doesn't say anything. She's looking at his father's eyes, her husband's eyes, and it must be difficult for her.

"I'm so happy for you," she says.

He doesn't say anything.

"Are you okay?"

"Yes," he says, but he's not okay. It doesn't matter that he can see. It doesn't matter that by the end of the day he'll be up and about. It doesn't matter what he does, because the curse is waiting to punish him for breaking the rules and sneaking into the land of the seeing. For a short time, he'll be allowed in as a guest, but the curse won't allow him to stay. He knows it's only a matter of time before this world he can now see will cast him aside and the curse will pull him back into the darkness from where he came.

THIRTEEN

—◆—

"You're late," his boss tells him.

Vincent looks at his watch. "Only by six minutes."

"Which means you're late."

"I'll make up for it."

His boss has a beard but not the mustache component that goes with it. It's a look Vincent has never understood. Given that he's also bald, it leaves a horseshoe of dark-brown hair on the bottom half of his face. Vincent imagines picking him up by it and swinging him around. They're standing out in front of the warehouse where deliveries are being sorted. Vans are racing into and out of the building. It's going to be another hot day, and Vincent wants this conversation over with.

"You had time off at the start of the week, and on Thursday you didn't even finish your deliveries. It's—"

"My friend died," Vincent says.

"Your friend was a homicidal maniac."

"The police got that wrong. Look, I'm sorry I'm late, but it's just six minutes, and it's Saturday."

"I don't care that it's Saturday," his boss says. "And it's not just six minutes. You're six minutes late here, which means people are waiting by their doors six minutes longer than they need to. Documents get dropped off in town six minutes later than they should, people have to delay their—"

"I get your point."

"I don't think you do, because if you did you wouldn't have come in late. People have to delay their lunch breaks by six minutes, they have to—"

"Like I said, I get your point, and I'm sorry. It won't happen again."

"I know it won't happen again, because we're going to let you go."

"Wait. What? Come on, you—"

"We should have let you go a few days ago when you didn't finish your run."

"But I had to go to a funeral," he says, and he thinks that's why he's being let go. Not for being late, not for taking time off, but because Simon was his friend, and nobody wants to work with people who hang out with killers.

"Get your gear and go," the boss says. "You'll be sent a severance check within the next two weeks."

All the jobs he's had, he's always walked away from them. They've gotten boring, or too difficult, or the work was outside when the weather was too cold, or maybe he didn't like the people he worked with. This is the first time he's ever been fired. "Come on, you can't—"

"I can, and I have," the boss says. "I've assigned your route to another driver."

Vincent shakes his head. "You can't do this. I have bills to pay. What the hell am I supposed to do?"

"Be on time with your next job," his ex-boss says, "and get new friends."

He stands motionless as he watches the fucker walk away—except for his hands, which are tightening into balls of rage. He thinks about the cabin, the isolation it gives him, the power tools he has. He could cut that son of a bitch up and wrap him in different packages and deliver him all across town. Of course, the problem is that he'd be the number one suspect. In six months' time it would be an idea he could revisit.

He walks to his car. When he pulls out onto the street, the engine shudders, hiccups, comes back to life, then dies. He twists the key and pushes the accelerator, and the engine turns over but won't catch. He feels like head-butting the steering wheel. Feels like leaning forward and biting it. Everything from the last week is starting to take its toll.

He can't believe Simon killed that woman on his own without including him, can't believe Simon is dead, can't believe he got fired . . .

He punches the steering wheel. And again. A woman pushing a pram walks past and stares at him. He punches the steering wheel again and she looks away and walks a little faster.

He takes a deep breath. He thinks about the cabin. The river. How peaceful it is out there and how, if he wanted to, he could drive there right now.

It doesn't work.

The anger is still there.

The car starts. He revs the engine a few times. He pulls calmly into traffic and doesn't gun the engine and doesn't run anybody over. He drives calmly all the way to the address he drove to last night and parks two houses away. Right now what this slightly upmarket street needs is a very casual murder.

He unclips his seat belt and stops with his hand on the door. "You're being stupid," he says. "You don't even know who's home. You can't act on emotion. This isn't the plan. This was never the plan. You're angry. You should leave."

He doesn't leave. But he doesn't go inside the house either. Probably just his luck there are twenty cops in there, all hidden behind furniture, getting ready to throw a surprise party for Detective Inspector Ben Kirk, who, right now, is on his way home. A surprise party to celebrate what Ben did to Simon.

He should leave.

He needs to leave.

He will leave.

He is turning the car around when there is movement from the driveway. Ben's girlfriend. The tall blonde whom he knows from somewhere. She's driving a dark four-door sedan. He waits for her to pass. He waits until she gets to the end of the block before he begins to follow.

FOURTEEN

— ◉ —

They wheel Joshua along the corridor. There are paintings on the walls, and he tries to figure out what the images could represent. Some are landscapes; there are some with what he thinks might be flowers in vases. There are people walking past them, towards them, people who all look different, and even though he knew everybody would be, it still surprises him how different they are. Of course, if they were similar, nobody would recognize each other, but it's not just ethnicity, or the way their faces look, it's their skin, their hair, the way they walk, how tall or short they are, the way they dress, the way they hold themselves—all of them unique. There are signs everywhere, on walls, on doors, some hanging from the ceiling on chains, all with symbols that could be numbers and letters—none of which he knows. There are posters on the walls, and when he gets home, he can put posters on his walls too.

There are thousands of things to take in, and he imagines most of them are irrelevant to everyone else. He looks at things others see so often they dismiss them. He sees the beauty in a window, in a door, in the buttons by the elevator, in trash cans, in stains on the wall, in the broken leaves of a potted plant. There are objects on the floor, stuff in people's hands, things in corners, things behind other things.

"I want to go outside," he says.

"And you will," Dr. Toni says. "But I'm going to need to examine you first."

"Then I can go outside?"

"As soon as we're done, yes."

He becomes as dizzy from trying to look at everything as he did from his earlier attempt to stand. They reach Dr. Toni's office. More items everywhere, things that weren't in the corridor. A desk. A computer. Office furniture. Things on walls. A big boxy thing that might be a filing cabinet. He takes it all in. Dr. Toni crouches in front of him, staring into his eyes, something that's been done other times in his life, but for the first time he doesn't know where to look. Not into her eyes, because that makes him feel uncomfortable.

"Look into the light," she says, then holds a small flashlight in front of him.

"It hurts a little."

"Just a few more seconds," she says, and then she checks the next eye. "Everything is looking good."

"Everything is good," he says. He's still smiling. Perhaps it's a side effect. He may smile for the rest of his life.

"I want you to look at something for me," she says, and she turns his wheelchair so he's facing the wall. There's a bookshelf full of books. A coatrack. More things on the walls that might be certificates, since he knows doctors usually have them on display. She walks over to a painting with symbols on it.

"First I need you to cover your right eye for me."

He covers his right eye.

"This is an eye chart," she says. "I want you to keep your right eye covered, and I want you to tell me what shapes you see."

The biggest shapes are on the top, and they get smaller as the rows go down. She points to the top one. As before, when she was holding up fingers for him to count, he has to come to grips with what he's seeing. He knows his shapes from feel, and he's imagined how they look—now it's a matter of lining them up.

"A circle."

"Good," she says, then points to the row below where there is a line of shapes.

He has to count the sides. Three of them. It has to be . . . "A triangle."

She points to something else.

"A rectangle, and now . . . a square?"

"Good," she says, then points to the next row.

"Square, circle, um . . . I can see it, but I can't figure it out."

"It's a pentagon," she says. "Next line."

"Circle again, triangle, umm . . . looks like the pentagon again, but with more sides."

"Hexagon," she says. "Keep going."

So he does. The shapes getting smaller, then getting blurrier as he gets a few rows from the bottom. He reaches the point where he's guessing, but two guesses into it she tells him to stop.

"That's good, Joshua. Really good."

"It is, isn't it?" his mother says.

"Very good," Dr. Toni says, smiling at them both. "Now let's do the other eye."

She turns the chart over to reveal the shapes in a different order, and Joshua covers his left eye and looks at the chart with his right.

"What's the top one?" Dr. Toni asks.

He doesn't answer.

"Can you see where I'm pointing?"

"Everything is darker."

"Can you see the shapes?"

His smile wavers. "I mean, I can kind of see them, but I couldn't tell you what they are. The top one might be a circle."

"Okay," she says. "That's enough."

He takes his hand away and can see that it's a square. She turns his wheelchair towards the desk, then sits on the other side. "First of all, there's no reason to think anything yet, other than we just need more time. Could be tomorrow your right eye will be as strong as your left, or it could take a week, or a month."

"Is there a problem?" his mom asks.

Dr. Toni smiles at them. "No, we just need to be patient."

"It's okay," Joshua says. "I mean, even if it never works, it's okay. I can see and everything is amazing, and I'm thankful for what you've done, more thankful than I can ever say."

"It really is a miracle," his mother says.

Dr. Toni smiles. Joshua gets the idea they're saying all the things that makes her job rewarding. "The good news," she says, "is there are no signs of any infection. The drugs we've had you on since the operation have been doing their job. You'll need to keep taking them for a while longer, but other than that, I can't see any reason you can't leave here tomorrow."

"Not today?" he asks.

"I want to keep an eye on you today." She reaches down to a desk drawer. "Here," she says. "I'm surprised you haven't asked already."

Even though he's never seen one before, he knows it's a mirror she's handing him. When he doesn't pick it up, his mom asks if something is wrong.

"I'm not sure if I'm ready," he says.

"It's common to feel that way," Dr. Toni says. "There's no hurry."

"No," he says, and he picks up the mirror. "I want to do this now."

He can feel his smile disappear. He doesn't know what to expect, and doesn't know what would make him happy. He angles the mirror and looks into the glass, and what should be a complete stranger looking back at him isn't. This is someone familiar to him the same way his mother was familiar to him earlier. This is Joshua Logan, the boy he believed he would never see. He has black hair, because he recognizes black, and because he's been told. His skin is white, but it's not how he imagined white would be, but some warmer version of that, similar to the tone he saw earlier when his eyes were closed and light started to come through. His eyes are blue because his dad's eyes were blue, and now he knows what blue is. He wonders for a brief moment where his original eyes are—those things that were part of him his entire life have to be somewhere, don't they? His lips are red because he's been told they're red, and his teeth . . . well his teeth are white, and his skin is white, but they are different types of white, just like Dr. Toni's coat is a different white. He doesn't know if the boy smiling back is a good-looking boy or an odd-looking boy—then decides none of that matters, and then decides that later on it might matter, that his thought process today will be different from what it will be in a month, or a year, because his ability to see is going to make him different. William and Pete were right—there is no way he can go back to his old school, and he wishes they could have what he has, but not at the same cost. The skin around his eyes is darker. He reaches out and touches it gently.

"The bruising will take another week or two to fade," Dr. Toni says, "and the swelling will disappear."

"Okay," he says.

"And you're going to need to wear protective glasses," she says, "for a few weeks. We don't want to risk anything getting into your eyes."

"I'll make sure he wears them," his mom says.

"And you're going to keep taking pills for a while, and eye drops too. You're going to have to come back in here every day for a few weeks."

He hands the mirror back to Dr. Toni. "Thank you," he says. "Thank you for everything you've done."

"You're welcome," she says, then hands him a pair of clear protective glasses. "Now, why don't you go and take a look around outside and put those new eyes of yours to use?"

FIFTEEN

Erin Murphy is running late. The kind of late that will annoy her colleagues, but it's the kind of annoyance that will disappear when she shows off the ring on her finger. Last night, Ben proposed. Proposed! The ring was hidden inside a fortune cookie given to her near the end of the evening, and once she opened it and saw what was inside, he got down on one knee and asked her to marry him. It was totally romantic, like something from a movie. For a moment they were the center of attention as everybody in the restaurant turned to watch, which was a little embarrassing, and everybody went quiet as they waited for her to give her answer—would she say yes? Would she say no? Was happiness to come, or disappointment? She said yes, to the relief of not just the crowd, but to Ben too, and probably also the waiters, who had probably seen people storm out without paying when things didn't go well. This morning she couldn't be any happier—even if deep down she questions if the proposal came because Mitchell's death put Ben's life into perspective. You have to hold on to what you have, because one day it might slip away—and what happened to Mitchell couldn't be a bigger reminder of that.

She winds down her window when she reaches the parking garage in town. The parking garage is a five-story concrete cube that looks like it could survive a nuclear bomb. There's a homeless guy hanging out front.

"Morning," he says, coming over.

"This is for you," she says, and she hands him a sandwich, which is part of her morning routine. Henry used to be a doctor, before he became a gambling addict, which led to him losing his job, losing his house, his wife, his kids. This she discovered a year ago when he helped her after the heel broke on her shoe and she fell over right in front of him, twisting her ankle and spraining her wrist in the process.

"Thanks, Erin," he says. "You're the best. Is that what I think it is?" he asks, looking at her hand, and she smiles even though deep down she feels bad that she's wearing an expensive ring while Henry can't sleep with a roof over his head.

"It is," she says.

"I'm happy for you," he says, and she wonders where his wife is now, his children, and wonders what it is he put them through in order for them not to want to help him now.

She reaches out her window for the ticket. The barrier arm swoops upwards. There are, of course, no vacant spots on the bottom floor. Are there ever? And none on the next floor up. Because it's Saturday, the parking lot is filled up by people coming into town to shop, and it isn't until she gets right up to the roof that there are any free spaces, where there's an entire row of them with a view out over the street. She hates working Saturdays, but the firm has been snowed under with work and the overtime is good, and, hey, now she has a honeymoon to start saving for so she can't complain. She grabs the closest one to the lift, a car pulling in next to her while she's unclipping her seat belt. She locks her car and reaches the lift and pushes the button and the guy who pulled in next to her is now standing beside her, a respectable distance away, the kind of distance guys will keep so you know they're not going to make conversation.

The lift arrives. The door opens. She steps in and the guy steps in. He smiles at her and presses the button, then stands in one corner while she stands in the other. She wonders when everybody jumped on the unwritten rule that you couldn't make conversation in a lift. People can chat in all sorts of situations, they'll say hi as they pass by on the street, they'll make chitchat buying groceries, or at a bar, or a sports game, or in a queue—but making small talk with a stranger in a lift is committing a cardinal sin, it's as if—

"Hi," the guy says.

At first she doesn't know how to respond, or even want to, for that matter. Who the hell talks to people in elevators?

"Hi," she says.

"Sorry, I didn't mean to startle you. I think it's crazy two people in a box no bigger than a bathroom can't make conversation for the ten seconds they're in it for. We're all in this together, don't you think?"

"That's exactly what I think," she says, and smiles at him. He smiles back. He's a good-looking guy. Finger-length hair that's carefree and swept back, like a surfer. A beard too tidy to be a hipster beard, and perhaps too short too, since it's only an inch long. He has smile lines around his eyes and a deep tan and he smells of pine. He's wearing a red-and-black checkered shirt, and for some reason she thinks this guy is good with his hands. There's something about him that's familiar, especially in his eyes, which are almost gray, and certainly intense. She's seen those eyes before.

"Anyway, we're almost at the ground floor," he says, "so it's not like we had to listen to each other for long."

She laughs. "That's true," she says.

"Also, if I hadn't started making conversation, I wouldn't be able to tell you that you left your lights on."

"I did?"

"Yeah, you did."

"Are you sure? I didn't even have them on," she says, but maybe she did turn them on. She was pretty distracted. Could have been an automatic thing.

"Maybe I'm seeing things. But I'd hate to have said nothing and they were on, then you come back later and the battery is flat." The doors open. He steps out. "Was nice talking to you," he says.

She stays in the elevator. Even though she thinks he's wrong, she'll have to check. The doors have almost closed when he puts his hand between them. With his other hand he's patting down his pockets. "Sorry," he says, "I gotta go back up too. I've either left my wallet in the car or at home. This is why my little niece calls me Crazy Uncle Vinnie," he says, and laughs.

"Well, I guess we get to make more lift small talk."

"What shall we talk about? Religion? Politics? Or chat about the weather?"

"We're already out of time," she says. The doors open. There's nobody else up here. "You're a courier driver, right?"

They step out of the lift. "How'd you know that?" he asks.

"You deliver to my work," she says.

He nods slowly, then smiles. "Ha—I thought I knew you from somewhere. It's such a small world. You're at that accounting firm. Goodwin, Devereux, and something, right?"

"Goodwin, Devereux, and Barclay," she says, "and yes, that's the one."

"This makes you a real person."

"Sorry?"

"It's something my best friend Simon said to me once," he says. "He said when you chat to a random person, you start bumping into them all the time. They go from being ghost people you never see to real people."

"Kind of like when you buy a car nobody else has, only to find every third person has one once you buy it," she says.

He snaps his fingers. "Exactly!"

He walks to his car and she walks to hers. "I think you're wrong about the lights," she says.

He turns back towards her. He smiles. "The one at the front," he says. "See?" She moves around the front, between the car and the wall it's facing. "The friend I was telling you about," Crazy Uncle Vinnie says, coming towards her. "Simon. He died."

"I'm sorry," she says, looking at the lights from a different angle now. They're definitely not on. When she looks back up the man is almost next to her.

"It wasn't your fault," he says, and his tone is different now; he's not the same guy she rode in the lift with. The smile lines look like frown lines. The hipster beard looks like a serial-killer beard, and whatever work he does with his hands involves dark and bloody things.

"My lights . . ." she says, "aren't on."

"I know."

She doesn't like the sound of that. Doesn't like being alone with him. Ahead of her are parked cars and empty spaces. Behind her, a waist-high wall and the city five stories below. She's getting a bad feeling about why his niece calls him crazy.

"I really should be getting . . ." she says, but then doesn't get to say anything else. The man, this now-real person, completes the distance between them, and before she even understands what is happening, he's lifting her up and pushing her over the wall. She fights with him while gravity pulls at her, and she's pulling at him, clutching at his arms, at his shirt, and then she's hanging on to the wall as she dangles. He puts one hand around her wrist and holds on tight, helping support her.

"Please," she says. "I don't want to die."

"Nor did my friend, but your boyfriend killed him anyway."

He pries her hands off the wall, and then she is falling.

SIXTEEN

—— ◉ ——

Oh boy! Oh boy oh boy oh boy! Is this a thrill or what? Vincent is amping. He wonders what Detective Logan looked like when Simon pushed him out the window and wishes he could have been there for that too—the look on the detective's face must have been similar to the look on this woman's face right now. A look of shock, of disbelief, a look of acceptance and at the same time a look of hope, that somehow she is going to land safely.

She screams. She reaches for the walls as if she can catch on, but she can't.

She collides with the large metal *P* of the PARKING sign. Her weight rips it from the wall, but it manages to hang there, her body sticking to the top of it, and he has time to think she isn't going to go any farther but then she does, she slides off the giant letter and continues her journey to the pavement, and at the same time she hits it the *P* hinges towards her and blocks his view. He focuses on the *P*, sees that there must only be a bolt or two still keeping it from dropping. He wills it to drop. He tries to Jedi the fuck out of it, but it keeps hanging there. He wants her to have survived. He wants her able to see the giant letter break away and come for her.

It doesn't fall.

People are making their way over to her. They're probably already calling the police. He needs to get the hell out of here. He gets into his car. He does his best to stay calm as he takes the ramps down to the exit. His hands are shaking so badly he's worried he's going to hit the wall on the turns. He slows down. If there's a car coming the other way and there's an accident, he'll be stuck here. But there is no other car, and there is no accident, and he makes it all the way to the exit. He puts the ticket into the machine and pays cash.

He has done well. Now all he has to do is drive away.

Except . . . he wants to go and take a look.

The exit is on the opposite side of the parking garage from where he entered. He takes it, then turns left, drives to the end of the block, then turns left again, bringing himself onto the street the woman landed on. He can't see her, but he can see the growing crowd surrounding her. Some are using their cell phones to call for help, some using them to take photos. It was a mistake to come this way. If one of those cameras should capture him . . . But what? What would happen? Probably nothing, but if he's not careful, one of those probablys will turn into an eventuality.

He drives past them all. He takes the next left and passes a music store and a bar and a lighting store with a display in the window so lit up it must be visible from space. He makes the orange light before it turns red. He heads for home. Soon he hears the sirens. He never sees the emergency vehicles, but he knows where they're going. This is something real. Something he needs to repeat.

He reaches into his pocket and pulls out the ring. It's an engagement ring. He wrenched it off her finger when he pried her hands off the wall. It looks brand new. He wonders if he gave it to her last night in the restaurant, and that's why they hugged and everybody was looking at them. He hopes so. It will make what happened even more painful for Detective Ben Kirk.

Of course, there's a small part of him that feels bad for the woman— she was always friendly to him at her work, she never complained when he was late, she always greeted him with a smile, saying things like *I hope you had a nice weekend* and *Have a great day!*

Well, he's having a great day now. It started off badly, but she's turned that right around. There are going to be more great days. Not for Detective Kirk, though.

No, for Detective Kirk and those close to him, there are nothing but dark days on the horizon.

SEVENTEEN

—◉—

Behind the hospital, the gardens offer a range of colors Joshua can't keep up with. There isn't just red, but light red and dark red and bloodred and apple red, there is light blue and sky blue and then there's just blue. How is he supposed to remember it all? Kids learn colors before they can even talk. Their little toddler brains absorb the information like a sponge. It will come to him—people have been saying that all morning—it will come to him, don't stress out about it. So that's what he's trying to do now. Learn and not stress.

"I want to stand up," he says.

"Are you sure?" his mom asks.

"I think so."

He pushes himself out of the wheelchair and gets to his feet. He's fine; at least he's fine until he moves his feet, and then he immediately loses balance and falls back into the wheelchair. He closes his eyes and keeps them closed as he gets back to his feet. Everything feels fine. He takes a few steps—no problems. He stands still and opens his eyes and lets the garden come into view. He takes a step. The gardens tilt and the skyline shifts, but he doesn't fall. He closes his eyes, takes another step—he's all good. Eyes open, he manages a few paces, then his mom helps him back to his wheelchair.

"How about you sit for a while and I can—"

"I want to learn as much as I can today," he says.

"There'll be plenty of time for that," she says.

"If I wake up tomorrow and I can't see again, or if something goes wrong with my eyes in two days, or three, or whenever, all I'll have left is my memory. I want to know what everything looks like, what colors are, how it felt to walk while I could see. I have to absorb enough information to get me through the rest of my life."

"None of this is going to be taken from you," she says, which suggests to him she doesn't know about the curse, or perhaps she does but doesn't believe in it. "I'm not saying we have to go inside and stop for the day, I'm just saying let's not rush the walking, okay?"

He knows she's right.

She continues to push the wheelchair. What are those people doing? They're smoking. What's that? That's a parking meter. What color is that car? Yellow. And those things in the lawn? They're mushrooms. He can hear a siren in the distance. It's getting louder, which means it's getting closer. It's more than one siren, perhaps more than two. Ambulances coming to the hospital. He heard one leave earlier, rushing somewhere into the city to help the sick and injured, and he guesses that if it's coming back with the sirens on, then somebody is fighting for their life. No siren would mean they fixed the person up already, or they're beyond fixing.

Their route brings them from behind the hospital towards the emergency department entrance. "I can wheel it," he says, and takes control of the wheelchair. When they round the corner there's a man walking unsteadily towards them. Joshua can't guess ages yet, but this guy must be between his age and his mom's. The guy's got black finger-length hair that looks messy, and stubble the same color. He's using a cane to keep balanced. Perhaps he's got a broken leg, or a prosthetic one. Joshua is unable to slow down in time and the man isn't able to move out of the way, and he clips the guy's cane and knocks it to the ground, and a moment later the guy falls down next to it.

"Oh geez, oh geez, I'm so sorry," Joshua says.

"No problem, buddy," the man says, and his mom is already crouching down to help him up.

"I'm so sorry," she says. "Are you okay?"

"Yeah, yeah, I'm fine," the guy says. "Ain't no big deal." He brushes himself down. Then he smiles. "I probably shouldn't have been daydreaming," he says, "or quicker on my feet." He laughs. "Looks like you're having fun in the chair, though."

"I'm really sorry," Joshua says, because he doesn't know what else to say.

"Seriously, buddy, don't worry about it." Then he pauses, then frowns slightly. "Do I know you?"

"I don't think so," Joshua says.

"Yeah, I do, I do."

"My son has one of those faces," his mom says.

"Well, that might be it, but I'm pretty sure I've seen you around." Then he shrugs. "I'm sure I'll figure it out later. Hope you get yourself a license for that thing," he says, and taps the wheelchair with his cane, then tells them to have a great day before he walks in the direction they came from.

"Geez, I hope he's okay," Joshua says, then he notices that his mom looks different. He thinks she might be upset. "Are you okay?"

"There's something I need to tell you," she says. "That man, he did recognize you."

"Who is he?"

"I don't know who he is, but he, and a lot of other people, know who you are." She crouches down to speak to him. "What happened to your dad, you know that made the news, right?"

"Yeah, of course."

"And the eye surgeries, you remember how they made the news because of how groundbreaking they were?"

"I remember," he says, and he knows where this is going. A police officer getting killed always makes the news. A cutting-edge surgery performed on a blind boy—that's news too. Two big stories made even bigger by the way they're connected. "I'm in the news," he says. "Because my eyes came from dad."

"It's everywhere," she says. "Not just the newspapers and TV, but all over the Internet. For the first few days following . . . following your father's death, it was all anybody was talking about. I've been inundated with interview requests for you from a bunch of countries. Magazines want to do feature articles on you."

"I don't want to do any of that."

"And that's what I've been telling them. The first few days the police put guards out in the corridor of your room to stop journalists from getting access to you."

"I had no idea."

"Because you weren't meant to. It's been your job to heal, and to mourn, not to answer questions. I've been getting police escorts to and from home because there is so much media camped outside there, and once they learn of your release, it's only going to get worse."

"They're waiting outside our house now?"

Out on the street, the traffic is parting for the ambulance. It pulls into the ambulance bay, a police car following it. He's never seen an ambulance or a police car before, but he's read about them enough times to immediately know what he's looking at.

"They will be," his mom says, "which is why we're going to stay with your grandparents for a while. We're going to have to get used to more people recognizing you."

"I don't want to be a story," he says.

"I know. And we'll . . . Oh my god," she says, and she stands up and stares at the police car.

"That's Uncle Ben," he says.

"He looks . . ." she says, but doesn't finish. She doesn't need to, because Joshua can see exactly how his uncle looks. He looks upset and concerned and panicked. A gurney is pulled out of the ambulance with a woman on it. There are pieces of medical equipment that look like they're holding her together. There's blood all over her. Sixty minutes into his new life and already Joshua is seeing something that makes him want to look away.

"That's Erin," his mother says, and puts her hand to her mouth. "Oh my god, that's Erin."

Uncle Ben is at Erin's side, holding her hand. The gurney is rushed through the main doors, and a moment later all that remains is the ambulance with the flashing siren that has now been muted and the police car with the door open.

"I can't . . . I don't know . . . Oh my god, that was Erin," his mother says. She moves towards the entrance, pushing the wheelchair. "I need to get in there."

They can't take the same emergency doors the paramedics took Erin through, so they go to the main entrance. They're almost at the reception desk when his mom stops pushing him. She moves in front of the wheelchair and crouches down in front of him. He now knows what completely serious looks like.

"How did you know?" she asks.

"How did I know what?"

"How did you know that was Ben?"

"I . . ." he says, but doesn't know how to answer. How did he know? He has never seen Uncle Ben before, and yet he knew that's who it was without even thinking about it. In fact, until just now, he wasn't even aware it was something he *couldn't* have known.

"Joshua, how did you know?"

"I don't know," he says. "I just did."

"But that doesn't make sense," she says.

He shrugs because he doesn't know what else he can offer. Then he apologizes. "I'm sorry," he says.

"You don't . . . it's not . . ." she says, and like Joshua, his mother can't seem to find the right words. "We'll discuss it later."

A nurse lets them into a large corridor where doctors and nurses are scurrying back and forth. There are gurneys parked along the walls, and thin tire marks where some have skidded across the floor. There are patients lying in some of the gurneys, others are sitting in chairs, some are being spoken to and some are in the process of waiting. There are sets of double doors in various directions. Joshua doesn't know what he's looking at. There's a nurse up ahead, and his mother approaches her. The nurse is wearing a green set of what his mother told him earlier are called scrubs. He wonders if that's because the people who wear them are always scrubbing vomit and blood off them.

"The woman who was just brought in here," his mom says, "Erin Murphy."

"Are you family?"

"Yes," she says, which is close enough to the truth. "What's happened? Is she going to be okay?"

"The doctors are working on her."

"Detective Ben Kirk came in with her. Where is he?"

"Follow me," she says.

She leads them through one of the sets of doors and to a waiting room half full of people. Uncle Ben is pacing it, having an animated conversation on his cell phone, using the kinds of words Joshua's parents would have grounded him for using. Ben sees them and wraps up the call.

"What happened?" his mom asks.

"Nobody knows. An accident maybe, or . . . We still don't know, but Erin fell . . . she fell a long way . . . The doctors are doing what they can but . . ." He runs his hands over his face, then uses his palms to wipe at the tears that are brimming in his eyes. "They don't know if she's going to make it. It's bad, Michelle, really bad."

She steps in and hugs him, and Ben wraps his arms around her and holds on tight.

"She wouldn't have jumped," he says, as if somebody had suggested she had. He pulls back and looks at her. "She was happy. I proposed to her last night and she said yes, and . . . and she wouldn't have jumped. I have to go," he says. "I have to go and figure out what happened."

"You need to be here for her," his mom says.

"If somebody did this to her, I have to find them. I have to . . ." He stops talking. Joshua knows what it is his uncle needs to do, the same thing his uncle did to the man who killed his dad. "Can you stay here? Can you be here for her? I can't be here . . . I can't be, in case . . . in case the doctors can't save her." For the first time he notices that Joshua is there too. "Your eyes," he says. "You can see."

Joshua nods.

"That's good," Uncle Ben says. "Really good."

Then he's racing back the way they came, leaving Joshua and his mother in the waiting room.

EIGHTEEN

Over the following week, Joshua learns.

He begins with children's books. A is for apple. B is for beach ball. It's not like he didn't know these things—he's always been a good speller—but what he's learning now is how to recognize the letters. How they look. The words they form. He's relearning things he knows from a different point of view. There's a tutor whom Dr. Toni puts them in touch with, who comes to see him every day. His name is Roger Lee, and Roger used to teach English before retiring two years ago. He retired young, at fifty-five, because both his parents died in their early sixties, he tells Joshua, and if the same thing was going to happen to him, he wanted to have at least retired first. So why does he tutor people now? That's what Joshua asks him, to which Roger tells him there are two reasons—the first is that when you retire at fifty-five, it becomes difficult to fill your days, and the second is that he does it to help Dr. Toni as a favor to her, because Dr. Toni saved his daughter's sight fifteen years ago. He comes in every day for six hours, and for Joshua it's like being at school, only a far more intense version of it. He likes Roger. The guy makes him laugh with stupid jokes and he pulls faces and fakes heart attacks when Joshua gets something wrong, but he smiles and congratulates him too when things are going well.

Joshua likes learning, but he doesn't like being at his mom's parents' house. It's warm and stuffy, as his grandparents prefer it that way. Anytime he opens a window to let some fresh air in, they close it a few minutes later. It always smells like freshly baked bread and cookies, though, so it's not all bad, and after six days of hospital food, every meal is a feast. His grandmother is always hanging around, offering him and

Roger food, asking if she can get them anything, which after a while makes Joshua feel like she thinks he's incapable of doing anything on his own. His mom tells him she's doing this out of love and is trying to be helpful. But he knows even she's getting frustrated with it, because he sees his grandmother doing it to her as well. His grandfather is never sure of what to say, so he often says nothing, spending time in his office doing whatever it is he does in there—even his mom has no idea. Some days Joshua sees him only around mealtimes.

"He probably sneaks beer in there and watches sports on his computer," his mom tells him.

Joshua is too busy studying to get bored, which makes the days go by quickly. His mom goes back to work, meaning his grandmother dotes on him even more. He's allowed to watch TV in the evenings, but they never put the news on. The first movie he watches is a Star Trek movie, and he can't see the resemblance between Captain Kirk and Uncle Ben, not until he watches an old TV episode where all the men wear pants that are too short and all the women wear skirts that couldn't get much shorter. He can see why his dad loved the show so much. He finds himself addicted to *Supernatural* episodes. In fact, he finds himself addicted to TV in general, and he no longer listens to audiobooks. He still reads when he can. He's moving on from *A Is for Apple* to *Zeddy the Zombie*, a book about a teddy bear who, after being bitten by a zombie, comes to life with an appetite for brains, but it's difficult when words are new to look at, and he manages only a handful of pages each day. Roger is impressed by his progress. He keeps telling him that he's going to catch up with all the other students he'll soon be studying with in no time. His other grandparents come over nearly every day to see him, and they bring books for him, and DVDs, and big smiles with which they try to mask the pain of losing their son. His grandfathers talk rugby and his grandmothers talk golf and he wonders if these are things he's going to play, and when he sees rugby on TV he hopes not, but golf looks okay. Every time his mom comes home from work she gives him a hug, but she never matches the smile she gave him when the bandages came off. He's listened to enough books and watched enough TV now to know that the shock of his dad's dying has worn off, and the reality of having him gone is kicking in. She's sad a lot of the time, and he wishes he could fix that. She's sad for Uncle Ben and his girlfriend too. Erin has been in a coma since the accident and nobody knows for sure whether she'll come out of it. Some days he goes online and reads stories about his dad, and what happened to him, and he watches the footage from the funeral and it makes him cry.

A week into Joshua's new life and he's able to read at the same level as other kids his age—just not at the same speed. Some mornings he wakes up and watches the sun rise. He watches it set in the evenings. He calls William and Pete a few times, but they say they're busy with school and homework. When he asks if he can come and visit, they tell him maybe later.

He misses them.

He misses his dad. He doesn't know how he's going to adjust to not having him around. Who's going to take him to the beach, or tell him about girls, or laugh about some weird stuff that happened at work that day, about how they arrested some guy dressed in a clown outfit trying to steal cars, or how they arrested a guy who tried to rob a bar that turned out to be a cop bar. Who's going to tell him what to do if some kid is picking on him at school? His mom will—of course she will—and Uncle Ben too—but it's not the same.

It will never be the same.

After a week at his grandparents' house his mom tells him that the news cycle has moved on, and that it's time to finally go home. Other than driving to and from the hospital, he hasn't been out in the car. Everything fascinates him. Other cars, other people, the roads, dogs being walked, cats sitting on sidewalks, prams being pushed, and mail being delivered. Stop signs, traffic lights, indicators, cars with dents in them, license plates, roundabouts. Big houses, small houses, old houses, new houses. Beaten-up gardens, dried-up lawns, weeds and flowers and pruned roses and sculpted bushes and leaves piling up in the gutters and brightly painted letterboxes and bark that looks fresh and bark that looks old. People see these things every day, but how often do they take the time to *really* see them as if for the first time? They don't. Of course they don't, and there's no reason why they would.

His house is in a suburb to the north of the city called Redwood, where most of the houses are single-story homes built in the seventies and eighties, most of them brick or summer hill stone, and most of them well kept. He's never known how it's looked, but he has always known it's slap-bang in the middle of Averageville, as his dad says—or used to say. Joshua has lived here his entire life—even his biological parents lived out here. He looks at every house they come up to as if it could be theirs, because it could be—he has no idea what it looks like.

They pull into the driveway of a brick house that's been painted light brown and has a black concrete-tile roof. There's an oil stain in the center of the driveway and weeds poking up from the edges of it. The lawn is ankle deep and there's a knee-high fence out front and trees on the boundary to the left and right as tall as the house. The house was painted a few years ago, back when his dad remodeled the kitchen and they had new carpets put in. All of that combines to make a forty-year-old house look ten years old on the outside and only five on the inside. There are bay windows catching the sun to the north, and a deck leading from a patio out back.

He climbs out of the car—any balancing and dizziness issues disappeared later the same day his bandages were taken off—and follows his mom inside. Everything is lined up exactly where he remembers it all being, only now it's like a magician has pulled back the curtain. He puts his hand on the kitchen bench. It's solid and feels the same and it is the same, only in another way it isn't. This is his home, he's lived here since he was a baby, it's familiar, but at the same time it's like he's never been here before.

"I want to see my room," he says.

"It's this way," his mom says, then laughs. "Sorry, I know you know that. I don't . . . I don't quite know why I said it."

"It's okay," he says.

"Go explore," she says. "I'll make you some lunch when you're ready."

He's seen teenagers' bedrooms on TV, and on TV the walls are covered in posters of musicians and athletes and movies, but he doesn't have any posters in his room. There are framed photographs of him with his parents, and there are framed photos of his biological parents too. His mom showed him some of these a week ago. His parents were strangers to him, and he found it difficult to connect to the pictures in an emotional way. They were people he never knew.

The bedroom faces north. The sun is coming in and hitting the bed. There are no books in here, no TV, but there's a radio and an alarm clock and a desk where he does his homework. Everything is straight and tidy and he tries to think about the last time he was here. He was packing his schoolbag and his dad was telling him to hurry up. He sits on the end of the bed and cries, and he knows his mom can probably hear him but she leaves him alone, which is exactly what he wants.

His second week out of the hospital has him spending more time with Roger. His reading speed gets faster, and he has no hesitation identifying the numbers or letters put in front of him. He finds more TV shows to become addicted to. He spends more time outside. He walks the streets in his neighborhood, his mom letting him go out alone, though reluctantly so. He goes to the park. One night his mom takes him to the cinema. The screen is so big and the action so loud and he loves every second of it. They eat at a restaurant the following night and the day after that she takes him into her work to show him around. He looks at the cats and dogs in cages and wants to bring every one of them home. She takes him to the cemetery where, for the first time this year, he can feel autumn approaching. His dad's gravestone is newer than any of the others surrounding it. He holds his mom's hand and neither of them says anything. There's a giant oak tree ten yards away that stands over them like a sentry. There's a small lake out to the right with ducks splashing about. The sun is out, and even though there's a cool wind whipping through the graves, he thinks it's a nice place to be buried. He thinks his dad would like it. He knows for a fact his dad saw people buried in other places—people found in shallow graves, in trash bins, in barrels in lakes. If you're going to be dead, Joshua figures this is the place to be doing it.

His grandparents visit the house and his neighbors pop over, as do cousins and other uncles and aunts, as well as aunts and uncles who aren't related to him but are close friends of his parents. Sometimes the phone will ring at home, and it will be a journalist wanting to write something about him, but his mom always says no, and thankfully the journalists don't come to the house. His story is no longer a story, at least not for those who don't know him.

His world keeps getting bigger.

As does his fear of school.

He's nervous about his new school and hopes he'll fit in, but he's worried that it may not be possible if everybody knows who he is. With his first day approaching, he tries to convince his mom to have him homeschooled by tutors over the next two years. She lists reasons why that's not possible, stopping once he admits he sees her point.

"You're going to like it there," she says.

"Nobody likes school," he tells her.

"Well, then you're not going to like it any less than anybody else."

On the Friday before his return, she takes him to Christchurch North High, the same public school where she and his dad and Uncle Ben met when they were kids. It has a roll of nearly a thousand students from all walks of life, but no doubt he's the first who used to be blind. The school is seventy years old, and Principal Mooney looks like he's been working there the entire time. While his mom chats with him, a teacher by the name of Miss Franklin shows Joshua around. Miss Franklin tells him she was a student here not even ten years ago. She has blond hair tied into a ponytail and a pair of glasses she keeps adjusting and she has so much energy he keeps thinking she's about to break into a sprint. She shows him the math block, the English block, the gym, the football field, the science labs, the hall, and the social studies block. She tells him that when she was here she was the captain of the netball team and the volleyball team, and she ran track. She tells him she coaches now. School is out for the day, but there are some students milling around, some chatting in small groups, others making their way to the edge of the grounds, some stare at him, some ignore him. She shows him the swimming pool, where the water looks clear and perfectly still.

"Can you swim?" Miss Franklin asks.

"I can float," he says. "If I fell off a boat I could doggy-paddle for five minutes before drowning."

She laughs. "We can teach you how to do better," she says.

"You mean you'll get me to six minutes?"

She laughs again. "Maybe even ten."

"The problem with swimming is I could never know what direction I was going in, or when the edge of the pool was on its way."

She shows him the arts department, the languages block, the wood-working and metal shops. "You're going to love it here," she tells him. "The other students are all very nice, very accepting. Of course, like any school, it has its troublemakers, but you're going to make a lot of great friends here."

"Cool," he says, because he thinks that's what she wants to hear.

"There is one more thing, though," she says. "You and your family have been getting a lot of media attention—"

"Not anymore," he says.

"No, but . . . but yes, that may change, in which case if any reporters approach you here, you come and tell us, but what I was going to say is it means the other students, they're all going to know who you are. A lot of them, or most of them, I guess, don't read the news. I was the same at that age. But what happened to your dad, and to you, it's not always being driven by the news. It's driven by social media, and most of the students here let their lives be ruled by it. What I'm saying is, be prepared for that, and if it becomes a problem, or you need somebody to talk to about it, or you have any concerns at all, you come and see me, okay?"

He promises her that he will.

They return to the office block and join up with his mother and Principal Mooney. Aside from looking like he's been teaching for seventy years, Principal Mooney is dressed like he stocked up on all his outfits back then too. He's wearing a red bow tie and suspenders. He also has his sleeves rolled up, showing arms so thin they look like broom handles. When they shake hands to say good-bye, Joshua's worried that the bones in Principal Mooney's hand are going to break.

"You're going to fit in well here, son," Principal Mooney says. "We're all looking forward to having you."

On the drive home he watches his mom operating the car, the way her feet press the pedals, the way she changes gear. There's a lot of timing involved, but his mum makes it look effortless.

"They all seemed nice," she says.

"I guess."

"You guess?"

"I mean, they probably say that same stuff to everybody who joins the school, right? What else are they going to say? 'We're not looking forward to having you, and the teachers actually hate children'?"

His mother laughs, and he realizes how much he's missed that sound. "I see your point," she says.

"Can you imagine if they were that honest?" he says, and now he's laughing too. "'You're not going to like Mrs. Smith, because she has a hairy mole on her face and she always smells like cheese, and the art teacher can't draw a stick figure but we employ her anyway because she gets us cheap drugs.'"

"Or, 'The metal shop teacher learned everything he knows from prison,'" she says.

"I want to learn how to drive," he says.

"What?"

"I want to—"

"I heard what you said," she says. "I . . . I guess I was expecting it, just not so soon."

"I'm old enough," he says. "And with all that's going on, I need something to look forward to. School's going to be difficult, but learning to drive will help me cope with it."

She laughs.

"What?"

"You've finally caught up to being a teenager," she says.

"What do you mean?"

"You're trying to manipulate me. You're using your angst at the new school to convince me to teach you to drive."

"Is it working?"

"It is," she says. "And you're right. How about once you settle into school, you study up and get your learner's license and I'll get you some lessons. Does that sound okay?"

"We have a deal."

NINETEEN

They drive to the hospital. On Tuesday Dr. Toni had told them they no longer needed to come in every day and could start putting two days between appointments. Two weeks ago when the bandages came off, the hospital and everything in and around it seemed wonderful. He was in awe of everything. Now he sees the mundane exactly how everybody else sees it. He's tired of coming here and he's hoping soon Dr. Toni will space the appointments out to a week, then a month, then a year.

They pull into the parking lot only to find the only free parking space is partly taken up by the SUV in the spot next to it.

"We call that asshole parking," his mom says, and it's the first time he's ever heard her swear. "Just in case it's on your test when you go for your license."

They park on the street and walk. Inside, they take the lift up to Dr. Toni's office, where they have to kill time in the waiting room. Joshua picks up a gossip magazine and flips through the pages. Over the last few weeks he's seen many of these people over and over, reality TV stars who are famous for reasons he can't understand, people earning millions of dollars for being who they are—and it makes him wonder how somebody can be so extravagantly rich for doing so little, when his dad died for this country and never made a fraction of that kind of money. How do athletes and movie stars earn more than nurses and schoolteachers? He keeps reading, purely for the practice. A magazine like this—there aren't any words that trip him up.

After fifteen minutes Dr. Toni comes into the waiting room and gives them a big smile. "How have you been, Joshua? It looks like the bruising has disappeared."

He'd noticed. Every day since getting the bandages off he'd look in the mirror to see how much it had faded. He tells her he's been good then asks how she's been, and she says the same. He takes a seat and reads the eye chart, using letters these days instead of shapes. He gets to the second-to-lowest line with his left eye.

"Still no headaches? Nothing like that?"

"Nothing."

They move on to the right eye. It's the same as it was on day one.

Dr. Toni sits behind her desk and smiles at him. "With my other patients, and with all transplants in general, the donors are vetted. We need to make sure the organs going in are healthy, and in the case of eyes, we'd want to make sure we are implanting those with twenty-twenty vision. In your case, we didn't get to do the preparation we'd normally have done. I know you think Mitchell had perfect vision," she says, looking at his mom, "but it's possible he didn't."

"Is there anything else it could be?" his mom asks.

"It's unlikely the eye was damaged during the surgery, and I know the surgery went well. It could be amblyopia, or the equivalent of that."

"Which is?" Joshua's mother asks.

"One in thirty people have it. It's when the eyes are at different strengths, so the brain switches off the optic nerve to the weaker one. If that's the case, then it's not going to strengthen by itself. Joshua, tell me exactly what you can see out of your right eye."

"Shape and color," he says, "but nothing definite. I mean, if you sat down next to me I'd know you were there, but I wouldn't be able to tell who was sitting there."

"The others you've operated on," his mom says, "did they have similar difficulties?"

"No," Dr. Toni says. "But I suggest we still give it some time. One option we can look at in the near future, if you're willing, is to patch the good eye and hope the weaker one improves."

"Patch?" Joshua asks.

"You'd wear glasses with a patch over the good eye. It's what we try with children. It means you can only see out your bad eye, with the hope of the nerve improving and bringing equal strength to both your eyes."

"I'd be blind again," he says.

"Not blind, no," she says.

"But all I'd see is color and shape."

"With the hope that it would strengthen."

The idea makes him feel ill. "I can't."

"How long would it take?" his mom asks.

"It's hard to know. In many cases with children it doesn't work at all, but we're talking about kids seven years and under. It's hard to keep them committed to wearing the patch. With adults—well, it could take some time. A year or two, if at all. Just like the surgery we gave you, curing amblyopia in adults is still a recent advancement in medical technology."

"I don't want the patch," he says. "Really, I don't, and I'm happy with the way it is. More than happy."

"We'll discuss it again soon," Dr. Toni says.

"I can't wear a patch to my new school. I can't be that guy."

She gives him eye drops to dilate his pupils, then gets him to sit in front of a machine with lenses that he looks into. He follows her instructions of looking left and right while she examines him. "Everything looks in great shape," she says. "How about I reward you by telling you I won't need to see you till next Friday? How does that sound?"

He smiles. "Really good."

"I'll try not to feel too hurt," she says, smiling back.

She walks them to the door, but then his mom stops them. "There's something else," she says.

"Mom . . ."

"I need to ask," she says.

"You promised you wouldn't."

"I know I did, but we have to know."

"Know what?" Dr. Toni asks, looking concerned.

"We've been reading online about organ memory," his mom says.

"You mean cellular memory," Dr. Toni says. "Where some people believe memory is stored not only in the brain, but in all the cells?"

"Exactly," his mom says. "The evidence is anecdotal, but I want to know, what's your take on it?"

"I don't really have a take on it. It's not something I've ever had any experience with. Why are you asking? You think Joshua is experiencing it?"

"We should probably get going," Joshua says.

"It was the day the bandages came off," his mom says. "Joshua had never seen Ben before, but when he saw him pull up in the car he recognized him. How is that possible?"

Dr. Toni says nothing as she considers an explanation. Joshua has thought about it over and over but hasn't come up with any answers. At least none that make sense.

"You must have called out his name without realizing it," Dr. Toni says. "Moments of shock can play tricks on us. What we say, what we remember, and what we repress can cause confusion."

"No," his mom says. "That's not what happened."

"Joshua has known Ben all his life, correct?" Dr. Toni asks.

"Yes," his mom says.

"And you've described to him what he looks like, I imagine, on more than one occasion."

"True. But Joshua didn't know what those descriptions meant, not really."

"Once those bandages came off, the descriptions he's had of people would have started making more sense. A backlog of information would have become relevant. The brain is an amazing thing," Dr. Toni says. "It has the ability to connect all kinds of dots. My guess is everything he'd learned about Ben slotted into place, and he recognized the description. Has it happened again?"

"No."

"Then it could also be that the next person Joshua saw who had anything remotely in common with Ben he would have thought was Ben anyway, and it just so happened it was him. Did he pull up in a police car?"

"Yes," Joshua says.

"It seems to me there was some memory association going on, and he was lucky with his guess. I think it's worth considering those possibilities before jumping to the conclusion of cellular memory."

"I can see how that makes sense," his mom says.

"Remember," Dr. Toni says, "all that anecdotal evidence you're reading is anecdotal for a reason."

TWENTY

"I thought we agreed not to tell anybody," Joshua says, as they step into the lift.

"I know we did," his mom says, and then, in a much softer voice, she says, "I'm sorry."

"Now she's going to think I'm weird."

"She won't think that, honey, but we needed to tell her. I should have told her earlier."

They step off the elevator. There are stripes of various shades painted on the floor to guide visitors to different areas of the hospital. They follow the green stripe to the intensive care unit. It's a difficult place to visit. There's so much emotion and pain in the air, along with hope, false hope, and the sense that Death is browsing the patient list looking for people to take on a road trip. People who've come to see their loved ones walk around with grim looks on their faces, and when they do manage a smile, there's nothing warm in it. The nurses and doctors who work here are amazing. He wonders how they stay so strong. It's in this ward that Erin is being kept. She's in a private room hooked up to a bunch of machines that monitor her vitals. Her head has been shaved, exposing stitched-up wounds and bruising. Parts of her body are covered in bandages, and other parts are covered in casts. Her body is in traction, both her legs elevated, her right arm the same. She has a cracked spine, broken ribs, shattered legs, and a swollen brain. Even if she does come out of the coma with no significant brain damage, months, if not years, of rehab are waiting for her. One of the machines connected to her is monitoring her heartbeat, offering a consistent and soft beeping sound. He wonders if she is dreaming, and if she is, he hopes it isn't of the fall.

There are plenty of get-well cards on display, most with pictures of flowers or teddy bears with Band-Aids on their arms. There are lots of flowers too, all fresh looking, as if they were delivered today. Michelle sits next to the bed, and Joshua leans against the windowsill. The window looks out over the parking lot, and beyond that the gardens of the hospital. Some of the trees are starting to change color. In the past, autumn has meant cool weather and the crunch of leaves underfoot and nothing more. He had no idea it could be such a beautiful mess.

"What did you think of Dr. Toni's explanation?" his mom asks.

He turns back towards her. "It makes sense. My fear is that doctors will start eyeing me up to be their next medical experiment."

"That won't happen."

"It will, if people think cellular memory is real. They'll want to study me."

"I'm sure they wouldn't."

"Scientists always want to study stuff like that. Usually for all the wrong reasons."

"Only in the books you read," she says. "In real life they're not going to strap you down and cut you open."

"Won't they?"

"They might ask you some questions, and run some tests, but that's all."

"What's all?" Uncle Ben asks, coming into the room. "What are you guys talking about?"

His mom gets up and hugs Uncle Ben. "How are you?"

"I'm fine," he says, but the way he sounds, the way his body slumps as he says it, tells Joshua he's not fine at all. If he were still blind, he'd have taken Uncle Ben at his word—he's learning people often say more without them.

Ben squeezes Erin's hand before leaning against the windowsill next to Joshua. "What were you talking about?" he asks. "About cellular memory?"

"Nothing," Joshua says.

"It didn't sound like nothing. I've heard the term before. It's like when a guy receiving the heart of a concert pianist will suddenly want to take up the piano, right?" He turns towards Joshua. "Is that what's happening to you, kiddo? You're getting the urge to join the police force?"

Joshua shakes his head. "No. It's nothing."

"Well, if it's nothing, then it can't be too hard to explain."

"The same day Erin was brought into the hospital," his mom says. "We were outside on the grounds. Joshua's bandages had only just come off. We saw the ambulance arrive. We saw you arrive."

"And?"

"And Joshua recognized you."

The smile on Ben's face vanishes. He tightens his lips and the beginning of a frown appears. "You recognized me?"

"I don't know how," Joshua says.

"Your mom must have said something."

"I didn't," his mom says.

"Maybe you did, but just weren't aware of it."

"I'm telling you, that's not how it happened," she says.

Ben's frown becomes full blown. "How is that possible? You think it's this cellular memory theory? You think it's real?"

"According to half the research on the Internet it's real," his mom says.

"And the other half?" Ben asks.

"The other half think it's crap," Joshua says.

"Joshua!"

"Sorry, mom, but it's true. We told Dr. Toni about it. She thinks it was some kind of lucky guess, because you were in a cop car."

"Cellular memory," Ben says. "So what or who else have you recognized?"

"Nothing else, really."

"Think," Ben says.

"I am thinking."

"Think harder," Ben says, an edge to his voice.

"Ben," his mom says.

Ben throws a glance in her direction. "This is important," he says, his words clipped. Then he sighs, looks back at Joshua, and carries on. "Look, this is important. I need to know, has there been anything else? Anything at all?"

"No," Joshua says.

"Are you sure?"

"He said no, Ben."

"There are dreams," Joshua says.

The room goes quiet, except for the faint beep of the heart monitor.

"What dreams?" Ben asks.

"I started having them before the bandages came off. I wasn't really aware of them at the time, but became aware later. My dreams used to be full of shapes and not a lot more, then suddenly there were people. I think I saw my dad."

"What?" his mom asks.

"There was one face I kept seeing, and when the bandages came off, well . . . Remember after we saw Uncle Ben and Erin, we went back into my hospital room? Remember what we did then?"

"I showed you some photographs," his mom says.

"You showed me Dad," he says, and he remembers thinking at the time he was looking at a dead man through that very dead man's eyes. Other than the eyes, which belonged to Mitchell, there were other similarities that ran in the family. Same wavy black hair, same jawline, same cheekbones. He can see those features in his granddad too. His grandmother tells him that he has the same smile as his biological mother, the same laugh too. She told him he even walks the same way his dad did back when he was a kid, and when she tells him things like that she smiles, but there's a sadness there too.

"And?" Uncle Ben says.

"That was when it came to me," he says. "After the operation, I stopped dreaming about shapes and started dreaming about people. That included Dad."

"You said there were others you recognized?"

"I knew who Mom was too." He looks at his mom. "When the bandages came off, I recognized you right away."

"You did? Why didn't you say anything?"

"It didn't . . ." He shrugs. "I don't know. I think I wasn't really aware of it. I remember that you looked familiar, but I didn't question why. With everything else going on . . . I don't know. I just didn't think about it."

"You're serious," Uncle Ben says.

"There's more," Joshua says. "As soon as we left the hospital and went to my grandparents' house, I started using the Internet. I looked up the man who killed Dad."

The room goes quiet again. He looks from his mom to Uncle Ben. They stare at him, transfixed by what he's saying. Or, more accurately, by what he's about to say.

"As soon as I saw him, I knew it was him. I know you're thinking that because I was searching for it, I already knew what I was going to be seeing. But Uncle Ben asked if there were other people, and there were."

"Who else?" his mom asks.

"I recognized myself too."

"The man who killed your dad," Uncle Ben says. "What was he doing in the dream? Did you see what happened to your dad?"

"I don't want to say."

"Please, Joshua, it's important."

"But it doesn't make sense," Joshua says. "Even if you believe in cellular memory, it doesn't make sense."

"What doesn't?" Ben asks.

"I saw him die," he says, and he can picture it clearly and he tries not to cry. "I saw those nails being shot into him, and then I saw him fall. But that's not possible, right? I should only be seeing things from Dad's point of view. I can see . . . I can also see the way that Simon Bower looked at my dad. I see it like he's looking at me. I see him standing over me, then pushing me with his foot. I see the look on his face, this completely expressionless look as I . . . as Dad falls. But I see the look on Dad's face too. He was confused. He was scared. He knew what was coming."

His mom has gone completely pale. She's starting to shake.

"I remember looking down and seeing nails, as if they were sticking out of my chest, but at the same time I remember pointing the nail gun at him. That's what I mean when . . ." he says, and his voice catches for a moment but he pushes himself to carry on. "That's what I mean when I say none of this makes any sense."

TWENTY-ONE

In the two weeks following his rooftop meeting with Erin Murphy, Vincent has done two things while refusing to do a third. The first is he's been panicking. Erin survived an impossible fall because luck intervened, turning one big fall into two smaller falls, thanks to the signage attached to the exterior wall. The second of those two smaller falls still should have been enough to kill her—and would have, if not for the fact she landed on some poor son of a bitch on the ground. She landed on a homeless guy who, it turns out, used to work at this very hospital more than ten years ago. That unlucky bastard had his back broken and his spleen and kidneys ruptured and is facing months of rehabilitation, and even then he may never walk right. Vincent figures the guy probably isn't in much of a hurry anyway—where's the desire to get back on your feet when you're going to get tossed out onto the street once you do? Maybe the guy will use the time in the hospital to turn his life around.

For some reason, Fate decided to keep Erin alive, and when Fate pulls some bullshit trickery like that there's often a reason, and he knows the reason might be so she can miraculously wake up and identify him.

The second thing Vincent has been doing is his homework on Detective Inspector Ben Kirk. Emotionally bankrupting someone to the point of oblivion requires serious preparation. It also requires a list. On that list are the names of Ben's parents, Erin's Murphy's parents, Ben's new detective partner, his dead partner's wife, his dead partner's son, his friends, two aunties, three uncles, even his cat. The cat might get a pass, but everybody else on the list will be getting rooftop performances of their own—though he knows he can't use the rooftop trick again. That would create a pattern and enable the police to make a list of their own—this one of suspects. At the moment, according to the news, the police don't know if she jumped, fell, or was pushed.

The third thing—the thing he has been refusing to do—is get a job. Not having a job gives him more time to focus on the crazy, and he knows that's what this is—a whole bunch of crazy balled up tight in his mind that can be cleared away only once he's finished with Ben. The thing is, he's happy with the crazy. He doesn't want it to fade. It all started with Ruby in the woods, and he wants to see how far he can run with it. Anyway, he has some savings. Not a lot, but enough to get him through this.

He walks into the main entrance of the hospital. There are security cameras out front and dotted around inside. Vincent has parked his stupid, good-for-nothing car a mile away and walked, thinking that the real bad guys in this city aren't throwing women off rooftops, they're setting the rates for the parking meters. But at least his car won't be captured on camera. Today he's gone with a pair of jeans that he'll throw out when he's completed his mission and a black long-sleeve shirt that will get the same treatment. He's wearing a baseball cap pulled down tight, revealing only the hair around the sides of his head, which he's brushed talcum powder into to make it look gray. He's brushed talcum powder into his beard too. He's carrying flowers he stole from the graveyard where he visited Simon earlier this morning. He keeps them at chest level to help block his face. He takes the elevator and steps into the corridor of the intensive care ward in time to see Detective Logan's boy and wife coming towards him. They don't pay him any attention on their way past.

He loiters outside the intensive care ward, holding the flowers in one hand, holding his cell phone to his ear in the other, and looking like he's on an important phone call. When nobody shows any interest in him, he heads into Erin's room.

"Why didn't you die on that pavement?"

She doesn't answer. Doesn't stir, doesn't twitch, doesn't do anything other than take up a hospital room and give a bunch of machines something to monitor. If he killed her right now, the machine would start beeping like crazy. Doctors and nurses would race here to save her.

That's why he brought the flowers.

He heads for the bathroom he passed earlier back down the corridor.

TWENTY-TWO

—— ◉ ——

Dr. Toni is sitting in her office with her feet up on the corner of the desk. She's staring outside but not taking in any of the view. She's tapping a pencil against her knee in random Morse code as she thinks about Joshua. She is thinking about the surgery, and how one eye works and one eye doesn't. There have been different results over the last two years from different doctors. Most operations have been a success. The rare few have not, and there are some with mixed results. Having one eye work and the other not isn't unheard of, and the operation will still be deemed a success even though she's disappointed it didn't go exactly how she wanted. The scientific community will understand that the likely cause could be any number of things and won't put the blame on her technique, or delay future surgeries.

Since Joshua's transplant, she's been inundated with interview requests. She enjoyed the spotlight when she did the first surgery in New Zealand last year—hell, back then the hospital even put on a press conference and her photo was in all the papers, so the spotlight was something she couldn't avoid. But this time the last thing she wants is to be put in front of a camera. Given what happened to Mitchell Logan, and given what they did to the man who killed him, she wants to be left alone and have the story fade away.

A knock at the door breaks her from her thoughts. She spins her chair around, and before she can say anything, the door opens. Ben Kirk steps into her office. He looks like somebody put him in the spin cycle of a dryer and left him in overnight. He's lost weight, he hasn't shaved, his hair is a mess. He obviously hasn't been sleeping much. She's known Ben a long time—they dated for a few years from their late teens into their early twenties, and the only other time he looked this bad was when his brother died.

"Can we talk?"

"You look like hell," she tells him.

"Then I look how I feel," he says, and slumps down into the chair in front of her desk.

"I know you've got a lot going on right now, Ben, but you really need to get some sleep, otherwise you're going to be no good for Erin."

"I'm trying," he says.

"Maybe you should talk to somebody," she says. "I can give you the name of somebody who might be—"

"I'll be fine," he says, "and anyway, I'm here to talk about Joshua, not me."

"I still think you should—"

"I know," he says. "And I will, and I'll get a prescription for some sleeping pills and—"

"It's not just getting a prescription, Ben, it's about talking to somebody."

"Right now I want to talk about Joshua."

"Okay, fine," she says.

"This cellular memory thing, is there anything to that?"

"They've told you?"

"Just now," he says.

"Do you believe them?" she asks.

"The kid has no reason to make any of this up," he says. "He's a good kid. I believe that he believes what he's saying, but I know from the job that people mix up the order in which they remember things."

"That's what I think this is, just him mixing things up."

"So you don't think it's possible."

"I think it's unlikely."

"What about the dreams?"

"What dreams?" she asks.

"He didn't tell you?"

She shakes her head. He tells her about the dreams. She sits silently as she takes it all in. "It's interesting," she says when he's finished. "But they're dreams. Nobody can explain dreams. All sorts of crazy things happen when we're asleep."

"If cellular memory is true, then Joshua saw the last thing his dad saw before he died."

She leans back. She's no longer tapping the pencil against her knee. Instead she's poking the eraser into her chin, as if it's holding her head up. Ben isn't here to discuss Joshua. He's here to discuss something else. "I have a really bad feeling about where you're going with this."

"I don't think you do."

"You're convinced somebody pushed Erin off the rooftop," she says.

"Somebody did."

"And now you think if you had her eyes that would give you a chance to see the person responsible."

"I'd only need one."

"Jesus, Ben . . ."

"I know how it sounds."

"I don't think you do."

"I know it sounds extreme."

"No, Ben, it sounds crazy."

"It's not crazy."

"It's worse than crazy, Ben, I'm sorry, but it is. You don't know if anybody else was there."

"Somebody was there," he says.

"Even if you're right, you don't know if she saw them and—let's run with your assumption that she did see them—we don't even know if cellular memory is a real thing."

"Then we do our homework and see if it is."

"Even if by some chance it is real, you can't control what you're going to see. You could see somebody she saw at the supermarket the day before and suddenly you're blaming them."

"But—"

"Let me finish," she says, "because we haven't even gotten into the ethics of it yet, let alone the possible complications, not just the fact that I'd get fired, then discredited, and on top of that it would put future operations in jeopardy. There's also—"

"We're beyond ethics," he says. "The things we've been doing—"

"Don't give me that," she says, pointing the pencil at him. "Don't sit there and say we're beyond ethics when everything I've agreed to was your idea to begin with." She leans back in her chair. "Sometimes I don't know how you and Mitchell ever talked me into this."

"You know exactly how," he says, and he's right. She does know. "Our job," he says, and he leans back too, and she doesn't think she's ever seen somebody in as much pain emotionally as he is right now. First with what happened to Mitchell, and now Erin. "It's reactive," he says. "We get to people after they've been hurt. This was a way for us to be proactive. A way to help."

"I bought that line back in the beginning," she says. "If I hadn't, then none of this would be happening."

"We've helped a lot of people," he says.

"At a great cost."

"You can't put a cost on something like that."

"No? You can't put a price on your soul? That's how it feels, Ben."

"These were bad people, Toni, and now they're gone and in their place we have good people," he says, his voice hard. "I haven't sold my soul, and I sleep better because of it."

This Ben isn't like the Ben she was in love with all those years ago. What he's doing now would never have seemed possible to Ben of the Past, but what she's doing would never have seemed possible to Past Toni either. Sometimes she wonders what life would be like if they had stayed together. He broke her heart when he left her to travel. When he came back five years later she was no longer angry with him, and of course you can't be mad at somebody who returns home to spend time with his dying brother. She was also far too busy with her studies to hold on to that kind of resentment, but whatever had been there when they were in love had disappeared for him, but not, it turned out, for her. There was still something there—still is—and that's why she agreed to help him when he and Mitchell came to her five years ago.

All of this, she thinks, started with Ben's brother, Jesse.

Now Ben has Erin, and she's happy for him. For them both. She wonders if Erin knows the reason Ben is sleeping so well at night.

"Please, Toni, I love her. I know I have no right to ask you, especially because . . . well, because of our past, but she means everything to me."

"Our past has nothing to do with it," she says, and she wonders if he ever felt this way about her. She doesn't think so. If he did, he never would have woken up that Friday morning back in the summer of their youth and told her over the pancakes he made for her that he was planning a trip. He never said the words *I'm leaving you*. No, he said, *I hope you'll be happy for me*.

"If it were simple, I would. You know I would. But this . . . this is too much. You can't expect me to unplug her eye and slot it into you long enough to have a vision and then switch it back. It's not like plugging in a TV, Ben. We're talking about serious operations here, with some serious healing time and some serious risk."

"I need to know what happened."

"I know you do." She softens her voice. "I know you do, and I know you love her, but what you're asking isn't about love. It's about revenge. Listen to yourself. You're asking to put Erin's body under more stress. What if something goes wrong with the operation? What if there's an infection and her body is too weak to fight it? What if she dies? What then? What if by looking for answers, you end up killing her? What then, Ben? What then?"

"I can't lose her," he says. "But I can't . . . I can't not know what happened."

"Then do what you do and find another way to figure it out."

"It's all I've been trying to do." He sighs, then hangs his head in his hands for a few seconds before looking back up at her. "I'm sorry I came to you."

"It was a crazy idea," she says, "but you had to ask."

"No, not about Erin. I mean I'm sorry I came to you five years ago. I know how hard it's been."

She isn't sure how to respond. She also wishes he hadn't come to her five years ago. She can't deny he's right about one thing—there are good people out there now who would be dead if he hadn't. She's still figuring out what to say to him when the fire alarm goes off. Without any hesitation, Ben jumps out of the chair and races into the corridor.

TWENTY-THREE

—— ◆ ——

Smoke comes out from under the bathroom door. On the other side, the flowers Vincent brought with him, along with all the rolls of toilet paper he could find, are on fire. He doused everything in lighter fluid before removing the central stem of the door handle so if anybody tries to turn it, it will turn without gripping any of the mechanics. It isn't going to open.

He walks calmly into Erin's room. He takes the syringe out of his pocket, extends the plunger so the tube is as full of air as he can get it. And he waits.

Somebody pulls the fire alarm.

He jams the syringe into her neck.

He presses the plunger as fast as he can.

Nothing happens.

Vincent is confused.

Outside the room, there are warning shouts, confusion, and a lot of movement. The fire alarm is loud, a whining *whoop*, *whoop* with the second part of the *whoop* increasing in pitch and intensity. People are running in different directions. Some away from the smoke, some towards it.

He puts the syringe into his pocket. According to all the crime shows, when somebody forces an air bubble into a target, the effect is quick. If the bubble is big enough, it can get lodged in the bloodstream and cause a blockage, which can lead to a heart attack. He's also read about it online. It comes down to the amount of air and how quickly it's injected. Sometimes it's fatal, and sometimes it isn't. If it works, it can be undetectable in an autopsy. In this case, Erin fell from a rooftop and probably crushed every organ in her body and broke every bone—why would they look for another cause of death?

Why isn't it working?

Maybe it takes time. Maybe it takes thirty seconds, or five minutes, or an hour. Maybe it doesn't work at all, and it's like one of those childhood myths that are frightening to kids but utterly ridiculous, like the one about blowflies laying eggs inside your ears and their babies eating your brain on their way out.

He has to do something.

There is a set of drawers against the wall with medical supplies on top. He grabs a roll of bandages. He will stuff the bandages into her mouth and let her choke to death. Sure, it won't be subtle, but he's here and he's not going to leave without getting the job done. He can't risk her waking up and remembering what happened.

He wads the bandages up into a ball.

Before he can open her mouth, the machine monitoring her heartbeat goes crazy.

TWENTY-FOUR

———— ◆ ————

Ben hits the staircase, not wanting to use the elevator if there is a fire. He pictures the ground floor ablaze and people trying to reach the roof. He pictures helicopters airlifting patients to safety. He imagines windows being broken and ladders being raised and water being pumped into every room. His imagination throws all these things at him, and in every scenario Erin is burning.

He leaps the final few stairs, then pulls open the door to the intensive care ward and sees right away that this is where the commotion is centered. He rushes into the corridor, almost knocking over a guy in a baseball cap, his shoulder instantly throbbing from the impact, but he doesn't look back to see if the guy is okay. None of the overhead sprinklers have been activated. They are designed to go off where they detect heat, which means the fire hasn't spread to this area yet, even though the corridor is foggy with smoke. He can't see any flames. People are coughing. People are calling out. The fire department will be on its way, but it's going to be at least a few minutes. People are saying "Stay calm, stay calm." He reaches the nurses' station and can hear another alarm, this one almost drowned out by the fire alarm.

He reaches Erin's room. The second alarm is louder in here. It's coming from the machine monitoring her vitals. If a machine could have emotions, this one's would be described as angry as hell.

Erin is dying. He is losing her, and nobody knows.

He races into the corridor. The doctors and nurses are busy moving patients. None of them can hear Erin's alarm. He grabs the attention of the nurse nearest him. A young blond guy who looks like he should still be in school. "You have to help," he says. "The alarms are going off in her room."

"There's no need to panic," the nurse says. "It's the fire alarm, if we all stay calm and—"

"That's not what I'm talking about!" Ben yells, dragging the nurse back towards the room. "You have to help me."

"Okay, okay, stop pulling me."

He relaxes his grip. The nurse follows him to Erin's room. "Oh no," he says, and pushes past Ben. He puts his fingers against her neck. Then he looks back at Ben. "Get anybody you can," he says. "Tell them we have a code blue."

"Is she going to be okay?"

"Go!"

So he goes. He grabs the next medical professional he can see, this one a doctor with slicked-back hair and bushy eyebrows so thick they look like they're growing on top of his glasses. "There's a code blue," he says, then pushes the doctor in the direction of Erin's room. Then there's a nurse and another doctor, but by now others are becoming aware. Within thirty seconds, half a dozen people are working on her.

A doctor grabs him by the arm. "You're the cop, right?"

"Can you help her?"

"You can help us. Figure out where the hell that smoke is coming from and let us do our job."

He dives into the smoke. Still none of the sprinklers have been activated. There's a door to his right where the smoke is at its thickest. A doctor is trying to open it with one hand, while in his other he's holding a fire extinguisher. Ben puts his hands on the door and tests to see how hot it is—he can remember something along the lines that if it's hot, he shouldn't open it, then he remembers that if there's smoke coming out from under the door, he also shouldn't open it because the smoke is toxic—but then he figures there's plenty of smoke out here anyway. He puts his hand on the handle, and when he turns it, it doesn't do anything. It feels like all the innards have been taken out.

"What's behind there?" Ben asks, then notices the sign on the door. It's the bathroom.

The doctor can't answer. All he can do is cough.

"Give me the fire extinguisher," Ben says. "Grab some wet towels and lay them along the floor to block the smoke."

The doctor hands him the extinguisher, then coughs some more and collapses. So much for getting any towels. The fire engines can't be too far away. At least he hopes so.

Using the extinguisher like a battering ram, Ben smashes it into the handle. The handle comes off after the first blow and it's like he thought—the central piece has gone. This is deliberate. His lungs are starting to fill with smoke. He's becoming light-headed. The doctor is on the verge of passing out. He punches the fire extinguisher into the door, and after a couple of blows the wood cracks. He gives it a few more, then he kicks at the cracks. The door folds inwards. Smoke rushes out. It feels like it's coming from the desert. His eyes start to water. He pushes the door open the rest of the way. The room is full of fire. He points the extinguisher into the heart of it and pulls the trigger. White powder sprays out, but it's not enough. He moves forward but there are too many flames. It's a losing battle.

A nurse appears next to him. She points a fire extinguisher into the blaze. They walk farther into the room. A third person shows up. They begin to get on top of it. The fire alarm is still going. The sprinkler system isn't working in the bathroom, because it's been disabled: someone has pulled the spout away from the wall and pointed it at one of the sinks, so instead of the water spraying out in an arc to cover the flames, it's running straight down the pipe and into the basin.

They kill the rest of the flames. He can't stop coughing.

The timing of all this, he knows what's just happened.

Somebody tried to kill Erin.

The same somebody who threw her from the rooftop.

Out in the corridor someone is helping the doctor who collapsed. Ben makes his way past them. In Erin's room the doctors and nurses are still working on her. He stands in the doorway coughing. There's nothing he can do but watch.

TWENTY-FIVE

———— ◉ ————

Monday does what it does best—it arrives quicker than any other day. Joshua is sure the physics behind that is something neither Albert Einstein nor Stephen Hawking could get a handle on.

He doesn't need the alarm clock to wake him, because he's hardly slept all night. It's seven when he drags himself out of bed. He dresses in the school uniform they shopped for last week and watches TV for an hour, flicking between the news that he isn't really interested in and cartoons made for preschoolers. When he sits at the breakfast table he has no appetite. He leaves his bowl of cereal untouched and divides his time between staring at the food and staring at the wall.

"You really should try to eat," his mom says.

"I'm too nervous."

"You have every right to feel nervous," she says. "Anyone transferring to a new school would feel nervous."

"I know." He puts a spoon into his cereal and stirs it around a little, then tries to balance the spoon to see if he can get it to stand on its own. "But knowing that doesn't make me any less nervous."

"The day will go fast, and the next thing you'll know you'll be back home, and remember what I promised you?"

He wants to learn to drive, but first he has to pass the written test, but before that there is something even simpler he needs to learn: to ride a bike. He must be one of the only sixteen-year-olds in the country who doesn't know how.

"I miss Dad," he says. The house has been set off balance in every way since his dad was killed. Joshua can no longer hear his father's footsteps, his voice, his laughter, he can't hear him singing in the shower or swearing at a quick-fix five-minute job that takes two hours. He can't smell his dad's aftershave in the mornings, can't smell the odor of fast food that would absorb into his clothes when he couldn't make it home in time for dinner, can't feel the weight of his dad's hand on his shoulder when he would ask him about his day. He can't taste his dad's cooking anymore, which he ate usually every other night because his parents took turns in the kitchen, and he actually thought his dad was the better cook. He has his sight, but there is a sensual void not having his dad around, and he feels it the way he imagines an amputee feels a missing limb.

"I miss him too," his mom says, and he knows she does. As much as he misses him, his mom must miss him even more, and he realizes that other than going back to work, his mom has had no other life. She hasn't seen friends. Hasn't gone out. She's dedicated all her time to him. Sometimes he can hear her crying during the night, trying her best to be quiet. He knows she's being strong for him, and he's grateful, because her strength is stopping him from curling up into a ball and breaking down every minute of the day. She's being strong for him, and he needs to repay her by being strong for her.

Starting now.

"You're right," he says. "About school. It will go fast, and I know it's going to be great."

"You'll make friends in no time," she says.

"I know. I know I said I'm nervous, but I'm excited too," he says, which isn't true at all. He's just nervous, but his mom doesn't need to hear that. Not anymore. "I'm actually looking forward to going."

"Good, Joshua, that's really good."

He picks up his spoon and eats his breakfast, which makes his mom look a little happier, and then it's time to leave.

There's lots of traffic on the roads—typical for this time of day. The one thing he's discovered about traffic is that it's less annoying when you're blind. There are lots of students about, some walking, some on bikes, others waiting at bus stops, all wearing school uniforms of various colors. His mom has told him that you could drive a circle through this and the neighboring suburbs and you'd pass primary schools, secondary schools, and high schools all within walking and biking distance of each other, a dozen of them in total. He sees kids who can be only five or six years old walking with their parents holding their hands. He sees ten-year-olds on bikes carrying bags almost as big as they are. The young boys and girls look full of energy and ready to ask questions and run into traffic and chase cars. The high school students look moody and cool, totally apathetic and as though they wished they were anywhere else but here. Some of those older ones are wearing the same uniform he is. He wonders if he'll be in the same class with any of them, whether or not he'll become friends with some of them.

When they're two blocks from the school campus, he asks his mom to pull over.

"You're embarrassed to have me drop you off at the gates?"

"Umm . . . it's not that . . . it's—"

"I'm pulling your leg," she says, and brings the car to a stop. She smiles at him while he reaches into the backseat for his bag. "You're going to be okay," she says.

"I know."

"I'll be back to pick you up when school finishes."

"I can walk home," he says. "I don't mind."

"I'll be here," she says.

"It's not that far. It'll only take me an hour at the most. Please, Mom, I want to walk home. I think it will be good for me."

"Are you sure?"

"Completely. I want to do this."

She gives him a smile almost as big as the one she had at the hospital when his bandages came off.

"What?"

"Nothing," she says. "Ring me if you change your mind."

He opens the door. "It's going to be okay," he tells her, the same words Principal Anderson said to him when all this began, and he's starting to think Mrs. Templeton got it right. Things will never be the same, but eventually they might just be okay. "Really, it will be."

"Be careful," she says.

"I will be."

"And call me if you change your mind, or get lost."

He climbs out of the car and begins walking, turning around to briefly wave good-bye. It isn't long before he's surrounded by the noise of the schoolyard, the buzz of a thousand students talking and laughing and arguing. Some of the kids start to take note of him, but no one says anything. He goes to the administration block. He talks to a reception- ist and she tells him to take a seat. The bell goes off to mark the start of the first period. A few minutes later, Miss Franklin appears.

She gives him a big Monday-morning smile and looks even more full of energy than she did on Friday. "Nervous?" she asks.

"A little, yeah."

"Understandable. How did you get on over the weekend?"

He'd spent time over the weekend going through the textbooks for his classes and trying to play catch-up. Roger helped him. The school year was two months old, and even though some of the curriculum he had already learned at Canterbury, there was plenty that was new ter- ritory for him. He's studied so much over the last two weeks that his brain wants to explode from it all.

"It was okay," he says. "And my tutor is happy to keep helping me."

"Remember, all the teachers here are aware of the situation. No- body is expecting any miracles, and none of them are going to be call- ing on you in class to answer something in front of the other students. It's not our goal to embarrass you, Joshua, but to help you. If you're stuck on anything, don't be frightened to put your hand up and ask, or hold back at the end of the lesson and ask then if there's time. Every- body here wants the best for you."

"Okay," he says, and it's a relief to hear all that.

"You ready to go to your first class?"

"As ready as I'll ever be."

"Remember, any problems you come and see me, okay?"

"Okay."

She leads him into another wing and down a corridor where there are lockers on one side and classroom doors spaced out on the other. He wonders if the Canterbury School for the Blind looks the same. The lockers have stickers on them and names and dates and symbols scratched into them; the floor is scuffed by the hundreds of feet that walk on it every day; and there are posters on the walls reminding students to wash their hands and not to litter. Every surface looks like it needs a fresh coat of paint. There are drinking fountains spaced out every twenty yards and bathrooms every forty. There is nobody else around. Their footsteps echo down the hall. Miss Franklin knocks on a door near the end of the corridor and opens it and he suddenly thinks of Mrs. Templeton and the morning she pulled him from class. He follows Miss Franklin in. Thirty students all turn to look at him. Miss Franklin chats with the teacher. There is a murmur as some of the students talk among themselves, until the teacher asks them if their brains are so scrambled from the weekend they can't remember how to be quiet. Then he looks at Joshua, then addresses the class.

"Everybody, this is Joshua, who I told you about on Friday. Or do you prefer Josh?"

"Josh is fine," Joshua says.

"Josh, this is everybody, and I'm Mr. Stone," he says, and Mr. Stone looks athletic and young and the male counterpart to Miss Franklin. Perhaps they studied here at the same time. He has brown hair that's eight or nine inches long tucked back behind his ears. He looks like he should be behind a guitar instead of in front of a blackboard. "You'll find everybody here quite accommodating, wouldn't you say, everybody?"

There is the general murmur of forced consent.

"I'll leave you to it," Miss Franklin says, and she smiles at Joshua before disappearing.

"So, Josh," Mr. Stone says, smiling at him. "Welcome to our little neck of the woods. The students know a little bit about you, but how about you tell us a little bit more about yourself?"

"Umm . . . sure, okay," he says, and turns towards the class. He's never looked out at a group of people before. Back in his old school, they had to give speeches, and he hated it. On days when he knew they had to do it, he'd act sick at home, hoping he wouldn't have to go to school—not that it ever worked. The only way he got through them was by pretending there were only two other people in the class. When you're blind, that's something you can do, but he can't do that now. Not unless he closes his eyes, and even then he doesn't think that would work. Somebody says something near the back that he can't quite hear, and a couple of students laugh. "Umm . . . my name is Joshua Logan. I . . . I, umm . . . well, I used to go to another school but . . . umm . . . but now I go here."

He stops talking. The class looks at him expectantly. When he doesn't add anything else, Mr. Stone takes over. "Well, I'm sure there's more to tell, but how about we tackle our Monday morning and get some work done. Josh, why don't you take a seat, there's a desk down the back waiting for you."

He walks to the back of the room, feeling everybody watching him, some with curiosity, some with hostility, some with amusement, some with looks he hasn't learned how to read yet. He takes a seat. He's in the middle of the back row, there's a girl to his left who keeps looking straight ahead, and a boy to his right who is running a fingernail over his desk back and forth, as if trying to scratch a hole through it.

"Okay, class, it's Monday morning, so you know what that means, right?"

There's a murmur of consent, and everybody reaches into their bags.

"That's right, it's biology time," Mr. Stone says, and Joshua figures he's saying it for his benefit.

Joshua reaches into his bag and flicks through the books. His heart beats fast and then almost stops. He can feel himself turning red. He puts his hand up.

"What is it, Josh?"

"Umm . . . I must have left my textbook at home."

Some of the other students laugh. Mr. Stone smiles. "No problem, Josh, I got a spare one here. Start handing this back, would you?" he says, and hands a textbook to the student at the front of the row, who hands it behind him and so on until the book reaches the student seated directly in front of Joshua, a boy much bigger than him, with short spiky hair and lots of pimples on his face. He hands the book back but doesn't let it go. He mouths a single word, but Joshua doesn't yet have the ability to lip-read. Joshua has to tug at the book to get him to release his grip. The boy sneers at him, then turns back towards the front of the class.

"Turn to page fifty-six, everybody," Mr. Stone says, and everybody does, including Joshua, and he's thankful he's looked through the beginning of this book over the weekend, otherwise right now he'd be feeling even more embarrassed than he does. Even so, when Mr. Stone starts talking, he feels immediately out of his depth. None of this makes sense.

This new world is going to chew him up and spit him out.

TWENTY-SIX

—— ◉ ——

"We don't know that for a fact, Ben. Doesn't matter how many times you watch it, it's not going to change—we never see him go into Erin's room."

Ben looks up from the screen to Detective Vega. They've interviewed staff and patients and visitors from the hospital without any luck, and are now once again watching the security footage. Ben is halfway through a bacon sandwich and a coffee and Vega is halfway through a salad and an organic smoothie, the components of which look like they washed ashore. Vega has been assigned as Ben's temporary new partner. It feels like a betrayal to be moving on after Mitchell's death, but he's not fool enough, or Hollywood enough, to argue that he works better alone. He thinks the trial partnership will become a full-time partnership. He hopes so. He likes Vega and he likes having a second set of eyes and somebody to watch his back. He's never known anyone like her—she looks more like an actress playing a cop in a movie than an actual cop, and with her long dark, wavy hair and big green eyes and smile that always makes others around her smile, she has the ability to flirt with her suspects and make them open up, and if that doesn't work, she can flatten that smile and tighten her jaw and look like somebody who could break you in half. Which, he thinks, she probably could. He's known Vega for five years but doesn't know anything about her outside of work, though it's obvious she spends a lot of her downtime at the gym beating the hell out of punching bags and benching more than her own body weight. Ben has always kept himself in shape, but he wouldn't ever want to go one-on-one with her in an arm wrestle.

"It's too much of a coincidence," Ben says.

She talks around a mouthful of salad. "That doesn't mean it's not just that—a coincidence."

"Somebody tried to kill her," Ben says. "Twice now."

"The doctors said it was an embolism. They said it's not that uncommon to experience one after surgery, and she did have a lot of surgery."

He puts his sandwich down. He hasn't had much of an appetite over the last few weeks, and today is turning out to be no different. "I know. I know that, okay? The doctors have said that a hundred times already. But this guy," he says, and he taps the computer screen where there's a paused image of the man with the flowers, "he hurt her. I'm sure of it. Why else go to the effort of setting that fire?"

"I'm not saying you're wrong," Vega says. "I'm saying you can't be sure."

He thinks back to the moment he came down the stairs. This man wearing the baseball cap—or Mr. Baseball, as they're now calling him—is the man he ran into. What did his face look like? He doesn't know. He saw him and dismissed him in a heartbeat—there was no reason not to—as he was focused on getting to Erin, and it was that focus that allowed the doctors to save her. Any delay could have cost Erin her life.

Either they're dealing with some whackjob trying to kill her, or they're dealing with some whackjob trying to burn down the hospital and kill everybody.

They can trace some of his movements using surveillance footage. They see him enter the hospital. They see him step onto the elevator and they see him step off on Erin's floor. There is never a good view of him; the peak of the baseball cap is covering his face. He spends time making a phone call before walking towards Erin's room, but then there are no cameras to cover the angles or to see if he actually enters the room. When he reappears he finds the bathroom, then reappears six minutes later, now without the flowers. He goes back towards Erin's room, and a short time later smoke comes out from under the bathroom door and somebody pulls the alarm.

There is even footage of the moment Ben ran into him a minute later by the stairs.

If it is a coincidence, it's one of the biggest ever. Why would Mr. Baseball risk returning to finish Erin off? Because she can identify him. That's what Ben thinks. Which suggests she knows who he is. His cop instinct makes him question if Mr. Baseball is an ex-boyfriend; if this were any other case, he would question if it was somebody the victim was secretly seeing. Proposing to her the night before, was that the trigger that sent Mr. Baseball into a rage? Did he steal the engagement ring out of some kind of resentment?

The last footage they have of their arsonist is him exiting the hospital towards the street.

"If that fire hadn't been contained—"

"But it was," Vega says, "and he didn't disable any of the other sprinklers. As soon as it spread beyond the bathroom door, others would have been activated."

"We don't—"

"Either way," Vega says, interrupting him, "he's going to go away for a long time."

"If he's responsible for what happened to Erin, he's not going away at all."

Vega turns to look at him. "What is that supposed to mean?"

Ben thinks about what he said. Then he shrugs. "It doesn't mean anything. I'm venting, that's all."

"Don't do anything stupid, Ben."

"I won't."

Vega stares at him silently.

"What?" Ben asks.

"Nothing."

"If you've got something to say, say it."

Vega puts down her bowl. The salad has gone. He's never understood how people eat them. "People are talking."

Ben leans back in his chair. "What people?"

"Other detectives. Other officers. There are rumors going around the department."

"What rumors?" he asks.

"I think you know," she says.

She's right. He does know. "They think I executed Simon Bower."

"They think you were so angry at what he did, that you staged the scene and killed him. They think you even shot yourself with the nail gun."

"And you? What do you think?"

"I think that you're at work when you shouldn't be. I think you shouldn't be on this case, because it's personal. I think that statements like the one you made thirty seconds ago don't make people want to believe you."

"What happened to Simon Bower was self-defense," Ben says.

"And I believe you," she says. "Even if it wasn't, there isn't a single person here who doesn't have your back. Bower got what he deserved, and nobody here will argue that." She pauses for a few seconds. "Look, I want you to know that I think it's a mistake for us to be on this case. I know you pulled some favors to be working it, but your judgment is clouded. You can't take a step back and look at things with an open mind."

"Anything else?"

"No. That covers it," she says.

He picks up a handful of printouts of Mr. Baseball. "Good. Then let's go talk to Erin's colleagues, see if anybody there looks like our guy, or if anybody can identify him from these pictures. Somebody has to know who he is." He gets out of the chair. Vega is staring at him. "It really was self-defense," he says.

"And like I said, I believe you. But if you have to take similar self-defensive actions against this guy, the walls of the police department aren't going to be thick enough to contain the rumors anymore. You're going to start making the headlines."

TWENTY-SEVEN

——— ◉ ———

"I said you're a freak, freak," the boy with the pimples says.

It's the same boy who was sitting in front of Joshua in class earlier, and now he realizes what word was being mouthed to him back then—*freak*. Joshua looks at his bag on the ground, his schoolbooks spilling from it. Then he looks back to the boy talking to him. One of his front teeth is sitting on top of the one next to it. His breath smells bad, and there are small blackheads dotting the sides of his nose. He's a big boy, a little shorter than Joshua, but solid looking, the kind of solid that makes him look taller than he really is and that in ten years will turn to fat. Joshua thinks this kid probably knows that. He can be mean to everybody he wants now, but in ten years' time he'll be eating pizza from the box in front of a TV, wondering why he has nobody in his life.

But that's in ten years. Right now the boy has him pinned up against a locker. Other students are walking back and forth, none of them paying any attention, making Joshua realize this must be such a common occurrence that everyone is bored by it.

"You going to do anything, freak?"

Never has anyone shoved him before. No one has ever called him a freak. He doesn't know what to say. He doesn't know what to do.

"Bet you think you're so special around here, right? All famous and everything because you got your name on TV and in the papers, but that don't mean shit around here. Around here you're a nobody, loser."

Joshua still says nothing, because he doesn't know what to say, and even if he did, he's sure it would be the wrong thing.

"So you got a new set of eyes but no tongue, is that it? Geez, you really are a freak."

"I'm not a freak," Joshua says, finding his voice.

"Well now, what do you know? The freak can talk," the boy says, then looks to his right, where his two friends are standing. One thing Joshua has learned from books and lately from TV is people bully only those they know they can intimidate. They don't bully those they think can or will fight back. Bullies are bigger. They're meaner. Bullies attract bullies and like to hang out in numbers. Good information to have in your back pocket, but fairly useless at the moment. What would help would be to have someone—preferably another bully—on his side.

"What do you want?" Joshua asks.

"It's not about me," the boy says. "It's about you, and what you want, and right now you want me to slap you in the face a little," he says, then slaps lightly at the side of Joshua's face, over and over. "You also want me to give you a titty-twister," he says, then reaches down and grabs Joshua's right nipple through his shirt and twists.

The pain is immense. "Stop it," Joshua says, trying to fight him off.

"Maybe you want me to do this," the kid says, and his friend hands him a can of soda, as if they've done this a hundred times already today. The boy points it at him and pulls the tab.

The soda erupts, and the kid aims it at Joshua's shorts, soaking the front of them. When Joshua tries to move away, the boy uses one of his meaty forearms to hold him in place, and with the other keeps the soda flowing.

"What's wrong?" he asks. "Did you wet yourself? Is that what you used to do when you were blind because you couldn't find the bathroom?"

Joshua tries to push forward, but is held in place. The boy tosses the can and what's left in it into Joshua's bag. "Calm down, freak," he says. "Unless you want me to knock you on your ass."

His shorts and underwear are soaking. So are his socks. He doesn't understand why any of this is happening. What did he do, other than show up at school? Then he realizes the enormity of the situation—as bad as this is, it's only day one. What if every day is like this? What if this happens before and after school, as well as on lunch breaks? What can he do?

He has to fight back.

He pushes himself off the locker, but right away his feet slip on the soda and he falls over, landing on his butt. People are laughing at him.

"Give me another soda," the big kid demands, and when he has one, he leans down and points it at Joshua's face. Before he can pull the tab, they're interrupted.

"That's enough, Scott," a girl says, the same girl who was sitting to the left of him in class.

Scott sneers at her. "Yeah? What are you going to do about it?"

"Tell everybody a little something that nobody is meant to know."

He pauses. "What do you mean?"

"I think you know, but if you don't, I can always tell you in front of everybody."

"Nobody would believe you," he says.

"How about we find out?"

Scott glares at her, then at Joshua. "We're done here anyway," he says, and he and his buddies walk away.

Joshua gets to his feet. He wants to crawl into a hole where nobody can ever find him.

"I'm Olillia," the girl says.

"Joshua," he says.

"No, I said Olillia."

"Huh?"

She smiles at him. "It's a joke," she says. "To cheer you up. I said I'm Olillia, then you said Joshua, and I acted as if you'd misheard me and that you thought I had said Joshua."

"Oh," he says, feeling lost.

"Let's start again. I'm Olillia," she says, and puts out her hand. Olillia is a little shorter than him, skinny, with dark hair tied into a ponytail. She has a great smile, and big blue eyes that seem to smile too, and he never knew such a thing was possible. He remembers his first thought when the bandages came off in the hospital, when he looked at Dr. Toni and thought she was the most beautiful woman in the world. A few days after that, he thought that the woman with the long red hair who read the news on TV late at night was the most beautiful woman in the world, and there have been others too, on TV and in magazines, but right now none of them can compare with Olillia.

"You're supposed to shake it," she says.

"Huh?"

She takes his arm and extends his hand and takes it with her other hand. "Like this," she says, and shakes hands with him. "Nobody taught you that?"

"Sorry," he says. His hand is wet from where he pushed himself back off the ground. Her hand is warm. It feels nice.

"Can I have my hand back now?" she asks.

"Sorry," he says again, and he lets it go.

"You apologize a lot," she says, wiping her hand on her bag. "And you're wet too."

He's about to apologize again, but catches himself. "Nice to meet you, O . . ."

"Olillia," she says.

He bends down and takes the soda can out of his bag. Whatever had been left in it has leaked through his books. His shorts and underwear feel uncomfortable, and he isn't sure what he's going to do. He has twenty-five minutes until the lunch break is over. He can't imagine drying out much in twenty-five minutes. What he can imagine is leaving a wet soda patch everywhere he sits.

"You don't talk much, do you?" Olillia says, still smiling at him.

"I guess not," he says.

"That's okay," she says, "I can talk for the both of us. My family says I talk too much anyway. My mom used to say it's because I'm a Sagittarius."

"What about your dad?"

"He's Taurus."

"I mean—"

"I know what you mean," she says, and laughs. "My dad thinks I talk too much because I'm a girl, and when I say that's sexist, he says it's not sexist, but hereditary. He says his mom was the same way, and his sisters too, who never stopped talking when they were growing up. Both of them are lawyers now, so they get to talk all the time. Only it means everything they say is pretty boring. Is it true? Everything the news said about you?"

He's still struggling to keep up with her, but he likes the feeling. He's embarrassed standing in his wet shorts, and he's humiliated that he's been bullied, but if it hadn't happened he wouldn't be talking to Olillia right now.

"I haven't read all the stories," he says, "but yeah, I used to be blind."

"Wow," she says. "I've never met a blind person before."

"You still haven't," he says.

She laughs, and it makes him feel great. "You're funny," she says.

He looks up and down the corridor, unsure where to go next. He wants to keep talking to Olillia, but he also wants to wring as much of the soda out of his clothes as he can.

"I'm sorry about what Scott did," she says. "He can be a real jerk, but I assure you there aren't many people here like that."

"You mean there are more?"

"It's a universal thing," she says. "You didn't have bullies at your last school?"

"Not really," he says.

"Then you're catching up," she says. "You should use a bathroom. You can rinse your clothes off and hold them under the hand dryer until you have to go back to class. It's probably your only option. Also, lesson 101 with bullies—it's probably not going to help if you go and tell any of the teachers. I mean, I don't know if that's what you were planning on doing. Was it?"

"I . . . I don't know," he says, and he really doesn't. His thought process has been distracted by Olillia.

"I've seen it before with Scott and other Scotts of the school," she says. "It'll have short-term gains. They might get into trouble and might even have to serve detention. Then they might leave you alone for a day or two, but then it'll be worse."

"So what do I do?"

Her smile fades. For the first time in the conversation, she looks sorry for him. "There's not a lot you can do."

"You could tell me what it was he doesn't want people to know."

She laughs. "There's nothing," she says. "I made it up. People like Scott, they always have something to hide."

"That's . . . that's really impressive," he says.

She smiles. "One of my lawyer aunts taught me it. I'll see you in class, okay?"

"Sure."

"It's nice to meet you, Boy Who Used to Be Blind."

"It was nice to meet you, Talking Girl."

She smiles at him and he smiles back. She walks away, but his smile remains. He hauls his backpack down the corridor and hardly notices the students giggling at the sight of his wet pants. He finds an empty bathroom. He locks the door and gives his underwear and shorts a quick rinse in the sink, then does what Olillia suggested—he holds them under the hand dryer. He's worried it's going to overheat and the insides will start sparking. He does the same with his socks. Occasionally someone tries the door, a couple of times people call out and hammer on it, but he ignores them and every time they go away. After twenty minutes his clothes aren't completely dry, but they're far better than they were.

The school bell rings. Lunchtime is over.

Two hours to go until he gets to leave.

Two more years until high school is over.

How bad can it possibly get?

TWENTY-EIGHT

━━ ◉ ━━

They separate when they get to Goodwin, Devereux, and Barclay. Detective Vega heads to Human Resources to try to figure out who was where on the two days Erin was attacked, and Ben goes to reception to talk to Erin's coworkers. Ben remembers it wasn't long ago that the company was in the news after one of its staff went on a killing spree. It's a piece of history that the firm has tried to forget, and he senses his professional presence here is unwanted, in case he's about to open old wounds.

"I'm so sorry about Erin," the receptionist says, and even though he's met her on more than a few occasions, he can't remember her name. Sharon, or Suzan, or Shelly. She's in her midtwenties and has shoulder-length brown hair that Erin once told him takes her an hour to straighten every morning. He knows she and Erin are friends, but it's a coworker friendship that doesn't extend into socializing much beyond gossip, Christmas parties, and the occasional after-work drink. "Is she going to be okay? She will be okay, right? I mean . . . she has to be. Why . . . why would this . . . I mean . . . everybody loves her, nobody would want to hurt her. Erin is one of the most beautiful people I know. Could it have been an accident?" she asks. "That's the only thing that makes sense, right?"

"You've heard about the fire at the hospital on Friday?"

"Of course."

"It was a distraction," he says, deciding to eliminate any *maybes* and *possiblys* to make it sound like fact. "Erin suffered a cardiac episode at the same time which was induced deliberately." He hands her a printout of Mr. Baseball's image from the hospital security camera. He watches for any sign of recognition. "This is the man that hurt her. Do you recognize him?"

"I can barely see him," she says. "His cap is in the way."

"It's the best angle we have," he says. "Perhaps you recognize the cap, or the clothes. It's possible he's been following Erin without her knowing it, or he could even work here."

"I don't know," she says. "It's really hard to tell."

The idea of what he has to ask next makes him feel nauseated. "Were there any long lunch breaks she was taking? Any out-of-office working trips? Things like that?"

"What are you getting at?" she asks, giving him a look that tells him she knows exactly what he's getting at.

"Look," he says, "the last thing I want to think is that Erin might have been seeing somebody, and I believe in my heart of hearts she wasn't, but what you need to realize is my job exposes people every day doing one thing when others think they are doing something else."

"She wasn't seeing anybody."

"Would she have told you if she was?"

"I don't know," she says. "Maybe."

"Would you tell me if you knew?"

"Of course. But she wasn't, and I'm not so sure why you would think she was."

He doesn't tell her his theory, but it's possible she was seeing somebody else, and it's possible after Ben proposed she broke off the relationship with the other man—and that other man, this man in the photograph, didn't take the news well. Perhaps they were meeting at the parking garage. Perhaps that was where he parked his car, that often they'd see each other in the mornings, that they'd share a lift down to the ground floor, then walk side by side to the office before sharing a motel room on their lunch break. Neither her phone records nor her credit card statements suggest any kind of affair, but that doesn't mean there wasn't one.

"Take another look at the picture," he says. "Take your time."

"I'm sorry," she says. "I really don't recognize him."

"Out of everyone working here, who is Erin closest to?"

"Cynthia," she says. "I can take you to her."

Cynthia is an accountant, and he follows Suzan or Sarah to her office. He's met Cynthia before, but he doesn't know her well enough to remember much about her. She's in her late thirties with makeup that looks like it was applied in a hurry and a black ponytail tipped with an array of split ends. Her desk is cluttered with papers and there are children's drawings on the wall done in crayon of people and cats and trees. She gives him a tired-looking smile when he shows her the picture from the hospital, then gives him a tired version of the same answers the receptionist gave him.

"Was she having any problems at work?" he asks, after he explains to her why he's here.

"What kind of problems?"

"With men, in particular. Anybody paying her too much attention? Anybody hitting on her? What about the bosses? Any of them inappropriate around female colleagues?"

"That stuff doesn't happen here," she says.

"That stuff can happen anywhere," he says. "Is it possible she was seeing somebody?"

"You think she was seeing this guy?" she asks, and looks at the photograph again.

"It's something I have to consider."

"If she was, she didn't tell me."

He makes his way through the rest of the office, asking the same questions and getting the same answers in return. No, Erin wasn't seeing anybody. No, the office of Goodwin, Devereux, and Barclay isn't the kind of place where female employees are given superlong hugs or told how good they look in a tight skirt. Vega's trip to Human Resources is also a bust.

They talk to everybody in the office. Ben becomes increasingly dejected. All he's achieved is a sense of betrayal, not from Erin, but from himself for entertaining the idea she was seeing somebody else. They're done here. They reach the elevators. When the doors open they have to wait for a courier carrying a package to step out. They step in and don't make any conversation on the way down. He knows Vega is sensing his frustration. They reach the ground floor and get outside. The day hasn't changed much since they arrived earlier. Same blue sky, same temperature, same traffic, same sense that the case isn't going anywhere.

Ben tosses his jacket into the backseat of the car. Vega climbs in, but he remains standing on the sidewalk staring at the courier van double-parked with the hazard lights blinking.

"What is it?" she asks.

"If Erin was seeing somebody who worked nearby, we should canvass the entire block."

"That's a lot of work," she says.

"I'm going to start with the courier driver."

"The one we passed on the elevator?"

"Why not? He probably delivers to all these buildings. It's worth a shot."

Ben walks over to the van and leans against it. The courier driver doesn't appear thrilled to see Ben leaning against his van when he returns. He looks less thrilled when Ben shows him his badge. He has a goatee and a pierced nose and a small hoop going through his eyebrow. He's the kind of guy who makes Ben wonder if all the packages in the back of his van have drugs in them. He's wearing a blue shirt with the company's logo emblazoned across the front: a van with a smiley face, and a parcel behind the wheel driving it, looking just as happy.

"I'm wondering if you can help me," Ben says.

"How's that?"

"You deliver to many offices around here?"

"I do."

"You recognize this guy?" he asks, and shows him the printout.

The driver takes a look. "Sorry, mate, but I don't, but I'm also not that good with faces." He hangs on to the picture. "Maybe leave it with me and if I see anybody, I can let you know. I'm still making my way around so haven't seen everybody there is to see."

"You mean you're new at this?"

"I've only been doing this two weeks," he says. "So maybe if—"

"Just two weeks?"

"Yeah."

"You replaced somebody?"

"The other guy got fired."

"When?"

"Like I said, a few weeks ago."

"But when exactly."

The driver scratches at his chin while he thinks about it. "I guess . . . it would have been two weeks ago. Maybe a bit longer . . . actually, I think it was a Saturday."

Saturday. The same Saturday Erin was thrown off the roof by somebody she recognized.

"Could this guy in the photo be the guy who's job you took over from?"

"Could be, but I never met him. You should go and talk to my boss," he says. "He might have a better idea."

"Give me his phone number," he says. "I'll give him a call."

TWENTY-NINE

—— ◉ ——

Joshua isn't sure which class he's going to dislike the most. Back at his old school, he hated math. Right now he'd give anything to be in a math class instead of this god-awful place—woodshop. Canterbury School for the Blind doesn't have this subject on offer, for obvious reasons. Until a guide dog can be trained to fire up a power saw, carpentry isn't going to be a first choice for a blind person. Now that Joshua can see, woodworking is apparently something he has to do and, for a New Zealander, being able to build a fence or make a garden shed from scratch is supposed to be embedded into your DNA. He's never swung a hammer or run his fingers over the grain and determined which angle to plane it from. He doesn't have the experience or the imagination to look at a piece of wood and see a birdhouse. His dad had dabbled a little. He could put up shelves but not make them. He could put kitset furniture together without any leftover parts. Joshua figures he'd be lucky if he could get to that level.

To make things worse, Scott is a gifted woodworker. Joshua figures that's always going to be the way—some of the meanest kids are also going to be the most brilliant, either superb athletes or brilliant with their hands. While he struggles with a tape measure, figuring out the dimensions for the stool he has to start making, Scott is using a lathe to shape the legs of his. He makes it look so easy, and when he finishes he scoops up a pile of sawdust with both hands, comes over to Joshua's table, where Joshua is still measuring things up, and blows the sawdust into his face.

Immediately it gets into his mouth and he spits it out, but, worse, it's in his eyes too. Scott is already laughing.

"I can't see," he says, trying to brush the sawdust away.

"Then it must feel like old times," Scott says.

The door has been opened for the darkness he's known his entire life to come back. He doesn't know what to do. When he opens his eyes they hurt, they hurt so bad, and everything is blurry. Have his eyes been damaged permanently? He should have been wearing the glasses Dr. Toni gave him.

Scott walks away, still laughing. Joshua wipes at his eyes, which have started to tear up.

"It's going to be okay," somebody says, another student, a boy he can't see. "Stay calm and I'll get Mrs. Thompson."

"I'll stay with him," a girl says, and it's Olillia. He doesn't have to be able to see her to recognize her voice—he figures it's like a superpower. "I'm sorry about Scott," she says. "I knew he could be a jerk, but not like this. I was wrong earlier. You should talk to a teacher about it."

"I can't see," he says, and he's starting to shake. What if his eyes *are* ruined? What if they're all scratched up and the nerves are getting shredded and the corneas sliced and . . .

"Did I tell you why I was named Olillia?" she asks.

Why is she asking him this now? "What?"

"It was meant to be Olivia, but my dad has bad handwriting, and the person typing it onto my birth certificate thought the *V* was two *L*s, or maybe the guy typing it was drunk, or maybe my dad was too—nobody really knows how it happened, they just know that it did. Olivia became Olillia, and my parents never got around to changing it, and by the time they did get around to it they decided not to. They liked the name."

"I like it too," he says, keeping his eyes closed and his face scrunched up.

"So do I. I like to think I might be the only Olillia in the world. Are you starting to feel better?"

"No," he says, then he realizes that's not true. She's been talking to him to keep him calm. "Maybe a little."

"It's going to be okay," she says, and he realizes then that she's holding his hand.

"Okay," he says.

She squeezes his hand tighter, then lets go.

"What happened here?" someone asks, and his superpower tells him it's Mrs. Thompson, the woodshop teacher.

"Joshua got sawdust in his eyes," Olillia says.

"You need to stop rubbing them," Mrs. Thompson says.

"I can't help it," he says.

"Did somebody do this to you, Joshua?"

Olillia starts to answer. "It was—"

"An accident," Joshua says, interrupting her.

Mrs. Thompson puts her hand on Joshua's shoulder and leads him through the classroom. He can feel everybody staring at him. All he can see are blurry shapes and color. She leads him out into the foyer between the woodshop and the metal shop, where all the schoolbags are stored during class.

"Tilt your head up," Mrs. Thompson says, and he does, and she dabs away around his eyes with something wet, perhaps a cloth or a tissue. "I'm going to put in some drops, okay? Try not to struggle."

"Okay," he says, and she puts a thumb on his left eyelid and puts in a couple of drops, then repeats it with the right.

"This should flush anything out."

"Okay," he says.

"There's a lot of sawdust, Joshua. It's in your hair, on your face, in your ears. You want to tell me what happened?"

"I don't know," he says.

"You don't know? That's the fallback answer of every kid I've ever taught in this school, Joshua. How about you try to be more original and tell me what happened?"

"I think . . . I think some flew off my workbench somehow."

"I heard you used to spend a lot of time listening to audiobooks. Is that right?"

He isn't sure where she's going with this. "That's right," he says, moving his eyes around. They're feeling better. Mrs. Thompson and her gray hair and blue eyes are coming into focus. There are three of her, but that's an improvement from a minute ago.

"What kind of books?"

"Crime and horror, mostly."

"Okay, now look at me," she says, and he does. She uses her thumb to open his eyes one at a time, stretching around them to look for more sawdust. "So you listen to lots of books, and telling me the sawdust came off your table somehow is the best story you can come up with?"

"That's what I'm telling you," he says.

"If somebody did this to you, Joshua, I can't do anything unless you tell me."

"Like I said, I really don't know how it happened."

"How do your eyes feel now?"

"They feel fine," he says, and the three of her have become one.

"Do you want me to get the school nurse?"

"No, I'll be fine."

"Are you sure?"

"I'm sure," he says. "I guess I just panicked a little. I'm sorry."

"No need to apologize, Joshua. Are you sure you don't have anything else to tell me?"

"Nothing," he says.

"Well, if you change your mind, you know where to find me."

Woodshop is the last class of the day, and when it wraps up he's achieved little on his project but believes he's achieved a lot in terms of accepting his fate. Mrs. Thompson asks Scott to stay behind, and Scott throws Joshua an accusing look, to which Joshua looks away. He grabs his bag and heads for the school gates, hundreds of other students doing the same thing, some on bikes, some walking, some being picked up, some being picked on, some ignoring him, some staring at him, none talking to him. His first day of school is over. His mom was going to teach him to ride a bike this evening, but he thinks before anything he needs to learn how to fight.

He will call Uncle Ben later and ask if he can show him how.

THIRTY

The logo from the courier driver's shirt is now staring down at Ben from a giant sign hanging outside the package depot. The smiley logo is a direct contrast to the man who manages the place, a guy by the name of Neil Proctor, who is the kind of guy who might know what smiles look like on TV but has never inspired them in real life. He tells them the guy he fired a few weeks back was Vincent Archer. Tells them it was a long time coming. Says he took an afternoon off work for a funeral, then came in late two days later and that was it. He had to let him go. That's the kind of thing in Ben's line of work that they call a *trigger*. The funeral, the boss tells them, was for Simon Bower. He gives them Archer's address, and tells them that whatever they think he did, he probably didn't do, but did something way worse instead.

"He's a strange son of a bitch, that one, and recently he's gotten even stranger."

"In what way?"

Proctor scratches at his beard while he thinks about it. He has the beard-but-no-mustache look Ben considers a mistake on anyone who sports it. "In every way," Proctor says.

"Can you be more specific?" Vega asks.

"I can't be. But there's a real creep show going on inside his head, that's for sure. Look who he was hanging out with."

On the drive to Archer's house, Ben calls Detective Kent, who was one of the detectives who interviewed Simon Bower's friends and coworkers and neighbors. Her opinion of Archer? She tells him that both she and Detective Travers thought he was a nice-enough guy, and cooperative. She tells him Archer has no criminal record. Ben tells her they're driving there now to interview him. He asks her to try to get a warrant so they can enter the premises if he's not home, or if he's unwilling to let them look around. She tells him she doesn't think they have grounds for a warrant, but says she'll do her best. He asks her to send a couple of patrol cars to the address as backup.

The houses in the neighborhood date back anywhere from forty to eighty years, some of them brick, some of them weatherboard, some of them bungalows, some of them statehouses. There are tidy gardens, messy gardens, overgrown gardens, sparse gardens. It's the same kind of street Ben lives on. The same kind of street a large percentage of the population of Christchurch lives on. A whole lot of average mixed in with a whole lot of ordinary. Except for Vincent's house. It's the exception to the rule. He lives in a bungalow that's around seventy, maybe eighty years old. It looks freshly painted. It has big windows so clean the only way he can tell there's glass in them is because of the reflection. The wooden framing is white and crisp and stands out from the dark-gray weatherboard. All of it is immaculate. There's a deck leading from the entrance that eats up half the front yard. There are flax bushes and ferns that are evenly spaced out, and the entire yard looks like a landscaper must come there twice a day. There are bark gardens and rhododendrons and yucca plants all around the edges. They drive past it and park half a block away and kill the engine and Ben can feel the tension in his body rising.

"Let's go have a chat," he says.

"We agreed to wait for backup."

"We can do this."

"I'm sure we can, and I don't know how to say this without sounding insensitive, but not waiting for backup is what got Mitchell killed."

That's not what got Mitchell killed, he thinks, but he can't tell her that. Calling for backup hadn't been an option for them. But if they had, Mitchell would still be alive and so would Simon Bower.

"You're right," he says. "We'll wait."

Backup arrives in the form of two patrol cars nine minutes later.

The officers are armed. They form a hard-and-fast plan. One officer will remain on the street in case Vincent Archer isn't home and he pulls up. One moves to the back of the house. Two stick with Vega and Ben while Ben knocks on the door.

Nobody answers.

"You reckon he's not home? Or not answering?" Vega asks.

"Not home," Ben says.

"We have to wait for the warrant," Vega says.

He walks away and calls Kent. She tells him she's still working on it. They could go ahead and smash open the door and storm inside, but whatever they find won't be any good to them if the warrant gets turned down. And even if he'd be able to keep his job afterward, he'd be ruining his partnership with Vega before it even began.

"I'm going to take a look around while we wait," he says.

"Don't break anything," she says.

He walks around the house, looking through the windows as he goes. Everything inside is as tidy as out. Some of the appliances look like they've just come out of the box. On the inside the house looks like it was built only a year ago. There's a large open-plan kitchen with an island in the middle and a double-door fridge, and the cabinetry looks handmade. There's a large lounge suite and a fireplace and no TV and some framed vintage movie posters on the walls. The carpet looks new, and there are potted plants in every room and a bookcase that takes up half a wall. Everything is neat and in its place and the bed is made and the house is full of right angles and there are no dishes anywhere.

The room at the back of the house has the curtains pulled. Could Archer be in there sleeping? Ben moves along the window trying to find an angle to see inside, and gets one between the curtains, though he has to drag a wooden picnic bench over and climb up onto it to do so. He can see newspaper articles and photographs and lists all pinned to the wall haphazardly.

He gets out his phone and calls Kent.

"How you getting on?"

"Not well," she says.

He describes the room he's just seen.

"Give me two minutes," she says. "I'll get it done."

He returns to the front door. "This is definitely our guy," he says to Vega.

"You saw something?"

"A whole lot of something."

Kent calls him back. She gives him the okay to go ahead. He hangs up and tells Vega it's go time. She swings the battering ram into the door. The result is devastating. The door separates from the jamb, the noise like a car being rear-ended. Splinters of wood shoot in every direction. She drops the ram and they storm into the house with their guns raised, identifying themselves loudly in case Archer is hiding. Three of them make their way from front to back, Vega and Ben clearing the lounge and kitchen and dining areas, the other officer clearing the hall, office, bedrooms, and bathroom.

Archer isn't here. They holster their guns. Ben pulls on a pair of latex gloves, and Vega follows him into the room at the end of the hallway, which features a display of Vincent Archer's madness.

"It's a Room of Obsession," Vega says, and Ben hasn't heard the term before but likes it. He'll use it in the future. The articles pinned to the walls are mostly about Simon Bower. There are articles about Andrea Walsh too, the woman Simon Bower killed whose body they still haven't found. Articles about Erin falling from the rooftop. About the fire in the hospital. There are photographs too, none Ben recognizes from the newspaper or online, but that Vincent must have taken himself. Pictures of the building site where Mitchell died. There is a picture of Vega outside her house. There's a photograph of Ben's mom and dad getting into their car at a mall, a photograph of Mitchell's mom in the garden and Mitchell's dad washing his car. There's a photograph of Josh and Michelle outside a school, a photograph of Josh with his grandparents, a photograph of Josh leaving the hospital. There are lists of addresses, birthdays, places frequented, anything and everything. He can barely feel his legs. He needs to sit down. The reason Erin was hurt was because of what Ben and Mitchell did to Simon Bower. What he's looking at here is a man's blueprint for revenge.

He realizes he's been holding his breath this whole time.

He lets it out.

In the center of all of this madness is a photograph of Ben Kirk made up of four separate pieces, printed out and pinned up in a two-by-two formation, each piece holding one-quarter of his features. It's the photograph the media kept running with, the one that's on his police ID. There are two things pinned to them. The first pin is holding the engagement ring he gave to Erin. Seeing it floods him with memories. They met four years ago when he was seated next to her at the cinema. She was wearing a white summer dress and her arms were tanned and her smile made his heart race. He'd gone with a friend but spoke to her during the previews. He'd made her laugh. He'd asked for her number. They'd gone to dinner the following weekend. He remembers taking the engagement ring to get sized the week before he proposed. It had belonged to his grandmother. She'd handed it down to his mom a long time ago, and his mom gave it to him when he told her he was going to ask Erin to marry him. He'd pinched a ring from Erin's jewelry box for the sizing, and his grandmother's was cleaned and the stone was reset and the band resized, and a few days later a chef was able to hide it inside a fortune cookie and now that ring is hanging from a pin on the wall of some messed-up crackpot's home.

"What is it?" Vega asks him.

He picks up the ring. "It's Erin's," he says. "It's the engagement ring I gave her."

"It's beautiful," Vega says.

The ring has been tarnished by Vincent Archer's sweat and by the toxic air in his house. Ben doesn't know if he'll ever be able to look at it the same way again.

"He must have kept it as a memento," Vega says.

Ben drops it into an evidence bag. What he does know is that it can't stay here.

The second item pinned to the two-by-two formation of his photograph is a list of names.

"Look at this," Vega says, reading a newspaper article.

But Ben doesn't look at it. He's too preoccupied. He unpins the list from the wall. On the top is Erin's name. The faint trace of a checkmark is next to it. Cleary the checkmark was made when Archer thought he had killed her, then he'd tried to erase it when he found out she was still alive.

"It's Ruby Carter," Vega says, still reading the article.

Ben doesn't answer her. He's focused on the second name on the list. This one has been underlined half a dozen times. Joshua Logan. He looks back at the photograph of Joshua outside his school. Not his old school, but the new one.

"She was your case, right?" Vega asks.

Ben looks at his watch. It's twenty-five past three. School has been out for ten minutes.

"I can only think of one reason why this guy would have articles of Ruby Carter pinned to his wall," Vega says. "He killed her. Maybe both he and Simon Bower killed her. I think we should . . . Jesus, Ben, are you okay?"

"We gotta go," he says.

"Go where?"

He runs for the door. "I think Joshua Logan is in danger."

THIRTY-ONE

"Hey, Josh, wait up!"

He turns around. Olillia is waving at him from a group of students he passed outside the main gates. He hadn't noticed her among them as they stood in a circle chatting. She says something quickly to them, then walks over to him. "You walking or catching the bus?"

"Walking," he says.

"Mind if I walk with you?"

"I'd like that," he says, and then blushes.

The street is full of parked cars with parents waiting to pick up students. There are other students walking and biking in all directions. His last school was different. Parents waited out front, but nobody walked or biked.

"How are your eyes?"

"They're fine," he says. "I guess I overreacted."

"You've been blind all your life, and you probably thought you were about to lose your sight again. If it'd been me I'd have been blubbing like a baby. I'm sorry about your dad, by the way."

The change of subject is so dramatic he isn't sure what she means at first. He's had so many things on his mind today his dad had slipped somewhere towards the back. "It's tough," he says.

"I know," she says. "I lost my mom. I was only five when it happened, so my only real memories are that she loved me and we made each other laugh, but sometimes when I try to picture her I can't. She got cancer. I don't remember her being in the hospital or anything. Just that she was always there and then . . . and then she wasn't."

"I'm sorry," he says.

"Then we're both sorry." She smiles. He wonders if her family has a curse too.

"So you live with your dad?" he asks.

They've walked a block. There are clusters of students around him, some in groups, some in pairs, some by themselves. Some are piling into a bus that's pulled over.

"And my brother," she says. "He's older than me. He's twenty, but he lives at home. He got the normal name."

"Yeah? What is it?"

"Normal," she says. "Strange name, huh?"

"Seriously? His name is Normal?"

"Yeah, crazy, huh? I don't know what our parents were thinking." Then she laughs and slaps him lightly on the arm. "No, just kidding. It's Zach."

He laughs too. He's never met anybody so weird.

"You got brothers or sisters?" she asks.

"It's just me and my mom."

"Any pets? We have three cats. Some days I think that three cats are three too many, and other days I think I'd like more."

"No pets," he says. "At least not full-time pets."

"They're part-time?"

"Yeah."

"So you mean half the day something will be a cat, and the other half it'll be something else? Like a table?"

"Exactly," he says. "But sometimes they might be a couch too."

"Part-time dog, part-time lounge suite," she says. "But what's the real story?"

"Mom is a veterinarian, and sometimes she brings kittens home, or puppies. It's kind of like foster care, especially if they're not well and she wants to keep an eye on them overnight. We'll have them for a few weeks or so. Sometimes a month."

"Must be hard saying good-bye to them."

"It is," he says. "I try to focus on the fact that they're in better health than when they arrived, and they're going to a good family."

"Do some of them die?"

"Sometimes, yeah, but not often."

"That must be really sad," she says.

"Yeah, it is."

"Your mom must be really brave," she says. "I'd be a mess."

There is a convenience store at the next corner, a black Rottweiler tied to a bike stand outside. It watches them as they walk past. It has a hungry look in its eyes. There's graffiti on the lampposts and chewing gum on the sidewalks and he can smell fresh bread and stale cigarette smoke. They hang a right past it. Olillia is telling him the names of her cats, and of previous cats that have been in her life. He likes the sound of her voice. Up ahead is a railway crossing. It runs along the top of an embankment that forms a parabolic curve. He sees some students from his school wander off and follow the tracks to the right.

"Out of the way, loser," somebody yells, and he turns around to see a student from his school riding his bike on the sidewalk, coming fast towards him. He steps aside just in time. The student races up the side of the embankment as fast as he can, gets some air at the top by pulling up on the bike, then disappears down the other side.

"You know him?" Joshua asks.

"Levi? No, not really. I know who he is, that's all. Kind of guy you'll be reading about in the papers one day for all the wrong reasons."

"Like Scott," he says.

"There is one advantage," she says. "Levi is a year ahead of us, so you've only got to put up with him this year."

They climb the embankment and stop at the top. He looks up and down the tracks. Where the tracks cross the road, there are long pieces of pavement between the rails, and of course the embankment is paved too, but beyond the road are sleepers that go as far as he can see and the embankment is made up of millions of fist-sized stones, all of them blocky and rough. There's no sign of a train, but he can see students in each direction. The ones he watched a moment ago have paused to light cigarettes and untuck their shirts.

"I live in that direction," Olillia says, nodding down the tracks to the left. He knows that the trains pass a couple of neighborhoods behind his. On quiet nights if the air is still he can hear them. He also knows that on occasion people underestimate how long it takes to cross the tracks and for some reason drunk people have been known to fall asleep on them, causing horrific accidents. "Which way do you go?"

"I'm that way too," he says, "but I was going to take the roads. I've never walked down train tracks before."

"You should try it," she says. "It's cool."

Cool. He thinks about that word, and realizes he's probably never done anything in his life that could be described that way. He could start by walking these tracks. Follow them in the direction of his neighborhood. It would be like an adventure, and it's not like he can get lost. Not really. And if he does, he can either use his phone to call his mom or use the map application to figure out where he is.

"Well?" she asks.

"Let's do it," he says.

"Great! Where do you live?"

He tells her. She thinks about it for a few seconds, then nods. "It's perfect," she says. "We walk down this section, which takes us to the road I want. Then you carry on to the next one. You'll cut twenty minutes off your trip."

They walk between the rails on the sleepers. The students heading in the same direction are now too far away for him to make out anything but the color of their uniforms.

"You ever been on a train?" she asks.

"Never," he says. "In fact, I've never even seen a train."

"Never?"

"I've heard them, and I kind of have an idea of what they must look like. I've still never seen one on TV or on the Internet. Not because I'm not curious, but there are plenty of things I haven't seen yet."

"I imagine there are plenty of things you'd look up online before looking up trains," she says. "I was on one with my mom once, but I can't—"

The sound of approaching sirens interrupts her. They turn to see a police car racing over the crossing at the intersection behind them. It reminds him of the day Uncle Ben sped into the parking lot of the hospital, following the ambulance.

"Geez, somebody's in a hurry," she says.

"Hope nobody has been hurt," he says, then thinks that if somebody has, hopefully it was Scott.

They carry on walking, Olillia balancing the left rail and Joshua the right. The stones forming the sides of the embankment peter out into ankle-high grass that's dry and patchy, and farther out are wooden fences separating all of this from the neighboring houses. Some of the fence palings are missing, some twisted and warped, and all are covered with graffiti.

"What were you saying? About the train?" he asks.

"Oh, yeah. I was going to say it was so long ago that I can't remember. I only know because Zach remembers and he told me about it once. I don't even know where we were going, or why. What was it like?" she asks. "Being blind?"

He can smell grease and can hear insects buzzing in the grass. There are beer cans and drink bottles tossed in every direction. He figures the only thing that isn't here but should be is a kid prodding a dead cat with a stick and a hobo drinking wine wrapped in a paper bag. The first autumn leaves are starting to pile up against the base of the fences. He wonders who litters more, people or nature.

"It wasn't like anything," he says. "I mean, it's how I always was. I didn't miss my vision, because I never had it, but yeah, I knew I was missing out. There were times when it was really hard, but most of the time I didn't think about it. Like, you know how you don't think about breathing, you just do it? Kind of like that. I didn't think about being blind, or dwell on it, it was who I was."

"And now?"

"And now everything is different."

"But not just because you can see, right? Because of everything else in your life?"

"Yes," he says.

"Do you still see your friends from before the operation? Or do they see you differently now? And when I say *see*, I don't actually mean *see*."

"That's . . ." he says, but doesn't finish.

"That's what?"

"That's really insightful," he says. "And no, I don't. They don't want to hang out with me anymore."

"Must be tough," she says. "Not just losing your dad, but feeling guilty that you can see after what happened to him, and feeling bad your other friends can't see too."

He wants to hug her, but doesn't. They keep walking. Occasionally one of them will lose balance and fall into the other one, knocking the other off the rail too, causing them both to laugh.

"Am I the first friend you've made since getting your sight?"

Her question makes him smile. It makes him feel good inside. It brings back the thought of hugging her. "Yes."

"You'll make others," she says. "I'll introduce you to some people tomorrow. They'll like you, I promise."

"Thanks," he says. "That sounds . . . cool."

"You won't have to be alone anymore, and you'll like them."

He's excited about making friends. He also thinks that having lots of friends is the best defense you can have against guys like Scott.

Soon Joshua and Olillia are batting away mosquitos and squashing the occasional sandfly against their arms. Joshua can't see any grasshoppers, but he can hear them chirping from all directions. He feels sweat dripping down his side, where his schoolbag is resting, but the sweating and the itching are the only downsides to this outing. He likes the heat from the sun, likes walking on the rails, and the sleepers, likes the sounds of insects coming from the grass. It's firing off his imagination the same way his audiobooks used to, and he wonders if that could lead anywhere, that perhaps of all the things available to him, being a writer is now one of them. Of course, he could have been a writer even if he had remained blind—but describing a world you've seen in the light is easier than describing one that's only ever been in your head.

"You always walk?" he asks. "Or you sometimes bike?"

"I walk," she says. "I could actually drive, if I had a car."

"Really? You can drive?"

"I got my learner's license two months ago, so I always have to drive with somebody older who's been driving a few years. It's fun. I guess you've never driven, huh?"

"Never," he says, "but I want to."

"My brother could teach you. He taught me."

She tells him about her brother. He's studying at teachers' college because he wants to be a physical education teacher. He loves sports, plays a bunch of them, not well enough to play professionally, but well enough to be able to teach others. The students they were walking behind leave the tracks at the intersection up ahead. A police car, perhaps the same one as before, shoots up the bank and races down the other side, part of it hitting the ground and creating sparks, its sirens blaring. Seeing it brings them both to a stop.

"Must be something pretty bad," he says.

"I hope nobody's been hurt," she says. "You think they're heading to an accident? Or a crime scene?"

"Could be either of those, or could be they're looking for some-body."

They reach the intersection. The houses up and down the street look similar to the houses on his street. They're mostly single-story homes with the occasional two-story scattered among them. Autumn is stripping the gardens and the hot sun is burning the lawns and some yards are in better condition than others.

"This is where we part ways," she says.

"Oh, yeah, of course."

They stand by the tracks staring at each other.

"Umm . . . do you want my number?" she asks. "In case you have any questions about school or homework? Or if you want to maybe walk to school together?"

He smiles. "Sure," he says. He takes his bag off and unzips the compartment along the side. His hands are shaking a little. He's nervous and isn't sure why. He takes his phone out. The screen is sticky from the soda poured on it earlier. He tries to switch it on, but it doesn't work.

"Give me your hand," she says, and he does. She writes her phone number on his palm and doesn't mention the fact his hand is shaking even though surely she must notice it. "It was nice walking with you, Boy Who Used to Be Blind," she says.

"I'll see you tomorrow, Talking Girl."

He watches her walk down the bank and then down the road. She's fifty yards away when she turns and waves. He feels like he's been caught out, but he's not sure of what. He waves back, then crosses the road and continues down the tracks.

This next section is the same as the previous, only there's lots more litter, more dried grass, more graffiti, and, as he begins sweating even more, more insects too. Every few seconds he has to slap at something trying to take a bite out of him. There's another student way up ahead. He focuses on him, trying to match his pace. After a hundred yards he realizes the phone number on his hand won't survive the walk home—his sweat has already smudged the first two digits. He takes his bag off, pulls out a notebook, and scribbles it down. When he puts his bag back on, he looks down the train line behind him. Somebody is running towards him. He can't tell who, but somebody from his school is making the most of the same shortcut. When he looks back a few moments later he sees that it's Scott.

This can't be good.

He runs.

"Wait up, freak!" Scott yells.

He's never run before in his life. He's walked quickly, and he's jogged a little bit over the last few weeks, but he's never run anywhere, not like this, not full on like his life depended on it. This means he's short not only on experience, but also on stamina. Already he's breathing hard. The student he was following is now in the next section of train tracks, too far away to help even if he wanted to. His feet pound heavily on the sleepers, and he keeps his eyes on them, knowing one false step will send him into stones. He can hear Scott catching up. Can hear his feet stomping on the sleepers. The road comes into view. He just has to make it there. Just has to keep running.

Scott ankle-taps him. He loses balance and flies into the air. He twists and manages to use his bag to take some of the impact, but not all of it. He rolls down the stony embankment and into the grass below.

THIRTY-TWO

— ◉ —

This is what it's like to be a stalker, Vincent thinks. An elevated heart rate, sweaty palms, and a constant case of the nerves. A stalker who is an idiot. Who has a lot to learn. A newbie.

Going to the hospital—that was stupid.

Injecting Erin Murphy—that was stupid.

He succeeded only in drawing attention to the fact that her accident wasn't an accident at all. He's let the police, the hospital, everyone, know that someone is trying to kill her, which would be at least somewhat bearable if he had, indeed, successfully killed her. Instead he's back where he started—living with the knowledge that she could wake at any moment and remember every detail.

There is an upside—the precautions he took at the hospital worked. The police didn't come for him. The woman not dying—that was bad luck. But not getting caught—that's good planning.

It will all go better with the boy.

He's been following Joshua Logan and other people close to Detective Benjamin Kirk over the last two weeks. It took him a while to determine the order in which they would all go down. It was a complicated process, but he has finally pinpointed his second target—the son of Ben's former partner, the boy who got his father's eyes.

Vincent looks like any other parent as he taps his fingers against the steering wheel while staring into the sea of students. It's easy to fit in. What isn't easy is knowing what Joshua will do. Is he getting picked up? Walking? Getting the bus? Well, that's why Vincent is there—to learn. The other thing that isn't easy is spotting the kid. There are so many of them all dressed the same.

But then there he is, walking out of the gates, and Vincent has to keep waiting because if he follows he'll spook the kid. He also can't keep catching up and pulling over. He knows the route the boy will take—he just needed to find out his mode of transportation. Walking is perfect.

He gives it five minutes, then pulls out. He passes Joshua near a convenience store where schoolkids are fattening themselves on meat pies and cans of soda. Joshua doesn't go in. Nor is Joshua alone. He's walking with a girl from school.

Vincent takes the next right and drives up and over a railway crossing a hundred yards down the road. He drives another twenty-five yards and pulls over. The girl could be a problem if the kid is always going to walk with her. Other students bike past his parked car. Some walk. He keeps looking busy by checking his watch and playing with his phone. A kid with dark spiky hair and a mean look on his face races past him on the footpath side of the car, and when Vincent glances at him the kid yells, "Loser!" and flips him the bird.

He considers following that kid home instead.

Joshua reaches the top of the railway tracks, and instead of coming down this side, he and the girl change direction and walk along them.

"Interesting," Vincent says, and pulls into traffic.

There is a light up ahead that's green, but nobody is going through it, and soon he sees why—there are police cars racing through the intersection. They turn and come his way, and for a moment he's nervous that for some reason they're coming for him, but they don't slow down. They're heading in the direction of the school, hitting the railway fast. Maybe one of the kids has stabbed a teacher, or one of them has stabbed a fellow student. Usually the biggest assholes were assholes as kids too, but the kind of shit that happens at schools these days is far beyond what the biggest bully would have tried back when Vincent was a student. He still remembers his first day at high school. He was thirteen. It was a couple of years before he met Simon. All his friends had gone to a public school, but his parents sent him to a private school, which meant he knew nobody there. On day one in the playground one kid pulled Vincent's pants down around his ankles, then knelt behind him, while a second pushed him in the chest, sending him toppling over the first and onto his back with his legs in the air. There wasn't a single student who didn't laugh. He pulled his pants up and knew there was a decision to be made—become the butt of everyone's joke, or get himself some respect.

The boy who knelt behind him was still on his knees laughing. Vincent kicked him hard in the face. He broke the boy's nose, split his lip, and knocked out two of his teeth. He dived on the other kid, and they were still swapping punches that mostly missed when the teachers pulled them apart. He knows his parents' money was the only reason he wasn't expelled that day, but nobody laid a finger on him again. Ever.

Traffic starts to move, and though he misses this green light, and misses it on the next cycle too, he gets it on the third. He drives north and gets held up at the next intersection, this time for another police car, and once again misses two green lights because of backed-up traffic. The kid who called him a loser earlier passes him again, and now that he's seen him a second time, he reminds him of that kid back in school whose teeth he kicked out. The traffic clears and he turns down the road, and up ahead the girl who was walking with Joshua is now walking towards him, and Joshua isn't here. He's probably carried on down the tracks. Vincent turns the car around and this time he times the light, then gets stuck at a red, but only for a minute before making the next left down a road that runs parallel to where he saw the girl.

Joshua will be all alone on those tracks, Vincent figures. Vincent's goal for the day had been to follow the kid and learn his movements, the same way he's been following the others, but really, you can follow people for only so long before they start to notice you. The point here isn't to follow, the point here is to act.

With the kid all alone on the railway tracks, the time to act is now.

He parks near the railway crossing and gets out of the car. He carries the knife wrapped in a rag. He had put it in the car earlier just in case, and, hell, this is a classic just-in-case moment. He climbs the incline, and when he gets to the top of the tracks he looks first to his right, and sees nobody in that direction. To his left, nothing makes sense. The boy is only about twenty yards away, lying in the grass. Another kid is moving towards him. With traffic and delays, the boy has covered more ground than Vincent expected. Maybe he's been running too.

He should just turn away and go back to his car. He can always pick this up again tomorrow, or next week. There's no hurry.

The second kid reaches down over Joshua, ready to punch him.

None of this is your problem, he tells himself, *and none of this was the plan.*

He's tempted to go down there, but leaving is the right thing to do. Keeping the knife wrapped in the rag, he takes a few steps back towards his car, then changes his mind. He'll wait and watch a little, and see where this goes.

THIRTY-THREE

Ben tries Joshua's cell phone again. The kid must not have switched it on since leaving school. Michelle, on the other hand, has been easy to get hold of, and he's managed to put the fear of God into her.

Officers have been sent to Joshua's house, as well as to the school, with others cruising the streets. They know the make and color and license plate number of the car Vincent Archer owns. A manhunt is under way, and they will find him—the question is, will Archer find Joshua first?

Ben and Vega are on their way to Vincent Archer's parents' house, hoping they can learn more about Vincent and, in doing so, perhaps learn where he might be—or where he would take Joshua. While Vega drives, Ben phones the others on the list Vincent made, warning them that they may be in danger. He's also placing calls to Joshua's friends, after Michelle told him how despondent Joshua has been feeling about the way they've ignored him. It's possible he's gone to see them.

Robert and Helen Archer live in a neighborhood full of big houses and tall fences, expansive yards and expensive cars. It's the kind of neighborhood that makes him feel like he's wasted his life by not winning the lottery. There can't be a house on this street with fewer than six bedrooms and three baths, and some with more, Ben expects, and some with tennis courts and pools out back. These aren't mansions, because Christchurch doesn't do mansions, but they are about as big as you can get in this city. He's never known anybody to live on a street like this, but he has visited these kinds of houses before, because rich people kill too. Robert and Helen Archer. For some reason the names sound familiar, but he can't figure out why.

The house is hidden behind a hedge that must be ten feet high. There's an opening in the middle of it, but that opening is filled in with a wooden gate. They pull up in front of it and Ben winds down the window and presses his finger onto the button of a video intercom.

A woman answers. "Can I help you?"

"It's Detective Inspector Vega and Detective Inspector Kirk," Ben says, and they hold their badges up to the camera. "From the Christchurch Police Department."

"What can I help you with?" the woman asks.

"We'd like to talk to you about Vincent," Ben says.

"Vincent? Why? What's happened?"

"We'll explain when you let us through."

"Yes, yes, of course," she says, and there's a buzzing sound and the gate rolls open.

It's a short drive to the house. There's a good half-acre of front yard, with the driveway curving around an oak tree that's taller than the two-story house. A tire swing that looks fifty years old and ready to break hangs from a branch as wide as a horse. Parked next to the tree is a perfectly rustic garden seat that looks ready to throw out of alignment the spine of anybody who might try sitting there. There are lines of manicured roses and knee-high hedges of clipped lavender being dive-bombed by bees. Large square patio tiles eat up the last ten yards of lawn towards the contemporary house where there's an outdoor table and a barbecue and a bar and a fireplace. A birdbath at the edge of the lawn is holding the attention of a black-and-white cat. The house, only a few years old at most, is made up of slate tile walls the color of sand. There are floor-to-ceiling windows, which provide a voyeur's-eye view of expensive furniture and high ceilings. It looks like a movie star could live here.

The entrance is two side-by-side doors with a column on each side. One of those doors opens, and a woman wearing a purple blouse and black pants comes out. She must be incredibly strong, Ben thinks, to be able to support the weight of the massive pearl necklace hanging around her neck. She has dark blond hair and designer glasses and a botoxed forehead and a smile that's had the same treatment. She reminds Ben of every real estate agent over fifty he's ever met. She introduces herself as Helen Archer and doesn't ask them to come inside, but instead leads them to a pair of outdoor sofas. Again he wonders how he knows her name, and he can't make the connection. He certainly knows he's never been here before, and she doesn't look familiar. She takes a couch and Ben and Vega take the other. Between them sits a low concrete coffee table with candles arranged perfectly in its center.

"Is your husband around?" Vega asks.

"Oh my god, is Vincent . . . Has there been an accident? Is he dead?" she asks, lifting a hand to her mouth. With the number of rings on her fingers, her arm muscles must be as strong as her neck.

"No accident, and he's not dead," Ben says.

"Your husband," Vega says. "Is he here?"

Helen Archer shakes her head. "He's working," she says. "He's in banking," she says, which is vague, and Ben suspects she keeps it that way because banking can be hard to explain and even harder to make sound interesting. It's probably why so many bankers are good at avoiding jail. "He won't be home until late. They're working on . . ." She pauses, then smiles. "I'm sorry," she says, "I'm blabbering. You still haven't said why you're here."

"Vincent was friends with Simon Bower," Ben says.

"Ah," she says, and she looks relieved. "So that's why you're here. Not to talk about Vincent, but about Simon. After what he did, well, I'm ashamed he was in our life in any capacity."

"You never liked him?" Vega asks.

"I can't sit here and say I'm disappointed that Vincent ever saw any-thing in him, and I can't give a speech about how you can't choose who your children become friends with, because the truth is we all liked Simon. He was a good boy. Always friendly, always polite. Throughout the years he came to birthdays and dinners because Vincent would often invite him and he was always more than welcome. If there was anything that needed doing to the house, or the previous house, Simon would always offer to help. In fact, he's the one who laid down this beautiful outdoor area," she says. "Only now . . . now I want to rip it up. What he did . . . it was so . . . so inhumane, it makes me ill. You must think I'm a harsh person when I say I'm glad the police killed him. Yet part of me . . . part of me still wants to believe he couldn't have done those things."

Which tells Ben she isn't going to believe what he's about to tell her. "Actually, he's not why we're here," he says, and her body tenses. "You watch the news?"

"I like to stay up on current events," she says.

"Then you'll know about the fire that was set in Christchurch Hospital last week."

"Where are you going with this?" she asks.

"And you'll know about the woman thrown from the rooftop of a parking structure in town."

"I've read about it," she says.

Vega takes her cell phone out of her pocket. She queues up a photograph she took of the walls in what Ben is now also thinking of as the Room of Obsession. She hands it to Mrs. Archer. "This is from one of Vincent's bedrooms," she says.

Helen Archer takes the phone. "What are you showing me here?" she asks.

"Vincent is responsible for the fire," Ben says, "and for the attempted murder at the car parking building."

"That's impossible," Helen says.

"That photograph," Vega says, "is full of people he's currently targeting."

"He blames the police for what happened to Simon," Ben says. "And he's out for revenge."

"You're insane," Helen says. "You both are."

Ben pulls a pair of evidence bags out of his pocket. "This is a list of people he's targeting. The name on the top is the woman he threw from the roof." He shows her the second evidence bag. "This was her engagement ring. We found it pinned to Vincent's wall."

"We believe that right now he's targeting the young man who is second on that list," Vega says. "He's the son of the police officer Simon killed and, as of right now, nobody can find that young man or Vincent."

"This is all some kind of mistake," Helen says. "I think I need to call my husband."

"There is also evidence implicating Vincent in the disappearance of another young woman," Vega says.

"Not my Vincent," Helen says, and she's made no move to get up, made no move to reach into her pocket for a cell phone.

"Then help us find him so we can clear things up," Ben says. "A young boy's life is on the line here, Mrs. Archer. Help us find Vincent so we can at least rule him out."

"Don't think I don't know who you are," she says. "You're the man who killed Simon, and I stand by what I said that I think that's a good thing, but it won't be a good thing if you're the man who shoots Vincent too. I'm not going to help you do that, not when you have your facts wrong. You're a shoot-first, ask-questions-later type of policeman," she says. "The worst kind of policeman."

"What happened with Simon was an awful thing he brought on himself," Ben says. "He killed my partner, and then he tried to kill me."

"For which we only have your word," she says.

"What happened to him was self-defense," Detective Vega says. "Please, Mrs. Archer, there are other lives on the line here. We're not wrong about him."

"I read the news, Detective," she says. "I know the woman who fell from the parking building is your fiancée. I'm sorry about what happened to her, but that makes this personal for you. It means you're not thinking straight. You don't want to arrest Vincent, you want vengeance, and that doesn't bode well for my son, whether he's done anything or not. Now, we're done here, Detectives. Any further questions can go through my lawyer."

She stands up.

Ben and Vega stand up too. "Your son," Ben says. "There's something not right with him. Maybe he's masked it well and you've never suspected, or maybe deep down you've always known something was off. Right now he's out there trying to kill a sixteen-year-old boy. When all of this is over, the police and the media and the Internet are either going to portray you as the woman who wouldn't help us and let that boy die, or as the woman who did the right thing and helped us save lives. Which is it to be?"

"You're a manipulative bastard, aren't you," she says.

"And one who's going to tell everybody how thanks to you, we were able to save the life of a young boy. That's the headline here, Mrs. Archer, if you work with us. How you turned your own son in, how heartbreaking it was, and how it made you a hero."

She looks down at her hands. "What do you want to know?"

"Is there anywhere isolated he might go? Somewhere he can take a victim? Somewhere he likes to go to get off the grid?"

"Not that I know of."

"When was the last time you saw him?" Vega asks.

"A couple of days ago," she says.

"What did he want?" Vega asks.

She sighs. She looks defeated. In the last few minutes they've punched a hole in her perfect life and told her that her son is a killer. "He came to drop off a present for his niece. It was her birthday recently and we had a party here and he didn't show," she says. Ben and Vega see her mind ticking over, wondering if the reason he didn't show might go hand in hand with the reason they are here. "He made her a rocking horse," she adds.

Ben says nothing. Nor does Vega. They say nothing in the hope Helen will fill the silence. She does. "He also borrowed one of our cars. His broke down, and he can't afford to replace it. We've offered to buy him a new car, of course we have, but . . . but Vincent sees that as charity. He never accepts anything, it's the way he is. He was willing to let us at least *lend* him a car while his was getting fixed."

"So his car is in the shop," Ben says.

"That's what I'm telling you."

If Vincent is right now following Joshua, it's no wonder he hasn't been spotted.

The police are looking for the wrong car.

THIRTY-FOUR

"Hey, freak," Scott says, and Joshua can't get his breath back, can't make sense of what's happening, can't get to his feet. His head hurts and his legs hurt and so does the rest of him. He can taste blood. Scott has punched him in the stomach. "You shouldn't have told on me."

Skin has torn away from Joshua's hands and knees. Bits of dirt and flecks of stone are stuck in the cuts. His schoolbag has twisted around his body and is restricting him like a straitjacket. He doesn't know what Scott is talking about. Doesn't know how far Scott is willing to go. Isn't he frightened of being expelled? Or being charged with assault? Joshua doesn't think so.

Scott punches him so hard in the arm, it goes numb. "If you tell anybody again, then this is how every day is going to go between now and the rest of your life," Scott says.

"I . . . I didn't tell anybody," Joshua says, and he sure isn't going to tell anybody about this. This is how bullies get away with things.

"You going to keep your mouth shut from now on? Or do I have to break your jaw?"

"I get it," Joshua says.

"What do you get?"

He gets that whether he tells anybody or not, Scott is always going to come for him. That's the thing about the Scott Bullies of the world—they do what they want because they can, because they don't care, because their empathy chip has been switched out with an asshole chip.

If he doesn't do something in this moment, then nothing will ever change.

He lashes out with his foot.

It connects with Scott's knee.

"Ah!" Scott cries out, and he drops his hands to it as he falls over. "You're dead!"

Joshua is already on his feet and running, but he's running farther from the intersection he was trying to reach earlier, the tumble down the bank having turned him around. He can't change direction now, because it would mean running back into Scott. He can hear him catching up. Last time he got his ankle-tapped, he hit the ground hard. The same thing is going to happen this time too.

Unless he keeps it from happening in the first place.

He comes to a stop. He fights his bag off and faces Scott. He separates his legs and makes a solid base and tightens his hands into fists. He pictures himself as a brick wall that can't be budged. He pictures his hands as sledgehammers.

Scott will slow down. He'll reassess.

Surely.

Won't he?

Scott keeps coming, and fast.

Joshua swings his fist as hard as he can the moment he's in range.

And completely misses.

The momentum takes him off balance. Scott punches him in the back of his head. Those two things combine to send him flying again into the air. Without his bag to take the impact, his head hits heavily against the ground.

Everything goes black.

THIRTY-FIVE

Vincent watches it all from his position up on the tracks—Joshua getting punched in the stomach before kicking the other kid in the knee, Joshua running, Joshua making an unsuccessful attempt to defend himself. The poor kid never had a chance—and suddenly Vincent thinks that, ultimately, he'll be doing him a favor by killing him. The world can be a big and scary place—too big and scary for Joshua Logan.

The second kid is bigger than Joshua. He's got fat and muscle to service his streak of meanness—he's seen it before in other kids, and he'll see it again. Joshua is starting to move, but slowly, and with his eyes still closed. The big kid is still standing over him, talking to him, but in a voice too low for Vincent to hear. Vincent makes his way down the bank, the stones noisy under his feet. The kid turns towards him.

"He fell," the kid says.

"He didn't fall," Vincent says. "You pushed him."

The kid's face tightens. Vincent can see all the nastiness in his features. This is an ugly kid made uglier by the way he sees people. "So what if I did?"

"Nothing," Vincent says. "But if you're going to beat up a defenseless kid, at least have the courage to own up to it."

"What's it to you, you piece of shit?"

Joshua is starting to groan. He opens his eyes and stares right at Vincent. He looks confused. He closes his eyes again. The groaning stops and he goes still.

"I'm sorry, kid," Vincent says. "You're in the wrong place at the wrong time."

"Actually, mate, you are. I suggest you mind your own business."

"Really? Is that what you suggest?"

The kid tightens his hands into fists. He sure has a lot of courage, Vincent has to give him that. Then he raises those fists and takes a step forward. "I am going to smash you, you pervert," he says.

"Run," Joshua says, groaning again, and now he's looking from Vincent back to the boy. "Scott, you have to run."

The boy—Scott—glances towards Joshua. "I'm not running from anybody," he says, which is also the last thing he says, because at that moment Vincent brings the knife out from under the rag and plunges it so deeply into Scott's chest that the blade gets stuck.

"No," Joshua says, but then his eyes close again and he goes still, as if he's the one who's been stabbed.

Vincent watches the look of shock on Scott's face, and he can't deny there's a spark of pleasure from taking this brat out of the world. He's sure half the people this kid ever came into contact with will want to give him a medal, and now that he thinks about it, he's pretty sure the other half will too. He watches the life fade from him. It leaves his eyes first, then his face. His mouth droops open. His final breath smells awful and sounds awful and makes Vincent want to take a shower. He puts the boy on the ground and wiggles the knife out. Annoyingly, he's getting blood on his hands and pants. He's definitely going to need to take that shower after he's done here.

Joshua's eyes are opening and closing as he fights to stay conscious. One dead boy—another about to die—Vincent needs to confuse the police as to what really happened here. He remembers a case in the news recently. A person was murdered and thrown in front of a train in the hope it would look like a suicide or, at the least, hide what really happened. It didn't work back then, but that doesn't mean it won't work now.

Let the train cut Scott into a dozen pieces.

Let the train finish Joshua off.

By the time forensics can piece them all together, he'll be much farther along with his list.

He grabs Joshua by the wrists and drags him up the bank.

THIRTY-SIX

They have their sirens on and are speeding towards the school when the police radio comes to life.

"Kirk here," Ben says.

"Detective, this is Officer Walker, we've got a location on the black Lexus you're looking for. It's parked up on Hillswood Road about ten yards east of the train tracks."

Ben closes his eyes for a second and lets his imagination run. He doesn't like where it goes. "I want you to get that car open and check if the boy is in there." He doesn't need to add *in the trunk*, because he knows the officer will know what he means.

"On it," Walker says.

Vega has already changed direction. Ben estimates they'll be there in two minutes. A long two minutes. He hears glass shattering over the radio. He hears the trunk pop open.

He holds his breath.

"Trunk is empty," Walker says.

He breathes out slowly. "Anything to suggest where Archer might be?"

"We're looking," Walker says.

"Look faster."

"Yes sir," Walker says.

"We're almost there," Vega says.

"Can't this thing go any faster?" Ben asks.

"Not if you want us to get there in one piece," Vega says.

"Did smashing the car window bring people out of their houses?" he asks Walker.

"Affirmative."

"Then start asking questions. What about the house the car is parked outside of? Could they be in it?"

"We got an elderly woman coming out that front door. I'll know in a moment."

"What about the train tracks?" Vega asks. "They cut through all those neighborhoods, and they would form a shortcut between the school and Joshua's home. Maybe he walked down them? Maybe this guy saw him?"

Ben talks back into the radio. "Get those train tracks checked out right now, Officer, and I mean right now."

"Yes sir."

Up ahead a furniture truck is backing into a driveway, the front end hanging into traffic and blocking both lanes. Their siren causes panic, and the more the other drivers try to get out of the way, the more congested the road gets.

"Move!" Ben yells, to no one in particular. To everybody. He waves his arms in a universal gesture for *get out of the way*. It doesn't help.

He keys the microphone on the radio. "Talk to me," he says.

"I'm on top of the train tracks and walking in the direction of the school," Walker says. "It's a dump back here. Lots of bottles everywhere, it's like—"

"We don't need a commentary," Ben says. "Can you see anybody?"

"Not yet," Walker says. "I'm still . . . wait."

Ben's heart stops pounding as his chest tightens and grips it, stopping it from beating. That's how it feels. The furniture truck gets more of its bulk into the driveway. Vega punches through the gap that has just formed, clipping the truck and smashing the headlights of both vehicles. The driver yells at them. Other cars are pulling out of the way. Vega hangs a hard left and Ben can see the railway line two hundred yards ahead.

"What have you got?" Ben asks. "Officer? Officer Walker? What have you got?"

There's silence, and then the radio comes back on. The tracks are a hundred yards away now. "Detective, I've . . . err . . . I've got Joshua Logan."

"Is he okay?"

"I'm . . . I'm sorry, Detective, but he's not. Joshua is dead, sir, and he's not the only body down here."

THIRTY-SEVEN

Joshua's body will be lying alongside the tracks. Blood will be all over his clothes, and his face will appear relaxed and his eyes will be open wide to the wonder of it all. It will take three police officers to hold his mom back, and perhaps they'll need a fourth. She'll collapse then, and the officers won't be able to hold her up. She'll lay on the ground with her forehead against it as her fists beat the pavement, and perhaps she'll beat on Ben too for not having done enough to save her family. First she lost her husband and now she's lost her son, and how can anyone move on after that? How can you possibly pick up the pieces of your life when those pieces are gone?

Ben will stand next to Joshua's body, wondering what he could have done differently. All that blood, all those tears, Michelle Logan screaming at him, saying he should have done more to protect her son, and she's right, he should have.

He can see it all playing out before it's even happened.

The blood. The screaming. The reactions.

It's all waiting for him over the next few minutes, but right now he's still fifty yards away from the train tracks in the car with Vega; they haven't even gotten to the scene yet. He hasn't called Michelle yet either, but he knows those wheels are already in motion.

There are no more furniture trucks. No more congested traffic. If only they had had more time. He thinks what they could have done differently, and there are some obvious answers. He thinks about Helen Archer, and wonders if she knew what her son was capable of. He tries placing her name again but can't.

They come to a stop behind the patrol car. There's an officer talking to a woman in her eighties, gray hair pulled tightly into a bun, hands making big gestures, a steely look on her face.

"Get the trains shut down," Ben says to Vega, as he jumps out of the car. He runs up the slope and down the other side, Vega somewhere behind him on her phone. He slows down when he's a few yards from Officer Walker. He can see legs in the grass, the flash of the school uniform. He was hoping . . . Well, he was hoping Walker was wrong.

"I'm sorry," Walker says.

Ben doesn't say anything. He reaches the body, praying this won't be Joshua, that somehow, somehow, if he hopes hard enough, if he gives it everything he has, then . . .

It isn't Joshua.

The knowledge hits him so hard and fast he stumbles in the stones. By wishing the body was somebody else, has he made it so? Has he fated somebody else? Then he remembers: Walker said two bodies.

"Ambulance is on its way," Walker says. "So is backup and forensics."

"Where's—"

"In line with us," Walker says, "fifty yards further down," he adds, nodding in the direction of the school.

Vega catches up with him as he walks down the tracks. He swats at the sandflies that buzz past his face. The neighborhood sounds like it's about to be overrun by grasshoppers.

"That wasn't Joshua," she says.

"No, but it's somebody from his school," he says. "Joshua is up ahead."

"I'm . . . I'm sorry," she says.

He doesn't say anything.

"Back at Vincent's house, you didn't want to wait for backup, or a warrant, and I'm the reason we did."

She's right. He wants to be able to tell her it's okay, not to blame herself, but things *would* be different if they had broken into Archer's house the moment they got there. He doesn't say any of that. He doesn't need to.

"I'm sorry, Ben. I'm really sorry."

"You get the trains shut down?"

"Yes," she says. "And we're setting up roadblocks at each intersection to make sure nobody walks down here. We'll get him, Ben, I
promise."

"I know we'll get him."

"It doesn't make sense for Archer to kill Joshua and leave his car
behind."

Joshua's body comes into view. Like last time, it's the legs he sees
first sticking out of the grass. Only these are in jeans, not the cheap
polyester blend of a school uniform. And they're longer than Joshua's
legs. He breaks into a jog. More of the body comes into view.

It isn't Joshua.

The legs and the jeans belong to Vincent Archer.

"What the hell?" Ben asks.

"So where is Joshua?" Vega asks.

"You hear that?" Ben asks.

"There's a train coming," she says, looking down the tracks.

"I thought you said you had the lines shut down."

"I did," she says. "Maybe that driver hasn't gotten the message."

"It's going to ruin our crime scene," Ben says.

He hikes up the stony embankment to the tracks. Best he can do is
run towards the train and wave his arms and hope the conductor will
see him, but already he knows it will be impossible for him to stop in
time. The train is going to blast through the scene and scatter some of
their forensics into the breeze, and mix dust and dirt into the forensics
that remain.

He runs anyway, the train getting closer, and as he runs, he finally
realizes why Helen Archer's name is so familiar: It came up in the investigation when they were searching for Ruby Carter. Helen and her
husband owned one of the cabins about five miles beyond the search
zone where Ruby went missing.

The train isn't slowing down. He keeps waving his arms, and that's when he sees him, Joshua, lying in the middle of the tracks fifty yards away with the train bearing down on him.

Ben is no longer waving his arms. Instead he's sprinting, desperate to reach Joshua before the train does, but already knowing there isn't enough time.

THIRTY-EIGHT

—◆—

Joshua hurts. He hurts from the blow he took to his head. His hands and knees hurt from where he fell. He hurts from Scott punching him. He hurts from being confused, from not knowing where he is. He hurts because his father is dead and there's a curse picking off his family. He hurts because he saw Scott murdered in front of him.

Most of all, he hurts from having his eyes removed.

They were never really your eyes, he tells himself, which is true, but it comes as no consolation. He has a headache. In the hospital, when he had the itch, it felt so deep it couldn't be scratched, like a splinter in his brain that couldn't be pulled. Now something is pulling on that splinter. Maybe it's the curse. It's jiggling the splinter back and forth so quickly it's producing a humming sound. He doesn't know what kind of technique was used to remove his eyes—whether it was something surgical like a scalpel, or something crude and dirty like a melon baller. He's too scared to raise his hands to his face to find out, too scared he will find a tangled mess of optic nerves and veins.

He reaches up and can feel the bandaging around them—and suddenly it all makes sense—he's in a hospital and the doctors are trying to help him. Only this doesn't feel like a hospital bed, because the bed is lumpy. It feels like wood and stone, plus . . . isn't that dirt he can taste? And why would a lumpy hospital bed be vibrating? The humming is getting louder. It's turning into rumbling. He can hear dull-sounding cars and muffled sirens and somebody somewhere shouting.

The rumbling gets louder.

He rolls onto his back. He pulls at the bandage and it comes away, revealing the most beautiful sky he's ever seen, and he's relieved, so relieved that his eyes haven't been taken away, that he can still see, that he doesn't have to go back into the darkness. The bandage wasn't a bandage at all, but a flap of his shirt that's been torn away from the bottom, right up to the collar. Why was it torn?

He isn't sure. He closes his eyes. What is the last thing he can remember? The humming in his head is getting louder. The splinter gets pulled, and the memories start tumbling through the hole left behind. He remembers Scott wailing on him. The stranger showing up—only he wasn't a stranger. He was the man from his dreams—the man with the fishing rod and the girl and the mountain bike. There are patches of memory that are missing after he was dragged up to the tracks. That explains why his back is hot and sore, and could explain how his shirt got torn. There are glimpses of memory of stumbling along the tracks looking for help.

He's holding the knife that killed Scott in his left hand. He has no idea why. When he tries to sit up, he feels seasick. He rolls onto his side, sure he's about to throw up.

A horn blares so loudly he's sure he's going to start bleeding from the ears. The ground is no longer rumbling, but shaking. The stones are rattling.

He looks up.

Even though he's never seen one, he knows exactly what it is barreling towards him. He rolls to his side and onto the stones as the train races by. He keeps rolling, down the bank and into the grass. Earlier he thought how strange it was that people fell asleep on train tracks, and perhaps this is how it happens—somebody knocks them out first. The knife is still in his hand. How did he get it from the man who was trying to kill him?

He vomits, barely avoiding his hands. For the first time he notices a deep graze on the back of his left hand, and now that he's noticed it, it hurts. He tears the flap of shirt off and uses it to wipe his mouth. The last carriage passes him by, the sound going with it, revealing a new sound. Somebody is coming. He can hear footsteps pounding, they sound muted and dull—in fact, everything does. The footsteps belong to the man who tried to kill him. They must. He's coming to finish him off.

He can see the man's shadow. It's moving across the ground. He holds his breath as the man leans down, and a moment later, a hand lands on his shoulder and tries to roll him over.

This man killed Scott, and now he's going to kill him.

He has to protect himself.

He rolls over and swings the knife.

Straight into Uncle Ben's throat.

THIRTY-NINE

— ◆ —

The blood is warm and sticky and flows freely and Ben tries to hold on to it, tries to keep it in, knowing that once it hits the ground it will be too late ... *too late* ... *just* ... *hold* ... *on* ... *to* ... *it*. He looks at Joshua, who is almost unrecognizable, this kid with the big scared eyes who narrowly missed being hit by a train. There's blood on Joshua's hands and flecks of blood and vomit on his face. His shirt is all torn up, and he's still holding the knife, holding it in Ben's direction as if he wants to take another swing.

The blood keeps flowing, like somebody turned a tap on full, and he thinks ...

Hell ... he doesn't know what to think.

"Joshua," he says, a spit bubble of blood forming on his lips and popping. He stumbles, one foot gets trapped behind the other, and a moment later he lands on his butt with his legs ahead, hands still tightly wrapped around his throat.

All he has to do is hold on to the blood.

All he has to do is bleed a little less.

If Erin can survive falling from a rooftop, then surely ...

"Uncle Ben!"

He opens his eyes. Joshua is moving towards him.

"I'm sorry."

Ben doesn't answer him. He can't.

Vega reaches them. She has her gun drawn. She points it at Joshua. "Put down the knife!"

"But—"

"Put it down," she yells.

None of this makes sense, and all of this is escalating at the same rate everything is disappearing, and Ben wants to sleep. How can he sleep with all this shouting going on? He can no longer hold on to his throat so tightly.

"Put it down!" Vega says again, screaming at Joshua, who, for his part, is looking less feral and more petrified now.

Footsteps pound the ground behind them. Somebody is coming. Probably Officer Walker. Or the Grim Reaper—he must be in a hurry with all that's going on around here. Joshua puts the knife down and moves away from it.

"Stay right where you are," Vega says, and holsters her gun. She moves to the knife to secure it.

Ben no longer has the strength to stay sitting. He falls onto his back and looks up at the darkening sky. The stars don't come out. Vega comes into view.

He wants to tell Vega that it was an accident. He wants to tell her that he doesn't want to die. That he doesn't blame her for the decision she made back at the house that delayed them, because it's his fault for not trusting his gut and kicking in the door and shaving ten minutes off the investigation. It's his fault, and Mitchell's too, because everything they've done has led to this. Perhaps this is karma. He wants to tell her to tell Erin he loves her, and that he was thinking about her in this moment.

"Hang in there, Ben," Vega says. "Promise me you'll hang in there."

He promises nothing.

Officer Walker appears. He pulls off his shirt. "Ambulance is on its way," he says, then balls up the shirt and crouches down. He pushes it hard against the wound. "Hold on, Detective," he says, and then he says something else, and Vega says something else too, but he can't hear them anymore.

It's okay now, Ben wants to say, but can't. I feel fine, he wants to add. It's true—he does feel fine. False alarm, everybody. He's going to be okay. He needs a nap, that's all, a little shut-eye and then he'll be as right as rain.

He watches the light disappear from the sky.

There are still no stars.

FORTY

—— ◉ ——

Joshua is shaking. It wasn't that long ago that he was sweating and destroying sandflies against his forearm with his hand. Now he's cold. A man and a woman are kneeling over his uncle. The man has his shirt balled against the side of Uncle Ben's throat. The woman is holding on to Uncle Ben's hand, telling him to stay with them. He can see a thin mist of dirt in the air, brought up from the ground by the train.

You did this, Joshua thinks. *You stabbed your uncle in the throat and now he's going to die.*

Or maybe he's dead already.

"I didn't mean to," he says, and if they can hear him they don't acknowledge it. He can see his uncle's face, how pale it is, his eyes open and staring. The only signs of life are his twitching fingers—and even that might not be a sign of life, but nerves firing after death. He's read that that's a thing. His hearing is returning. He can hear sirens. An ambulance comes to a stop by the tracks, its doors fly open, and two paramedics sprint towards them, each of them carrying bags.

"Move aside," one of them says, and the two officers helping Uncle Ben make way. The paramedics talk quickly to each other using incomprehensible medical jargon. They pull instruments from their bags that Joshua can't identify. More police cars arrive. An officer is carrying a stretcher towards them. A cell phone is ringing. It's coming from Uncle Ben's pocket.

"Is he going to make it?" the woman asks, and now that she's not shouting at him, and that his hearing is returning, he recognizes the voice. She's the detective who picked him up from school the day his dad died.

"He's lost a lot of blood," one of the paramedics says.

"Is he going to make it?" she asks again.

The paramedic doesn't answer. Gently they move Uncle Ben onto the stretcher and then slowly carry him towards the ambulance, each footstep carefully placed. The detective turns towards him. The look of anger on her face has disappeared. She looks tired, and sad.

"Joshua," she says. "You probably don't remember me, but—"

"From school," he says. "Detective Vega."

"That's right," she says. "I'm sorry I pointed the gun at you. I'm sorry I yelled."

"I didn't mean to hurt him," he says. He feels numb. He wants to cry. And scream. "I thought . . . I thought it was . . ." he says, but suddenly the energy required to talk disappears. He doesn't have the strength to stand. He sits in the grass and pulls his knees up to his chest. He feels stupid and angry with himself. He swung the knife without checking to see who he was hitting, and what kind of person does that? "I didn't know it was him."

"I know you didn't," she says, and she crouches down so she can face him. There is blood on her blouse, and a smudge of it on her cheek, and it's all over her hands too. He looks at his hands and sees the same, some of the blood his uncle's, some his own. He studies the graze on the back of his hand. It's the first time he's ever seen a wound on his own body. His hands are shaking badly.

"Is he going to die?"

"The doctors are going to do everything they can to save him."

"That sounds like he's going to die," he says.

"He might," she says.

"Is my mom coming?" he asks.

"I'll call her, but first I need you to tell me a few things. The other boy, who is he?"

"His name is Scott," he says. "He goes to my school. Is he . . . is he dead?"

"I'm afraid so, Joshua. Did you stab him?"

"No."

"You had the knife."

"There was another guy—I don't know where he is, but he attacked us." He looks behind him, looks up and down the path running parallel to the tracks. "That's who I thought was behind me when . . . when I . . . I hurt Uncle Ben. We have to be careful, because that other guy might be around."

"You're safe," Vega says.

"You don't know that."

"Yes, I do, Joshua. How did you get the knife?"

"I . . . I don't know."

"Tell me what you do know."

"I know I might have just killed my uncle," he says. "I know it's all my fault. I know I just want to curl up and die."

"Tell me what happened," she says.

He tells her everything, from walking home with Olillia to being chased and punched by Scott. He was dragged up onto the train tracks, but he was so far out of it he hardly even noticed he was being moved. He walked down the line for a while, but isn't sure why. He thinks he passed out again. He thinks his shirt got all torn up from being dragged.

"I must have picked up the knife along the way," he says.

"Tell me about this man. Did you recognize him?"

"Kind of."

"Kind of? Do you know from where?"

"Not really," he says.

"Do you remember struggling with him?" she asks.

"I want to go home," he says, and gets to his feet.

"Please, Joshua, it's important you try to remember. Did you struggle with him?"

"I don't think so."

They are on the other side of the embankment from where Scott died. They begin to walk, passing the blood left behind by his uncle.

"Have you found him?" he asks. "The man who did this."

"Yes," she says.

"Where was he?"

"On the other side of the tracks."

He looks in that direction, but can't see anything except the hill of stones, the tracks, and the tops of the fences beyond. "What did he say?" he asks.

"He didn't say anything," she says, and she's looking at him funny now. Like she's examining his expressions. "He's dead, Joshua."

"Oh," he says, then he isn't sure what else to add. Then he figures it out. "That's why you asked if we struggled. You think I killed him and took the knife off him."

"Did you?"

"No," he says. "At least . . . at least I don't think so. Why did any of this have to happen?" he asks, but he knows why. It's because of the curse. "Just who was that guy?"

"There's a more important question," she says. "If you didn't do this, then who did?"

FORTY-ONE

The splinter comes back. It makes Joshua's head pound, and it gets worse with every footstep. He rubs his temples, only to find that rubbing his temples doesn't help.

"An ambulance will check you out while you're here," Vega says.

"It's just a headache," he says.

"You were knocked out," she says. "You can't take that lightly. You'll need treatment and observation."

The grasshoppers are no longer making any noise in the grass, or perhaps his ears haven't recovered enough to hear them. The sandflies aren't bothering him as much either, but perhaps that's because they're all drinking from the blood that's been spilled. "Will I go to jail for what I did to Uncle Ben?"

"Is everything you told me true?"

"Yes."

"Then no. You won't be going to jail."

To his right, the graffiti on the fences changes in style, different patches representing different artists, some of it intricate, some of it swear words, the rest of it various caricatures of the human anatomy that Joshua finds hard to keep his new eyes off of.

He pulls those eyes away. "So what will happen?"

Instead of answering, she asks a question of her own. "Have you thought any more about how you knew the man who attacked you?"

He remembers telling Scott to run, because he knew the man who had found them was a bad man. He was the man from his dreams, but he can't tell Detective Vega that without sounding like a crazy person. As she did to him, he answers her question with one of his own. "Do you know who he is?"

"His name is Vincent Archer," she says. "Do you know the name?"

He thinks about the name. Visualizes the man, tries to find a connection between the two things, but can't find one. "I've never heard of him."

They come to a stop. "Tell me," she says.

"What?"

"You're holding something back, Joshua. This is not the time to do that. I knew . . . Are you okay?"

He crouches down onto his hands and knees and vomits into the grass. His body goes from heaving to shuddering, and he feels light-headed. Detective Vega crouches down next to him and puts a hand on his back. He finishes throwing up, then gets upright onto his knees. He tears off another flap of his shirt and uses it to wipe his mouth, then, unsure what to do with it, leaves it on the ground next to the mess he made.

"I'm fine," he says, and he's still shaking.

"You don't look fine," Vega says.

"I guess I'm not. What I did to Uncle Ben, it just makes me feel so ill."

"I know, Joshua, I know. But the best way you can help him right now is to be honest with me. I need you to tell me what you're not telling me. I knew your father, I worked with him, I respected him, and if he were here he'd be telling you the same thing, and that's to be honest."

Joshua isn't sure that's true. There are tons of people stuck in jail cells right now who shouldn't be, all because they spoke up when they shouldn't have. The proof of that is in the news stories that cover the eventual release of the lucky ones. The rest are left to pay the price for crimes they didn't commit. He thinks that if his dad were here, he'd be telling Joshua he needs a lawyer.

But his dad isn't here.

"Whatever it is, Joshua, I would rather hear it from you than learn it from somewhere else. You need to tell me."

"You'll think I'm weird," he says, as she helps him to his feet. "That I'm a freak."

"I won't, I promise. I would never do that."

He takes a breath and exhales slowly. He looks into her eyes and watches for a reaction. "I've dreamed about him."

The reaction is there. A flicker of disbelief. She tries to cover it. "What kind of dream?"

"You don't believe me."

"Please, Joshua, tell me."

He thinks about the forest, the fishing rods, the mountain bike, and the woman. "I recognized him, the same way I recognized the man who killed my dad, and the way I recognized Uncle Ben the first time I saw him."

"You recognized Ben when you first saw him?"

"Yeah, the day Erin fell from the roof. I think my dad and this guy today, somehow they knew each other. Maybe dad arrested him in the past."

"I'm not sure what you're saying," she says.

"It's called cellular memory," Joshua says. "And I knew you wouldn't believe me."

"Cellular memory?"

He starts to explain it to her, but doesn't get far before she interrupts him. It turns out she has heard of it—just not by that name.

"You're saying it's a real thing?" she asks.

"I don't know what else to think," he says.

"Vincent Archer doesn't have a criminal record," she says. "Your dad never arrested him, and there's no reason for them to know each other."

"You asked me to tell you," he says, "so I told you."

"And now you believe you're seeing what your dad saw."

"I don't know what to believe," he says. He resumes walking and she stays with him. "I can't tell you anything more than that. But you haven't said why he was coming after me."

She tells him they discovered Vincent Archer is the man who hurt Erin. They entered his house. They found photographs of Ben and those close to him pinned to a wall. There was a list, and Joshua's name was on that list.

"We couldn't find you," she says. "We sent police cars looking."

He remembers the cars racing up and down the streets.

"We tried calling you," she says. "But your phone was off."

How different things would have been if his phone had worked. Perhaps Scott had a curse of his own. He's the one who broke the phone, and the events that played out were allowed to play out because of that. "It's broken," he says.

They reach the intersection. There's an ambulance pulling up. "Let's get you looked at," she says.

"Has anybody called Mom? Does she know?"

"What's her number?"

He knows his mother's number from memory, but when he tries to recite it, he can't.

"It's okay," she says. "I'll be able to get hold of her."

The ambulance comes to a stop and the doors open. A paramedic helps him climb into the back. Joshua sits on the gurney. Because Vega's hands are covered in blood, she gets another detective to photograph Joshua's hands and take swabs of the blood on them before she disappears. Despite everything he's said about the attack, he knows she's skeptical. That's her job.

The paramedic has muscles that poke through his uniform, making Joshua think he's the kind of guy the Scotts of the world would never pick on.

"Joshua, right?" he asks, pulling on a pair of latex gloves.

"Right."

"I'm Sven," he says. "I hear you were knocked out."

"I guess so."

"I want you to do something for me. I want you to repeat these words after me. Okay?"

"Okay."

"Fish, tree, house, five plus five equals ten."

"Fish. Tree. House. Five plus five equals ten," Joshua says, wondering what the point is.

"Good. Now tell me what happened," Sven says.

Joshua tells him about getting punched, about hitting the ground and everything going dark, about coming to and passing out again a few times.

"Do you feel sick? Nauseous?"

"I threw up earlier, a couple of times, but I feel okay now. Just the headache."

"Dizzy?"

"Not anymore."

"But you were," he says.

"Yeah."

"How many fingers am I holding up?" Sven asks, and holds up three fingers.

"Three," Joshua says.

"Now how many?"

"Still three," Joshua says.

"Good. What about hearing? Notice any hearing loss?"

"A little," Joshua says, "but that's because a train raced past. It's better now."

"Let's take a look," Sven says, and leans over and moves his fingertips slowly through Joshua's hair, revealing where he was hit. "There's some blood up here. We're going to have to clean you up, but it doesn't look like you're going to need any stitches. Your hands and knees hurt?"

"They do, but mostly my hand."

"Okay. Let's get those cleaned up too."

The paramedic soaks some pads in a chemical out of a bottle, then wipes Joshua's hands clean. He replaces the pads a few times, then moves on to his knees. The pads go into a plastic bag that the paramedic seals up tight. Joshua figures it's all part of the evidence gathering. When the wounds are clean, the paramedic applies ointment and puts some bandaging on his hand. He cleans Joshua's head wound but doesn't bandage it.

"They'll take a closer look at the hospital," he says. "Can you remember my name?"

"It's . . . umm . . . no," Joshua says.

"Can you remember how many fingers I was holding up earlier?"

"Three."

"Remember the words I asked you to say earlier?"

"Yes."

"What were they?"

"Fish, tree, umm . . . fish?"

"You remember the numbers?"

"Ah, yeah, five."

"Is that it?"

"I think so."

"Okay, Joshua."

The paramedic climbs out and goes and talks to Detective Vega. She's using a bottle of water and a towel to clean the blood off her hands. His mom comes into view. She rushes up to the detective, who points in Joshua's direction. She runs towards him, Joshua already climbing out.

She wraps her arms around him. "I was so scared," she says.

Over her shoulder he can see crime scene tape being strung up. Crowds of people are gathering. An army of bystanders. His mom is hugging him so hard he's struggling to breathe. He tries to imagine how he looks, with blood and bandaging on him, his shirt missing large sections in the front.

"I couldn't have lost you," she says. "I couldn't have."

"You're going to if you don't stop squeezing me so hard."

She loosens her hold. "Detective Vega explained everything on the phone. What happened to Uncle Ben wasn't your fault."

It feels like his fault. After all, he was the one holding the knife.

"What did the paramedic say? Are you okay?"

"He said Joshua needs to go to the hospital," Vega says, coming over. Her hands are clean, but there's still blood on her shirt and on her cheek. "He's going to need some tests, and he'll need observing and may have to stay the night. We'll also need a statement."

Joshua sees Olillia standing in the crowd. He fights the urge to run over and hug her. Her face is pale and she looks like she's been crying. She waves at him. He waves back. His mom and Vega look into the crowd. "Can I go and see my friend?"

"Who is she?" Vega asks.

"Olillia."

"Olillia?"

"From school. She walked some of the way home with me."

"She was with you? On the tracks?" Vega asks.

"Not all the way. She left at the previous intersection."

"I'm going to have to interview her," Vega says, "which means you can't talk to her now. Perhaps later. Right now we need to get you to the hospital."

"I think . . . under the circumstances, I want Joshua to have a lawyer before giving a statement," his mom says.

"Joshua isn't in trouble," Vega says.

"Even so, I think it's for the best."

Vega nods. "Okay."

"And Ben?" his mom asks. "Have you heard anything?"

"They're still working on him," Vega says. "At this stage it could go either way."

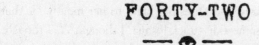

FORTY-TWO

Vega watches the ambulance drive off with both Joshua and his mom in it. The crime scene is filling with people. The train that came through earlier will have destroyed some of the evidence on the lines, but she's confident there'll be enough here to either support or betray Joshua's version of events. At the moment, officers are canvassing the houses that back onto the train tracks, as well as ones located on the streets the train tracks cross. Somebody must have seen something.

She walks to the barricade and to the girl who waved earlier. The girl has dark hair tied into a ponytail and a pretty face and big blue eyes. She reminds Vega of her kid sister. "You're Olivia?" she asks.

The girl looks concerned. She nods. "Olillia," she says.

"I want you to come with me," Vega says.

"Okay."

Vega leads her to a patrol car away from the crowd. She places Olillia with her back to it, so she is facing away from the spectators. "Wait here for me," she says, then heads to her car. From the back she grabs her backpack and the fresh blouse she keeps inside it for moments like this. Ben has a backpack just like it in the trunk too. There's another ambulance here, and she goes into the back of it and peels off her bloody blouse. She uses the towel she cleaned her hands with earlier to wipe herself down, and pulls on the fresh top, then throws her stuff back into her car just as the medical examiner pulls up. They exchange a small wave just before the medical examiner starts getting briefed by one of the detectives. Vega heads back to Olillia. "You walked home with Joshua?"

"Yes. I mean, kind of. Not all the way. Is it true somebody died?"

"Whose idea was it to take the train tracks?"

"Oh no," Olillia says, and raises her hand to her mouth. "Is that what happened? Did somebody attack Joshua? I thought . . . I thought he'd be okay. I mean, I always take the tracks, but never this far, and . . . I . . . I don't know what happened. Is this . . . Did this happen because of me? Josh was going to take the roads, but I convinced him . . . I talked him into taking the tracks."

The girl is on the verge of losing it. Her big blue eyes look even bigger as the tears shimmer on the edges of them. Vega puts her hand on her shoulder. "Please, tell me what you know," she says.

Olillia confirms she and Joshua parted ways at the previous intersection. She got home and saw on social media a few minutes later that somebody had died. There were photographs of a dead boy in uniform taken from people poking cameras over their fences, but she couldn't tell who it was, and she didn't know if it was real.

"I was sure it was going to be Joshua," she says. She borrowed her brother's car and drove here, parking as close as she could, then running the rest of the way. "If it's not Joshua who was killed, then who?" Olillia asks.

It's only a matter of time before the dead boy's name is released anyway—perhaps by somebody who gets a better look at one of the photographs that these sightseeing neighbors have taken. Vega figures she may as well tell the girl. It might also give her a better idea of what happened.

"The victim is Scott Adams," she says, and she watches Olillia for a reaction and gets one. A huge one. The girl's hands fly to her mouth and her eyes go even wider. "You knew him?"

She nods.

"How well?"

"Not well," she says, wiping at the tears. "But we've gone through school together. He lives . . . He lives on my street."

"Do you know why Scott wouldn't have turned off at the same road, then?"

Olillia shakes her head. Then slowly she nods. "Maybe," she says, and looks down at her feet.

"Olillia?"

"Scott . . . Scott was being mean to Joshua all day. He . . . soaked him with a can of soda, and ruined his cell phone by pouring the rest into his bag. Later, in woodshop, Scott blew sawdust into his eyes. I told Joshua not to say anything, because . . . because I've seen it where that makes it worse. But then . . ." She raises her hands to her mouth again.

"What is it?"

"Later in class I told our teacher what Scott had done. I had to . . . because . . . well, I just had to. She made Scott wait back after school. I think she told him off. Maybe Scott thinks that Joshua told on him? Maybe he was following him to . . . to beat him up. Is that what happened? Was there a fight? Joshua . . . I only met him today, but he couldn't have . . . he wouldn't have done this, and if I hadn't said anything to Mrs. Thompson, then Scott wouldn't have followed him. None of this would have happened."

Vega opens up the back door of the patrol car. "I need you to wait here for a while, okay?" she says.

"Is Joshua going to be okay?" Olillia asks, climbing in.

"I'll be back soon."

She tells an officer to keep an eye on the girl before walking to the tracks. The medical examiner, Tracey Walter, is making her way up the bank to the other side. Vega first met Tracey a few years ago on a case that involved a guy who'd been so high on pain medication he thought he could fly—something he tested from the roof of his house, and something that had proven more difficult than he'd thought. Tracey had been the one to perform the autopsy, and then their paths had met again a few weeks later, this time at a barbecue, where they had friends in common. Their paths kept crossing after that, mostly for work, and then at the gym, then in more social situations, and for the last year they've been dating—not that anybody in the department knows. She knows they'd give her shit about it. They've both been so busy these last few weeks they've hardly had time to see each other. In fact, the last time she saw Tracey was a week ago, and back then her hair was red. Now it's blond. Tracey had told her she'd had it dyed, and it looks good. It's the third change in the last year, and sometimes it makes Vega feel like she's dating different women.

She catches up to Tracey as she reaches the first body. The school was contacted and a photograph shown to the principal earlier; that's how the identification was made. They learned from the school that Scott Adams was bright and was well liked, but further questioning revealed that Scott was well liked only by his fellow teammates on the school rugby team, and wasn't really that bright at all. Even further questioning showed that he was a notorious bully.

"Hey," Vega says.

"Hey," Tracey says. "This is awful." She looks down at the boy, and whenever they're confronted with a scene like this, Vega wants to hug her so they can both remind themselves the world isn't as bad as it looks. Of course, she can't hug her. When they're in the field, or at the morgue, they only ever talk work and they make no references to their personal lives, and when they're on a date or around friends, it's the opposite. She doesn't tell Tracey she likes her new hairstyle, because it's the last thing she wants to say right now, and it would be the last thing Tracey would want to hear. She'll tell her later. Tracey crouches down over the boy. "Amount of blood here, looks like the kid never had a chance. Position of the wound," she says, "I'm guessing the knife sliced right into the aorta, but I won't know for sure until I get him on my table. He would have gone into shock immediately, and would have died within a minute."

"You'll be able to tell from the angles who stabbed him? If it lines up with the other victim?"

"There are a lot of variables," Tracey says, "but I'll do my best."

They walk over to Vincent Archer. Tracey reaches into her pocket and pulls out a small sachet. She tears it open and hands Vega the wet wipe from inside. "Your cheek," she says, and taps her own cheek to indicate to Vega where she means, and Vega wipes it and sees that it was blood.

"Thanks," she says. She balls it back into the packet and then into her pocket.

Tracey crouches over Archer's body and looks him over. There's a fist-sized dent in his skull that will likely line up with the bloody rock a yard away. The rock hasn't been fingerprinted yet. Nor has Joshua. But they will be. Vega imagines how quickly it all unfolded, this quiet section of train tracks becoming a battlefield—and how close did that train come to hitting Joshua?

"Are you okay?" Tracey says, standing back up.

"I'm fine," Vega says.

"Ben's a strong guy," Tracey says. "He won't give up easy."

"I know."

"There's something else bothering you."

"No, really, I'm fine."

"Are you sure? You look . . . not so great."

"I'm okay," she says.

Officers begin erecting tents over the bodies to protect them from the elements, as well as from the neighbors poking cell phones over fences to snap photographs. Tracey goes back to examining the body. Vega thinks about what Olillia said about Scott bullying Joshua at school. That's what they call in the business a good ol' fashioned motive. It's possible Joshua stabbed the boy out of anger, and it so happened Vincent Archer arrived not long after—but she doesn't think so. She thinks Vincent Archer brought the knife to the scene. She thinks Vincent Archer figured killing two boys instead of one would have helped hide what really went on here today, the same way he was able to hide what really happened to Erin.

"What do you know about cellular memory?" she asks Tracey. "You in the for or against column?"

"I ever tell you dad had a heart transplant ten years ago?" Tracey asks.

Vega likes Tracey's parents. Tracey's mom competed in the Olympics thirty-something years ago and came in fourth in the 400 meters, and still jokes about wanting to go back there to try to get a bronze. Her dad practiced medicine until a couple of years back, when he retired.

"No," Vega says.

Tracey stands up and faces her. "He got really sick," she says. "We thought he was going to die, actually, but he was lucky. He got a new heart. A few months after, he started getting a craving for German beer. Nothing else tasted right to him, had to be German, then he started eating German food too. So I pulled some strings and got hold of the donor file. Want to take a guess as to where the donor was from?"

"Germany."

"Australia," she says. "Sometimes we see things that aren't there. Dad's cravings came from somewhere, though. Could be the donor spent time in Germany. Could be he loved German food. Keep in mind people get transplants every day and never develop any desires, but with Dad it was definitely like somebody threw a switch. Was that craving on a cellular level? Anecdotally, I'd say yes. As somebody who opens up and examines dead people for a living? I'd say no."

"So you're unsure."

"I don't believe in it, but not enough to dismiss it."

FORTY-THREE

—— ◉ ——

Joshua changes out of his uniform and into a hospital gown. What's left of his shirt along with the rest of his clothes are placed into a paper bag and handed to a police officer who's so pale he looks as if he might catch fire if he stepped into the sun. Before the officer leaves, he takes Joshua's fingerprints, then hands him a paper towel to wipe away the ink.

"It's so we can figure out which prints belong to who," the officer says, but Joshua knows what he really means is, *It's so we can figure out if you killed anybody.*

The bandage on his hand is replaced, and the wounds cleaned up again and patched over. Doctors do memory tests. Reflex tests. How many fingers are being held up, can he count from a hundred backwards, what's today's date, can he walk in a straight line without feeling dizzy? His mom keeps questioning the doctors, the worry in her voice obvious. He spends forty-five minutes in an MRI having his brain scanned. Afterwards they wait for an hour in an examination room. He feels fine. He wants to go home.

Dr. Toni comes to see him. She's edgy and distracted.

"It's so . . . so awful," she says. "I . . . I can't believe it."

Joshua tells her he can't believe it either. She shines a light into his eyes and looks at them closely. Then she gets him to read from an eye chart. The results are the same as last time. The blow to his head hasn't made his good eye worse. It hasn't made his bad eye better.

"Do you know how Ben is doing?" his mom asks.

"There's been no update," Dr. Toni says.

"It's been a few hours."

"And it may be a few more," she says.

When her exam is done, she leaves Joshua and his mom in the examination room, while a different policeman, this one not so pale, stands outside in the corridor with the door closed. Similar to when his dad died and Joshua had the operation, the media are stalking for interviews, but so far they're being kept at bay outside the main entrance. The policeman is there just in case someone is able to sneak through. With the door closed, it's the first chance they've had to be alone since everything happened, and in the quiet his mom begins to softly cry. She's sitting in a chair while he's sitting on the bed with his legs dangling over it. He gets down and pulls up a chair next to his mom and takes her hand.

"I'm sorry," she says. "I should be stronger. It's just that after everything . . . I could have lost you."

"But you didn't. It's going to be okay," he says, even though it may not be, but he gets now why people say it all the time.

"I should never have let you walk home."

"It's the curse," he says.

"What?"

"Why do you think all of these bad things keep happening? Me being born blind, my biological parents dying, now Dad has been killed. I'm connected to all of it. The curse is because of me. It follows me everywhere. It got to Erin, and now it's caught up with Uncle Ben. It even got its claws into Scott, and I only knew him for one day. Doesn't matter what we do, the curse will always be there."

"It's not a curse," she says.

"No? Then what is it?"

She thinks about it for a few moments, and he doesn't interrupt her. Then she sighs, as if she's figured out the answer and is resigned to accepting it. "It's a combination of bad luck," she says. "A combination of good people trying to do bad things, and bad people doing worse things."

"What do you mean by that?"

"Nothing," she says.

Before he can ask her again, the door opens, and Dr. Hatch—the doctor who gave him the MRI—walks in. Dr. Hatch looks like a slightly younger version of Joshua's grandfather—which, he guesses, makes him an older version of his biological dad. He has a ring of gray hair around the sides and back of his head, and no hair on top, just like another Star Trek captain he's seen on TV. Joshua wonders if Mr. Fox continued his genetics lesson with a lecture on baldness. If his grandfather is bald, then would his dad have gone bald too? Will Joshua go bald in twenty or thirty years?

"I have two pieces of good news for you," Dr. Hatch says. "The first is that you seem fine, and we're going to let you go home tomorrow morning."

"I can't go home tonight?" Joshua asks.

"It's best we keep an eye on you overnight."

"What's the second piece?" his mom asks. "Is it Ben?"

"Actually, no, but I've heard the surgery is going well. The news is about Erin. She came out of her coma thirty minutes ago."

His mom leans forward and hugs the doctor tightly before pulling back. She looks embarrassed. "I'm sorry," she says. "I didn't mean to do that, but that's great news."

"It's okay," Dr. Hatch says, smiling at her. "Makes me enjoy giving good news even more."

"Is she okay?"

"She can't remember anything, and there's a long way to go, and it's too soon to know how badly damaged her brain is, but we're hopeful. I'll get a nurse to come and get you soon, Joshua, and we'll get you admitted for the night. Okay?"

"When can he go back to school?" his mom asks, and Joshua hadn't even given that a thought. Today they thought he was a freak—what will they think tomorrow?

"I'd give it a couple of days," Dr. Hatch says, but Joshua knows there's more to it than that—it will come down to when the police will let him return. "The nurse will be through soon."

"Erin's going to be okay," his mom says, when Dr. Hatch has left the room. She turns towards Joshua and hugs him. "See? There is no curse. Erin's going to be okay, and Ben's going to be okay too, I'm sure of it, and we're going to get past this, I promise."

FORTY-FOUR

— ◉ —

Vega interviews one of the neighbors as a pretext to get inside, and then she asks if she can use the bathroom. Every part of her being feels it. The guilt. She can feel it in her chest, where it squeezes her heart, and in her stomach, where it feels like a boulder. It's heavy and confining and there's just so damn much of it. There's guilt for not having done more to help Ben. Guilt for the way she pointed her gun at Joshua, for the way she yelled at him. Guilt for staying at the scene and not going to the hospital. Guilt for not having faith in her partner when he first started saying he thought somebody was trying to kill Erin.

She throws up into the toilet and washes her face and stares at her reflection in the mirror. She told Tracey earlier that she was fine, but she isn't, and she wanted to tell her what was upsetting her, but she couldn't, not out there with everything going on. All that guilt . . . none of it compares to the guilt she feels for delaying the decision to enter Vincent Archer's house. The boy on the tracks, even Archer, they'd both still be alive if she hadn't insisted on waiting for backup. Ben wouldn't be fighting for his life. She knows there's a fine line between doing what's right and bending the rules. She did the right thing—technically—but doing the right thing came at a huge cost. She dries her face, thanks the woman for the use of her bathroom, and returns outside, where the crowd has doubled.

She makes her way over to Olillia and thanks her for her time, gets her phone number and address off her, and tells her she's free to head home. "I'll have some more follow-up questions and will be in touch," she says.

"When can I see Joshua?" Olillia asks

"That's up to the doctors," Vega says.

"I don't . . . I don't know what you think happened, or what did happen," Olillia says, "but Joshua wouldn't have done anything wrong."

"I'll give you a call later on today, okay?"

"Okay."

"You said you drove here in your father's car?"

"I think I'll walk home," Olillia says.

"I'll have somebody drive you," Vega says, and signals for an officer to come over and escort the girl from the scene. "One more thing," she says. "Don't talk to any media, okay?"

"Okay."

"You promise?"

"I promise."

When Olillia has gone, Vega waves over another couple of officers to let them know she's leaving, and to ask them to join her. The officer and his partner follow her to Vincent Archer's parents' house in case things get out of hand. Giving death notifications is the worst part of the job, even when the person who's been killed is a rotten son of a bitch.

She buzzes the gate and this time it's Robert Archer who answers. He stands with his wife by the door and they watch her and the patrol car roll in. They have their arms around each other, and she knows that they already know what's coming. Helen collapses into the couch she sat in earlier that day when Vega tells them. She bites her knuckle; sounds of pain occasionally get stuck in her throat and are expressed in large gulps. Vincent's father fixes himself a glass of scotch and stares out into the yard and doesn't say anything.

"If I had . . . If I had helped you the moment you showed up," Helen says, "you would have found him on time. I could . . . I could have saved him."

"Yes," Vega says, and she knows she shouldn't say it, but she can't help herself. "Your son would still be alive, and so would the boy he killed."

Helen cries harder then, and Robert turns red and tells her to get the hell off their property. The two officers, a guy who's been on the force for only two years and a woman who's been on it for almost ten, give Vega disapproving looks as they go back to their cars. She feels disgusted at herself for saying what she said, but she said it to share the blame. After all, there's plenty to go around.

She's out on the street and on her way to Vincent Archer's house when Kent calls her. She asks Vega how it went, and Vega updates her, omitting the final bit of the conversation, then Kent tells her how it went for her. She had gone with Detective Travers to break the news to Scott Adams's family. They found a three-year-old boy and a six-year-old girl looking after themselves. When asked, the six-year-old said their mom had gone out for a quick drink, but, because the girl was six, she wasn't able to tell them where or when. They finally found the mother feeding coins into a slot machine at a local bar with a glass of wine in her hand—obviously not her first. She was stabbing at the buttons trying to win back the rent money she had already lost. She broke down in tears and they drove her home to where her kids were being watched over by a social worker Kent had called. During the trip back, the mom pulled herself together enough to ask if she would be compensated for the loss of her son, either by the man who killed him, or by the police, or by the justice system. "I still have two other mouths to feed," she had said. "It certainly feels like somebody owes me something."

There's an unmarked patrol car parked out front of Vincent Archer's house, but no tape or barriers cordoning the house off from the street. It's been kept that way to avoid any attention being drawn to the scene. Somebody has pulled the front door shut as best as they could after Vega smashed it open earlier today. There's a mess of splintered wood on the floor next to it. She pulls on a pair of latex gloves and turns on the lights as she moves from room to room. Everything is immaculately tidy. She opens the fridge. It's full of plastic containers that have been carefully stacked and labeled with the type of meat inside and the expiry dates. An egg carton has the expiry date written on it too. The vegetables all look crisp and clean. There are no dishes in the sink, and she checks the dishwasher to see it full of clean dishes. Perhaps he ran a cycle today. She checks the rubbish bin. It's empty. There are two large bags of dog food on the dining table but no dog. There's a knife block with three blades missing. Two of those are in the dishwasher. The third she can't find. She gets her phone out and sends off a text message.

In the lounge there's no TV. There's a brand-new lounge suite and a log burner and a bookcase that takes up half the width of one wall. There's a peace lily in the corner that looks healthier than any plant she's tried to keep alive. The bookcase looks handmade, a collection of modern horror and crime novels fills all but the top two shelves, where carpentry books all neatly stand side by side, except for one that's lying facedown. She picks it up. It's a book about reupholstering furniture. Perhaps the lounge suite isn't new at all, but has recently been given a new lease on life. The coffee table looks handmade too, and, now that she thinks about it, she thinks she can smell paint. The source of the smell is coming from the garage, where a drop cloth is on the ground covered in splashes of paint. This is possibly where Vincent worked on the rocking horse Helen Archer told them about. Looking around the garage at the other things Vincent has created, she has to admit that for a psychopath he was good with his hands.

In the main bedroom the bed has been made and there are no clothes on the floor, not like her house, where clothes pile up next to the bed over the course of the week. She goes through his drawers. Everything is neatly folded. On the wall is a framed black-and-white poster of a kid looking beyond the window of a house out towards a hill where trees are being felled. On the adjoining wall above the drawers is a framed photograph of Vincent standing next to Simon Bower, a river next to them, a cooler with a fishing rod leaning across it by their feet. They're each holding up a fish. She can't think of many men who would have photographs in their bedrooms of their friends, and she wonders if the connection between Simon and Vincent was more than just a friendship. She looks at the photograph. Both men are smiling, and in this moment the camera hasn't captured who these men really are beneath the surface. Wouldn't it be great, she thinks, if one day technology advances to the point where you could put a photograph like this into a scanner and it would strip away the masks the people in it are wearing? She wonders if the photo was taken by a camera with a self-timer, or if a third person took it, then wonders if that third person was at the railway line today.

In the office there's an out-of-date computer sitting on a desk that looks old but has been lovingly restored. There's a wooden captain's chair with leather upholstery. She turns on the computer and sees right away it's going to take time to boot up. Perhaps it's as old as the desk. She heads down to the Room of Obsession. It smells like sweat. This room is so different from anything else here, it's like it should be in a different house. Perhaps Vincent Archer is a different person when he's in here. In a house full of straight edges and elegant curves, the articles pinned to the wall could have been clipped from the newspaper by a four-year-old. Vega looks over the newspaper articles about Ruby Carter, surer than ever that Vincent had something to do with her disappearance. She searches for other pieces of jewelry that might be hanging from the walls but finds none.

Her phone beeps. The message she sent earlier has gotten a response. She's been sent a photograph of the murder weapon. It's a match to those she saw in the kitchen. Vincent Archer brought it with him.

She goes back into the office. The computer has warmed up. There's no password, and she has instant access to Vincent's email. It's a pathetic affair. His inbox shows messages from his parents, work, a couple of carpentry newsletters that he's signed up for, emails from his bank, his insurance company, one from his dentist saying it's that time of the year again. There are emails from a dating website that Vincent signed up to a year back but never finished completing his profile for, as if he got bored or distracted or nervous. There are emails from Simon, but they're mundane. They talk about catching up to go fishing, or for a drink, or to go and catch a movie. The emails don't mention any conflicts with other people. There are no references to Ruby Carter. No references to Andrea Walsh. She clicks the icon to look for new messages, and two come through, one from the mechanic about his car, and the other another carpentry newsletter that promises subscribers tips on how to make the perfect jewelry box for Mother's Day.

She minimizes the email screen. There are photographs saved on the desktop of Vincent fishing, laughing, drinking. There are photographs of this house being renovated, and Simon is in some of them. There are other pictures with a few other faces in them, group events that look like summer barbecues with his family.

Her phone beeps again. Another text. This one saying Vincent Archer's prints have been run against those on the parking chit used immediately before and after Erin was thrown from the rooftop. The prints are a match. It also says Joshua's prints have been run against the rock that killed Vincent Archer. Those prints are *not* a match.

In the Room of Obsession, she stares at the wall. She is missing something, she's sure of it. Something important. The dots are here somewhere—she just can't connect them.

She gets out her cell phone. She calls the hospital and is transferred to Dr. Coleman, who is still in her office.

"What can I help you with, Detective?" Coleman asks.

"Tell me," Vega says. "What exactly are your thoughts on cellular memory?" After a few seconds of silence, she thinks Coleman might have disappeared. "Doctor? Are you still here?"

"I'm here," Coleman says. "Listen, I think it's probably better if you come and see me. There are some things I need to tell you."

FORTY-FIVE

— ◉ —

Outside the window is a darkening city. This time of the year, it's light until almost eight o'clock, but every day moving forward a few minutes of sunlight will be shaved off until the city is on the other side of its June winter. It's this time of the year when Dr. Coleman often regrets not having done more with her summer.

Only now she has other regrets to focus on.

There's a knock on her door, and a moment later it opens.

"Dr. Coleman?"

"You must be Detective Vega," Toni says. "Please, take a seat."

The detective must be around her age, Toni thinks. She's attractive and muscular and right now she also looks tired. It's been a long day for everybody.

"Can I get you a drink?" Toni asks.

"No, thank you."

"You mind if I have one? I think I need it."

"Go ahead."

From her bottom drawer she pulls out a hipflask of gin. She pours some liquor into a glass. From a small fridge in the corner of her office, she takes out a bottle of tonic and adds a couple of splashes to the gin, along with some ice cubes. She hated gin when she was younger. She always thought of it as an old man's drink. Jesse drank it, though. Because Jesse drank it, she drank it too, near the end, when his life expectancy went from months to weeks. She sips at her drink, remembering what it was like back then, while restraining herself from gulping it down now. Vega says nothing, and Toni knows she is waiting her out.

"In a lot of ways," Toni says, staring into the glass, "it's hard to know where to start."

"How about at the beginning?"

"The beginning," Toni says. "I guess that's as good a place as any." She takes another sip. She knows what she wants to say, but isn't sure how to say it. "What you need to know is that we thought we were doing a good thing. Did you know that Ben had a brother?"

Vega shakes her head.

"His name was Jesse," she says. "He died. It was a little over ten years ago. They were twins."

"He's never mentioned him."

"It hit him hard. He came back from overseas to be with him, and Jesse . . . Jesse lasted almost five more years with the heart he had. It was awful. Watching somebody close to you slowly dying when there's nothing you can do. He was on a waiting list, of course he was, but waiting lists are long. They teach you in school about supply and demand. It's an economic thing, but it's a medical thing too. There are more people needing organs than there are people giving them up, and then you have to be compatible too. Have you ever lost anybody close to you?"

"My parents," Vega says.

"Then you know what it's like. How'd they die? Were they sick?"

"It was a car accident," Vega says. "My dad, he liked to drink. He'd get behind that wheel so drunk he could barely see. It caught up with him. I was young at the time. They were too. I'll be the age they were when they died in a couple of years."

"I'm sorry," Toni says. "People often wonder if it's better to lose a loved one quickly or slowly. With Jesse it was slow, and the stages of grief that came with him dying bounced from acceptance to denial to hope. He was so sick all the time, and he was on the waiting list but . . . but there are always people on the waiting list. Hope strung out is still hope, but it feels like hell. In a way, Jesse died well before his last heartbeat. He knew. You could see it in his eyes."

"You knew them, didn't you, back then," Vega says.

She nods. "I used to date Ben. Truth is, he broke my heart. This was back before Jesse got sick." She laughs softly and gently shakes her head. "It was twenty years ago. I can't believe it's been that long. The thing is . . . about a year after he left, I started seeing Jesse. It wasn't romantic, nothing like that. It could have been. Jesse loved me, and in a way I loved him too, but he wasn't Ben. In the beginning I used to allow myself to see him as if he were, because they were so similar, and after all, they were twins. It was stupid, of course. I wanted him to find a nice girl, but whenever he did he'd want me to meet them, and right away they could tell there was something between us. I think that's why he always made the introductions—it was a way of sabotaging his own love life. When he got sick, I cried almost every night for him. I would have done anything to have saved him, but what could I do? What could anybody do?"

She takes another sip. The office is quiet. Vega is watching her. She seems aware that whatever it is Toni wants to say, she hasn't gotten there yet.

"It felt like a hole was ripped in my chest when he died, and Ben . . . he was in so much pain I thought . . . Well, for a while there I thought we were going to lose him too. He kept asking how it could have happened. They were twins, they were designed the same way, one couldn't get sick without the other getting sick. He stuck to that notion for a long time. How could his heart beat strong when Jesse's had failed, and at such a young age? It didn't matter what you said to him. He blamed himself. It was stupid, but he did. He had classic survivor's guilt. In the end he turned that blame to the system that had let Jesse down."

She takes another sip. Her drink is half gone.

"'Bad people are doing all kinds of shit in this city while good people are dying when their organs get tired.' Those were his exact words when they came to see me. He'd been a cop for a few years by then, and as you must know, you see a lot in those first few years."

"Not just the first few years," Vega says, "but that's when it's the most shocking."

"The thing is, Jesse got sick around the same time Mitchell's sister died. Her name was Myra. She was Joshua's biological mother. It was a brain embolism. Nothing anybody could have done. So she died, and of course Joshua's dad had died not long before that. Then Jesse got sick and between Ben and Mitchell there was all this loss. Nothing could have been done for Joshua's parents, but Jesse could have been saved, if the resources had been there. That's why Ben said it, that line about good people dying because their organs got tired while bad people keep doing what bad people do. I'm not sure if it was Ben's idea, or Mitchell's, and I'm not sure if they knew either. I think it's one of those places conversations can go on days where things are dark. But the conversation did go there, and they came up with a plan, and they brought that plan to me."

She pauses and takes a drink. Vega is studying her.

"You've already figured it out, haven't you?" Toni says.

"I still need you to tell me," Vega says.

She finishes her drink. She can feel her mind starting to swirl. When was the last time she ate?

"It was a victimless crime—that's how they put it, and I was willing to buy it. After all, there were no victims. They needed somebody to adjust the donor records of those killed during the commission of a crime. Such a simple thing, and it was simple. Somebody is fleeing from the cops and their car hits a tree, then why not use the organs that survive the crash to save somebody else? Somebody breaks into a house to steal something or rape somebody and they cut their arm on the broken window and bleed to death, why not give their heart to somebody like Jesse? The waiting list is so clogged, Detective, you have no idea, and this wasn't going to solve that, but it would make a difference."

"And you went along with it."

"What you have to understand is how much I missed Jesse, and how much I missed the person Ben used to be. I know you see a lot of hurt, Detective, but so do we. Every day somebody in a hospital dies. These corridors are haunted by the ghosts of those we could have saved if we'd had more time, or more resources, or more people willing to donate their organs. So yes, I went along with it."

"But you're an eye surgeon," Vega says.

"One who they could trust, and one who could connect them with others who could also be trusted. I knew the risk, but I also knew the rewards."

"How many others are involved?"

"I'm not going to tell you," she says.

"You have—"

"No, I don't have to."

"Any medical examiners involved?"

"No. Not that I know of."

"What do you mean not that you know of?"

"I mean this was Ben and Mitchell's thing. If they involved other people outside this hospital, I don't know who they might be. But it's unlikely, because they wouldn't have needed one to be involved. Once the donor records are altered, any medical examiner looking at the bodies should expect those organs to be missing."

"Those missing organs might also hide cause of death," Vega says. "So when you say it's unlikely they needed a medical examiner involved, it's also just as likely they did."

Toni doesn't say anything.

Vega leans back in her chair. "I should have said yes to that drink."

"I can still make you one."

She shakes her head. "Why are you telling me any of this?"

"I don't know."

"Do you want me to arrest you?"

"I'm not sure."

"You don't think I will, because you know if I arrest you, then I have to arrest the others too, including Ben."

Toni twirls the base of the glass around on the desk, watching the ice slowly melt. "Maybe that's what we deserve."

"There is no *maybe* about it. But arresting you . . . it tarnishes Mitchell Logan's memory. Every case he and Ben ever worked on will be reopened and examined because they're corrupt cops who—"

"They're not corrupt."

"I don't think you get to make that judgment, Doctor."

She doesn't say anything.

"So, again, I ask you," Vega says, "why are you telling me this?"

Toni sips at the water that's now in the bottom of her glass. How to explain? She isn't sure.

"You look like somebody who wants to be punished," Vega says. "Is that it?"

"Yes," she says. "A boy is dead because of us. Ben has been critically injured, stabbed by another innocent boy, and it's all because of us. That's why I'm telling you."

Vega starts to say something, but stops. Her eyes widen. She leans back and slowly nods. Toni can see the pieces all fitting into place. "The ambulances," Vega says.

Toni takes another sip of her drink. She should make a fresh one, but she doesn't want to. She doesn't want to numb herself for the accusations that are about to come. She says nothing and lets Vega carry on.

"It's why they arrived so quickly when Mitchell and Simon were killed, isn't it? It's why the bodies were gone before the rest of us even arrived."

Toni doesn't say anything. It's taking all of her strength not to turn away and stare out the window. She faces the detective. She has to.

"It's why Mitchell and Ben went in without backup," Vega says. "Why they didn't share their lead. Why they were armed. Simon Bower was shot in cold blood out of revenge, but if he hadn't been, he still would have died that day anyway. There was an ambulance waiting around the corner to whisk the body away to be harvested, only neither of you foresaw Mitchell being hurt. Did somebody need some organs that day, Doctor?"

"It wasn't like that. It's not like they called the day before. We'd get the news after it had happened, and we'd be scrambling to make use of the organs, but that's the way it always is, no matter where the organs come from."

"It was premeditated," Vega says.

"I never knew that for sure," Toni says.

"Because you didn't want to know. You were happy to turn a blind eye," Vega says.

"All I knew is that sometimes bad people, really bad people, get killed, and it's okay, isn't it, if their deaths can save others?"

"Let me ask you something," Vega says. "You ever ask them why the ambulance got to the scenes so fast?"

"No."

"No," Vega says. "You didn't ask because you didn't need to. You knew what was going on."

"It wasn't like that in the beginning," she says.

"I'm sure it wasn't. But where does it end? You have a sweet little child who needs a new heart, so then what? Ben goes out there and executes the next bank robber or wife-beater or shoplifter he finds?"

"It's not like that," Toni says.

"That's exactly what it's like. I ask you why you're telling me this, and you say a boy is dead because of you. It means you've figured it out. These are the consequences of everything you all put into action years ago. It's why you think you deserve to be punished, and you're right—you do. If Simon doesn't die that day, then Vincent doesn't get angry. He doesn't go looking for revenge. He doesn't track Joshua down and kill an innocent schoolboy in the process. He doesn't toss Erin off a roof."

Toni stares into her glass. There are no answers in there. "Are you going to arrest me?"

"I should, because I've had the worst damn day, and it all stems from what you and Ben and Mitchell were doing. There's a dead kid out there that I've been blaming myself for, and even though it all comes back to what you guys were doing, it still feels like it's my fault, so for that I'm angry. For that I shouldn't just arrest you, I should shoot you and give your organs to some people with better ethics than either you or I have, and maybe I'll do that, I don't know. I really don't know. I'll sleep on it."

"We were trying to help people," Toni says, and she really should have poured that second drink. "I'm sorry."

"I know, I know you are," Vega says, and she takes a deep breath and calms herself. "Look, right now I want to talk about Joshua. Can we do that?"

"Yes," Toni says.

"You're not going to give me any of that doctor-patient confidentiality bullshit, because if you are, then—"

"No. I'll tell you what you want to know."

"Is it possible he's really seeing these things that his dad saw?"

"Ben believed so. In fact . . . he wanted me to perform an operation on him and Erin."

"What kind of operation?"

"He wanted one of Erin's eyes. He believed it would give him the ability to see who had pushed her off the roof."

"Two minutes ago I thought I'd heard the most insane thing I've ever heard," Vega says. "You've just managed to top it."

"I told him it was crazy, and that I wouldn't do it."

"I'm glad you at least have some kind of moral compass," Vega says, not giving Toni a chance to respond before carrying on—not that she would have. "I want to take Joshua out of here."

"You can't. He's under observation."

"It's important. I've been updated on his condition. The MRI and tests are all clear. There is no reason he needs to be kept in here."

"There is a reason," Toni says. "'Better safe than sorry' might not sound like much of a reason, but it's a valid one."

"Look, Doctor, we now know there's another killer out there. Did he save Joshua, and is he a hero? Or is he just another criminal? I don't know. This thing you've been involved with, this little . . . Frankenstein business of yours, it's gotten people killed."

Toni knows she's right. In the beginning they'd harvest organs and save lives and there was something good in that, but then the darkness of it all crept in.

"They say the road to hell is paved with good intentions, and right now that's a road you're a long way down. Me, I have my own demons to get under control because of today. You and me, we need to do this. Right now. There's a killer out there, and we need to find him right now."

"By putting Joshua in danger."

"By getting Joshua to help. If we do nothing and this guy kills again and you could have done something to prevent that, are you going to be able to live with yourself?"

"It's not me I'm worried about," Toni says.

"I promise I'll keep him safe."

"We," Toni says, pushing her empty glass aside.

"Sorry?"

"It's *we*, Detective. *We* will be keeping him safe. If you're taking Joshua out of here, I'm coming with you."

FORTY-SIX

—◉—

It's after visiting hours, and Joshua's mom is no longer allowed to stay. His mom arranges a ride back to the railway tracks because her car is still there. They hug good-bye, and she tells him she loves him. For a while he doesn't think she's going to let go.

He lies down on his bed and turns on the TV, hoping for a distraction, hoping to see something other than the endless footage in his mind of Scott being murdered. All that's on are reality shows. There's one about renovating houses, one about cooking, another one about renovating houses, and another one about cooking. During breaks he sees advertisements for reality shows about mass dating, shows about teenagers partying, shows about heavily tanned housewives swearing at each other, shows about cops pulling people over with blurry faces and potty mouths. It's the kind of TV that makes him miss being blind.

The day is catching up with him, and he's feeling exhausted, but when he turns off the TV he finds he can't get to sleep. His mind is racing in such an uncontrollable way, he would be seriously surprised if he ever slept again. His hand itches, but unlike when his eyes itched after the operation, he's able to dig his finger under the bandaging to scratch at it. When Dr. Coleman comes in, he's surprised to see her—and he thinks somehow she's found out he's scratching at himself and she's coming to tell him off the same way people were telling him off when he scratched at his eyes—but then Detective Inspector Vega walks in after her, which tells him something else is going on. He sits up.

"How ya feeling, Joshua?" Vega asks.

"Has something happened? Is Uncle Ben still okay?"

"He's still in surgery," Dr. Toni says.

"Joshua, I want to ask you about something," Vega says.

"Is he going to be okay? Uncle Ben?"

"We're hopeful," Dr. Toni says.

He crosses his arms and nods. "What do you want to ask me?"

"It's about cellular memory," she says.

"I didn't think you believed me."

"I'm keeping an open mind," she says. "I want to know, is it possible if you saw a picture of the other man who was there this afternoon, you might recognize him?"

"You want me to look through mug shots?" he asks.

"No, because we found prints at the scene today that don't match anybody—all the people in our mug shot books have names and fingerprints, so we're dealing with someone who doesn't have a record," Vega says.

"So somebody else *was* there," he says, and even though he knew he couldn't have been the one to kill Scott, it comes as a huge relief to have proof. But who did? And why kill Vincent and save him? "It's just like I told you."

"We believe somebody else is involved, yes," Vega says, and suddenly his relief disappears. It sounds like Vega is still making room for the possibility he's been lying to her, because *we believe somebody else is involved* isn't the same as *we know it wasn't you.*

"So what are you asking me?"

"Would you be willing to come with me to Vincent Archer's house to take a look around?"

He thinks about it for a few seconds. "You think I'm going to see a photograph of the person who killed Vincent Archer?"

"It's possible."

"But I didn't see who killed him, and even if there is a photograph in Vincent's house, it's probably going to be a picture of a friend of his, right? Why would a friend kill him?"

"Most people who are killed are killed by somebody they know," Vega says. "Also, Archer has been taking photographs of other people he was following. I think that if you come to the house you might see something that I can't see."

"But like I said, I never saw who killed him."

"No, but you might recognize something, or somebody, from your dreams."

"Okay," he says. "I'm in."

"I'll call your mom and run it past her."

Vega makes the call. She explains to his mom what their plan is. His mom tells Vega she'll call back with a decision in a few minutes, though Joshua isn't sure what it is she needs to think about. Dr. Toni sources some clothes for him. A pair of jeans that are a little too long and a faded T-shirt that is a little too tight. The shoes and socks fit okay. He wonders who they belonged to and what happened to that person. He likes the idea of being able to help. He thinks his dad would be proud of him.

His mom calls back. She tells Vega she's not willing to let Joshua go. Joshua can't understand why, and nor can Vega, who argues the point. His mom can't be convinced. Joshua feels all the energy leave the room. He's upset with his mom. He wanted to go.

"Your mom has agreed that we can talk about it again tomorrow," Vega says after she's hung up. She sounds disappointed. "She said she wants to run it past your lawyer first."

"I don't need her permission to go," he says.

"No, but I do. You're sixteen years old, Joshua. If I took you to Vincent Archer's house without her consent, I'd lose my job." She looks like she wants to say more but can't seem to figure out what. She takes a deep breath, then sighs slowly. "On that note, I suggest we call it a night. Joshua, I'll have someone escort you to the station in the morning to meet with your mom and your lawyer, and then we can interview you and get a formal statement."

"I think mom is going to meet me here," he says.

"Either way," Vega says, sounding dejected, "I'll see you at the station tomorrow."

FORTY-SEVEN

---◆---

Vega feels flat. And angry. And tired. She wants to drive to Michelle Logan's house and shake her by the shoulders until she changes her mind. For the life of her, she can't figure out why Michelle said no. Sure, she wants to protect her son, and that's understandable, but Vega questions if there's something more going on.

She walks with the doctor and they part ways at the elevator. Vega makes her way to the waiting room outside the operating theater where Ben is being operated on. Several off-duty officers are hanging about, even though visiting hours are over. She updates them on the case. Nobody here holds any malice towards Joshua—their blame is directed at the man responsible, but she can't help but think some of it should be directed at Ben Kirk as well. Despite his claims that killing Simon Bower was an act of self-defense, she now knows it was an execution. She spends time with their colleagues, swapping stories about Ben— stories that don't reveal what he was truly capable of. She wonders if any of them knows what Ben and Mitchell were up to. She wonders if Tracey knows.

From the hospital she drives back to the railway crossing. Lights have been set up along the railway line. Crime scene tape has been strung up with patrol cars guarding the intersections. Somebody in the crowd of onlookers is eating a pizza out of the box while watching. She wants to grab him by the collar and show him up close what death looks like and tell him it isn't entertainment. Police officers are stationed along the fence line, pacing back and forth and asking people to stop taking photographs and threatening them with arrest if they don't comply. The photographs of the bodies posted online earlier have been removed from the source—but those photographs were copied and shared thousands of times already. The exercise isn't completely pointless—those who took and uploaded the pictures will all be charged, and hopefully it will send out a message to others willing to do the same stupid thing. Only she doesn't think it will. The kind of person who takes a photograph of a dead teenage boy and puts it online isn't the kind of person who understands how society should work. Some of those photographs were selfies, the photographers standing on the fence smiling into the camera with the crime scene behind them. It's the kind of behavior that gives her grave concerns for civilization.

For the briefest of moments, she thinks those photographers would make great candidates for Ben and Mitchell's organ-transplant program.

Detective Travers is talking to Officer Walker, the officer who found Vincent's Lexus. Detective Kent, Travers's partner, is standing with a forensic technician a little way down the tracks. Vega walks over to Kent. She's always had somewhat of a crush on Kent, and that crush never lessened after the detective was left with a horrible scar on the side of her face after somebody tried to kill her a while back. She thinks back to her conversation with Dr. Coleman earlier, about seeing all kinds of bad things on the job, and seeing Kent now makes her think how easy it must have been for Ben and Mitchell to justify to themselves what they were doing. She isn't sure what she would do to somebody who hurt Tracey in such a way, but she suspects if she were truly honest she knows the answer.

Vega has met the forensic guy on other cases. His name is Mike Peterson, and Peterson is one of those guys who use their hands a lot when they talk. He's in his fifties, completely bald with a pointed head like the end of a rugby ball. He's always friendly and happy to talk, and not the kind of guy you want to get caught on the phone with if you're in a hurry. Together, Kent and Peterson walk her through the scene and give her what Peterson calls the "most likely scenario." He gives the phrase air quotes to stress that the word *likely* means there's a factor for error.

They show her disturbances in the stones and grass, and tell her whose blood is where, and whose shoes made which impressions. Peterson does most of the talking. The "most likely scenario" supports what Joshua has been saying, that Scott chased him down the train tracks, tripped him, and sent him down the stony embankment. There are blood marks on stones that Peterson tells her came from Joshua's hands and knees. There are signs of a struggle, then footprints where Joshua tried to run. They come to a stop farther down the tracks—the spot where Scott Adams was killed. It's here where Joshua dumped his schoolbag. The body has been removed.

"It's hard to tell what happened next," Peterson says, as they walk to the location where the second body was found. "We think Archer dragged Joshua Logan up to the tracks. We got clothing fibers and trail marks that lead up the bank."

"There are grazes on Joshua's back," Vega says.

"On his uniform too," Kent says, "which was badly torn."

Peterson is nodding. "All of it indicates he was on his back and dragged by his hands."

"One possibility," Kent says, "is that Archer was planning on letting Joshua get hit by a train to hide what had really happened. I've seen it happen before."

"Only at some point Joshua gained partial consciousness and made his way further down the tracks," Peterson says.

"But not right away," Vega says.

"No, not right away," Peterson says.

"Between him getting dragged up here, and ending up down there, we think that's when our unknown subject showed up. He takes care of Archer. We think because Archer dragged Joshua up the slope, he had his back to the tracks and the path on the other side, so never saw his attacker coming. The blood trail suggests he was hit with the rock before making his way down the hill to flee. It's why there's a distance between the bodies."

"Have you spoken to Tracey?" Kent asks.

"Not yet," Vega says, but she needs to. And not just about Vincent Archer.

"My guess is Archer's attacker caught up and hit him again with the rock, perhaps a few more times. Tracey will be able to confirm," Peterson says.

"We can't explain why Joshua had the knife," Kent says.

"I think I can. He told me he can vaguely remember being dragged up onto the tracks, and after that he thinks he walked along them."

"It would explain why he was so far down," Kent says.

"I think it's possible Archer put the knife in Joshua's hand hoping that when the train hit it would somehow stay in there, or at the least have Joshua's fingerprints on it. He had no idea we were looking for him and, if we hadn't been, and it had happened that way, we'd all be drawing very different conclusions. My guess is Joshua held onto it as he walked along the tracks before collapsing. Any witnesses?" Vega asks. "Any of these camera-happy neighbors have anything useful to say?"

"Nothing," Kent says. "There's something else that even makes less sense than this guy coming along and saving Joshua and then fleeing. Why leave Joshua out on the tracks where he could be killed? Why not drag him off to the side?"

"He fled the scene because of us," Vega says. "He heard the sirens and he figured the police would find Joshua before the next train did."

"It's one hell of a gamble," Kent says.

"Well, it wasn't his life he was gambling with," Vega says.

"It still doesn't make sense," Kent says.

"It does if you factor in that the guy who saved Joshua is a Good Samaritan with something to hide."

FORTY-EIGHT
— ◉ —

Joshua wakes up at six a.m. He sits by the window, watching the city come to life. He had no idea how many people would be up and about at this time. There are people jogging on the streets, making their way to or from the nearby park. There are delivery trucks, taxis, police cars, perhaps people finishing work while others are starting it, perhaps people on their way to the airport to fly a few thousand miles for work or holiday. He's been on a plane a few times. Two years ago his parents took him to Tahiti, and he's been to Australia twice; he rode some roller coasters at a theme park there and it was one of the best days of his life. He wants to go back.

Dr. Hatch comes in a little before eight. He smells of coffee and there's some kind of stain on the lapel of his white jacket, perhaps chocolate. He smiles at Joshua and asks how he's feeling, and Joshua replies he's feeling fine, and doesn't mention how tired he is, or how sore he is. During the night the headache came back, but if yesterday's was a ten, then last night's was a three. It was uncomfortable enough to make falling asleep difficult. It didn't help that whenever he closed his eyes he saw the look on Scott's face when he realized he was dying, and other times he would see the look on Uncle Ben's face as he was bleeding out. The cuts on his hands are hurting too, as are the scrapes on his back.

"Your uncle is going to be fine," Dr. Hatch tells him. "The operation was a success, and he's going to make a full recovery. It will take some time, but he'll get there."

"Can I see him?"

"Not yet, no. He's still in intensive care, but he's stable. Perhaps later today, or tomorrow."

Dr. Hatch runs some basic tests, and after fifteen minutes tells him he can leave once his mom arrives. They shake hands good-bye, with Dr. Hatch applying only slight pressure so as not to hurt him, and then he disappears. Joshua returns to the window, but gets in only a minute of staring before a nurse with a pair of glasses so large they almost reach her hairline walks in and hands him a note. "This was dropped off for you last night, sweetie," she says, and her smile stays on her face as she watches him unfold it. Then she winks at him. "Apparently the girl who dropped it off was quite pretty."

He reads the note. *Hope you're doing okay, Boy Who Used to Be Blind. I'm really sorry I took you down those tracks . . . and I'm sorry I told Mrs. Thompson what Scott did to you. I'm not going to school tomorrow, so maybe if you want to, you can call me. I'll understand if you don't want to talk to me again, or if you hate me. I feel so bad and it's all my fault and I want to crawl into a cave and hide. But I would like to talk to you if you want to. Here's my number in case you lost it. Olillia* ☺

He traces the smiley face with his finger. He hates the idea that she's blaming herself.

"Can I borrow a phone?" he asks.

"When we're done here," the nurse says. "Now let's take a look at those bandages."

She removes them one at a time, examines the cuts, cleans them down, and re-dresses them. His left hand still requires a bandage, but his right hand and knees she covers again with plasters. She checks his head and cleans around the lump that's still painful to the touch. She's in the process of finishing when his mom shows up. She asks how he is, and he tells her the same thing he told Dr. Hatch. The nurse finishes, winks at him again—a wink that's magnified by her glasses to become the biggest wink he's seen since being able to see—and tells him to be careful today, and then Joshua changes into the clothes his mom brought with her while she waits out in the hall. He almost forgets about the note from Olillia, and has to go back into his room to fetch it from the pocket of the borrowed jeans when they leave.

"You've heard about Uncle Ben?" she asks him.

"Doctor Hatch told me," he says.

"Hungry?" she asks.

"Starving."

They walk to the cafeteria. It's a different policeman outside his door today from the one last night, a guy who walks with small, jerky movements, as if his joints are made of tin. The policeman doesn't make any conversation along the way, but he does eye everybody suspiciously, as if they could be the person who attacked Vincent Archer. When they reach the hospital café, Joshua orders a bowl of muesli and some fruit and an orange juice because they don't have the one thing he really wants—a breakfast burger. His mum has no appetite and orders only a coffee.

"Here," she says, and reaches into her handbag. "I got you something."

She hands him a small package. He unwraps it. It's a new phone. He remembers his old phone and what Scott did to it, which makes him think of Scott and his last moments. He tries to push the image from his thoughts. He leans across the table and hugs his mom. "Thanks," he says.

"Now tell me more about last night," she says. "I want to know what Detective Vega had in mind."

His breakfast shows up while he's telling her. The muesli tastes like cardboard but he's so hungry he eats it anyway. His mom has to constantly blow across the surface of her coffee to cool it down.

"I think I should have gone," he says, when he's given her the details. "I would have been okay."

"You would have, until you weren't," she says. "That's what happened with your dad."

"It wouldn't have been like that, and I might have been able to help."

"I don't want you going to that house."

"Why not?"

"I've already told you why. Now finish your breakfast."

He finishes his breakfast and his mom finishes her coffee. There's a bunch of reporters outside the main entrance, so they take the staff entrance out into the parking lot behind the hospital. The police officer drives them to the police station with the same robotic movements he had when walking. His mom leaves her car at the hospital. Joshua sits in the backseat, switches on his new cell phone, and is happy to see it's half-charged. He unfolds the note from his pocket and copies the phone number into the phone. His mom bought him a SIM card too, and he slots that in. The phone finds the network, and he composes a short text.

Hey, Talking Girl—it's Josh. I'm doing okay. Talk later?

It's only a couple of minutes to the police station. He's been here before, but he's never seen it. It's a concrete block with windows that's as wide as it is tall, and it looks like it might have taken longer for the architect to find his pencils and ruler than to actually design it. From the outside he counts nine floors. It looks dirty, as if all the exhaust from the passing traffic has stuck to the sides of it. A gate rolls to the side so they can enter the parking lot behind it, then the police officer leads them upstairs to a room where Joshua's lawyer is waiting.

She introduces herself as Natalie White. Natalie has a thin smile and short dark hair and expertly applied makeup. She looks like she'd fit in with the people he's seen on the covers of entertainment magazines. Her hand is warm when he shakes it and she asks him if he needs anything, and he tells her he's fine. The room is four concrete-block walls. Half of one is taken up by a mirror. Joshua suspects the building's architect was the same guy hired to do the interior design. He also suspects someone is on the other side of that mirror observing them. There's a table set up with two chairs on each side. There's a video camera on a tripod in the corner. His phone vibrates in his pocket, but he doesn't check it. He sits next to the lawyer, and his mom drags one of the seats around so she can sit next to Joshua.

"Are the police going to charge him with anything?" his mom asks. "Do they think he killed that boy?"

"Joshua is just here to give a formal statement," Natalie explains, "but let's see what they say before we plan for things we don't need to plan for. Remember, Joshua, don't answer anything too quickly. If there's a question I don't like, I want to be able to interrupt. If there's something you're unsure of, you say nothing. If I don't like what you're saying, I'll tell you to stop. Got it?"

"Yes."

"It's important that you really do get it, Joshua."

"I get it," he says.

The door opens and Detective Vega steps in. She's carrying a cup of coffee and she looks tired. Her clothes are wrinkled and there are bags under her eyes. She sits opposite him and his mother and his lawyer.

"How are you feeling this morning, Josh?" Vega asks.

"I'm fine," he says.

"Can I get you something? A drink maybe?"

"I'm good," he says.

"Okay, okay, good. Well, then let's go over everything that happened yesterday, shall we?" she says. "Joshua, I want you to start by telling me why you decided to walk down the train tracks."

"I told you all this yesterday."

"I know you did, but yesterday you were suffering from a concussion."

"Which means anything he said yesterday can't be—"

Vega puts up her hand to interrupt. "I know what it means, Counselor, and that's why we're here this morning, to go over everything again."

"What does it mean?" Joshua asks.

"It means you weren't in a fit state of mind yesterday to be giving statements," his lawyer says.

Vega ignores her. "Okay, Joshua, why don't you tell me what happened yesterday, starting with why you took those train tracks?"

He tells her everything he told her yesterday. He tells her about leaving school, about meeting Olillia, about walking the train tracks.

Occasionally Vega will jot something down. He tells her after Olillia left, Scott chased him, and he tried to defend himself but didn't know how. He slows down, as if by holding back the story it will end differently, that if he doesn't reach the point where Vincent Archer arrived then perhaps it doesn't have to have happened. Only it did happen, and again he can see Scott's face at the moment he knew he was dying.

"Tell me what happened at school," Vega says. "Concerning your altercations with Scott Adams."

"What altercations?" his mom asks.

"Joshua?" Vega says.

"There weren't any altercations," his mom says.

"Mom," he says, looking up at her. "It's okay."

"I want a few minutes with my client," his lawyer says.

"It's okay," Joshua says.

"Joshua—"

"It's really okay," he says, and then he tells them about yesterday. The shoving. The can of soda. The sawdust. He's embarrassed as he tells them. His mom looks upset.

"I was going to ask Uncle Ben to teach me how to fight—at least that's what I was thinking before I . . . you know, hurt him."

"He doesn't blame you," Vega says.

"You've spoken to him?"

"No. But I know him well enough to know he won't blame you in any way."

"Okay, Detective," his lawyer says, "Joshua has given you a statement and, as you just said, Detective Kirk doesn't blame my client. Joshua has done nothing wrong, so if there's nothing else, it's time we wrap this up."

"There is one more thing," Vega says. "I'm hoping Joshua might be able to help us with our investigation."

"In what way?" his lawyer asks.

"We believe if we take him to Vincent Archer's house he might see something that can help identify who we're looking for."

"I don't see how he could identify anything or anybody at a house he's never been to, belonging to a man he'd never met before."

"He might be of great help, and we still have a killer out there we need to find."

"No," his mom says.

Everybody turns to look at her.

"It will be completely safe," Vega says. "We'll have plenty of—"

"I said no."

"I'm happy to do it," Joshua says.

"Joshua, I said no," she says again.

"You want to tell us why?" Vega asks.

"Perhaps give me a few minutes alone with Joshua and his mom," Natalie says.

Vega stands up. "I'll be back in five."

"You want to explain your objections?" his lawyer asks, once Vega has closed the door behind her."

"I'm not going to expose Joshua to the danger of visiting the house of the man who tried to kill him when the police don't understand the connection between that person and this other person who showed up yesterday. I also don't want Joshua seeing something and the police department creating a whole new context for it, and suddenly Joshua is facing charges for something he didn't do."

"I understand your concern," his lawyer says, "but I think there's an opportunity here to help the—"

"It doesn't matter what you think," his mom says, and he's never heard her talk like this before. "All that matters is that I've said no."

"It's your call," his lawyer says.

"And I've called it."

Natalie knocks on the door to let Vega know they're done. Vega comes back in and sits down.

"The answer is still no," his lawyer says.

"I don't see why," Vega says. "What's really going on here, Mrs. Logan?"

"What's going on," his lawyer says, "is that jail has its share of innocent people because things were taken out of context. Lives have been ruined when the police misread the evidence."

"That's not happening here."

"Can you honestly sit there and tell me innocent people have never ended up in jail?"

"I'm not here to debate the injustices of the system," Vega says.

"Well, you should. Every cop should. Every time a jury finds somebody not guilty, that's somebody the police believed to be guilty, and somebody's life they've tried to ruin because they didn't get the facts straight. Until the police are held accountable for arresting the wrong people, that will never change, and do you want to know why that will never change?"

"I'm sure you're going to tell me," Vega says.

"If the police were held accountable then nobody would ever get arrested. You'd all be too scared to do your jobs," Natalie finishes.

"You're discussing one thing when I'm trying to discuss another," Vega says, "and by doing so you're blowing this way out of proportion. Joshua can help us by visiting the house. Don't you want us to get this killer off the streets?"

"That's a manipulative question, Detective. You know better than that."

"We're not the enemy here," Vega says.

"I'm sorry, Detective, but my client has given you an answer, and it's no."

"Sorry isn't going to help the next person this guy hurts," Vega says.

"That won't work on me either, Detective. You have your job to do and I have mine. My client is tired, and yesterday was a long day for him. It's time for him to go home."

FORTY-NINE

—— ◉ ——

The same policeman who drove them to the station drives them back to the hospital so Joshua's mom can retrieve her car. They don't make any conversation on the way. Somebody must have tipped the media off that Joshua was no longer at the hospital, because they're all gone. When they get to her car, the policeman follows them back home.

"I really wanted to help," Joshua says, staring out the window. They pass a flattened hedgehog, and up ahead is another. He wonders if they made a pact.

"And what if something happens?"

"Like what?" he asks, turning towards her. "There'll be plenty of other officers there."

"People have been dying and getting hurt all because somebody else wants revenge," she says. "We don't know what this guy wants, or how crazy he is. I don't want you getting involved."

She keeps looking ahead, eyes on the road, not willing to even glance at him.

"If this guy wanted to hurt me, he would have done it yesterday," he says.

"If he wanted to help you," she says, "he wouldn't have left you on a set of train tracks to get run down."

"Dad used to say the world was full of good people willing to do nothing."

"Your dad is dead, Joshua."

He feels like jumping out of the car at the next set of lights and walking the rest of the way.

"You're upset with me?" she asks.

"No," he says, but he is.

"It sounds like you're upset with me."

"I'm fine," he says, but he isn't.

"I want what's best for you."

"I know," he says.

"You'll understand one day."

He's not sure he will. His phone vibrates. He had forgotten that it went off earlier, but he leaves it in his pocket, not wanting to read the message in front of his mom.

"You're wrong," he says.

"About?"

"About me understanding one day."

His mom says nothing.

"I'd have thought you wanted this guy found so you could thank him. I'd have thought . . ." he says, then stops talking. He focuses on what he's just said. He looks at his mom. She doesn't look back. An idea is forming. He scrambles to get hold of it. *I'd have thought you wanted this guy found so you could thank him.*

"We never spoke about school," his mom says, changing the subject. "Why don't you tell me more about your day?"

I'd have thought you wanted this guy found so you could thank him.

"Joshua?"

Why would she not want to thank him? He said a moment ago he would never understand, but that's not true. He's making sense of it.

"Are you still awake over there?"

"You don't want him found," he says.

"Excuse me?"

"The man who saved me. You don't want him found."

"That's ridiculous," she says.

"That's what this is about," he says. "It's not that you think I might be in danger, or that I'll see something the police will take out of context and blame me for, it's that you do want to thank him, only not in person. You want to thank him by not helping the police find him."

"I don't want to talk about it anymore, Joshua."

"You don't want him found."

"I said I don't want to talk about it."

"Because he saved my life, and that makes him a hero."

"A real hero wouldn't have left you on the tracks."

"He couldn't have known a train was on its way, and anyway, maybe he didn't leave me on the tracks. Maybe I stumbled back onto them."

She says nothing.

"Aside from that, I think you approve of what he did. You think we're all better off with this guy out there because he took a really bad guy off the streets."

"So what if that's what I think?" she asks, taking her eyes off the road for a second to glare at him. "Having somebody out there ridding us of these monsters, that's a good thing, Joshua. If he's done this before, and somebody else had given him up, then he never would have been there yesterday to save you. Right now you'd be laying out cold and dead on a slab in a morgue, maybe you'd be in pieces, and I don't think you really get what it's like for me knowing how close that came to being a reality. You could have died, Joshua. I remember what it's like being your age. You feel immortal. You think stuff like that can't happen to you, but it can, and it almost did. This man, he saved your life. We have to pay it forward. We have to do our best to make sure he's around to protect the next person who's in danger."

Joshua isn't sure what to say. It's almost like this isn't his mom anymore. Has she always felt this way? "We don't know if he was following me, or Vincent Archer, and we don't know why."

"None of that matters. It doesn't matter what kind of man he is, we owe him for what he did."

"Is that what Dad would want?"

"Yes," she says, and she sounds sure of it.

Joshua needs to know why this man saved him. Needs to know his intent. Is he a good man or a bad man? Is he neither? Was he following him or Vincent, or was he just somebody passing by? "What if—"

"Let it go, Joshua. I'm asking you, please, just let it go."

FIFTY

—⟨◉⟩—

Before Joshua left the police station, Detective Vega gave him back his schoolbag. He now tells his mom he's going to do some homework, and he carries that bag to his bedroom and closes the door. This time of the morning, the sun is blanketing his bed and almost touching his desk. He gets himself comfortable on the bed, propping a pillow between his body and the wall. He pulls out his phone and checks the messages.

Hey! Glad you're doing okay. Sure, looking forward to talking! Then, later, the second text. *Hope you're still doing okay.* ☺

He replies. It takes him a little while to compose the text because his left hand is still in a bandage, which makes the phone harder to hold. *Just got home. I still don't understand what happened yesterday, but I'm okay. How are you?*

It's barely a few seconds until she texts back. *I can't believe Scott is dead.*

I'm sorry, he texts.

If I hadn't told Mrs. Thompson what he had done to you, or if I hadn't convinced you to use the train tracks, none of this would have happened.

His texting speed is getting faster. A few weeks ago he'd never sent a text in his life, and now he's wondering how people managed to socialize without it. *It would have happened in a different way. It's not your fault. Are you going back to school tomorrow?*

I don't know. Want to catch up today and talk about everything? I can come to your house, or you can come here?

I'd like that, but I'm not sure mom will. I'll find out and text you.

Okay. See ya!

See ya!

He decides to wait until his mom is in a better mood before asking if he can see Olillia. He gets out his homework and realizes he can barely remember anything from school yesterday, other than Scott, and Olillia, and getting bullied in the corridor, and bullied in woodshop. He puts his homework aside and figures his teachers will forgive him for not getting it done. Instead he sets up his new cell phone, playing with the settings and entering the contact details of people he knows. When he's done, he carries on with a book he's been reading. It's about a boy who stows away on the wrong boat, and has to keep hiding from the crew once he realizes the meals the crew eats consist of other people who stowed away on the boat. The boy, Danny, is coming to realize it wasn't skill or luck that enabled him to sneak onto the boat, but the design of some very hungry sailors. The book is called *The Cannibal Cruise* and it ticks all the right boxes literature-wise, yet today he can't get into it. Unlike the cannibals in the book, his tastes, apparently, have changed.

"Hey," his mom says, knocking on his door, then coming into his room.

"Hey."

"I'm sorry we argued earlier. I just want what's best for you."

"I know," he says.

"I just got a phone call," she says, "from Principal Mooney. He was apologetic, but he said that, well, under the circumstances he doesn't think you should return to Christchurch North."

"Till when?"

"He means permanently. He said it's more for your benefit than anybody else's."

He thinks of Olillia. "I liked it there."

"It doesn't sound like you liked it," she says. "What you told Detective Vega made it sound awful."

"There were some nice people there too."

"Like this girl you met."

"Yes," he says.

"So you want to go back there?"

"Yes."

"Because of this girl?"

"Because it's going to be the same no matter where I go," he says. "I can't run from it, I have to face it."

She looks happy with his answer. "Then I'll talk to Principal Mooney in person. I think it will help if I go there now, before his decision is set in stone."

"Should I go with you?"

"I think it will go better if you're not there," she says. "Right now that school is emotionally charged, and you showing up will only inflame it. That much he got right, but to not let you go back at all? You didn't ask for any of this, and you can't be responsible for the actions of a psychopath. Before I go and plead your case, are you sure?"

"I'm sure."

"Good."

"Umm . . . while you're at the school, is it okay if I see Olillia? She's at home today, and we could do our homework together. Plus, I think it would be really good for me because I don't really know what I'm doing plus I think you'd really like her and not only that but she was there yesterday before the attack and it could have been her and not Scott if the guy had chosen the previous set of tracks and I think it will help to talk about it and—"

"Okay, okay, slow down," his mom says, putting up her hand. "You keep talking like that and you're going to run out of air and faint. You've convinced me."

"So she can come over?"

"Why don't you meet her at the library? I can drop you off, and pick you up when you're done."

FIFTY-ONE

— ◉ —

Vega is tired. And hungry. And irritable. After the interview with Joshua, she's been brooding all morning, and what really isn't helping is this churning feeling in her stomach, brought on by the idea that the woman she loves has played a part in all that has happened. She didn't call Tracey last night, and hasn't called her this morning, so by now Tracey surely knows something is wrong, but she'll have no idea about what. Earlier Vega even asked Detective Kent to pick up the two autopsy reports so she wouldn't have to face Tracey herself. Vega knows she's being stupid. She should go and see her, and ask her outright if she was involved with Ben and Logan and Dr. Coleman. The problem is Tracey might say yes, and then what? Do they break up? Can she be involved with somebody who was doing something not only illegal, but questionably immoral too? And if Tracey says no, will she believe her? Of course Tracey might not be involved, and probably isn't, in which case—

Questionably immoral?

Did she really just think that?

Yes, she did. She thought that because she's seen what people like Vincent Archer can do. She thinks that because Simon Bower took a power saw to his victim. She thinks that because yesterday she said to Ben at the station that Bower got what he deserved, and nobody there would argue it.

No. You're thinking that because you're tired. Because your partner is in the hospital, and because your girlfriend might have been involved with harvesting body parts illegally, but if you ask her about it, the question itself could be seen as a betrayal, because it would tell her that you think she's capable of it.

It's a no-win situation.

She needs to calm her thoughts and focus on the investigation at hand.

The autopsy reports show that Scott Adams died almost instantly from the massive injury to his chest, and Vincent Archer was clubbed in the head four times for his own set of traumatic injuries. Detectives have been back out in the field talking to friends and colleagues of both Vincent Archer and Simon Bower. They've been taking fingerprints from those who allow it. So far the ones holding out aren't looking suspicious, just unwilling to help. *It's hard to save the world when the whole world is against you*—that's something Vega's foster dad told her years ago when she joined the police force. They're making plenty of progress proving what happened yesterday, they're just not making any progress determining who the other person involved is.

That's what brings her to Christchurch North. It's lunchtime when she arrives, and she sits in the parking lot finishing off a takeaway salad that looks like it was made yesterday and tastes like it was made last week, but she's so hungry she powers through it anyway. She checks her phone when it beeps. It's a message from Tracey. *Are you okay?*

She feels better now that she's eaten, and calmer, and she sends back a reply. *Yep—just busy. Talk later?*

Looking forward to it.

The grounds are littered with students. She reaches the administration building and is led into Principal Mooney's office, where he tells her what a shock it is, that over the twenty years he's been at the school this is the second time a student has been murdered, that he has lost others too—three to car accidents, one to imitating a "don't try this at home" moment he had seen on television, and two to cancer.

"It's always a difficult time," Mooney says. "But something like this, something so senseless, it's hard for the students. It makes them feel lost, that the ground can be pulled out from under them at any moment."

He goes on to say he questions whether Joshua should return. "It will be difficult for him," he says. "I know it wasn't his fault, none of it is, but the fact is if he hadn't come to this school, Scott Adams would still be alive."

"You're right," she says. "It wasn't his fault. Out of everything you've said, that's the one line you want to cling to."

Lunchtime ends and all the students are led to a special assembly. Vega follows the principal into the school hall, where it's ten degrees cooler than outside. It's like being pulled back through time, because even though she didn't go to this school, the hall and everything in it is almost identical to the one she did go to. Same wooden seats that sit four students apiece, all of them side by side in rows, same drab banners hanging from the walls with similar school colors and a crest, brown wooden walls and brown linoleum floor and the smell of dust that makes it feel like an old, abandoned gym. It's probably looked this way since World War II. There's a stage up front, and she guesses school plays are put on in here. At the moment the hall is full of chatter. Mooney steps up on the stage and walks to a podium and tells everybody to quiet down, which they do.

"Yesterday was a tragic day for all of us," Mooney says, looking out over the room. "Losing Scott . . . it's heartbreaking for all of us. Senseless for all of us. Scott was a good student and was well liked," he says, which sends a small murmur through the crowd. "He will be missed. We have counselors on hand if any of you would like to talk to them at any time during the day. Right now it's the priority of the police to build up a better picture of what happened, and to that end I'd like to introduce you all to Detective Inspector Vega. Detective?"

She takes the podium. She hasn't spoken to a roomful of people like this since her own days in high school. She hated it then, and she isn't too fond of it now. Unlike the speeches at her high school, when the students were whispering or messing around, she now has everyone's full attention. These kids are looking at her expectantly, like they want her to spill all the gory details. In which case they're out of luck.

"I'm sure many of you have heard different accounts of what happened yesterday afternoon," she says, "but the fact we haven't released any information to the public means whatever you've heard is rumor and hearsay. What I need from all of you is information. I need to know two things: Who uses those train tracks to walk to or from school? Who has seen anybody unusual hanging around?"

Nobody says anything. No murmuring. Just absolute silence.

"When Principal Mooney dismisses the assembly, I want all those students who can answer yes to either of those questions to stay behind."

There's a boy in the front row with a look on his face that makes her want to find some reason to arrest him. He's sneering at her when he puts up his hand. He's tall and skinny and has black spiky hair that looks like it was styled to look like it hasn't been styled. He has the shadow of a mustache on his upper lip that looks too frightened to grow in case it touches some of the pimples festering away there.

"Yes?"

"Is it true that Scott died saving that blind kid?"

"Do you take the train tracks?" she asks him.

"No."

"Did you see anybody hanging around outside the school?"

"No, but—"

"All of you need to understand I'm not here to answer questions or comment on the case," she says, looking from the boy and out over the rest of the students. "I'm here so we can start piecing things together. I'm here for Scott."

"That's unfair," the boy says.

"Excuse me?"

"You're saying you expect us to answer your questions, but won't answer any of ours. That's a dick move," he says.

"Levi," Mooney says, "I think you've said enough. I want you to stay behind with the others so we can have a word."

Levi says nothing, but he keeps glaring at Vega.

"Any other questions?" Mooney asks.

No hands go up.

"Anything out of the ordinary," Vega says, "I want you to come and tell me. No detail is too small," she says, and she feels like a salesperson.

Mooney wraps up the assembly. The school has 986 students. Eighteen are absent. Of the 968 students remaining, 951 of them walk out the door. *Seventeen isn't a bad number*, she thinks. It only takes one to have seen their Good Samaritan.

There are twelve boys and five girls. She steps off the podium.

"How many of you use the train tracks?" Vega asks.

Ten boys and two girls put their hands up.

"And the rest of you, you saw something unusual? You saw somebody hanging around outside the school?"

There are murmurs of yes, and some nodding.

"Okay, good. We're going to go through this one by one, and while that happens, I want everybody else to wait quietly."

The first student is a girl named Lelei, who keeps scratching at the back of her neck as she talks. "There was this guy, he was like, you know, hanging around outside the school. He kept looking at his phone, and his watch, as if he was trying his hardest not to be noticed."

"So why did you notice him, Lelei?"

"Because I hadn't seen him before, and because he was parked behind my mom."

"I want to show you some photos, and I want you to tell me if you recognize him, okay?"

"Okay."

At Vincent Archer's house last night, she made a copy of a photograph of him. That photograph is now mixed in with random mug shots. The photographs are on her phone. She swipes through them.

"Him," Lelei says, when she gets to the seventh photograph. It's Vincent Archer.

"Are you sure?"

"Positive."

"What did this man do? Did anybody get into his car?"

"No. That's what was weird about it. We had to wait ages for my brother, but that guy left before we did, without picking anybody up."

Archer must have left to follow Joshua.

Vega goes through similar interviews with the rest of the students from that group, each of them picking out Archer from her phone. All it does is confirm what she already knew.

She starts with the next group, but right off the mark she learns that of the twelve who use the train tracks exactly six of them went right instead of left. She interviews them anyway, but they offer nothing useful. The other six are more helpful, with a group of three saying they always take those tracks, and that they recognized Olillia following them with a student they didn't know, and they turned off at the next intersection and noticed a while later Olillia had turned off too. Had they seen anybody else? No. What about on other days? Yes. Sometimes there's a couple of old drunk guys who like to yell abuse at them, and there's often a guy there sniffing glue, but not yesterday.

Principal Mooney comes over and interrupts her. He has the boy who asked the question earlier in the assembly. He tells her that Levi has something to tell her that might be useful. She hopes he does, because so far nothing has been helpful.

Levi tells her he wasn't completely honest when he said earlier that he hadn't noticed anyone strange hanging around. As he begins to talk, it becomes apparent to Vega that coming here hasn't been a waste of time after all.

FIFTY-TWO

—◆—

Joshua's mom tells him that her grandmother was on the team of build-ers who built their local library. It was back in the sixties, and it was a time when construction and architecture were fields dominated by men. She tells him her grandmother was one of the toughest women she's ever known, and she had to be because men would undermine her all day long while also hitting on her. In the years that followed, the library's carpets were updated twice, and the color palette for the interior walls was updated in the early eighties, but other than that it looks almost identical to when she was kid, she says. She tells him it was one of the last libraries in the country to move on from books being listed on a catalogue of cards set in dozens of small wooden drawers to an updated computer system. Stuff like that is from such a different time, and the idea of it is so foreign he's not even sure he can believe it could have existed. She drops him off outside it and waits until he's gone in before driving away.

There's not a lot of life in the library. A few old-looking people sit-ting near the windows, reading old-looking books. Some young moth-ers quietly reading to their toddlers with toys nearby that look chewed on and torn. A librarian with a glazed look in her eyes slowly pushes a cart around, shelving returned books back in their proper places. The place is warm, though, and smells of books, and despite it looking old he's comfortable here. Olillia waves to him from near the back, and he joins her. She's wearing blue jeans and a white T-shirt that has a silhouette of a woman's face on it. It looks better than her uniform. She hugs him tight and he hugs her tight back and he likes the way she feels and the way her hair smells. They sit down and face each other and she asks him the same kinds of questions Detective Vega asked him, and he gives the same kind of answers and this is way better than texting, and he wonders if some people have forgotten that. A second librarian glances at them every time she passes, which is oddly frequent, as if she suspects them of committing some horrible, book-related crime.

"So you think your mom is wrong?" Olillia asks when he's done telling her everything, including his mom's reaction to him wanting to help Detective Vega.

"I don't know. I mean—I guess I see her point. The guy did save my life."

"By killing somebody," she says.

"True."

"Then he left you on the tracks to get run over."

"I'm not so sure he did. I think I might have wandered back onto them."

"Even so, you *were* on the tracks and almost died. There is one thing, though, that you haven't explained," she says, and he knows what's coming. "Why would Detective Vega think you might recognize somebody from Vincent Archer's house?"

It's a difficult question to answer. He wants to be able to tell her the truth, but he's frightened of her reaction. "If I tell you, you have to promise not to think I'm a freak."

"Surely you don't think I would ever think that," she says.

"No, but you might think I'm crazy, because it's a crazy thing to tell. Promise me you won't get up and leave, that you'll let me explain everything to you before you do anything."

"Now I'm worried," she says, and she looks worried. "Did you do something yesterday you haven't told me about?"

"It's nothing like that," he says.

"Then what?"

"Have you ever heard of cellular memory?"

She tells him she hasn't, so he tells her what it is. He gives her the racing car–driver analogy. A guy with a sick heart gets the heart of a racing car driver who died, then wants to become a racing car driver. Since they're in a building full of books and plenty of computers wired up to the Internet, he figures he can back up everything he is saying with anecdotal evidence, but it turns out there's no need. She's fascinated. He can tell she knows where he is going with it before he begins to talk about his own surgery. She doesn't ask any questions. She sits patiently while he tells his story, eyes big and face full of amazement.

When he's done she nods a few times, and smiles. "Wow," she says. Then the smile disappears. "It must have been scary for you, going through that. So what do we do now?" she asks. "Is there some way to stop it from happening?"

"You believe me?" he asks.

She looks confused by his question. "Why wouldn't I?"

"Because it all sounds insane."

"But you said it's true," she says.

"It is true."

"Then why would I think it was insane?" He isn't sure how to answer, and before he can figure it out, she carries on. "So you see your dad dying."

"Yeah."

"That must be horrible," she says, looking upset at the thought. "Do people think that cellular memory fades?"

"I don't know. Nobody really knows anything for sure."

"It must be . . . I don't know. I don't think I could handle seeing what you see. You're way stronger than anybody gives you credit for," she says, and he doesn't know how to respond to that, nor does he get the chance, because she carries on. "Let me ask you something. When you saw photographs of Simon Bower, you recognized him. How did you recognize Vincent Archer?"

"Detective Vega said he didn't have a criminal record, but my dad must have dealt with him at some point."

"Yeah, I guess that makes sense. Your dad knew a lot of people," she says. "Who else do you recognize?"

"Mom and dad, and Uncle Ben too. And me. We're all people my dad saw not long before he died. Maybe there's a time limit on it."

"Which would mean Vincent was somebody your dad must have seen not long before he died."

"Maybe he was. Maybe he was there that morning, and Uncle Ben didn't see him."

"So Detective Vega thinks you might recognize someone from the photographs in his house?"

"Somebody, or something. I want to help too, but I guess Mom is right, we could end up causing trouble for the person who saved my life. Doesn't seem fair."

"What if we find him first?"

"What?"

"We find him," she says, "and we figure out if he's a good guy or a bad guy, and then you know whether you should be thanking him or phoning the police. At least it will give you some answers. Not knowing who he is or what he's capable of will only keep you awake at night."

"How are we going to figure it out?" he asks.

"The same way Vega wanted you to figure it out."

"Wait, wait a second, are you saying we go to Vincent Archer's house?"

"Why not?"

He almost laughs. "I can think of a hundred reasons why not."

"And I can think of one really good reason why we should."

The thought of breaking into a house gets his heart racing. What if he gets caught? Aside from getting a criminal record, and having Principal Mooney absolutely forbid him to return to his school, his mom will ground him for the next two years. Olillia is staring at him. He wants to do it so as to not disappoint her. Plus, she might think it's cool.

"What you need to ask yourself," Olillia says, "is how much you want to find this guy. I'll help you, if you want me to."

"I have no idea how to break into a house."

"Nor do I, but I'm sure we can figure it out. Or, if you like, we can stay here and start on our homework."

"Okay," he says, the word escaping before he can hang on to it. Still . . . he can take it back if he wants to . . . Only he doesn't want to.

"Okay what?"

"Okay, let's figure out where he lives."

They use the online phone directory and come up with two possibilities. Olillia pulls out a set of car keys. "Let's do this," she says.

They grab their bags and take the back door into the parking lot. Olillia's brother took the day off from teachers' college and let her borrow his car. Because she's only on a learner's license, she's not allowed to drive by herself, or with passengers who aren't experienced drivers. They figure if they're going to break into a house anyway, they might as well start the adventure by driving illegally. The car is a red two-door coupe that sits low to the ground and doesn't have any backseats. They put their bags into the trunk. Olillia looks cool, he thinks, as she swings in behind the steering wheel, and it makes him even more eager to learn how to drive. She puts on a pair of sunglasses and manages to look even cooler before plotting the first address into the GPS on her phone. A moment later they're heading for the exit of the parking lot. He lowers himself in the seat so the policeman in the patrol car parked out front won't see him. He's never been driven in a car by someone his age before, and it's weird, like they're kids playing grown-ups. The policeman doesn't follow.

It takes ten minutes to reach the first address, a single-story house in a street of single-story houses, only this one looks better maintained and has an immaculate garden. "Hard to know," she says, as they approach it. "Should we go look at the other one too?"

"This is the one," Joshua says.

"You recognize it from a dream?" she asks.

"No. That parked car we just passed is an unmarked cop car. It has somebody sitting in it."

"You can tell that?"

"Same car that Uncle Ben drives, and Detective Vega, and the same kind of car we got driven to the police station in this morning. Makes sense they'd want to keep watch on the house. So much for taking a look around."

"Do you always give up this easily?" she asks.

"Only when I'm breaking into houses owned by murderers."

She drives around the corner and pulls over. "Let's give it a few minutes," she says.

"Until what?"

"So what do you want to do after you graduate?" she asks, not answering his question. "What do you want to be?"

"I don't know," he says.

"I want to be dancer," she says.

"Really?"

"Yeah. I mean, it's just a dream, really, but I love ballet. I've been practicing most of my life. I really want to perform onstage one day, at least that's the goal, and there are so many others out there with the same goal . . . the bar is just set so terribly high."

"I bet you're amazing," he says.

"You're sweet," she says. "Wait here."

She jumps out of the car. He hears a hissing sound from the back. He opens the door. She's crouching by the back wheel letting the air out of the tire.

She smiles at him and says, "It's all part of the plan."

He climbs out. "What plan?"

"We're not giving up on getting into that house."

"And how are we going to do that with the police officer watching?"

"It's not *we* anymore," she says. "It's *you*. And he won't be watching." She stands up and puts a hairpin back into her hair. "In one minute, I want you to walk up to the house and find your way in."

He sucks in a deep breath but can't get his racing heart under control. It was a mistake coming here, but he can't bring himself to say that. Olillia has already seen him being bullied; he doesn't want her to see him chickening out of this. His fear of breaking and entering is dominated by his enjoyment of having an adventure with her. "Okay," he says.

"Are you sure?"

"Yes. If I get caught I'll—"

"You won't get caught."

"Well, on the chance that I do, I'll say I was trying to help them out."

"Which you are."

"In a way my mom wouldn't find out."

"Exactly what we're doing."

"And I won't mention you at all," he says.

She leans forward and kisses him briefly on the cheek. He feels himself turning red, and when she pulls back, he sees that she's blushing too. "You won't get caught. See you on the other side," she says.

She hops back into her car and does a U-turn. Joshua's face is still feeling warm from the kiss. The flat tire makes a slapping sound as it goes around. She takes the corner and goes back in the direction they came from. He walks to the intersection and watches. She drives past the parked car then pulls over twenty yards past the house. She gets out and puts on a big show of looking dejected when she sees the flat tire. She opens the trunk, gets out the jack, then studies it as if it's the first time she's ever seen one. She drops it, pulling her foot out of the way in time, then picks it back up. She carries it to the side of the car, studies the area around the flat tire, then studies the jack, then looks confused by it all. By the time she has the tire iron out and is struggling to move the lug nuts, the officer on duty has stepped out of his car. He walks over and Joshua can't hear what they say, but a moment later the officer crouches down with his back towards the house and begins to loosen the nuts.

Joshua walks to the house. He goes through a gate into the back-yard. His hands are shaking. He shouldn't be here. Shouldn't be doing this. He should go back through the gate and leave. He checks the windows. Locked. The back door. Locked. Putting a rock through the window will draw attention. Sweat is dripping down the sides of his chest. His forehead is damp. This would be easier if he were here with the police. They'd kick in the door and . . .

That's it!

He races back through the gate. The police officer is still hunched over the wheel. Joshua crosses over the front lawn to the door. Sure enough, it's been smashed in. That's how the police gained access yesterday. It's closed, but he can see the lock has splintered away from the frame. The door makes a soft groaning sound when he opens it and does the same when he closes it behind him.

FIFTY-THREE

---◆---

"First of all—"

"Levi," Principal Mooney says, cutting the boy off. "We don't need one of your diatribes here. Let's show Detective Vega what a great student you can be, and show her what kind of good young man this school produces."

Vega is sure the school produces lots of great young men but is doubtful Levi is going to turn out to be one of them. She's tempted to tell him if he gives her something useful, she'll cut him some slack when their paths cross again—which no doubt they will. He's that kind of kid.

"Fine, whatever," Levi says. "There's this guy who was hanging outside the school, right? Creepy-looking guy."

"Creepy?"

"Yeah. I figured he was offering candy so he could fiddle some of the ugly kids."

"Levi . . ." Principal Mooney says.

"Did you tell anybody about him?" Vega asks.

"No."

"If you really thought he was there to hurt somebody, why not report him?"

"Because it wasn't my problem," he says, which is something Vega thinks sums up this generation of kids. Anything happening beyond the range of a selfie doesn't affect them.

"That's a disappointing attitude," Principal Mooney says.

"Yeah, well, whatever," Levi says. "Do you want me to tell the rest or what?"

"Please, go ahead," Vega says.

"So I'm keen to get home so I can do my homework so I can become a doctor or a lawyer or such, but I'm hungry so I go to the convenience store, right?"

"Which store?" she asks.

"The one with the giant homo who works there," he says.

"Levi . . ."

"What?" he says.

"Just tell me what happened," Vega says.

"So it's the store on the corner of Lambrose Street, you know it?"

"I know it," Vega says. It's between the school and the turnoff for the train tracks.

"Wow, you really must be a great cop," he says.

"Goddamn it, Levi!" Principal Mooney says, then he sighs and looks up at the ceiling before looking back at them. "I'm sorry," he says. "I shouldn't have said that, but please, Levi, can you behave yourself long enough to tell Detective Vega what it is you told me."

"Sure, I can do that," he says. "So, I see this guy drive past again when I'm on my way out. So I start heading home, and then—"

"You're walking? Biking? Driving?" she asks.

"Biking," he says. "Suddenly I'm seeing him again. He's parked up on the opposite side of the road on the other side of the train tracks, waiting all over again."

"And still you did nothing," Principal Mooney said.

"Like what exactly? Ring the police? Tell them there's a guy in a car? Yeah, right."

Principal Mooney sighs heavily but doesn't have a response, because the kid is right.

"So I'm heading home, and Mikey calls to say he's got my smokes . . . I mean, not smokes, I mean stuff . . . stuff for homework, and . . . ."

Principal Mooney is grimacing.

"Mikey?" she asks.

"Yeah, Mikey. So I'm heading there, and wouldn't you know it, here's this guy again, he's pulled up a couple of streets down from where he was last time, and he's walking to the train tracks."

Vega loads up the photographs on her cell phone. "Show me this man," she says, and Levi swipes through the images.

"Any in here of you?" he asks.

"You've earned yourself detention for the rest of the week, Levi," Principal Mooney says.

Levi doesn't answer him. He keeps swiping, then stops on the one of Vincent Archer. "That's him," he says. "But here's the thing, you take the detention off the table and I'll tell you what else I saw."

"Fine," Principal Mooney says.

"Okay, so every time I saw this guy, I saw another guy further down the street. Outside the school this other guy was parked a hundred yards away. Creepy, but not as creepy. Same when I came out of the corner store. This guy was on the other side of the train tracks facing the same way as that other guy, just watching."

"So there were two guys," she says.

"I don't know if they knew each other or what, but there were definitely two of them."

"When you saw this first man entering the train tracks, did you see this other man?"

"He was getting out of his car and starting to follow too."

Another teacher comes into the assembly hall, followed by Michelle Logan. Michelle looks at Vega, but then quickly looks away. Principal Mooney excuses himself and walks over to greet her, leaving Vega and Levi alone.

"You think you can give me a better description of this guy?" she asks.

He turns to see if any of the teachers are in hearing range. There aren't. Vega knows he's about to say something to annoy her. "My memory will work better if there's something in it for me."

She frowns. "Like what?"

"You know what I mean," he says.

"No. I don't."

"It's like in the movies," he says. "The amount people remember is equal to the amount they get paid. It happens all the time."

"Are you seriously doing this?"

"It worked a minute ago for getting out of detention," he says. "Plus it's not a free world, lady, despite what people say. You want something, you gotta pay for it."

"How about this. You tell me what it is I want to know, and I don't break your arms for calling me *lady*," she says, poking a finger hard enough into his chest that he can feel all those hours she puts in at the gym. His face goes pale. She hopes it leaves a bruise. She knows he won't dare say what she did, because it would dent his pride. "I know how cool you think you are. How tough you think you are. You don't help me and I'm going to find a reason to throw you into a holding cell where you'll learn what a tough guy really is."

"You're bluffing," Levi says.

"You really think so?"

He stares at her for a few seconds, and then his body relaxes. "Okay, okay. Fine. Whatever. So what do you want from me? To talk to a sketch artist or something?"

"Something like that," she says. She pulls her phone out of her pocket and asks for his mom's phone number.

"Why?"

"Because we're going to go on a field trip, and I need your mommy's permission."

Levi looks annoyed at her for saying *mommy*, before begrudgingly reciting the number. Vega makes the call. She introduces herself, and Levi's mum immediately asks, "So what's he done now?" Vega explains the situation, and she's given permission to take Levi out of school to visit Vincent Archer's house. It's a whole lot easier than dealing with Michelle Logan. In fact, it's so easy that she's left with the impression she could have taken Levi into a war zone and his mom still wouldn't have cared. It reminds her of what Kent told her yesterday after giving the death notification to Scott Adams's mom. Some kids just don't have a chance.

She updates Mooney, then leads Levi to her car.

"You got a boyfriend?" Levi asks, before they're even out of the parking lot.

"I'm not going to discuss that with you," she says.

"A hot chick like you, you must, right? How old are you?"

"That's none of your business," she says.

"I'll be eighteen pretty soon. You're what, forty?"

She's thirty-one. "How about we remain quiet until we get there."

"How about we go out afterwards, huh? Grab a couple of drinks?"

"I don't think so, Levi."

"Why? You're a lesbian?"

"No. Because it would be inappropriate. Because you're a small boy trying to act all grown-up. Because you have a big mouth. Because I simply don't want to. I could give you a hundred reasons. A thousand."

"So you are a lesbian," he says.

"Let's kill the chitchat, Levi. I don't want you tiring that brain of yours out before we get there. And I don't want to have to pull over and shoot you."

FIFTY-FOUR

— ◆ —

Joshua pauses and listens for signs of life. He should have knocked first, then fabricated a story as to why he was here if somebody answered, but it's too late now. He just has to hope the house is empty and, after a few moments, he's satisfied that it is. His heart is still racing. He figures if he doesn't get out of here soon it might even explode.

He takes the bandage off his left hand, and wraps it around his right hand and fingers, but not so tight he can't flex them. Now it's like he's wearing a glove, which means he can touch things and not leave fingerprints behind. There's still padding on his left hand, but, with the bandage no longer holding it in place, he peels it away and folds it into his pocket. The graze on his left hand is exposed, and starts to sting. It looks shiny and raw and gross. As soon as he's out of here he'll bandage it back up.

The kitchen is to the left. All the appliances are modern, and the kitchen itself is spacious. Everything is so tidy he's wondering if anybody even lives here. He checks the walk-in pantry and sees it's stocked with food, as is the fridge. The only thing out of place are the two bags of dog food on the table. In the lounge there's no TV, which he thinks is strange. The bookcase has a few books he's listened to in the past, and a whole bunch more he wants to read. There's a really cool movie poster on the wall that has a giant monster striding through a city knocking aside buildings. It has to be fifty years old at least. There are some handmade wooden toys on some shelves against the wall, the kinds of things he'd never be able to make not even after twenty years of taking woodshop. The carpets are soft and the furniture looks comfortable and none of this is what he was expecting. He was expecting the place to smell like old pizza. He was expecting dirty dishes stacked in and around the sink and flies buzzing through the rooms and T-shirts hanging over the backs of chairs and beer bottles on the coffee table. He goes down the hallway and opens the wardrobe door in the master bedroom. All the clothes have been ironed and the shoes on the floor have been cleaned. The bed has been made and there are no crumbs anywhere, no empty cans on the nightstand. The room is so clean it doesn't make sense anybody could sleep in here and dream the kind of evil dreams Vincent Archer was having.

In the office he sits down in front of the computer. It's already running. He nudges the mouse and the screen comes to life. His experience with computers is still limited, but his skills have increased over the weeks. He flicks through a bunch of photographs, recognizing Vincent Archer and Simon Bower, but not recognizing any of the other people he sees in them. Every time he sees Simon Bower, he wants to scream. This is the man who killed his father, and there's no outlet for his anger over that. He forces himself to keep looking. Whatever needs to happen to draw a connection between these faces and his dreams isn't happening. He thinks about what Olillia said earlier, that he's recognizing people his dad saw not long before he died. If that's true, then other than Vincent and Simon, his dad didn't see any of the other people in these photos the day he died. Perhaps not ever.

He looks at his watch. He's already been here ten minutes.

He goes into the adjacent room. This is the room he was told about. It's so vastly different from the rest of the house. Photographs and newspaper clippings line the walls. Some faces look totally unfamiliar, but there are those he recognizes. There's a photograph of Dr. Toni in the parking lot of the hospital. There's an article next to it about the work she's been doing with eye transplant technology. There's a picture of his mother, and it sends a shiver through him. She's in the parking lot of the veterinary clinic, stepping out of her car . . . and here's another one, this time of her checking the mailbox at home. There are photographs of Detective Vega, of himself, there are more photos of Erin, of his grandparents. There are some of Uncle Ben, including a large one in the middle of it all that is made up from four separate printouts.

There is so much wrong here. This guy, Vincent Archer, how could he have been a part of society for so long? What mask was he able to wear to hide his obsession? The answer is simple: the same mask he wore when he was in the other rooms of this house. Joshua doesn't want to be in the house anymore, and he doesn't want to leave the photographs of himself—or his mother—behind. They're like a contagion, spreading the sickness that plagued Vincent Archer.

His eyes stop on an article on Ruby Carter. He knows the name because his father was working on the case. He remembers they never found any trace of her or her bike. She went into the forest and never came out. He uses his phone to take a photograph of the article, then sends it to Olillia. A minute later he calls her.

"Hey," she says.

"Hey. How you getting on?"

"Almost done here," she says.

"I recognize somebody," he says.

"The woman in the article you texted me?"

"Yeah. There's this room in here, it's crazy. It's full of photographs and articles. This guy was planning on hurting a lot of people."

"You think he hurt her?"

"That's exactly what I think."

"So . . . why would you—hang on a second."

The phone is muffled, and he can hear her talking. There's a man's voice responding, a small laugh, then Olillia laughs to, and he hears her thank him, and a moment later he hears a car door close.

"I'm back," she says. "What was I saying? Oh yeah, I was going to ask how you would recognize her. You think your dad knew her?"

"It was his case."

"So he would have seen heaps of photographs of her."

"That's true. Except . . ."

"Except what?"

"Except I'm sure she's the woman from the dream I had after the operation. It's like . . . it's like I can picture her in the forest with her bike. I can picture Vincent there too, and their fishing rods. But how could I picture something like that with my dad's eyes if he wasn't there?"

It takes her a few seconds to respond, and he knows what she's going to say, and then she says it. "Maybe . . . maybe your dad was there."

"Then that would mean he was part of what happened."

"There'll be an explanation that makes sense," she says. "But if you dreamed about what happened to her, then it means you can see things further back than the morning your dad died."

"That's true," he says.

"I better move the car," she says, "before the policeman gets suspicious. Your father, was he a good detective?"

"Yes."

"And you have his eyes now," she says. "So why don't you use them the same way he would have? To detect?"

They hang up. He takes photographs of the room, then in the office he sits back in front of the computer and takes photographs of the photographs on the screen. He thinks about what Olillia said to him, about using his eyes the same way his dad would have used them, and there is something here that's bugging him. He goes into the bedroom and opens the wardrobe and looks at the clothes. He doesn't see what he's looking for. He takes pictures of the room, then returns to the lounge and looks at the couch and the chairs. Again he doesn't see what he's looking for. There's a door with internal access to the garage. The room smells like paint. There are tools everywhere of different designs, hand tools, power tools, things to shape and sculpt and build. There's a birdhouse on a shelf, a wine rack half-complete, a coffee table on its end with clamps holding it together, even a stool like the ones they're all making in woodshop. There's a toy car carved out of wood, some spheres the size of soccer balls that might be part of a larger project or just spheres, there's a small windmill that looks ready to be nailed to the roof of the garage. He has the urge to run his fingers over the tools. He doesn't know what they're called, but he knows what they do. He hated woodshop yesterday, and he thought earlier that even with twenty years under his belt he still wouldn't be able to make a single thing, but all of that has changed. Looking at everything, the materials, the tools, he wants to start making things. He *really* wants to start making things.

He goes into the hallway. He opens the closet and pulls out the vacuum cleaner. It's a bagless one, the kind with all the dust and dirt sitting in a central cylinder. Since being back at home, his mom has given him a list of chores he can do, and vacuuming is one of them. He pops open the cylinder and uses his finger to search for what he suspects he won't find, and he doesn't find it, and now he knows for sure. He puts the vacuum cleaner back and goes to the dining room where the two bags of dog food are still on the table.

No dog. No fur on the couches. No fur on Vincent Archer's clothes. No dog kennel anywhere and no fur in the vacuum cleaner and no dogs in any of the photographs. Not even a dog bowl.

Question—why dog food and no dog?

Before he can come up with any answers, the front door opens.

FIFTY-FIVE

Joshua knew this was a mistake. He knew he would get caught.

You're not caught yet.

Footsteps in the hall. He has a couple of seconds to hide.

Where?

The pantry. There's room enough for him. He gets inside and surely whoever is out there is going to hear his breathing. He can hear voices. One of them belongs to Detective Vega. The other he doesn't recognize. They don't come into the kitchen. He considers stepping back out of the pantry and telling Vega he's here. What's the worst that could happen? Well, aside from being grounded, it could lead to the man who helped him being arrested, even if that man is a good man. More important, it could lead to Olillia getting into trouble too.

He takes his phone out of his pocket and puts it on mute.

Vega and her companion move deeper into the house.

He texts Olillia.

Vega is here! In the house!

What? Has she seen you?

No. I'm hiding in the pantry. She's here with somebody.

Stay where you are. There's no reason for her to check the pantry, right?

What if more people are on their way?

Stay calm. Hopefully she'll leave soon.

He can smell tea bags and cornflakes. The bottom shelf is digging into his calves. He can hear voices from the other side of the house, but he can't make out the words. He opens the door. The voices become a little clearer. People have always thought that because he was blind, he would have superhuman hearing—but his hearing, and that of all his friends, wasn't any better than anybody's who could see. His phone vibrates. He closes the pantry door.

We're going to have to think of a way to get you out when she's gone. The cop outside will see you if you go out the front.

He realizes that was always going to be the case. *Any ideas?*

Go out the back when you get a chance. Either that, or stay in the pantry until they get bored with the house.

Don't want to let down another tire and drive past?

LOL.

His phone vibrates again. It's his mom. *Where are you?*

At the library. We'll be a few more hours. Where are you? Hopefully she won't say she's at the library too.

On my way home. Call me when you want me to come and get you.

Okay. How'd it go?

Should I call?

I think the librarian will tell me off if you do.

It takes a minute for her response. *Principal Mooney is thinking about it. Detective Vega was there earlier and put in a good word for you. He said she reminded him how none of this is your fault. I think it'll be okay.*

That's good. I'll call you in a few hours.

In that case, I'll go to the hospital and see Ben and Erin. Ben is awake today. Apparently he can't remember anything that happened yesterday. I'll come get you when you're ready. Be careful.

I will.

He doesn't like lying to his mother and also doesn't like how easy it is. The good word Detective Vega put in for him with his school will disappear if she finds him here. He definitely can't go out there now and tell her that he's here. He texts the photographs he's been taking to Olillia. He's sending the last one when the voices get louder. Now he can hear footsteps too. He opens the door a crack so he can hear what they're saying.

". . . drive you to the station," Vega says.

"What? Why can't you?" the person with her asks.

"Because I'm busy."

"I didn't have to help, you know. I could have said nothing."

"But you chose to help, which proves what a nice person you are," she says.

"Nice enough for that drink, then?"

"Not that nice," she says. "The officer will drive you to the station and once you've given the sketch artist a composite of the man you saw, you'll be driven back to school."

Man you saw? Did somebody see who killed Vincent Archer?

"And then what?"

"And then nothing," she says. "Unless you have more information to offer."

The front door opens. They walk outside. The conversation fades. He creeps out of the pantry and peers into the hall. The door is still open. He can see Vega and somebody from his school walking towards the parked car with the officer inside it.

He calls Olillia.

"They're outside," he says, "but Vega is coming back."

"Can you go out the back?"

"That's the plan. Then what?"

"Then you climb the fence directly behind the house."

"What?"

"I'm parked outside the house behind you. I don't think there's anybody home. It's your only option."

He heads down the hallway to the back door. There's a sliding lock. Once the door is shut behind him, he won't be able to slide that lock back into place. But he has no choice. He gets outside and closes the door. He runs for the back fence. The garden has been barked, and there are flax bushes and ferns that run the length of it. The fence looks like it's been recently painted. The planks are nailed in a way that means the beams are exposed on this side. It makes it easy to climb. On the other side is a house similar to the one he's just left. He drops into the yard, landing in a vegetable garden. He picks his way through it. From the edge of the garden he can see into one of the bedrooms, where a woman is standing with her back to him. She has a baby over her shoulder. The baby stares at him, and points, but the woman doesn't turn around. He moves to the corner of the house. The street is out there, and the only thing between him and it is a gate and the front yard.

He goes for the gate, staying low.

It's locked.

He reaches up, puts a foot on the beam, and pulls himself over. He runs across the front yard to the sidewalk where Olillia is waiting like a getaway driver with the door open.

FIFTY-SIX
— ◆ —

Vega sees Levi off in the car with the police officer, who has agreed to take him off her hands. She's glad to be rid of him. He had looked at the photographs on the computer, and those on the walls, and wasn't able to identify anybody in them. Still, it was worth a shot. She wishes she could take that shot with Joshua too. There's still a chance Levi can work with the sketch artist and come up with something useful.

She goes back into the house. She's thinking about Tracey, and the fact she still hasn't called her, and that's because she still hasn't decided what she's going to do. Ask her? Not ask her? Tracey might be completely unaware, and all Vega would be doing is implicating her before any evidence has hinted at her involvement—a really bad thing for a cop to do, she thinks. She'll give her a call now. She'll tell her everything is okay, and then ask her if she's heard any rumors in the medical examiners' office about organs being illegally harvested and see where the conversation goes, and hope Tracey doesn't think she's accusing her of anything. She gets her phone out and is at the threshold of the Room of Obsession when she notices it—the sliding lock on the back door is in the open position.

It was closed earlier. Wasn't it?

She puts her phone away and removes her gun from her holster and points it at the ground. She twists the handle on the back door. It opens. She steps outside. The back garden is as tidy as the front. Archer certainly looked after the place. She walks along the fence line, and there, right in the middle, are scuffmarks on the fence. The ferns next to it have some broken fronds. She climbs the fence the same way she suspects somebody else climbed it. There's a blond woman looking at her from a bedroom. She frowns at Vega and opens the window. In the far distance the sky is turning black. There's a storm coming.

"Can I help you?" the woman says, looking nervous.

Vega holds up her badge. "Has anybody come through here recently?"

"No. Like who? When?"

Vega looks down into the garden. She can see heavy footprints in the dirt and a few flattened vegetables. "Recently," she says.

"Wait there," the woman says.

Vega puts her gun into the holster. She stays up on the fence. The woman comes outside and approaches her. "You think somebody came through my yard?"

"Yes."

"Who?"

"I'm not sure," she says, but she has an idea. It's the Good Samaritan. Only . . . why would he? "Have you been home all day?"

"Yes," the woman says. Then she frowns a little. "A few minutes ago Sandy started pointing out the window."

"Sandy?"

"My daughter."

"Can I speak to her?"

"She's thirteen months old." The woman looks into her garden. "My vegetables," she says. "Some of them are ruined."

"Is there anybody else home who might have seen anything?"

"No," she says.

Vega hands the woman her card. Whoever climbed the fence is long gone. "Call me if you notice anything," she says.

"Will do."

The woman slowly makes her way back to her house, shaking her head as she eyes her garden. Vega lowers herself down. She is at the back door when the woman calls out over the fence. "Are you still there?"

Vega climbs it again.

"This isn't mine," the woman says, holding up a cell phone. "It was lying on the ground by the gate."

Vega wants to tell her she shouldn't have picked it up and gotten her fingerprints all over it, but it's too late now. She reaches into her pocket, grabs a latex glove, and pulls it on. The woman reaches up and hands her the phone. It looks brand new. She thanks the neighbor, then goes back inside. She switches the phone on. It takes only a few seconds to see who it belongs to: Joshua Logan. What the hell was he doing here? She reads the messages. He was hiding in the pantry while texting his friend Olillia. He sent her photographs he took in the house. At one point his mom texted him and he lied to her. He must have come here to try to figure out if he recognized anybody. He was trying to help without his mom knowing, but he couldn't have done it in a more stupid way. She isn't sure how hard to come down on him. She drops the phone into an evidence bag and tucks it into her pocket and makes her way to the front door. She's going to find him and ask him exactly what it is he thinks he's up to.

She is walking past the office when she is pushed hard up against the wall, and a moment later is thrown facedown onto the floor. The carpet absorbs some of the impact, but it still has her head buzzing. She can't stop her gun being taken out of her holster. Can't do anything but roll over and stare down the barrel as it's pointed back at her.

FIFTY-SEVEN

For the next few blocks, all Joshua can do is stare out the window looking for cops. He's too winded to talk. He's so nervous, he's trying to recall if he's ever heard of incidents in which sixteen-year-olds have had heart attacks. When he gets his breathing under control, he tells Olillia about what he saw in Vincent Archer's house. He tells her it defied all his expectations, that he was expecting the rooms to be blacked out, that there would be a pit under the house where Vincent kept his victims, that the fridge would be full of fried fingers and hearts. He tells her how normal it was, and in a way that made it more frightening—how can you find monsters when they can live like anybody? Then he tells her about the one room that was different, with all the photographs pinned to the walls, how it made his skin feel cold seeing the pictures of his mom up there. He tells her about the dog food and no sign of a dog. He takes the bandage off his good hand but doesn't reapply it to his bad hand, because he doesn't want it to stick to the wound, and he doesn't want to reapply the padding he took off earlier. He tells her more of the dream he had of Vincent and the missing girl. By the time he's done she's been driving for ten minutes and he doesn't even know where they're heading.

"It has to all be connected somehow," he says. "I just can't place it." He pauses and looks out the window. "Where are we going?"

"I'm not sure," she says. "I figured we'd drive back towards the library. Is that okay?"

"I have another idea," he says. "My dad used to bring work home with him, his personal case files and notes. Mum hasn't touched his office yet, so they might still be there."

"You want to go and look?"

"There's nobody home. Mom's visiting Uncle Ben at the hospital."

"Let me ask you something," she says. "Are we looking for the guy who saved you yesterday, or are we trying to figure out what happened to Ruby Carter?"

"I think both."

Joshua doesn't know the way home by sight, so he gives Olillia his address, which she types into her phone. When they arrive he gets them a couple of drinks and he thinks about how his dad renovated this kitchen a few years ago, and how Vincent Archer's kitchen looked renovated too. He grabs the first-aid box from the bathroom and applies some fresh padding to the back of his hand, and Olillia wraps the bandaging back around it. They head to his dad's office, where they pause outside the door. It's the one room he's never seen. He was in here often in what he's now starting to think of as his old life—the life when he was blind but at least nobody wanted him dead. Since coming home after losing his dad, he hasn't been able to cross its threshold.

"Are you okay?" Olillia says.

"I'm fine," he says, and he opens the door.

The room is tidy. It's on the south side of the house, so it's cooler in here, never getting any sun. He puts his drink down on the desk and rubs at his arms to try to help with the chill. There are photographs on the walls of him, and his mom, there are photographs of them together with his dad. The desk is the shape of an L, and sits with the length of it under the window and the side against the wall. It faces into the backyard. There's a jade plant on the corner of it, and golfing trophies sitting on top of the filing cabinet to the side. His dad tried to sneak away for a few hours every weekend to play. Joshua went with him a couple of times. He enjoyed the walk, and his dad would ask him to keep count even though he knew his dad was keeping count anyway, and sometimes he'd joke and ask Joshua if he'd seen where that shot went, and Joshua would always say it went so far he lost sight of it.

There's a cardboard box with Ruby Carter's name on it on the floor next to the filing cabinet. There's a couch on the wall opposite the window and desk, and sometimes he'd sit in here with his dad when his dad was working, as long as he stayed quiet, though sometimes his dad would talk to him about what it was like being a cop. His dad once told him the best thing a detective could do was stay in tune with his surroundings. "It's not just sight, buddy," his dad said once. "It's all the senses, and even then sometimes it's a sixth sense. That's why I think you'd make a great detective, if you wanted to be." His dad used to tell him he could be anything he wanted to be if he put his heart and soul into it. He never used to believe him, and of course his dad must have known it couldn't possibly be true.

"Are you sure you're okay?" Olillia asks.

He stares out the window. "I haven't been in here since Dad died," he says.

She moves beside him and puts a hand on his shoulder.

"It's crazy," he says, "but I still expect him to come home."

"That's not crazy," she says.

"We should probably get started," he says, "in case Mom comes back early."

He picks up the cardboard box and sits it on the desk. He removes the lid. On top is a map that covers the area where Ruby disappeared. He unfolds it and it becomes larger than the desk, so they lay it out on the floor. It covers ten square miles, most of it forest and farmland. It's north but mostly west of the city by about forty-five minutes, so his dad had said. The forest is parallel with a stretch of the Waimakariri River, a river that runs a little short of a hundred miles, starting from the heart of Te Waipounamu, the South Island, and ending in the beaches just north of Christchurch.

"Dad told me a little about the case," he says. "And about Ruby."

"I remember a month after she went missing it was her birthday," Olillia says. "It was in the news how her friends and family still held a party for her. They wanted to celebrate her life, but I bet without any kind of closure it would have felt so sad."

"I remember it," he says. "My dad went along. He was nervous about it, because he thought he'd be a target for their grief since she hadn't been found, but he said they were all welcoming and they shared stories with him of what she was like. He said it was sad, like you said, but there was laughter too. He thought some of them had accepted she was dead and had found closure, but others still had hope she had gotten lost but was managing to stay alive out there. I remember how hard he hugged me when he came home, and how he locked himself in his office all weekend working the case."

He pulls out an eight-by-ten glossy photograph of Ruby from the box. In it she's wearing a jumpsuit and standing in front of a small plane. She's smiling at the camera and has her hand outwards, her fingers forming a V.

"She was a skydiving instructor," he says. "Dad said she was a real adrenaline seeker. Whenever she had enough money, she'd travel to some faraway country and jump out of a plane or BASE jump off a cliff."

He sits the photograph on the desk so they can both take a good look at it. He wonders how long it was taken before she died. "It's why she was single—she never wanted any long-term commitments, and she figured doing what she did, she might not be around long enough for one anyway. Her mom told Dad every time Ruby went away she'd expect a phone call from somebody they didn't know saying there'd been an accident."

"Did your dad have any theories as to what happened to her?"

"There was never proof one way or the other whether she got lost, or if there was an accident, or somebody killed her. There's a lot of forest out there. He said they searched and scoured, and that if she'd been out there they would have found her. But if she'd been biking along the river and fallen in," he says, looking at the map, "it's possible both she and her bike were swept downstream. Nobody reported her missing for a day. He said her body could have floated a hundred miles, or she might have been swept under and snagged on some rocks. He said she might have floated downstream and managed to pull herself out only to get lost in a whole new part of the forest. It was impossible to prove foul play, and impossible to rule it out."

Olillia points to an X partway into the center of the map, around five miles from the river and a few miles from the motorway. The X is in his dad's handwriting. "What's that?" she asks.

"It's the inroad into the forest. It dead-ends a mile in," he says. "Dad said visitors can park their cars there. It's where her car was found. This map must be the range she would have biked," he says. "But she would have stayed in the woods, or along the riverbank, and wouldn't have gone into any of the farms."

"So there would have been other people out there on the day," Olillia says. "Maybe one of them saw something?"

"People saw her in the parking lot when she had first arrived, but that was it. Dad said she would go off track because they were too easy. He said she was somebody who always pushed themselves, and that pushing had turned her into an exceptional athlete. Supposedly she went out there at least once a week and would ride for three or four hours or more. She'd cover a thirty-mile loop—which I guess is the range of this map. That's why it was so bizarre she disappeared. She knew this forest well."

Olillia smiles at him.

"What?"

"I said before to use your dad's eyes because he was a detective. Now I bet you're sounding like him too."

He smiles. He likes that she said that. It makes him feel closer to his dad.

She pulls her phone out of her pocket. She swipes through the photographs he sent her earlier. "You said in your dream Vincent and Simon had fishing rods, right?" Then she stops on one of the photographs. "Look at this," she says, and zooms in on the image.

It's the picture that was hanging on the wall in Vincent's bedroom. It's Simon and Vincent by the riverbank, each of them holding up a fish, and again seeing a picture of Simon Bower makes him feel ill. There are beer cans on the ground and fishing rods lying next to them. Vincent has his foot up on a cooler, displaying a heroic pose. The photograph is taken from a lower angle, suggesting the camera is resting near ground level.

"Are you okay?" she asks.

"Yeah, yeah, I'm fine."

"It must be tough seeing him," she says, "the man that killed your dad."

He doesn't say anything.

"They must have been out there fishing," she says, "and she ran into them, maybe somewhere between the river and the parking lot."

"Look at the cooler," he says.

"What about it?"

"My granddad used to go fishing. He and his friends would go out there with a cooler full of beer and ice, and return with one full of fish and ice. See those beer cans on the ground? They probably did the same thing. Granddad loved his fishing, but he never would have lugged a heavy cooler through five miles of trees to get there. They'd have found somewhere more accessible so they could drive."

"So they parked somewhere else. Somewhere closer."

"Only there is nowhere else," he says. "There are no other roads."

"Not main roads," she says, "but places like this are normally full of tracks."

"How can we tell?"

"Let's use your dad's computer."

They switch it on. Olillia sits in the chair while he stands next to her. She goes online and finds a satellite map. She finds the parking lot. She zooms in. He can see two cars there. The images are clear enough to tell what color they are, but that's about all.

"That's now?" he asks.

"No. It could be a few months old, or older, I don't know. But they update it all the time."

"That's amazing," he says.

They spend ten minutes slowly scrolling left and right, up and down, studying the forestry. The mountain bike and horse tracks are covered by the tops of the trees, though sometimes they can glimpse them. What becomes apparent is there are no tracks wide enough for a car.

"She could have biked farther," Olillia says. "Maybe these guys were miles outside of the search zone. Can you remember anything else from the dream?"

"No."

"You're sure?"

"The dog," Joshua says.

"You remember a dog?"

"No, but Vincent must own a dog, right? But as I said, there was no dog at the house."

"Maybe the dog belonged to Simon Bower, and that's where it was kept."

"Or it's kept somewhere else, like a cabin."

"You think they have a cabin they visit when they go fishing?"

"It's possible," he says. "They drive there directly, hang out and fish, maybe spend weekends and holidays there. They keep a dog there and leave enough food out for it when they're not there."

"So they leave their dog there all alone? That's cruel."

"They're cruel men," he says.

"There are no cabins in the search zone, and anyway, wouldn't your dad already have considered the cabin theory?"

"I'll check his notes."

He digs his hands into the cardboard box and pulls out more files. Olillia keeps searching the map. She zooms out. There are farmhouses across the motorway, but they both agree they seem unlikely candidates because his dad would have checked them out. Plus, there's still the issue of there being a track to get to the river. Olillia scrolls beyond the range of the circle. She goes farther west, away from the city. The river continues in a straight line to the west for several miles before angling to the north. There are no cabins. No buildings. No track. Just a whole lot of trees. She brings the map back to where they started, then goes east, towards the city. Five miles outside the search range is a building. It's the first of three in the woods, each spaced half a mile apart, each overlooking the river. It's impossible to tell if they're cabins or houses from above, but Joshua figures there isn't much of a difference. There is an access road from the motorway that enters the forest, then branches out in three directions, one left, one right, one straight ahead, one for each of the cabins.

"Zoom in on that one," he says, and points to the westernmost one of the three. She zooms in. "There," he says, pointing at something next to it, a blue rectangular shape. The dream is coming back to him now, it's light on details, but there is one thing he's starting to remember.

"What is that?" she asks.

"I think it's a boat parked up on a trailer."

"You can see that?"

He shakes his head. "I can remember it."

"You remember it?"

"From the dream," he says. "Ruby Carter didn't bike any farther than normal. She had fallen off her bike and had come to them for help. They didn't help her. They put her in the boat and they hurt her."

"Are you sure?" she asks.

"Yes."

"How can you know this?" she asks. "How can you have seen something that your dad didn't see?"

He doesn't know.

"This guy who saved you, you think he might be at this cabin?" she asks.

"I don't know," he says.

"Should we go out there?" she asks.

"We should call Detective Vega. If they killed Ruby there, then we're going to be contaminating a crime scene. Only I don't have her number. Though Mom will have it."

"I have her card," Olillia says. "If we call her, it means we have to confess to everything we've been doing."

He nods. "Let's call her," he says. "And hope what we tell her will make her let everything we've done slide."

FIFTY-EIGHT
— ◆ —

It's the second time in her life that Detective Vega has been inside the trunk of a car. The first was when she was seven years old, well before her detecting years, and her foster brother thought it would be funny if they hid in the trunk of their babysitter's car. She climbed in first, and then instead of him climbing in, he closed it shut, and told her it was a game and she had to be quiet. Which she was, for a while, but then she got scared so she asked him to let her out. He wouldn't, because he wasn't there. She screamed and cried and nobody could hear her. Her foster brother had gone inside intending to leave her in the trunk for a few minutes, but he had fallen asleep. Instead of keeping a close eye on them, their babysitter had been keeping a close eye on the TV and the pizza that had been left in the fridge. Vega spent two hours in that trunk in which she cried and wet herself and thumped against the roof. On occasion she still dreams about it, and, a few weeks ago, she accidently threw an arm out in her sleep, dreaming she was hitting through the roof of the trunk, only she was hitting Tracey in the face.

And now that dream . . . it's happening again.

The back half of the car is parked inside Vincent Archer's garage, the other half of the garage is full of Vincent's projects. The man, who she assumes is the Good Samaritan, drove it in so nobody could see her being put inside. It could be his car, or one he stole. After the initial attack, the guy has been nothing but polite—well, other than the fact that he's handcuffed her and hog-tied her with duct tape. He did that so she would wait patiently while he went and retrieved his car.

Her wrists hurt bad, and the angle of her shoulders from having her hands behind her is pinching off her circulation and making her arms go numb. She is scared. As scared as she has ever been. Her optimism is burning bright—if anybody can get out of this, she can—but her pessimism is burning bright too; she has seen what happens to people when they've been stuffed into the trunk of a car. She tries to focus on all those hours she's put in at the gym. All that strength training. She just has to break the duct tape, snap the handcuffs, and she's free. Failing that . . . once they're on the road she can kick at the roof of the trunk and the side of the car and hopefully, unlike twenty-four years ago, somebody will hear her.

It's a good plan.

Somebody will hear her.

Somebody will call the police.

Somebody will save her.

The Good Samaritan is looking down over her. He's still wearing his sunglasses. He has a big grandfather smile and dark hair that's thinning in the middle and graying on the sides. There's a light dusting of freckles on his cheeks and a small cleft in his chin. He has nice straight teeth and is dressed well and looks like the kind of guy who might sell you insurance. He looks as though he keeps himself in good shape. Maybe he goes to the gym. Maybe even the same gym she goes to.

"We're going to go for a little drive," he says, smiling at her, and she wants to break his teeth. He takes his sunglasses off, revealing a set of blue eyes she wants to poke with her fingers. He has dark bags beneath his eyes that she wants to tear at. "It should be quite pleasant, yes, quite pleasant, and I won't drive too fast or take any corners too quickly so you should be okay back here. Are you comfortable?"

She shakes her head. No. She's not comfortable.

"Oh, well now, that is a shame. Perhaps I can find you something," he says, and he walks away from the car and goes inside. She tries to get up but isn't able to. He returns with a pillow. "I don't imagine you *really* want your face in the same pillow that Vincent Archer used, and I'm terribly sorry to do this, but I believe it will be better this way." He leans in and props the pillow under her head. He's right—the idea of using the same pillow Vincent Archer used makes her stomach curdle. But she can't deny it's a hell of a lot more comfortable.

"There, that looks much better," he says.

He's crazy, she thinks. *Full-blown mental.* A guy this unstable could as easily decide to cut off her ears and eat them as he would kill her.

"Whatcha thinking?" he asks, then reaches into the trunk and taps her on the forehead. "Want to share what's inside that neatly packaged brain of yours?"

She nods. He's about to take the duct tape off her mouth when her phone rings. He reaches into her pocket. "Who's Olillia?" he asks.

Even if she could answer, she wouldn't. Olillia's name has come up on the display because during an investigation Vega programs the names and numbers of everybody she's spoken to into her phone for immediate access.

"Silly me," he says. He peels the duct tape away from her mouth.

"Don't do this," she says.

"Please tell me who Olillia is. Do I need to worry about her?"

"A witness from an old case," she says. "She doesn't even live in Christchurch."

"Are you sure? You have a believable face but sometimes people with believable faces can say the most unbelievable things."

"It's the truth," she says.

"Okay," he says. "I had to ask though, so please, forgive me for that. And don't hate me for this either," he says, and he puts the phone on the ground and stomps on it, then stomps on it again. He picks it back up and works at it until he's able to break it in half. He tosses the pieces into the trunk. She can't call for help, but it also means he can't go through her contact list and start building a room of obsession of his own.

"You need to let me go," she says.

"Listen, I know you don't know me, but I'm a reasonable man. I can understand why you'd be scared, and I understand how unfair this is for you. You must be feeling quite put out by it all, and I don't blame you. I think you'd do well to accept early on that when it comes to me letting you go, that isn't going to happen." He puts the duct tape back over her mouth. He strokes the back of her head, the same way somebody would pat a cat. "The thing is, I've been having these really weird dreams, and they come with some rather strange impulses." He smiles at her. "I can explain more later, because it will be easier when I can show you. Now, I know you're thinking you can start banging against the trunk, bang bang banging," he says, his voice low and soft, almost hypnotic, and she wishes he would put the sunglasses back on because she doesn't want to see his eyes anymore. "But I'm going to have to insist you don't. I'm going to show you some respect and politely ask you not to make any sounds. Now, please, don't take this the wrong way—and this, of course, will only happen if you don't do what I ask—but I will kill you if you disobey me on this." He shakes his head, still patting hers. "I hate that I had to say that, and I don't like the way it made me sound . . . all nasty and evil, when that couldn't be further from the truth. To be clear, though, I will kill you if you try anything. I will also kill anybody who tries to help you. I know people can send mixed messages, that there can be breakdowns in communication, so why don't you nod if I've made myself clear."

She nods. He couldn't be any clearer.

"Good, that's really good. We're going to get along so famously!" He almost squeals when he claps his hands together. "We have to make one stop along the way, and this is when I'm going to need you to be a really good little girl and not make a peep. Nod if you understand."

She nods.

"You remember what I said would happen if you made a sound?"

She keeps nodding.

"Hmm . . ." he says, and tightens his mouth. "The more I think about it, the more I'm coming to understand this isn't the greatest idea. I hate to do this, I really do, and I must apologize in advance here, but the thing is I don't really know I *can* believe you." He reaches in and gently removes the pillow. "You can have it back in a moment," he says. "I'm awfully sorry, but I'll try to make this quick."

He grabs her head and bangs it as hard as he can into the bottom of the trunk. It's an instant headache, and she can't see straight, and her ear takes the impact and is squashed. She can hear a ringing sound.

"I so wish you weren't making me do this," he says.

He bangs her head a second time.

Nobody is going to hear her.

Nobody is going to call the police.

Nobody is going to save her.

He bangs her head a third time, and she passes out without the need for a fourth.

FIFTY-NINE

—— ◆ ——

The call goes to voicemail. Olillia doesn't leave a message.

Joshua continues sifting through the files. "Dad did look into the cabins," he says, finding the information. "Two are summer homes rented out to people on holidays. Of those two, one was empty, and the other had French tourists who hired the place out for a week. Dad and Uncle Ben interviewed them and they were able to look around."

"Guess they didn't find anything," Olillia says.

"The two cabins were . . . Oh geez, look at this!" He turns the paperwork towards Olillia so she can read it too. "Look who owns the third cabin."

"Robert and Helen Archer," she says, reading off the notes. "You think they're Vincent's parents?"

"Probably," he says. "It says here they used it as a holiday house, but hadn't been out there in years."

"Did the police search it?"

"There's no record of it," he says. "I guess they didn't feel there was any reason to. It was outside the range they were searching, and nothing suggested Robert or Helen Archer were involved."

"Wouldn't your uncle have made the connection when he learned of Vincent Archer?"

"He might have," he says, and then remembers what his mom texted him earlier. If his uncle had made the connection before Joshua stabbed him in the throat, then for now that connection has been forgotten.

"Let me try Detective Vega again," Olillia says.

"I'll check the drawers, in case there's something more current," he says.

While Olillia makes another phone call, he opens the desk drawers. The top one is full of stationery, as well as USB sticks and the family passports and receipts and blister packs with vitamin C tablets. He opens the second drawer. The only thing in here is a folder. He pulls it out and opens it. It's full of newspaper clippings and has a list of names written on the inside cover.

"Still no answer," Olillia says. She doesn't leave a message. "What have you got there?"

"I'm not sure," he says. He hands her some of the clippings and he looks over the others. They're all of people who have been killed over the last two years. Six in total. Three shot dead by the police—one a guy strung out on drugs waving a gun in a street, one a woman with a machete threatening to kill her daughter, the third a father who pulled a gun on the police after they went to speak to him about the bruises and broken bones his children were showing up at the hospital with. There's a serial killer who killed himself when Uncle Ben and his dad were closing in on his house, there's a guy who fell through the roof of a Salvation Army shop he was robbing who was in a coma for two weeks before life support was turned off, and there's a guy who abducted a small girl and, after being caught and hand-cuffed by Uncle Ben, tried to run away but ran into traffic and was killed by a car.

Why would his dad have these?

"So who are the names on the other list?" she asks, because the names in the articles don't match the names on the list on the inside cover.

"I don't know. Victims of those people maybe?"

"Let's find out."

She types the names into the computer one at a time. There are fourteen of them. Some she finds no information on. A couple were featured in news stories, plenty have personal pages on social media websites. It doesn't take long to figure out what they all have in common—each of them was sick, and now each of them is okay—their lives saved by organ transplants.

Olillia turns away from the computer and faces him. "When you look at the dates these criminals died, and the dates these other people were helped, it looks like they were all organ donors who, in death, were able to help others. That's admirable," she says. When he doesn't answer, she looks concerned. "Are you okay?"

"I need to sit down," he says, but before he makes it to the couch his legs give way and he ends up sitting on the floor in front of it. He turns himself so he can lean against it and looks up at her.

"What is it?" she asks. "You look awful."

He's thinking about his conversation with Dr. Toni. She knew his dad, but she said she didn't see him much, only when he was in the hospital. What did she say? *Sometimes criminals get injured and he'd be in here.* She said she had known his dad a long time. The morning he woke up after the operation there was a nurse. He asked where Dr. Toni was, and the nurse said she was performing the same kind of operation she had on Joshua, but with another patient. Somebody else was getting a new set of eyes. That means somebody else had to have died that day.

And somebody had, hadn't he? The man who killed his dad.

What did Uncle Ben say when Joshua came into the hospital that morning?

He got what he deserved, okay? After that he said, *I've made sure he's being put to good use. Do you understand what I'm saying?*

Back then, Joshua didn't know.

Now he does.

Uncle Ben killed Simon Bower out of anger, but also to serve a purpose. And now that he's made the connection, he can see it. He can see Uncle Ben standing opposite him, pointing a gun at him before moving around behind him.

What do you weigh?

What?

*You look like you run. You look like you hit the gym a little too. What
about smoking? Are you a smoker?*

How can he remember this if his dad was already dead? Olillia is
sitting next to him now, one hand on his shoulder, holding his good
hand with the other. "You're shaking," she says.

The others in the articles, were there similar conversations with
them? Did the child abductor run out in front of a car, or was he pushed?
The serial killer, did he really shoot himself? The man in the hospital,
did he not wake up because the injuries were too severe, or did he not
wake up because somebody needed a heart?

He thinks about the book he was listening to when he was in
the hospital after the operation. Frederick the vampire who didn't
want to feed on people, but when he did he chose only those who
were bad. Was his dad doing a similar thing? Did his dad kill bad
people to help others? When he told his mom yesterday at the hospital about the curse, she told him it wasn't that, but a combination of good people trying bad things and bad people doing worse
things.

She knew what his dad was doing. She had to know.

On the scale of good people and bad, where do his parents fall?

"Joshua? Talk to me. What is it?"

"I'm okay," he tells her.

"You don't look okay."

"I'm fine," he says.

"Should I try Detective Vega again?"

"No," he says. "Let's go to the cabin."

"Are you sure?"

For the first time since leaving the library, she looks concerned. At
school, and on the train tracks, and all afternoon she's been incredibly
strong. Sure, she was devastated when he saw her behind the police
barrier yesterday from the ambulance, and she was obviously upset
when she wrote the note for him, but the one thing he's never seen in
her is any sense of fear. She's done so much for him in the twenty-four

hours he's known her, and he can't ask her to do any more. Not this. Not when he could be putting her in danger.

"No," he says. "Not so sure."

She smiles at him, and perhaps she can read his mind, because she says, "I'm not scared about going out there," she says. "Just concerned, but I want to go. I think that we need to, you know, be more careful than we've been. I've seen way too many horror movies where going to a cabin doesn't work out well for anybody, but Vincent Archer is dead, so is Simon, so to be scared of them hurting us is silly. I'm just scared of what we're going to see out there because some things you can never un-see," she says, and he thinks of Scott, the look on his face as his life drained away. "I don't want you to say you're not sure about going because you think that's what I want to hear. Do you want to go?"

"I think I need to. Dad was never able to figure out what happened to Ruby Carter, but I think we can. I want to do this, for him."

"Maybe we should leave it to fate. We'll try Detective Vega again, and if she doesn't answer, then we'll go."

He doesn't believe in fate. He just believes in curses. She tries calling Vega again, and it goes straight through to voicemail. When she hangs up, he tells her the other thing that's on his mind. The dreams— the fact that he can identify Ruby Carter in that moment she was abducted, the way he knew Vincent Archer . . . and that feeling that came over him in Vincent Archer's garage around all the power tools, the same kind of power tools that Simon Bower used, that compulsion to cut and build and create. "I know why I'm remembering things my dad never saw," he says.

"How?"

"The day I was given the operation, there was a second operation. Somebody else got another set of eyes. Simon Bower was an organ donor that day too, like the people in these newspaper articles."

"What are you saying?"

"I'm saying I think there was a mix-up."

"You think you got Simon Bower's eyes?"

"Did I tell you that only one of my eyes works?"

"No," she says.

"I think the one that works is the one that belongs to my dad," he says, "and I think the other one came from the man that killed him."

SIXTY

Joshua and Olillia put everything back where they found it, switch the computer off, finish their drinks, and then hit the road. He feels numb, learning what he has about his dad, and even though he knows why his dad did it, he'll still question it over the coming weeks as he tries to come to terms with it.

They're quiet as they drive. Joshua knows Olillia is thinking the same thing he's thinking. They're driving out to the cabin where Ruby died, and perhaps there'll be evidence of that. Perhaps there'll be blood. Perhaps there'll be nothing out there, or maybe they can find out what happened to Ruby. His mom said to him in the beginning of all this that by getting his father's eyes he would have to honor him by being the best man that he could be. He's going to honor his dad by giving closure to a grieving family.

The rest of it, finding the man who saved him, finding out if Dad and Uncle Ben really killed those people, that can wait. Perhaps it can always wait.

They drive through parts of town he hasn't seen before. They pass shopping malls and industrial warehouses. They enter suburbs where there are big homes and small churches and run-down homes and no churches. Before long, they're on the motorway driving west, where there is faster-moving traffic and less of it, then they turn onto the Old West Coast Road, which forks off to take them in a similar direction. Farther to the west, storm clouds are gathering over the mountain ranges, but that part of the country would take another two hours of driving to reach. This part is flat, it's mostly dominated by lines of trees and lines of fences bordering farms. There are fields of sheep, fields of cows, fields of animals he doesn't recognize because he's never seen them, but Olillia tells him some are deer, some are alpacas, and ostriches, and emus. The ostriches look so odd with their long necks and fat bodies they make him smile, but then that smile disappears when she tells him the ostriches get slaughtered and eaten like any other animal they're driving past. His mom's a vegetarian, but his dad never was, and nor is he, but right now he's thinking it might be time to reassess that. There isn't as much greenery as he would have thought. It was a hot summer, one that burned the ground out here in the Canterbury Plains, and that's obvious now. Most of the fields are wheat fields, empty now, as they were harvested during the summer, and now some of those fields are being prepared for the next crop. He sees tractors plowing through them, leaving huge clouds of dirt in their wake.

After a while the distance between the road and the Waimakariri River gets narrower; at times the only thing between them are rows of beech trees. There are moments during the drive when his breath is taken away by the beauty of it all. He's lived in New Zealand his entire life but has never seen it, and now he wants to see all of it. The mountains in the distance will soon have snow on them, the rivers and the lakes, the big, open skies, miles of isolation, it's no wonder people fly thousands of miles to come here.

Olillia's GPS tells them that the turnoff is coming up on the right. They've been driving for forty minutes. She takes the entrance and stops a minute later where the road branches off to the three different cabins.

"We should go in on foot," she says, "and we stay quiet."

"The cabin is still half a mile away," he says.

"Good point," she says.

They continue to drive. After a quarter of a mile they decide they've driven far enough. They carry on by foot. Before leaving Joshua's, they had decided it would be wise to bring some dog food with them in case it was hungry. There was some at the house, as there always is, for when his mom brings her work home with her. Joshua carries the dog food.

They can hear the river, and every now and then he can glimpse it between the trees. The river gets louder as the road angles towards it. They walk for five minutes. The cabin comes into view. He feels like he's been here. They move into the trees and stay hidden so they can study it.

"You recognize it?" she asks.

"Yes."

The cabin looks more modern than anything on the street where he lives. Bigger too. It's two stories with a balcony up top that looks out over the river. It's north facing, getting the sunlight, though that sunlight is going to be overtaken by the clouds fairly soon. Parked out front on a trailer is the boat. It has an outboard motor on the back, and the entire thing is covered by a blue tarpaulin, as they saw online. There are no signs of life. No car in sight. If anyone is here, they either walked, biked, or swam.

"You think anybody is home?" she asks.

"No reason for anybody to be," he says.

"Yet we still parked a quarter of a mile away," she says, "and we're whispering."

It's a good point.

They approach the cabin, both ready to run at the first sign of trouble. The ground is hard and dry and covered in leaves and pine needles. Joshua lifts the tarpaulin off the boat. The ice cooler is in there, but there's no sign of the bike. They reach the cabin and press their faces against a window. They see furniture and potted plants and paintings. They don't see a dead body or Ruby Carter's mountain bike, and the walls aren't covered in blood. They don't see anybody inside. Of course, all that stuff could be upstairs.

"So now what?" he asks.

"Now this," she says, and she knocks on the front door.

"Why would you do that?"

"To confirm there's nobody here," she says.

Nobody answers. She tries the door. It's locked. "We could smash a window," she says.

"Or we could look for a key," he says. "Dad says people leave keys out all the time."

"Let's look."

The first place they look is under the doormat. Nothing. They start walking around the cabin. They don't find a key.

"It's possible they don't have one," she says.

"They do," he says. "Being all the way out here, you can't risk locking yourself out. There'll be one somewhere."

"Your dad would know where to look," she says. "I know we checked under the mat, but I bet there must be somewhere else where people leave keys all the time."

"Under rocks near the door," he says. "Dad said that once."

They check under all the rocks. Nothing.

"Where else?"

"Well, if it were a car key, Dad would say check on top of one of the wheels."

"People really hide them there?" she asks.

"Apparently."

"Wait here," she says.

She walks over to the boat and the trailer. She crouches down and checks on top of the wheel of the trailer on one side and finds nothing, and then checks the other side. She comes back and smiles and holds up the key.

"Your dad was right," she says.

She opens the door and he picks up the dog food and they step inside.

"Don't forget to breathe," Olillia whispers, as they step inside.

He realizes he's holding his breath. "Why are you whispering?" he asks.

"So the dog won't hear me."

"I don't think it's here," he says. "It would have come to the windows."

"True," she says.

"What's that smell?" he asks, but he already knows what it's going to be. The smell of something dead. The smell is the first thing that tells any character in any book or movie that they're about to find something bad. Only it's not as bad as he thought it would be.

"I kind of recognize it," she says.

"Maybe the dog died," he says.

"It's not that," she says. "It's . . . it's beer."

"Beer?"

"Yeah. It's fermenting. They must brew their own beer in here somewhere."

Now that she's said it, Joshua realizes it is a yeasty odor, and not a decaying-dog odor. Still, he finds it unpleasant, but perhaps it's the kind of thing you get used to. Vincent Archer must have. He wonders if the fermenting beer is masking any other smells.

They step deeper into the cabin. Olillia has closed the door behind them. This place is as neat and as tidy as Vincent's Archer's place. Everything looks modern and the cabin looks fresh, as if nothing can be more than a few years old, from the appliances to the paint on the walls. The kitchen and dining room are open plan, with the staircase for the second story in the center. There's a hallway ahead leading to more rooms. Other than the kitchen, which has a hardwood floor, the rest of the ground floor, including the stairs, is carpeted.

"Upstairs or the hallway?"

It's a fifty-fifty call and he has no preference. "Hallway," he says.

The smell of yeast and hops gets stronger as they take the corridor. All the doors are open, revealing two bedrooms and two bathrooms and what looks like a TV room, since all it houses is a large-screen TV mounted on the wall with two over-sized armchairs in front of it. The views from the rooms to the right look out over the river; the rooms to the left look out on the forest.

At the end of the hallway is the only closed door, and he puts the dog food down and opens it slowly in case the dog is locked in there. It's a utility room with a hardwood floor and no windows. There's a washer

and dryer and a sink and a toilet and a dog kennel. There are two metal
containers that he guesses must contain the fermenting beer. On the
floor are two dog bowls, one half full of water, the other half full of dog
food. Even over the beer he can smell the dog food. It's almost enough
to make him gag. He puts his hand up to his face as if he can block the
smell. He'd open a window if there was one. Because the only source of
light is from the doorway behind them, the room is dimmer than the
rest of the cabin. He looks at the kennel. If there's a dog here, then it's
either super shy or very dead.

Olillia opens a bag of dog food and holds it out from her body. She
crouches down.

"Hey, big fella, hey, it's okay," she says. "Hey, it's going to be okay."

They both jump when they hear movement in the kennel. Then a
low growling comes from it. Olillia drops the dog food on the floor and
the biscuits go everywhere. They each take a step back.

The growling gets louder, but the dog doesn't come out.

Olillia lowers herself again.

"Be careful," Joshua warns.

She gets down on her knees. Joshua tenses his body, ready to jump
in front of her if the dog strikes. She peers into the kennel. "Oh my
god," she says. "Oh my god. Joshua, you are not going to believe this."

Joshua crouches down and looks inside.

Olillia is right. He doesn't believe it.

SIXTY-ONE

—— ◆ ——

"They were going to cut off my feet," Ruby tells them. "But I convinced them I would die." She laughs, a little hysterically. "I told them I'd bleed to death no matter what they tried to do! They said that they could stem the flow, that they'd burn the stumps and I'd survive but I told them they couldn't know that for sure. I mean, how could they? Really, how could they?"

They are still in the utility room. The chain around Ruby's neck is thick and heavy and is held in place with a padlock. The other end is bolted to the inside of the kennel. There's enough length to crawl out of the kennel and drink her water and eat her food from the bowls, and to use the toilet in the corner. She can reach the sink too, only the handles have been removed from the taps, meaning she can drink only from the bowl. She can also reach the freezer, not that she had any desire to—in the beginning the only thing kept in there was meat that would make her sick if she defrosted and ate it raw, but a while ago, perhaps a few weeks, Simon cut a woman up and put her in there, and more recently Vincent took her out and buried her. "He was the real crazy one," she told them earlier. "They're both crazy. Simon's was an outwards crazy, but Vincent's was inwards. Outward crazy is scarier because it comes with blood."

She's wearing the same bike clothes she went missing in. On occasion those clothes would be washed, and she'd have to stay naked until they were returned, but she's never been given anything else to wear. On day one they shaved her head, and now her hair is almost the length of his smallest finger. She's lost weight, and muscle tone, and she reminds him of some of the people Joshua saw around the hospital, the ones who would shuffle along the corridors with their IV stands on wheels and not a lot of life in their eyes. There are sores on her neck and arms and rashes on her cheeks. There are small cuts on her hands, and her nails have been chewed down to the quick and there is blood under some of them. Her skin is pale white, except for under her eyes, where it's dark, like a bruise, but isn't, she tells them, a bruise.

"They never hit me," she tells them, "at least not much, and only in the beginning."

She looks nothing like the woman in the photograph Joshua saw earlier, and she's nothing like he imagined she would have been. This adrenaline junky who traveled to faraway places plummeting towards her death only to pull a rip cord that would save her life, and how strong and how brave she must be, until Simon Bower and Vincent Archer took all of that away from her.

But the worst . . . the worst is what they did to her feet.

"Simon was a builder and an engineer, so he made them," Ruby says, showing them the metal shoes. They wrap around her feet and ankles and are held in place with bolts. They look heavy. "There's a spike on a spring inside of each one," she says. "If I try to walk, the spike will go right through my foot. So I crawl around like a dog. That's what they wanted—for me to crawl. To be their dog. That's why I have to eat and drink out of the bowls. That's why I have a leash, and why they wash me outside under the hose." She laughs again, a laugh that gives Joshua the chills, the kind of laugh that people can't always come back from. He glances at Olillia, who glances back. "And it's better than having my feet cut off."

Her laugh peters out, and is replaced by a big grin. Then the grin disappears, and she cries. Her voice softens. "Help me," she says. "Please, you have to help me."

"We will," Olillia says, and she puts her hand on Ruby's shoulder, only to have Ruby pull back and snarl.

"Woof," she says, then she cries again.

"You're safe now," Olillia says, and her voice betrays her confidence, because she sounds scared. This isn't what she was expecting, and she doesn't know what to do, or say. Joshua can see her hands shaking. He was thinking earlier that Olillia was fearless, but he can see the fear is there now. Of course it is. How can you not look at Ruby and ask yourself, *What if that were me?*

Ruby growls again. "Woof," she says, then laughs.

Joshua reaches over and grabs Olillia's hand. She looks at him. He can see she's close to crying. "We've saved her," he says, "and it is going to be okay." He looks at Ruby. "We're going to get you out of here. We're going to get you to a hospital, and your family are going to come and see you. The men who did this to you, they're dead. Both of them. My dad, he was one of the detectives looking for you. He used to tell me about you, about the things you would do, about how courageous you are. These guys are dead, Ruby, and you survived, and your life and everything you had before this is waiting for you. I promise."

"Woof."

He squeezes Olillia's hand and looks back at her. The tears are coming from his friend now, a mixture of emotions all bubbling over, but they still have work to do. She's been the confident one all day, and now it's his turn. "Let's start looking for a key," Joshua says, "and if you can't find one, maybe we can find something to undo these bolts."

"I'll go. You stay with her," Olillia says. She disappears. An uncontrollable sob escapes her throat as she moves through the door. A moment later Ruby is on her hands and knees drinking from the bowl of water. Joshua's stomach twists into knots. Vincent Archer and Simon Bower were insane. The bad things he thinks his dad might have done, well, seeing Ruby like this, he forgives him. In this moment he accepts that the world needs people like his dad, like Uncle Ben, like the man who saved him on the train tracks. The world needs people to fight its monsters. They need vampires like Frederick. What it doesn't need are people who chain women up in kennels.

He no longer blames his mom for not letting him help Detective

Vega. Nor does he need to find out who that man was. He's happy knowing he's out there.

"I'm glad you came back," Ruby says. "I didn't think you would."

"What do you mean?" he asks.

"Sometimes they walk me," Ruby says. "They put me on a leash and take me into the woods. They gave me dog food. I refused to eat it . . . but in the end I had to. I was so hungry."

"I'm so sorry this has happened to you," Joshua says.

"You get used to it," Ruby says. "It could have been worse. I know that. They showed me that with the other woman," she says, looking around the room.

"It's going to be okay, Ruby."

"Don't call me that," she says, and she cries. "They took that away from me."

"What do you mean?"

"They took my name away. You're not allowed to use it."

"I'm giving you your name back," Joshua says.

She lowers her voice. "Can you . . . can do that? Do you think you're allowed to?"

"I'm allowed to."

"Can I tell you a secret?"

"Yes," he says, and he leans forward so he can hear her better.

"When Master killed that other woman, she was screaming and crying and . . . and it was so awful, and through it all I kept thinking, I just kept thinking I was glad it was happening to her and not me."

She starts to cry. Before Joshua can say anything, Olillia comes back. She holds up a key. "I found this next to a leash," she says. "And we can use these on her shoes," she says, holding up a set of box wrenches.

Ruby looks up at Olillia. "I didn't want to eat the dog food, and I swore I wouldn't, but in the end I had to. I just had to."

"You did the right thing," Olillia says.

"Did I? If I'd starved to death, this would have been over ages ago."

"It's over now," Joshua says, and this feeling he has, this must have been how his dad felt when he saved someone.

"Let me undo the chain," Olillia says.

Ruby tilts her neck to give Olillia access to the padlock. The skin around her neck is chaffed and raw looking, speckled with flecks of dried blood. She smells like dog food and vomit. Aware of how she must smell, Ruby says, "It's been days, maybe weeks since they hosed me down."

The lock pops open and the chain falls away.

"I kept thinking the police would come, but they never did. I used to scream for help in the beginning, but I stopped after . . ." she says, then stops talking. She lifts her left hand. With all there is to look at, Joshua hadn't noticed it. Her pinky finger is missing. "They cut it off. They said if I screamed again, they'd cut my entire hand off. They used to set up a recording device to catch me out, but I wouldn't let them catch me out, so I didn't scream anymore." She laughs. "I beat them," she says.

"You beat them," Olillia says.

Ruby gingerly touches her fingers to her neck. Her knees are red and sore looking from when she's crawled. Joshua picks up the box wrenches and finds them difficult to hold with the bandage on his hand, so he strips it away and stuffs it into his pocket. Then he starts with the left shoe, putting one ring spanner on the bolt, and one on the nut. He increases the pressure, and when he thinks he can't push and pull any harder, he thinks about where he is, what Ruby has gone through, and it gives him an extra boost of strength, enough to loosen the bolt. He spins it off with his finger and pulls the shoe away. It looks like a metal clog, but it's designed exactly how Ruby said it was—with a spike coming up from the center that's two inches long. There are scabs and holes in her foot from where it's pricked her. Her foot looks infected. If she had tried walking, that spike would have gone through her foot and up into her ankle.

"Can you walk?" he asks, once the second shoe falls away.

"I . . . I don't know."

They help her to her feet. Her legs resist straightening, and even then she can't support her weight on them.

"I could crawl."

"I'm sure we can manage to—"

"I want to crawl," Ruby says, interrupting him. She struggles. "Please."

They lower her back to the ground. "The lounge is this way," he says.

"I know where it is," Ruby says. "Sometimes the masters would let me watch TV with them."

Joshua's stomach twists again as she watches Ruby crawling into the lounge. He has the urge to help her, to carry her, to do something. To have spent three months like a dog . . . he knows his dad saw a lot of bad stuff, but he wonders if he ever saw anything like this. He suspects he did. He suspects his dad saw something like this too many times, and it changed him.

They reach the lounge, but Ruby doesn't stop there. She continues to crawl up the stairs on her hands and knees. He forces himself to watch her. He wants to feel her pain, as if in a way he can lessen hers by taking some of it. She makes it to the top.

"I want to see the river," she says, making her way to the balcony. Joshua is reluctant to open the door, fearful Ruby is going to use the rail to try to get to her feet, then drop herself over it. But Ruby doesn't show any desire to go outside. She sits on the floor near the window with her hand on the glass and gazes beyond it. "It's so beautiful," she says. "The way the sun hits the water, the way the water is always moving . . . it's an ever-changing view. My masters, what view do you think they had? Would they have seen what we see? Or some twisted version of it? Did they only see dead branches and decaying leaves and mud and dark skies? How can they have seen the sun and the beauty and still have done the kinds of things they did?"

"I don't know," Joshua answers.

"They're not your masters," Olillia says.

"They're not my masters," Ruby says. "You're right."

"And they never were," Olillia says.

"Do my friends and family think I'm dead?"

Joshua drags a coffee table over so he can sit on the edge. Olillia sits next to Ruby on the floor.

"You said before my old life is waiting for me, but how can it be if everybody thinks I'm dead? How long has it been?"

"It's been over three months," Olillia says.

"They had a birthday party for you," Joshua says. "They celebrated you because they were sure you were still alive."

"Then why didn't they come and find me?" she asks, and she doesn't look at them, she keeps looking out the window as the river moves and the leaves fall. "Why did they leave me out here?"

"They tried," he says.

"They didn't try hard enough. Nor did your dad."

"I'm sorry," he says.

"Why isn't he the one here finding me?" she asks.

"Because Simon murdered him," he says.

She doesn't say anything. Her face is expressionless. He wonders how close his dad, or Uncle Ben, came to this house. Did they knock on the door? Or just speak to Vincent's parents? They had no reason to search it, the same way they don't search every house in the city when somebody disappears.

"I want to ask you something, Ruby, okay?" Joshua asks. "You said before you were glad I came back. What did you mean by that?"

She finally turns to face them. "I want to go now," she says.

"We'll call the police," Olillia says. "We'll have to wait here."

"No," Ruby says. "No, we have to go. I can't stay here."

"But—"

"No," she says, and she starts crying. "Please, please, no. I have to go."

"There's no way she'll be able to walk all the way out to the car," Olillia says. "I should go get it."

"Are you going to be okay?" Joshua asks.

Olillia gives a brief nod, gets up, and quietly makes her way down the stairs. He wants to run after her and hug her.

"Ruby, when you said before you were glad I came back, what did you mean?"

"I want to go," she says.

"We will, I promise. Olillia is getting the car. What did you mean?"

"What?"

"When you said earlier you were glad I came back."

"It doesn't matter," Ruby says, "because you came back today."

"Please," he says. "Just tell me."

"It was maybe a week ago. Somebody started knocking on the wall outside the room I was kept in. It was you." Ruby turns back towards the river. She picks at a piece of skin sticking up from the side of her fingernail. "You didn't knock anywhere else. Just that wall, like you knew where I was going to be, and when you knocked, you asked, 'Are you really in there?'"

"It wasn't me," Joshua says.

"Then who was it?"

"Did you answer them?"

"I didn't say anything. I thought it might be Vincent testing me, and I didn't want to lose any more fingers and all I could think about was what had happened to that other woman . . . so I held my breath and said nothing."

"What did he say next?"

"He said, 'I've been having these strange dreams about you. I think they're real.' He told me it confused him, and he thought he was going crazy. He begged me to speak to him. He told me he'd come all this way to speak to me, and that if I proved I was there, he would help me. So I told him. I begged him to help me."

"What did he do?"

"He didn't do anything. He left. I thought . . . I thought I must have imagined it. All of it."

"You said he was dreaming about you," Joshua says, and his skin has gone cold and a lump has formed out of nothing and gotten stuck in his throat. He is thinking about his own dreams. Things he's seen from his father's eye, things he's seen from his father's killer.

If he has one of each, then doesn't it stand to reason there is somebody else out there with the other set?

Somebody else who is having the same dreams?

"Yes," she says. "I'm sure of it."

What he doesn't understand is why the person who came out here would save him from Vincent Archer, but not save Ruby Carter. He knows he's been seeing the world the way his dad has been seeing it, but in what way does the other recipient see it? "I need to make a call," he says, and that's when he realizes he's lost his cell phone.

SIXTY-TWO

———— ◉ ————

It's been a long day. A stressful day. Dr. Toni canceled a surgery because her nerves were so shot that she couldn't keep her hands still. She's pushed scheduled appointments to later in the week. This morning she woke with a stomachache and a headache that made her feel a hundred years old. She's struggling to think straight. She couldn't eat breakfast, and then threw up on an empty stomach, and then crawled back into bed and considered not coming into work at all, but she had to—she couldn't hide from what she had done. She hadn't really known that Mitchell and Ben were executing bad people for the parts they could provide—because she didn't want to know, which, she admits, isn't really the same as not knowing. She wonders if Michelle knew. She's always liked Michelle. They were never close, but she always enjoyed spending time with her back when they all used to hang out together, her and Mitchell and Ben, back before everybody grew up and everything changed. She can't imagine Michelle ever being part of those conversations. Can't imagine Michelle being complicit in what her husband was doing, or every day dealing with the risks that Mitchell could be hurt, or caught. But maybe she did know. Maybe she was there that day when the conversation between Mitchell and Ben turned dark, and the idea for all of this was born. Toni never asked. There's a lot she's never asked. All she wanted to think about were the lives she was saving, not cold-blooded murder. Detective Vega was right about that.

So she came to work and felt nauseated the entire day, waiting for the authorities to show up and arrest her, waiting for her career, her life, to be over. She didn't tell any of the others she knew of who were involved. She didn't think there was any reason to alarm them with something that may not even happen. But either way, whether she's arrested or not, everything they've been doing has already come to an end. It did the second Mitchell Logan was pushed out of the fourth floor of that building.

And now, standing outside in the parking lot, she finds that her day has gotten worse. The tires on her car have been slashed. She leans against it and covers her face in her hands. She doesn't know what to do. Someone out there—the universe, perhaps—must be teaching her a lesson. Officially paranoid, she wonders what else might be waiting for her. Maybe a bomb strapped to the engine. At the very least she knows Karma is going to throw her a string of red lights once she does get to drive home.

She can't deal with this right now.

What she can do is find a bar, have a few gin and tonics, then get a taxi home. Sort everything out tomorrow.

"Dr. Coleman!" The voice is familiar, but still makes her jump. She turns towards it. It's Dustin Moore. The second patient she operated on the day Mitchell Logan was killed, though she didn't perform the entire operation. Her colleague Dr. Holland removed the first eye, and after Joshua's operation was complete, she attached the first of Dustin Moore's new eyes before napping for a few hours before she was required to attach the second. It was the longest day of her career, yet today has felt longer.

Dustin is smiling and waving. He's in his midtwenties, with thick dark hair pushed back by his fingers. He has a day's worth of stubble and a tan you don't get without real commitment to the sun. He's wearing a white linen shirt that looks ruffled, and blue jeans, and he looks like he's been on an adventure somewhere. He's a good-looking guy, and it's hard to imagine he's the boy she first met when he was thirteen and his parents brought him in to see her. He was having problems with his vision. She diagnosed with him Coats's disease, a disease that affects one in every hundred thousand people that damages the blood vessels behind the retina. In most cases it affects only one eye, and in rarer cases, both. Dustin had one of those rarer cases. Year after year he came in for a checkup, and year after year there was nothing she could do other than monitor the progress as his vision faded. He was legally blind by the age of twenty.

Now he has Simon Bower's eyes. She wonders if he has his dreams too.

"Hello, Dustin," she says.

"Is that your car back there?" he asks, reaching her.

"Sadly, it is."

"Boy, somebody has it in for you," he says. "You want a hand with it? I mean, I can't really do anything on account of the fact I don't know anything about cars, and I'm guessing you only have one spare wheel and you need four." He shrugs, and gives an embarrassed smile. "I guess I can't really give you a hand."

"I'll deal with it tomorrow."

"You sure?"

"Yeah, I'm sure."

She starts walking. He walks with her.

"How are the eyes?" she asks.

"Good," he says.

"Sorry I had to cancel your appointment this afternoon."

"Hey, it's no problem, it freed me up to do other things."

She stops walking. He stops too. "Let me ask you something," she says.

"You want me to give you a lift? Sure, more than happy to. I'm a pretty good driver. Was one of the last things I learned before I became legally blind, and one of the first things I was desperate to do once you gave me back my sight. I owe you everything, Dr. Toni. Everything."

"I appreciate that," she says, "but that wasn't what I was going to ask. Have you . . . Have you experienced anything strange?"

He frowns. "Strange? Like what?"

"Like . . . strange, is all."

He laughs. "I think you're going to have to be a little more specific."

"It's okay," she says. "Forget I said anything."

"You mean like headaches and stuff? Blurry vision? My left eye still doesn't work, if that's what you mean."

"No. It's not that," she says.

"Then what?"

"Nothing," she says. She starts walking again. He falls in beside her.

"Hey, look," he says. "Let me be a gentleman and give you a lift," he says.

"It's fine. I'll get a taxi."

"You sure? I'd drive you to the moon and back if I could. Everything you did for me . . . My mom says I should be offering to mow your lawns and paint your house and make you lunch every day and deliver it to you."

Dustin is reminding her exactly why she has been doing all of this—to help people. Instead of focusing on the bad things that got her here, she needs to focus on the reasons why. The positives. "Your mom sounds like an extremely intelligent woman," she says, and they both laugh.

"I'll be sure to pass it along. But seriously, Mom would give me one humongous kick in the behind if I didn't help you out here. A pretty doctor with all her tires slashed? Hell, Mom would try to ground me for a month if I didn't help you out."

Maybe it's because she's tired and stressed, maybe it's because Dustin is making her smile, or maybe it's because he called her pretty and nobody has said that to her in a while—whatever it is, she smiles. "Okay. A lift would be good. I really appreciate it."

"Car's over here," he says, smiling back. "Word of warning, though, it's my mom's car—it's not quite as flash as yours. But at least the tires haven't been slashed."

She laughs. "I'm sure it's fine," she says.

They walk to a red four-door sedan. He unlocks the doors and they climb in. "So where to?"

"Home. It's been a long day. Time to relax and get some sleep."

"Yeah? That's a good idea," he says. "Sounds really good, actually. However, I have something else in mind."

"Yeah? What's that?"

"Well, I kind of fibbed a little back there," he says. "About when you asked me if I'd noticed anything strange."

Her smile disappears. He pulls a gun out of his pocket, and Toni has never seen one before, not in real life. It's amazing how something so small has the power to instantly provoke fear. She actually flinches when she sees it, and tries to pull back a little, but there's nowhere to go. In that moment Toni knows that it wasn't Karma or the Universe that slashed her tires. It was Dustin.

"I've been having these strange dreams," he says. "And they come with some pretty strong urges."

SIXTY-THREE

— ◉ —

Joshua pats his pockets one more time. He looks at the floor, at the couch, on the stairs. It has to be here, doesn't it? And if not here, then in the car, or back home, or in his schoolbag, or . . .

Or at Vincent Archer's house. That was the last time he used it.

"Oh no," he says.

"What is it?" Ruby asks, looking panicked.

"I've left my phone somewhere I shouldn't have," he says, and she looks relieved that's all it is, and he can't blame her. If he has left it at Vincent Archer's house, it doesn't matter. They're going to be telling Detective Vega everything anyway.

"Your girlfriend will have one," Ruby says. "We can call the police on the way." She leans forward and takes his hand in both of hers and looks up at him. "Where is your girlfriend? Is she coming back?"

"She's coming back. She's getting the car," he says. "Also . . . she's not my girlfriend."

"She likes you," Ruby says. "I can tell."

"I like her too."

"Yeah, I can tell you do. I hope you pluck up the courage to tell her."

He tries to help her down the stairs, but she says no, and instead she crawls. She gets to the bottom just as a car pulls up outside. "Olillia's here," he says.

Within seconds, Olillia rushes through the front door. "It's getting cold out there," she says, rubbing at her arms. "And there's no easy way to say this, but we have a small problem. The car doesn't have a backseat." She looks at Joshua. "I can come back for you," she says. "Or we can call your mom. Or Detective Vega."

"Let's call Detective Vega," he says.

"Help me get Ruby out to the car first," she says.

Ruby lets them help her out to the car. They support her between them so she has one arm around Joshua and one around Olillia. It's a struggle, but they get her into the passenger seat. Olillia was right— it is getting cold out here. The wind is picking up. Leaves and twigs and pinecones are falling to the ground. Olillia tries calling Detective Vega. There's still no answer. She leaves a message, saying it's urgent.

"I guess we'll drive directly to the hospital," she says. "Maybe Ruby can call her parents on the way too."

"Good idea. Just one thing—I've lost my phone. So make sure you come back, huh? Or at least send somebody back," he says. "I don't recall seeing a landline in there."

"You think your cell could be inside? Maybe it slipped out of your pocket since we've been here."

"I don't think so."

"I'll dial it."

She dials it. It rings for a while. They listen, but don't hear a ring inside the house.

"It was on vibrate," he says.

She calls it again. They listen harder. Nothing.

"Is it set up to be tracked if you lose it?" she asks.

"Oh yeah, it is!"

"Let's track it," she says.

She launches an app on her phone. Joshua puts in his details and a moment later a map appears on the screen. There's a blue dot in the center of it. It's moving.

"Somebody must have it," she says. She zooms out. "Look, it's coming towards us!"

"It must be Detective Vega," he says. "She must have found my phone. She would have seen all my texts to you."

"You didn't have a passcode on it?"

"It does, but it wasn't set to activate for five minutes. If she found it within that time she'll have had access to everything."

"We didn't know about the cabin at that point," she says.

"She must have figured it out the same way we did."

"Well, at least it means you won't have to wait as long out here by yourself."

"Also means I start getting in trouble even sooner."

She leans forward and hugs him and holds on for a while, then pulls away. "You did good, Boy Who Used to Be Blind. Your dad would be proud."

He thinks his dad would be.

"I'll see you at the hospital," she says.

He watches them drive away, and then he goes back inside and waits for Detective Vega.

SIXTY-FOUR

———— ◆ ————

Detective Vega has a real doozy of a headache, one that follows her from a dream she can't remember into the back of a trunk she only wishes she could forget. She doesn't know how long she's been unconscious—maybe a few minutes, maybe half a day. If the man who took her is the person who saved Joshua yesterday, she can no longer think of him as the Good Samaritan. He is now the Politely Spoken Bad Samaritan. She can't escape the idea that this is exactly the kind of guy Ben Kirk and Mitchell Logan would have donated to medical science.

Even with the pillow, she's still getting beaten up by the drive. She always figured it would be an uncomfortable way to travel—worse, even, than flying economy on a long-haul flight. She wonders if they've already stopped to pick up whatever—or whoever—it is the Bad Samaritan wants to pick up.

Something is buzzing in her pocket, and it takes her a moment to make sense of it since her own phone is broken—it's Joshua's phone. It's inside an evidence bag inside her jacket pocket. It stops buzzing. If she can get to the phone, she can call for help.

The car takes a bend, accelerates, then stays on course. They're traveling fast. They're probably on a motorway. She wriggles her body, twisting into different angles, but the handcuffs and duct tape make the phone impossible to reach.

At least for now.

The car slows. It turns off. The surface of the road changes from smooth to bumpy. They continue at a slower pace. The car hits a hole and she's thrown up against the ceiling of the trunk. It's like being inside a washing machine. After a couple of minutes, the car slows even further, then it comes to a stop. The engine dies. She can hear it pinging and ticking. She can feel the weight of the car change as the Bad Samaritan climbs out. She can hear his footsteps. He pops the trunk, and right away she can hear the wind through the trees and a river nearby.

"Hey there, welcome back," he says, the big smile still on his stupid face. "I hope that wasn't too bad. Take a look at what I stopped off to get you on our way." He holds up a dog collar and a leash. There's a price tag hanging from it. "I know, it's not conventional," he says, "but you'll get used to it, I promise, and I did make sure to get one in your color."

The collar is pink. She's never been a fan of pink, and never been a fan of people who think all girls should be.

He attaches the collar around her neck.

"There," he says. "It looks good. You look like a real princess. Come on," he says, and he tugs on the leash, pulling her forward, the collar tightening around her throat. She rolls out and lands heavily on her shoulder.

"Oh no, oh no, I'm so sorry, I didn't mean for that to happen," Mr. Bad says, "but really it's both our faults. Your fault for not trying hard enough, and mine for expecting more from you." He tugs the leash again. "Come on, up you get, nobody likes a straggler."

She can't get to her feet—there's still duct tape around her ankles and legs, some of it connected to the cuffs around her wrists. Best she can do is get upright onto her knees. She looks around, trying to get a sense of where he has brought her. There's a modern cabin with a boat parked on a trailer out front. She must be far outside the city, in an isolated area where one could make a lot of noise without disturbing any neighbors. The wind is getting stronger. Mr. Bad Samaritan cuts through the tape holding her legs together.

"Stay on your knees," he says, and he tugs the leash and she shuffles towards the cabin, following him. Her knees hurt. They're digging into pebbles and hard dirt and twigs and other annoying, natural debris. She's always loved nature before, but now she hates it. The first few drops of rain hit her face.

They reach the cabin. Mr. Bad tries the door.

"Well, this is fantastic," he says. "It's unlocked! I have more good news, too—the previous owner has passed on so there's nobody to disturb us."

She suspects that the previous owner may have been Vincent Archer. Perhaps the cabin belongs to his rich parents, who, in all their wisdom, didn't feel like telling her about this place. It's hard to think of an innocent reason for that, even though there must be many, including the simple one of them just not thinking about it. But the cop inside her, the one who knows how things really are, pictures Mr. and Mrs. Archer coming out here and doing all the same kind of weird shit their son was doing.

Mr. Bad leads her inside. It's nice in here. The carpet is friendly to her knees. There's nice furniture and nice appliances that she gets to see from her level. There are no articles pinned to the walls, so maybe this place doesn't belong to Vincent Archer.

"Why, this is spectacular," he says. "All the modern comforts of home," he says, and he removes the duct tape from across her mouth. She doesn't say anything. "First thing we have to do is get rid of the dog," he says, and pulls the gun out of the waistband of his pants. "I don't want one that somebody else has already loved."

"Don't," she says.

"Sadly, I must," he says. "It'll be better this way, trust me."

There's a kennel in the utility room. She thinks about the bags of dog food on the table in Vincent Archer's house. Mr. Bad crouches down so he can see inside. "Well now, it's empty," he says, and he seems unsure what to do next. "I used to dream about her," he says. "The woman who lived in the kennel. They treated her like a dog. I mean, quite literally like a dog. Isn't that the most wonderful thing?" he asks, and his big smile gets bigger. "Such a grand idea! They put a chain around her neck like the one I have around yours. They gave her water out of a bowl to drink and they made her eat dog food, and I saw all of this, I saw it so vividly in my dreams. I came here, and it was the same building, the same river, the same boat parked up outside. I called to her through the wall, and she was here!"

"Ruby Carter," she says. The woods, the river—this must be out in the forest where she went missing.

"I never knew her name."

"Is she still alive?"

"How would I know that?" He bends down and picks up what looks like some kind of metal shoe. "My, look at these!" he says, and his face brightens into a big smile. "How wonderful they've been left behind! They're even in your size! Come on, let's get these on."

He removes her shoes and, with the use of some box wrenches lying on the floor, puts the metal shoes onto her feet and tightens the bolts. There are large spikes on the inside making it impossible for her to stand. She wonders where Ruby is. Is she buried out here? Is that one of the last things Vincent Archer did? Is Andrea Walsh buried out here too?

"From now on, you crawl like a dog."

"I need to use a bathroom," she says.

"Why? So you can try something?"

"I really need to pee, that's all."

Slowly he nods. "I will have to watch you, just to make sure you don't try anything."

"I'm not going to try anything."

"I'm still going to have to watch you. I know it sounds horribly inappropriate, but I'm afraid there's no other way."

"I can't go with you watching me."

"Also, it can't be in the bathroom, it has to be outside, up against a tree."

"I'm not doing that," she says.

"Then don't go," he says.

"You're being unreasonable," she says.

"Excuse me? I'm the one here giving you options, and I'm the one being unreasonable? You have a lot to learn about manners."

"You want me to go all over the floor?"

"Do you want me to put you down?"

"I'm not your dog," she says.

"That's where you're wrong," he says. "The sooner you accept it, the easier it will be."

He tugs on the leash. Her instinct is to get her feet under her, but the spikes will sink into her. She tries to imagine how far she could get with them like that, and decides not far at all.

"You need to uncuff me," she says. "How can I crawl like a dog with my hands cuffed behind me?"

"Not well, I admit," he says, "but I'm not uncuffing you."

"You can handcuff my hands in front of me."

He thinks about it for a few seconds. "I guess I was always going to have to do that," he says. "But if you try anything, I will beat you."

He undoes the cuffs and does them up in front of her. In that moment she wonders if she could try something, but decides against it. She has the phone. That's where her escape lies. Mr. Bad pulls forward on the leash and forces her to crawl like the dog he wanted. He leads her into a lounge and he stands by the window and tells her she has to sit on the floor. She thinks about Tracey, and wonders if she'll ever see her again.

"Can you tell me who you are?" she asks, doing her best to sound friendly.

"Until a few weeks ago, I was nobody. Now I'm somebody with a pet."

She wants to tell him he's insane. Instead she says, "You don't need to do any of this."

"Need to? No, I don't suppose I *need* to do anything, but I want to. You do see the difference, right?"

"From down here on the floor chained up like a dog, it's hard to," Vega says.

He laughs. "Like a dog," he says. "Like a dog. Isn't it all so terribly wonderful?"

"You're half right," she says.

"I don't understand," he says, turning from the window to face her. She can see her gun tucked into the waistband of his pants.

"It's just terribly," she says. "There's nothing wonderful about it."

"Oh, I see, I see!" He claps his hands together. "That is quite funny, quite quick. I like that. I have chosen well."

"You want to tell me about the dreams?" she asks, because when he mentioned them earlier it reminded her of Joshua.

He looks confused. "What dreams?" he asks, still smiling his big ol' smile.

"You said before you'd been dreaming about the woman who was kept out here."

"The dog," he says.

She's not going to say *the dog*. "What did you dream about?"

He crouches down to her level. "Are you sure you want to know? They were quite unpleasant."

"Tell me," she says.

"Now, I don't want to be Mr. Negative here," he says, "but I'm pretty sure you only want me to tell you because you're hoping to learn something that will help you."

"No," she says. "I think that if I'm to be a good pet, I need to know how to keep you happy. To keep you happy, I need to know more about you. I want to be a good doggy," she says.

Mr. Bad laughs. "My, you really are quite something, aren't you," he says, but what that something is, he doesn't say.

"The dreams," Vega says.

"The dreams. Very well, then. They were full of blood. You wouldn't believe the amount of blood there was." He turns away and looks back out the window, but she can tell he's not looking at the view, he's looking back at the dreams. "Buckets of it, all if it getting splashed around. It made no sense. I started to dream of women screaming. I used to hate horror movies, you know. My wife . . . I should tell you that I'm married," he says, and she looks at his hand and yes, sure enough, there's a gold band on his ring finger, and she wonders if he's killed her. "And before you ask, I know that she wouldn't approve of this, of any of this."

"Do you have children?"

"Yes," he says, and she wonders if he's killed them too. "A boy and a girl. Seven and four."

"If you let me go, you can go back to them. You haven't hurt me. You've done nothing wrong."

"You don't get it," he says, "and I understand that, because I didn't get it either, not at first. Not until I had the dreams, and the urges that came with them. Before then, well, as I was saying, I couldn't even watch a horror movie. All that blood . . . I'd have to turn away. I can't watch or read anything that's too violent. It upsets me. I'm the person who faints at the sight of blood, can you believe that? You ask who I am? Well, that's who I was. Can you imagine the effect dreams of blood have on somebody who faints at the sight of a cut finger? To dream of women screaming, of all that blood . . . can you imagine?"

"What's your wife's name?"

"I know what you're doing," he says. "You're trying to get me to talk about my family. You're hoping we can relate, and that I'll let you go. That's not going to happen."

"The dreams," she says, "did they start after the surgery?"

The cabin goes so quiet it's as though somebody has thrown a switch to kill every tiny bit of sound. Five seconds pass. Ten. It's not as quiet as she thought, because she can hear the wind swirling around outside. "How did you know about the surgery?" he asks.

"You had it what, three weeks ago?"

"Do you know me?" he asks.

"It's called cellular memory," she says. "The dreams are real, but they're not yours." She explains it to him. Memory being stored in all the cells of a body. Cellular memory is a guy wanting to take up ice skating after receiving an ice skater's heart. It's a woman wanting to take up painting after receiving a painter's liver.

"It's a man wanting to take up killing after receiving a serial killer's eyes." She can see him thinking about it. She can see him making the connection. "Your donor," she says. "He was a murderer. When he died, his organs were harvested. What you're experiencing are his memories. Your desire to do this to me, to keep me like a pet, that's not your desire. That belongs to the man who died. How did you find this cabin?"

"I was drawn to it," he says. "I came here a week ago. I had to, to make sure the place was real. I thought I was going crazy, but hey, the place is real. I spoke to the dog and she spoke back, and I must admit that scared me. She didn't scare me, and the cabin didn't scare me, but the entire situation scared me. How could I know about this place? All I know is that I did."

"And Vincent Archer? You were drawn to him too?"

"No," he says. "I was driving back out to the cabin the following morning when I saw him coming out from the turnoff. I recognized him from the dreams, so I turned the car around and followed him. Now that he's dead, I figured, you know, that this cabin could be mine."

"That's why you were at his house today," she says. "You were going to look for any reference to the cabin and, if you found it, you were going to destroy it, so nobody would come out here."

"You really are a clever one," he says. "I wasn't expecting there to be anybody inside."

How differently this could have gone had she not been outside talking to the neighbor when he sneaked inside, or if she hadn't sent the only other officer away to drive Levi to see the sketch artist.

"When I saw you, that's when it happened."

"When what happened?" she asks.

"When this new life presented itself. In the smallest of moments, I saw how desire could become reality. Don't you see? Most of us don't reach for the stars. Most of us settle for lesser lives because we don't think we can achieve the unachievable. I didn't go there to find you, but once I saw you I knew I had to have you. The old me would have snuck back out of the house and regretted it with every passing day. In fact, the old me would never have broken in in the first place. The new me is one who acts. Who makes something out of nothing. A do-it-yourself kind of guy."

"Don't you see? That's not the new you, that's the old Simon Bower."

He shakes his head. "I know it's difficult for you to understand, but I'm doing what I want. Being who I want. If what you're saying is true about cellular memory, then I owe Simon Bower my thanks. He saw what he wanted and took it."

"It got him killed."

"Being foolish is what got him killed."

"Which is what you're doing. You didn't plan this. You knew the cabin was here, but didn't know for sure who owned it. You went to Vincent's house to remove any evidence he owned a cabin, not knowing if he was the one who even owned it, or if anybody else used it. You thought there'd be a girl tied up here, but there isn't. You had to buy a dog leash on the way because you didn't have one. You saw the metal shoes and thought they were a great idea, but they weren't *your* idea. You're making decisions on the fly, and trust me when I tell you, that always works out badly. You're going to make a mistake and probably already have. Where does your wife think you are right now? How are you going to explain your trips away from home to come out here? What if somebody else shows up?"

"Is there?" he asks.

"Is there what?"

"Evidence of the cabin at Vincent Archer's house?"

"Plenty of it," she says, which isn't true. She had no idea this place existed. "Anyone could come here at any point. Bringing me out here was a really bad idea."

He says nothing.

"You have a wife, you have children, you have a productive role in society. You're not a monster, and these desires aren't yours. The old you hasn't gone, it just needs to wise up and know this isn't the way you're supposed to be. I can help you," she says. "The doctors can help you."

"No."

"But—"

"I said no. The desires might have come from Simon Bower, but they're mine now. Would you tell a starving man he couldn't eat from the plate full of food you sat in front of him?"

"No, but I wouldn't give heroin to a heroin addict going through withdrawal."

"Nothing you say changes the fact his desires have become my desires. I like the way they make me feel. I like the things they're making me do."

"Will you let me go when you're done with whatever it is you're doing?"

He smiles at her, the kind of smile that makes her skin crawl. "I'm sorry to be so blunt, but eventually killing you is also part of the desire."

SIXTY-FIVE

———— ◆ ————

Joshua rolls out from his hiding space under the bed. Earlier, when he saw Vega pulled out of the car on a leash, hiding was the only thing he knew how to do. He looks around the room now for a weapon, but what is there? There's an alarm clock, some coat hangers, some sheets, a chair. When they were in the utility room, he could hear them. This is the man who dreamed about Ruby and knocked on the wall by the kennel. It stands to reason that it must also be the man who got the other set of eyes. The same man who saved him yesterday? He doesn't know. Now that they're out in the lounge, they're out of earshot.

Olillia will be at the hospital in half an hour. She'll explain what has happened, and the police will get involved. At least now he knows why they weren't able to get hold of Detective Vega. Hopefully Olillia will have given up trying, and will call the police. Hopefully she's called them already, and they're on their way out here to save the day. If so, they won't be in a hurry. They won't be speeding through traffic with their lights flashing. If she's called them, then they're forty-five minutes away at the earliest.

Or perhaps this maniac arrived while Olillia and Ruby were still on the road between the cabin and the motorway. Perhaps he waved them down. Maybe he stabbed them, or beat them, or tied them up before they could call anybody.

The thought of something having happened to Olillia makes his blood run cold. It makes his body shake. His stomach rolls and there's a weird taste in the back of his throat and for a few moments it's like it was when he first tried to walk after the bandages were taken off and he couldn't find his balance. He sucks in a few deep breaths. He closes his eyes, and he pictures Olillia being okay, and Ruby being okay too, and if he's to believe anything different, he won't be able to do what has to be done. He can't wait for help to arrive, because he doesn't know if it will.

He sneaks into the hallway. The wind is pushing at the cabin, trying to pick it up and carry it away. He gets closer to the lounge. He can hear them talking again. He crouches down by the door but doesn't look around. If he's seen, it could go badly for both him and Detective Vega.

"I know you saved Joshua Logan," Vega says.

The man doesn't answer her.

"Yesterday, on the train tracks," Vega says. "It proves you're a good person. It proves you can still be the man you used to be."

"You're wrong."

"I'm not wrong," Vega says. "You need help."

"No, I mean you're wrong about . . . what did you say his name was? Logan?"

"Joshua Logan," she says.

"I don't know any Joshua Logan," the man says, "and I don't know anything about any train tracks."

Joshua can no longer resist looking. Staying low, he peeks around the corner. The man is standing by the window with his back to the door, half turned towards the view and half towards Vega, who is sitting on the floor near the couch facing Joshua's direction. He can see raindrops hitting the windows. He can see trees bending in the wind. The sky is getting dark.

"You saved his life," she says. "You were following Vincent Archer, and you stopped him from killing Joshua."

"Detective, honestly, I have no idea what you're talking about, and this is quickly becoming very unamusing."

Detective Vega has eyes only for her abductor, but then she looks Joshua's way. They make eye contact for only a fraction of a second before she looks back at her captor. Her expression doesn't change. Joshua holds his breath and holds his ground.

"You really don't know what I'm talking about," she says.

"I really don't."

"Joshua is the kind of boy who should never try anything by himself and should always find a way to call the police."

"Now you're making even less sense."

"The police would have helped him. He had to find a way to call them, but given he didn't have his cell phone, he could have flagged down a car on the motorway, and of course he would have warned them that the man had a gun."

"Are you mad?" he asks. "Nothing you say makes any sense."

"Your eyes came from the man that killed Joshua's father."

"What are you talking about?"

"Your eyes," she says. "They were donated. They—"

"I do apologize, but I'm going to have to stop you there," he says, holding up his hand. "I'm afraid we're on completely different pages. I wasn't given any eyes. I don't know who Joshua Logan is."

"I thought . . . didn't you have an operation? You said as much."

"Yes, I did say as much," he says.

"I don't understand," she says.

"There was never anything wrong with my eyes," he says. "It was my heart. The doctors, they gave me a new heart."

SIXTY-SIX

— ◉ —

Plastic ties keep Dr. Toni's wrists tethered to the passenger door in a way that keeps her hunched forward slightly, and to the side. She has no movement. All she can do is sit in the passenger seat with her arm crossed over her body and stare out the window as they make conversation. Trying to look at Dustin strains her neck, and she wants to look at him. She wants to try to see what she's obviously missed since that first time he came in with his mom and dad to see her. They are driving west, having now gone past the edge of the city and into the land of the farmer. Even if she could unlock and open the door, she'd only end up being dragged along the road.

"At first, the nightmares kept me awake," Dustin says, and she tries to see him as the shy thirteen-year-old boy who once drew a portrait of her from memory. He told her back then he wanted to be an artist, and there was no denying he was good at it, just as there was also no denying those talents would be taken away once his sight disappeared. She tries to see him as the boy whose school uniform looked too big for him, and whose hair was always a mess. "That week in the hospital after the surgery was difficult. My eyes kept itching, and the only relief from the itch was when I slept, but when I slept there were the dreams. People I didn't know dying in the most horrible ways. It wasn't until I was at home a week later that I was able to figure it out—they weren't dreams, but symptoms. People call it cellular memory. Do you know of it?"

"Why didn't you tell me?"

"Yeah? What was I going to say? Excuse me, Dr. Toni, but I've been having some bad dreams."

"That's exactly what you should have said."

"And what would you have done?"

"I don't know. Something."

"You should have warned me, doctor."

"What?"

"You should have warned me what was going to happen."

"I didn't know back then."

"But you know now."

"Yes."

"Because your other patients have the same dreams."

She doesn't answer him.

He reaches over and strokes her hair and she flinches away.

"Some say the whole idea of cellular memory is a crock," he says. "Others support it, but there was nothing describing what I was experiencing. The stuff I was reading about was subtle, it was people who hated bananas suddenly liking bananas. But nothing about dreams, or knowing faces and locations, and I think it's because it was the eyes, right? They are a window to the soul, they are a lens that views the world. It makes sense that if any organ is going to experience cellular memory, it would be the eyes. I had to know—where did my new eyes come from? I asked you, you remember that?"

She remembers. He asked her before the surgery.

"You wouldn't say anything."

"I couldn't."

"Because all that information is confidential," he says.

"Exactly."

"Or is it because those eyes came from a killer?"

She doesn't answer him.

"They came from Simon Bower," he says. "He died the same day I got the eyes. The dreams . . . without them, I'd never have made the connection. I'd probably have thought they'd come from a car accident victim. Since getting them, Doctor, all I've seen is the blood and the pain of his life. There is a girl he tied up and kept as a dog. Can you believe that? What kind of person comes up with that? Then there's a woman he cut into pieces with a power saw, and there's a girl, much younger, and I think it was a long time ago that he tied her up, but he didn't kill her. She escaped. There are limits to what I can remember, but I have a theory as to why. Do you want me to tell you?"

It's too much to take on board. Girls being kept as dogs? People being cut into pieces? "Yes, Dustin, of course. I want to be able to help you."

He laughs. "I'm sure you do," he says. "All the memories have one thing in common. Violence and domination. I think the emotion of those memories is what causes them to stick. See, people think memories are stored in the brain, and they're right, but memories of such dark significance, they're the ones that are stored in the cells. What do you think?"

"I think you've put some real thought into it," she says, but what she really thinks is that his theory doesn't cover why normal people take on the normal hobbies of those their organs came from. Still, it explains why Joshua remembers his dad dying and was able to recognize Ben and Simon Bower.

"Imagine, if you will, Doctor, having those memories as if they were your own. Who killed that woman? Simon Bower killed her, but it feels like I did. Can you imagine what that's like?"

"No," she says, "but what you're doing now, this isn't Simon Bower, this is you."

"Simon—he wanted a different dog. He was tiring of the first one. He was going to kill her and replace her, only it didn't go to plan. The replacement fought back. When I close my eyes I can see it all. I see it the way you picture things when you read a book. She fought too hard, and he killed her. I don't just see what he saw, Doctor, but I see his intentions too. Do you know what else I saw?"

Before she can answer, he carries on.

"I saw the policeman kill him in an act of revenge. And that thing about intent . . . I know the two detectives planned on killing the person responsible for cutting that new dog into pieces. How many?"

"How many what?"

"How many others are there with these same dreams? How many organs got transplanted from Simon Bower?"

"I don't know," she says, but she does know.

"For me to have the memories of two different people . . . Well . . . tell me, Doctor, when did you figure out the mistake?"

She doesn't answer him. The mistake is something she's recently begun to suspect.

"Are you going to deny my eyes came from two different people?"

"It's called heterochromia," she says. "At least, that's what I put it down to. Or wanted to."

She tells him she noticed it during an exam last week. It was so fractional she almost missed it. The fact is, people can have different-colored eyes—heterochromia. People can have one green, one brown, they can have slightly different shades. She assumed the difference in shade was a condition Simon Bower had. Then she saw the same thing with Joshua. She suspected it, she just didn't see how it was possible. Mistakes like that don't happen.

Only, mistakes happen all the time.

"And you did nothing," Dustin says, "because you knew it would open up a lawsuit if you did. You knew people would look into where the eyes came from, and it might lead to you being found out."

"Yes," she says.

"So rather than be a good doctor, you decided to cover it up."

"I'm sorry," she says.

"I bumped into Joshua outside the hospital. It was the day my bandages came off. He was with his mom. I was walking with a cane because my balance was off after getting my sight back, and he knocked me over in his wheelchair. When I got up, I saw this was the kid from my dreams. I didn't know right away that's who he was, but I knew I'd seen him, I just couldn't figure out from where. That came later. He wasn't in the dreams with the blood, though. He was in the background, not really doing anything, like I was looking at a portrait of him. Then I kept seeing his face all over the place—in magazines, on the Internet. How?" he asks. "How did this happen?"

"There was a mix-up."

"Of course there was a mix-up," he says. "But I want you to tell me how there was one."

"I don't know," she says.

"That's not a great answer," he says.

"Somewhere between them being removed from the bodies and delivered to the operating rooms they were switched up somehow."

"That's a marginally better answer," he says, "but still not a great one."

"I don't know, not for sure." She changes subjects. "You saved Joshua yesterday."

"Yes."

"Why?"

"Because of the dreams, Doctor. Because of the way they make me feel."

"I don't understand."

He keeps staring ahead as he talks. The rain is getting heavier, and he has to speed up the wipers. "I couldn't let him die out there. He'd have stayed at the crime scene for hours, his body decomposing while you all tried to figure out what happened, and that would be no good to me."

"No good to you?"

"You've got another surgery to perform, Doctor. I want that boy's eyes, and you're going to get them for me."

"Wait . . . what?"

"You heard me, Doctor."

"You want me to operate on you?"

"I want that other eye, Doctor."

"Impossible," she says.

"Nothing is impossible if you have the right motivation. You do what I ask, and you get to live."

"It's not possible."

"It is possible. You refuse, and I kill you and everybody you love."

"There is nobody I love," she says, and it's true. She never got over Ben leaving her. She never got over Jesse dying. She doesn't have any family left.

"Then I'll choose an innocent bystander, perhaps one of your former patients."

"I'm not going to help you," she says. "If you're going to kill me, you may as well get it over with."

"Okay," he says, and the speed at which he answers surprises her.

He continues to drive. They say nothing for a minute.

"You don't really have to kill me," she says, breaking the silence. "You could let me go."

"I have no reason to let you go," he says. "If you're not going to perform the surgery, then I have no reason to let you live. No reason to let Joshua live either."

"You have no reason to hurt him."

"This is on you, Doctor. Me hurting him, that's on you."

"Don't hurt him. None of this is his fault."

"I'm not hurting him because I think it's his fault. I'm hurting him because you won't help. You know, Doctor, I really should be thanking you," Dustin says.

"Why would you thank me?"

"Because I like the dreams. I've gotten used to them. I like how they make me feel. I like the new person I'm becoming. The operation opened up a whole new way of life for me—a life I used to think about back when I was blind."

"What do you mean?"

"The things I've been dreaming about, these were things I used to *fantasize* about. What you've given me is the strength to follow that up."

"Then why do you want to get rid of Simon Bower's eye and replace it?"

He laughs at that. "Oh, you misunderstand," he says. "I don't want the other eye that belonged to the cop, I want the one that belonged to Simon Bower. Having both of them will make the dreams even more intense."

"You're insane," she says.

He sighs. "I suppose, deep down, I always knew you were going to say no."

"Then why go through any of this?"

"Because I want to turn dreaming into a reality. I want to know what it's like to kill somebody, and I think it's fitting that you can be my first. In a way, it's giving you the chance to make up for all that you've done wrong."

SIXTY-SEVEN

———— ◉ ————

Joshua hits the ground outside the bedroom and closes the window behind him to stop the storm getting inside and alerting the crazy man to his presence. He struggles to stay upright as the wind pushes him in the opposite direction from where he's trying to go. When all this is over—if it's ever over—he's going to take up running, he's going to start exercising, he's going to go to the gym and he's going to be prepared for the next psychopath who enters his life. He circles the cabin and hits the road a hundred yards away, where the cabin is out of view. Already he's puffing. Already he's soaking wet.

Pinecones are hitting the ground around him. One clips his shoulder. Leaves and twigs are flying horizontal to the ground. Flakes of dirt and grit hit him in the face. The cabins were half a mile apart. How long does it take to run half a mile? Superfit athletes can do it in under two minutes. He figures they'd run it faster under life-and-death circumstances.

He reaches the spot where Olillia parked earlier. He's been running for two minutes. At this pace he guesses the fork in the road is maybe another two minutes away. If there's nobody home at the next cabin, he'll smash a window and make his way inside and use the phone. If there's no phone, he'll go to the next cabin. Or is it better to run for the motorway and flag somebody down? Somebody would have to stop, wouldn't they? And that somebody would surely have a cell phone.

He's still running and still short of the fork in the road when he sees a flash of light through the trees. It gets stronger as the road straightens out. A car is coming towards him. Hopefully it's the police. He stands in the middle of the road and waves both his hands in the air. It slows down. It comes to a stop. He can hear it now over the rain. The engine switches off but the lights stay on. He can't see into the car. It could be like one of those circus cars and have twenty clowns inside and he wouldn't know. The driver door opens and no interior light comes on. A man steps out. Joshua tries to shield his eyes from the beams that have already half-blinded him, and the half of his vision that does remain has weird colors floating through it.

"You okay?" the man asks. He closes the car door and walks towards him. He comes into focus. Joshua's eyes hurt. He doesn't think the man is a policeman. "Buddy? You okay?"

He struggles to get his breath. "I. I need. Help."

"What kind of help?" the man asks.

The guy looks familiar. Where's he seen him from? A dream? No, somewhere real, only the guy was much paler back then, and it was a few weeks ago, but he can't figure out anything more than that. "We need to call the police," Joshua says, getting his breathing under control.

"What for?"

"There's a man with a gun," Joshua says, "back at the cabin. He's going to kill somebody. We have to call for help."

"Calm down," the man says. Is it somebody from the hospital? One of the doctors or nurses? "Tell me what's happening, but a little slower this time."

Joshua doesn't tell him everything—how can he?—but he gives him some basic facts. A man has dragged a policewoman into a cabin up ahead and is threatening to kill her. He has to talk loudly to be heard over the storm, and even then sometimes he has to repeat himself, shouting as he does so. The man is soaking wet now, and he has to keep wiping the water out of his eyes. He looks athletic, like he could run ten miles or swim for an hour.

"I'm sorry, kid, but I don't have a phone."

Joshua wants to ask who doesn't have a phone these days, to which the guy would probably point his finger back at Joshua.

"Is there anybody else in the car?" he asks.

"Nobody. How far is the cabin?"

"Not far. A couple of minutes if we run."

"Then let's go take a look."

"What we need is to get hold of a phone. We should drive to the next cabin, or go out to the road and—"

"And it might already be too late," the man says. "Come on, let's go take a look."

"We can't. The guy has a gun."

"A gun?"

"Yes," Joshua says.

"I'm in the army, kid. Guns don't scare me." He walks in the direction of the cabin. After a few paces he turns back to Joshua. "You coming?"

Joshua is torn between running for the next cabin or going back to the one he's come from. He tries weighing it up—going back he at least has somebody to help him, going forward he might not find anybody else. Or he could flag somebody down, only to have the police arrive too late. And if this guy is army, then he probably knows what he's doing.

He decides to follow.

"Try to keep up kid," the man says, breaking into a jog.

"Shouldn't we take the car?"

"In this weather we'd have to have the lights on so we don't hit a tree, and then he'd see us coming."

"What exactly are we going to do?" Joshua asks.

"Army stuff," he says. "It's important you keep up."

Once again Joshua is running. Once again his heart is pumping hard and his chest hurts. The rain is thicker now, colder. He thinks he's made the wrong decision, but they'd lose even more time by turning back. The car Vega arrived in comes into the view. The trunk is still open. The boat comes into view. Then the cabin. It's dark behind all those windows, and unless the man inside has night vision, it would be impossible for him to see them in the trees. The colors that were floating in his field of vision earlier have disappeared.

"Should we sneak in around the back?" Joshua asks.

"I have a better idea," the guy says. "Let's go in the front door."

"But—"

"Keep up," the man says. "I have a plan."

The man is still moving towards the cabin, almost pushing Joshua along with him. They're only twenty yards away now. He doesn't like this. This guy is going to get them both killed. "No," he says.

"Come on, kid."

Joshua comes to a standstill. "No," he says. "This is crazy."

"You said the guy has a gun, right?"

"Exactly. We can't—"

"Yes we can," the guy says, and pulls a gun out from his jacket pocket.

Seeing the gun makes Joshua uncomfortable. It puts him even more on edge. There's something here that's not right, but he can't say what. "I think this is a bad idea. We should have gone for help."

"I have a plan," the man says. "We head to the door, you go in first and draw his fire, then I come in after you."

"Wait . . . what? What are you saying?"

"I said you go in and draw his fire, and I'll be right behind you."

"That's crazy," Joshua says. "I'll end up getting shot."

"Here's the thing," the man says, and he turns the gun so that it's pointing directly at Joshua, and Joshua goes from feeling something isn't right to feeling something is incredibly wrong. "You go in and maybe you get shot and maybe you don't, but you stay out here and you catching a bullet is a definite."

"It was you," Joshua says, remembering him now, "at the hospital. You're the guy I knocked over with my wheelchair."

"You're right," he says.

"You recognized me, but it wasn't from the newspapers, was it? It was from the dreams. You have the other set of eyes."

"I do."

"And it was you yesterday, wasn't it?" Joshua says. "You're the one who saved me."

"Guilty as charged," the man says.

"Then why are you doing this?"

"Shut up, and let's get moving," the man says.

"Are you really in the army?"

The guy laughs at him. "No, I wasn't, kid, and stop stalling for time. We've got a job to do."

The rain keeps getting into Joshua's eyes, and he has to keep wiping it away.

"Hurry up, kid. Remember, if it weren't for me yesterday, you'd be in a hundred pieces by now."

"Why save me?" he asks, "just to do this?"

"Listen, kid, I don't owe you any explanations, okay? Now cut the chitchat and let's get this done."

There's a real sense of betrayal—how can somebody who has part of his dad treat him like this? There's another flash from the sky and this time the thunder is almost immediate, the heart of the storm directly above as it moves towards the city, the thunder so loud it makes him jump, and for a second, just a brief second, he thinks he's been shot.

They exit the trees and approach the door. The ten yards become five. Then two. Then they're there, with his hand on the handle and a gun jammed into the center of his back and Olillia hopefully fifty miles away by now and the police maybe on their way—or maybe not. He has to play for time.

Slowly, he turns the handle.

Slowly, he pushes open the door and waits to be shot.

SIXTY-EIGHT

— ◉ —

Dr. Toni can't break the plastic ties. They dig into her wrists as she pulls against them, tearing skin and drawing blood. The last thing Dustin said when he exited the car was to stay low and be quiet. He said if she called out to Joshua, he would kill him. She stayed low and quiet, but not low enough that she couldn't peek over the dashboard. She felt like a coward as she sat there watching them talk, but she believed him that if she tried anything, Joshua would bear the brunt of his anger. She could see the outline of the gun in his pocket the entire time. Nobody would hear the shot over the storm.

Where they've gone, she doesn't know. She didn't even know anything was out here, other than rivers and trees, but there must be something for Joshua to be out here too. Seeing him made no sense, and still doesn't. What the hell is going on? Why would he be out here? The headlights are still on, and they light up trees and dirt and swirling leaves and swirling rain, but nothing more than that.

She can't stretch her fingers to open the door, but she thinks maybe she can get to the handle with her feet. She kicks off a shoe and twists her body as far as she can, getting her foot up to the door. It's easier than she thought, and a moment later the door opens.

And now what?

Good question. She's still attached to it, only now she's getting wet too. She needs to find something she can cut the plastic ties with. She uses her foot to pop open the glove compartment. Inside there's a box of tissues, some CDs, a pair of women's sunglasses, and a paperback. Nothing useful.

She opens the door fully and the wind gets hold of it, pulling it all the way and pulling her out in the process. Her knees bang hard into the ground. There's a flash of white as the sky lights up, and five seconds later comes the rolling thunder. She knows there's a way to figure out how far away the thunder is by counting the seconds between the flash and the rumble, but it's one of those things she's never been able to commit to memory. She gets to her feet, leans into the door, then uses her foot to pull up the lever next to the seat, making it swing forward. Balancing herself on one foot, she reaches with her other into the backseat and hooks her toes under the handle of her handbag. She settles it onto the ground outside. She uses her hips to put the seat back into place and sits down. She empties the contents of the handbag on the floor of the car and flicks through it all with her foot.

Her phone isn't in there. Dustin must have taken it out earlier. She looks through the contents for something to cut the plastic ties.

Nothing.

She looks back through the glove compartment.

Nothing.

She looks as best as she can through the car.

Nothing.

Another flash of lightning, and this time the thunder is closer.

She thinks back to the contents of the glove compartment, and the CDs she saw in there. She uses her foot to pull one out. Johnny Cash. She places it inside the doorframe of the car and apologizes to Johnny, then closes the door on it, breaking it into several pieces. She uses her toes to transfer one of the bigger pieces to her fingers. She angles it towards the plastic tie. It's not exactly a scalpel, but she wouldn't be a surgeon if she wasn't an expert with a blade.

She goes to work.

SIXTY-NINE

If there's a way to get through to him, to convince him not to hurt her, Detective Vega doesn't know what it is. She will stay calm and keep trying, because at the very least it's buying her some time. Joshua will get hold of the police and then her colleagues will save her. Soon they'll be sneaking through the woods and training sniper rifles into the cabin and, if they have to, they'll take this man down. She hopes they can take him alive. He hasn't killed anybody, and what's happening to him isn't his fault. It could be that with therapy and drugs he can go back to being the man he used to be.

Stay calm. Stay patient. Don't make him mad. Don't make him upset. Those thoughts are on a loop. The storm is in full force now, with flashes of lightning so low she keeps expecting one to turn the cabin into kindling.

Her captor is staring out the window. She doesn't even know his name, but tomorrow it will be splashed all over the papers. Every time there is another flash of lightning, she can see his reflection against the glass. With her hands in front of her, she has access to Joshua's cell phone, but for now it can stay in her pocket. If he catches her reaching for it, he'll take it off her. Maybe he'll even kill her. Of course, the other possibility is that somebody might call it, and if they do it's going to vibrate. But with the storm raging at the walls, he might not hear it if it does.

When the sky and forest light up again, Vega sees two figures moving through the trees. Both she and her captor jump when they see them. One of them is Joshua. The other person she doesn't recognize. Why didn't Joshua call the police? What was he thinking?

"Well, this is a shame," Mr. Bad says. "It means this cabin isn't as secure as I had hoped. It means maybe I can't keep a pet out here after all. I didn't even get to name you, but you know what they say, right?"

She doesn't know, but she does know he will tell her.

"It's easier to kill something that doesn't have a name."

"Don't hurt them," she says. "They've done nothing wrong. They're probably seeking shelter from the storm. All you have to do is tie them up, and then we can leave. I'll go willingly with you, whatever it is you have in mind."

"There is nowhere else."

"I have a name," she says. "It's Audrey."

"Well, Audrey, I hope it brings you comfort knowing you'll live on in my thoughts."

He turns back to the door. She reaches into her pocket and slips the phone out of the evidence bag, only to be confronted by the need for a passcode, brought about by the phone being inactive. What can she do? Well, she can crawl, but what will that do? Sneak up behind Mr. Bad and bite him on the ankles? She tries to loosen the bolts, but even with a thousand years of strength training they would be impossible to undo with only her fingertips.

The front door opens. The storm intensifies. She can see Mr. Bad's arm pointing ahead, but cannot see beyond that. He pulls the trigger without any hesitation, and no doubt he will pull it again before turning it on her.

He's probably killed one of them, and he's about to kill the other, and then he's going to kill you. You know what you have to do.

She does know.

She puts her notebook into her mouth and bites down hard before driving her feet down into the floor. The pain races through her nervous system. She knew it would be bad, that it would be the worst pain she's ever experienced, and she prepared herself for it, only there's no way she could really have prepared herself for it. It's far, far worse than anything she could have imagined. Her mouth tightens so hard her teeth are in danger of breaking, but she doesn't scream. There will be time for screaming and throwing up and passing out soon enough, if she's successful. The pain radiates up through her legs. It feels like every bone between her toes and her hips has been broken. Her knees feel like they're going to pop. Every cell in her body is screaming at her to sit back down and slide her feet off the spikes, but if she does that she's going to die. If she does that, then standing up in the first place was for nothing.

She runs for the door, hoping the ringing gunshot and the storm will mask her approach. The angle changes and she can see Mr. Bad is now pointing the gun at Joshua. Joshua has his hands up. He says something, but she can't hear what. All she can hear is the storm, and the blood pumping through her body as it carries nothing but pain with it. Her feet are stomping across the ground, the spikes widening the holes and leaving behind a trail of blood, the metal shoes banging heavily with each step.

Nobody can ever say she didn't go out fighting.

She is three paces from Mr. Bad when he hears her and pivots towards her.

She is two paces away when he takes aim at her.

One pace away when he pulls the trigger.

She slumps to the floor, different parts of her body crying out to be heard, but there is pain everywhere, she is so overloaded with it she doesn't even know where she's been shot, all she knows is she has been. She watches Mr. Bad turn towards Joshua where, behind the boy, the man who came to help is lying on the ground with a bullet hole in the center of his forehead, looking in her direction.

The pain, the disappointment of failure, the knowledge she's going to die and Joshua too, it all becomes too much for her then, and she gives in to it all and a moment later everything inside her switches off.

SEVENTY

— ◆ —

Detective Vega hits the ground clutching her chest with one hand and clutching Joshua's cell phone with the other. The man who shot her turns back towards Joshua.

Come on, Joshua thinks. *You not only have your father's eye, but Simon Bower's too. Look at the scene the way the man who killed your dad would.*

He has to be like Simon Bower.

"You killed your dog," he says, barely able to hear his own voice over the storm, over his ringing ears, over his scrambling thoughts on what to do next.

The man relaxes his grip on the gun, but just a little. "What did you say?"

"I said you killed your dog," Joshua says, trying to sound calm and collected, trying to sound like it's just another day, trying to sound how he imagines Simon Bower would sound all while trying not to throw up. He nods towards Detective Vega and does his best impersonation of someone not only older than him, but cold and crazy. "You're going to have to get another one."

"Explain yourself."

"I've been keeping a dog here," he says, "but it escaped. We were out looking for her."

The man looks unsure. "Did you find her?"

"Can I grab a drink?" Joshua asks, trying to derail this man's thoughts.

"You want a drink?"

"I'm thirsty," he says.

"No. You can't have a drink."

"Can I at least come inside?" He smiles, but surely the smile must look flat on him, like something poorly painted on. But isn't that how Simon Bower and Vincent Archer got by in society? By painting on emotions that weren't real? "This is my house, after all, so really I shouldn't be the one having to ask for permission. I need to grab a towel."

"Your cabin? I thought it belonged to Vincent Archer."

"It does, but I stay here sometimes. It's certainly more my house than it is yours."

"So who's that then?" the man asks, nodding towards the dead man on the ground.

"William," Joshua says, using the first name that comes to mind. "We stay out here sometimes. He and Vincent are friends."

The man slowly nods, perhaps taking all of it in, perhaps taking it in and not believing a single word.

"You never did say if you found your dog."

"We found her. We had to . . . put her down. We were coming back to grab a shovel, and now thanks to you I'm going to have to dig the hole by myself. I'm coming inside now," he says. "I didn't dress for this weather."

He moves forward, and the man takes a few steps back. He closes the door behind him. They both step over Vega's body and move into the lounge. He barely looks at her. He can't, because if he does it will betray his real thoughts.

"So do you want to tell me what you're doing in our cabin?" Joshua asks, and he moves to the window and looks out at the storm. Nobody is coming.

The man doesn't answer him. The sky lights up again, and when the lightning disappears, it makes the room seem even darker. Soon they won't be able to see anything at all. As it is he has to strain to see things clearly. The thunder is close enough and loud enough it vibrates through the floor.

"You shouldn't have come here," Joshua says, and turns to face him.

"You've killed my friend, and you shot your dog and got blood everywhere," he says, and he looks over to Vega, where blood is pooling beneath her feet and under her back, and she walked on the metal shoes. She's driven the spikes into her feet, and his hands are shaking so much he balls them up into fists behind his back so the man can't see. It's taking all his strength and willpower to stay standing upright, because his legs feel so weak. He thinks he can see Detective Vega's chest still rising and falling, but really it's too dark to know for sure. If she is alive, it's doubtful she will remain that way for long. He needs to find an excuse to examine her. That way he can get his phone. "Who is she?"

"She's nobody now."

"You should leave and take her with you," Joshua says. "She's your mess, not mine. I already have two bodies to bury, and I don't want my next dog seeing her."

"Your next dog?"

"I have to replace the one we put down," he says. He pauses, and then he smiles. "Actually, you know what? I think maybe we can help each other."

"How?"

"You need a new dog, and I need a new dog. I help you, and you help me. But first we need to get rid of the bodies. We should bury them. If you like, you can keep your dog out here at the cabin. There's plenty of room. We could even look at having a couple of dogs each," he says. "As many as we want."

"I could just—" There is more lightning, then more thunder, the time between them a little longer than before. "Could just kill you."

"There will be days when you can't look after the dogs when I can. Plus you owe me."

"Owe me?"

"You killed the man who was helping me."

The man nods. "I like the idea of lots of dogs," he says.

"So what do you say? Partners?" Joshua asks, and puts his hand out.

The man does nothing. Just stares at Joshua deep in thought, then after a few seconds he lowers the gun. He tucks it into the waistband of his jeans. He steps forward and puts his hand out. "Partners," he says. "My name is Gregory."

"Levi," Joshua says, and pictures the kid from yesterday who almost ran him down on his bike. Then, to reassure this guy that he's still the alpha, he defers the next option to him. "You want to bury the bodies now? Or wait till it's stopped raining?"

"You look familiar, Levi. Do I know you from somewhere?"

"I'm not sure," Joshua says. "So . . . do we bury the bodies now?"

"Let's wait till it's stopped raining."

"Then we shouldn't leave William in the doorway. I'll drag him inside."

He takes a few steps for the door, knowing Gregory will tell him to stop because it isn't just a dead man at the door, but a dead man and a gun. He's made it halfway when Gregory tells him to wait. He stops and turns around.

"I'll get him," Gregory says.

Gregory steps over Vega to get to the door, which gives Joshua the chance he needs. He crouches down and takes his phone out of Vega's hand. He enters his security code. He dials 111 and turns the volume down low and slides the phone into his pocket.

"What are you doing?" Gregory asks.

Gregory has stepped back into the lounge and is staring at him. He now has two guns.

"Nothing."

"It doesn't look like nothing. It looks like you were trying to make a call. Whose phone is that?"

"It was in the dead woman's hand," he says, trying to give detail to whoever answers the phone. "I was putting it into my pocket so it wouldn't get left behind."

"You're lying," Gregory says.

"It's true. I was turning it off so nobody could trace it. The police might figure out she's missing, and they might use it to figure out where she is."

"Have you been lying to me all along?"

"I'm not lying."

"She didn't have a phone on her, because I took it off her earlier."

"It was in her hand," he says. "I promise you."

"No. It wasn't. I think it's your phone."

Joshua can feel the tension in the room rising. "It was in her hand," he says. "I was turning it off."

"Then show me."

"What?"

"Show me the phone and how it's switched off. It really is a simple request, Levi. Hand it over. Keep in mind, if you're lying, you're dying."

He reaches for his pocket.

"No," Gregory says. "I'll get it. Put your hands up."

"But—"

"I said put them up, Levi."

He puts them up. While keeping a gun pointed at him and the other tucked under his arm, Gregory reaches into Joshua's pocket for the phone. He tries to think of something to say or do, but can't come up with anything. Seeing the world from his dad's or Simon Bower's points of view doesn't help.

There's another flash of lightning, and a moment later the window smashes inwards, glass spraying into the room. Gregory takes his fingers off the cell phone and turns the gun towards the broken window and fires four shots through it, the thunder sounding like a fifth. Joshua can't believe his luck, and takes the chance to reach into his pocket and hold down the power button. With the window gone, the curtains billow into the room. Rain starts coming in. Gregory bends down and picks up the broken branch that came through the window. The storm must have torn it from a tree and thrown it at the cabin. Joshua is relieved it happened, but disappointed it was only a branch, and not the police opening fire.

Gregory tosses the branch aside, then takes the phone out of Joshua's pocket. He looks at the display. He taps at it, getting nothing.

"I'm sorry I doubted you," Gregory says.

"We should bring William inside," Joshua says. He wonders how far away the police are. Wonders how much they heard. Did they listen, or hang up? Is Detective Vega dead or alive?

They reach the door. Gregory watches him, but Joshua doesn't have the strength to move the dead man. He considers running for it. If he can get a head start, he'll be difficult to find. That's if he can get a head start. Even if he can, that isn't going to help Detective Vega.

Gregory moves ahead of him so he's closer to the door and helps him with the body. They dump him on the floor inside the doorway, and when Joshua straightens himself up Gregory is pointing the gun back at him. "You said the dead woman," he says.

"What?"

"You said the phone was in the dead woman's hand, not the dead dog's hand. Everything you've been saying—I have to be honest, son, but it feels like you're playing me for the fool. I think it's best we part ways. You made a good effort, you really did, and I'm never going to be sure one way or the other about you. This is for the best. At least the best for me."

"I've been having the dreams too," Joshua says.

"What?"

"The dreams of blood."

"How do you know about my dreams?"

"I had an operation. I received a kidney," he says, because if he says *eyes* he knows this man will figure out who he is.

"When?"

"Three weeks ago, almost four."

"No, no, that's not right. I know where I recognize you from. You're the kid that's been in the news a lot."

"None of that matters," Joshua says. "All that matters is we have the same desires, and if—"

"Small world how we both ended up out here," Gregory says. "Too small for both of—" he says, but then he stops talking. He stares at Joshua as if confused by all of it, the operations, the dreams, confused by why he's out here. He lowers his gun. Then his body sags. A moment later he hits the ground.

Standing behind him soaked to the bone in the doorway and holding a tire iron is Dr. Toni.

SEVENTY-ONE

───── ◉ ─────

While Dr. Toni goes to work on Detective Vega, Joshua pats down Gregory, finding the handcuff keys in his left jacket pocket. He uses them to remove the cuffs from Vega and puts them on Gregory. He asks Dr. Toni where she came from, but she tells him there'll be time to explain later.

"The branch. You threw that through the window?"

"Yes," she says, "now find a phone and call for help."

He finds his phone and he calls for an ambulance and the police and tells them they need to hurry. He's told there are already police on the way to his location, and an ambulance too. They tell him Olillia called, and that she and Ruby are at the hospital, and that they heard his call a few minutes earlier. He tells them to hurry, and they tell him to stay on the line.

Dr. Toni is leaning over Detective Vega, but it's too dark for him to see clearly. "What can I do?" he asks her.

"Find something to loosen the bolts on those shoes."

He leaves the phone on the floor. He finds a light switch. The cabin lights up and hurts his eyes. He retrieves the box wrenches from the utility room. In the light he can see how bad Vega looks. Her skin has gone gray. There's blood everywhere. Dr. Toni is applying pressure to the wound in her chest.

"Is she even still alive?" he asks.

"Barely."

He loosens the bolts.

"Leave the shoes on for the paramedics," she says. "If you pull them out, it might speed up the amount of blood coming out of her feet. Can you drive?" she asks.

"No."

"I came in the same car you waved down," she says. "You're going to have to move it so the ambulance can get past."

"I don't know how."

"You're going to have to figure it out. Please, hurry."

He gets the keys out of the other man's pocket. He runs out into the storm. The wind pushes at him. Once again he finds himself running. He keeps running until he reaches the car. He gets behind the steering wheel and is upset to find the car has a manual gear stick. He turns the key and the car lurches forward, almost throwing him into the steering wheel as the engine dies. The same thing happens when he tries it again. He presses down on the pedals and when he pushes on the left one and tries starting the car, it doesn't lurch, and when he slowly pulls his foot away the car rolls, but then lurches again and the engine stalls.

This is useless, he thinks. If Olillia were here, she'd be able to do it.

Behind him, the flashing lights of an approaching police car.

He gets out and waves his hands, not that they could have driven past anyway. The police officers step out of the car.

"I'm Joshua Logan," he says. "I'm the one who called."

"Whose car is that?" one of the officers asks.

"It belongs to one of the dead men. Detective Vega has been shot. We have to get to the cabin."

"It's up ahead?" the other officer asks.

"Yes."

"Get into the passenger side," the officer says, then the officer gets in behind the wheel and drives.

It doesn't take long for both cars to get there. Not even half a minute. Joshua explains quickly about the situation they'll be driving into. Dr. Toni is still on the floor when they get there, still applying pressure to Detective Vega.

"We're losing her," she says.

The police officers quickly do what they can to help as Joshua stands back and watches. The storm continues to rage on outside, and somewhere out there is an ambulance making its way through it—he doesn't see it getting here on time.

He looks down at Gregory. There's a huge dent in the side of his skull that wasn't there a few minutes ago. There's a pool of blood that also wasn't there. He looks at his phone and sees that the call to the police department has been disconnected.

Dr. Toni has done what he imagines his dad would have done.

And he's not real sure how he feels about that.

EPILOGUE

——— ◆ ———

The storm that hit the region on Tuesday lasted two days, and let up only last night. It tore through the city, ripping branches from trees and damaging houses; it pulled a roof partway off a supermarket and was the catalyst for dozens of fender benders. This morning, though, it's all blue skies in every direction, which makes it hard for Joshua to believe the weather was so bad. But in its place came autumn. It couldn't be any more evident out here in the cemetery where Joshua and Olillia are standing in the trees fifty yards back from the graveside holding hands, out of earshot of the funeral. The ground is awash with leaves, the winds and the cold have stripped the trees bare, and he remembers thinking recently how autumn could be a beautiful mess—whereas now it just looks like a mess.

Joshua's mom opted out—not only did she not want to come, but she didn't want Joshua to go either. Neither of them would be welcome there, so she thought, and he had to agree—which is why he's standing fifty yards back. The media are here, of course, hanging out on the fringes getting footage as they try connecting the dots between those who died and those who killed, and as they question what made two mild-mannered men with no history of violence act in such violent ways.

Joshua is struggling to come to terms with what his dad and his uncle were doing. It's been a difficult few days, but his mom and Olillia have been helping him. To suddenly learn your dad is a serial killer . . . It's a crass label, but the sad truth is it's also an accurate one. His dad was killing people, and even though they were bad people and he was doing it to help those who were good, it still makes him a serial killer.

Perhaps when Uncle Ben is out of the hospital, Joshua can talk to him about it, and perhaps he can find a way to make peace with it. The media haven't made the connection between Gregory King and Dustin Moore and the fact that they were both organ recipients, but Joshua suspects it's only a matter of time. These men had been sick, and they were cured, only to have the cure make them a different kind of sick. If investigators do make the connection, they may also link it to what his dad and Uncle Ben were doing. He isn't sure if Detective Vega will say anything. He doesn't think so, though he hasn't gone to the hospital to see her yet. With each passing day, Joshua thinks it's becoming more likely she won't report Uncle Ben to their superiors.

He loved his father—still does—and misses him greatly. He can't help be angry that his dad brought his own death upon himself. If he and Uncle Ben hadn't gone to kill Simon Bower that day, then none of this would have happened.

Joshua and Olillia have been praised for saving Ruby Carter, but they've also been thoroughly reprimanded for placing themselves in such danger. Other than school and the funeral, he's been grounded for a month, as has Olillia. He suspects charges won't be laid against them. He knows Detective Vega has put in a good word for them, and he knows their story has been the headline all week, blasted out on all forms of media—there's no way the police could charge the teenagers who found Ruby Carter and not have a riot on their hands.

Yesterday, Dr. Toni came to see him. He didn't ask her what happened while he was outside the cabin trying to move her car. She came to tell him that Ruby is recovering well. Other than her severed finger, most of her wounds are psychological. She's remaining positive too. She knows there are worse things Simon and Vincent could have done to her. Both Joshua and Olillia would like to see her again, and Dr. Toni suspected Ruby would like that too.

The funeral ends. Vincent Archer's body is lowered into the ground. The small crowd consists of family—Vincent's parents, his brother, even his niece. There have been photographs of them all over the news. Vincent's mom turned him in to the police, but even so, thousands of people have gone online to write comments, calling her the worst things imaginable. None of the Archers are showing any emotion right now. After what they've been through, they probably want to at least have some semblance of control over their feelings. The only sign of life is coming from the little girl, who looks like she's just itching to run around and chase the leaves, anything to get way from the circle of sadness that is her family. The funeral ends and Vincent's dad throws a flower into the grave but no one else does, and then they walk away.

Joshua can't rightly say why he's here. It was more a feeling that he needed to be, and he suspects the urge came from the DNA in his body that once belonged to Simon Bower. He thought about asking Dr. Toni to remove the eye, but he's decided to keep it. The same way some people wear scars to remind them of something in their lives, he's going to keep the eye to remind him of what his father did. Olillia told him he's only punishing himself by thinking that way, and he suspects she's right—but he's still going to keep it.

When the curse came for Joshua, it took Vincent instead, but he knows it's still out there waiting for him. He knows this because of what Dr. Toni came to tell him yesterday.

Joshua and Olillia turn around and switch hands and head back to the parking lot.

As they drive away from the cemetery, he thinks about that conversation. Dr. Toni told him it wasn't just him and Dustin and Gregory who received new organs that day, thanks to his father's benevolent execution.

There are six other patients with organs from Simon Bower out there who could be having weird dreams of their own.

ACKNOWLEDGMENTS

A *Killer Harvest* has been a different outing for me—but boy, have I enjoyed it! Five or six years ago, I was having lunch with Tim Müller, my friend and German editor, and another buddy, Craig Sisterson, who has done more than anybody to put New Zealand crime fiction on the world map. We were at a Crime Writing festival in the UK. I can't remember what we were chatting about when Tim asked, "Have you ever considered writing a young adult novel?" to which I said, "No," to which Craig said, "You should really think about it," to which I said, "It's not my thing," to which I then followed up with, "But, if I were to write one . . . maybe I could write it about a boy who is blind from birth and gets his father's eyes after his dad is killed chasing a serial killer. Wait . . . wait . . . what if he had one eye from his father and one from the killer?" Just like that, completely out of thin air, this novel came to be. Often that's the way.

I wrote a few chapters and then shelved the idea for years to work on other books back then. It was in 2015 when I was hanging out in Sydney with my US editor, Sarah Branham, that the book became "unshelved." I told her about it, and she said, "Write it." So I wrote it—my very first young adult novel. I remember later that year I was hanging out with the folks at Atria in New York and telling them how the book had turned out . . . and everybody kept saying, "Hmm . . . that may not be young adult, but adult . . ." It turned out they were right.

A *Killer Harvest* exists firstly because of that lunch all those years ago, but it also exists because of the team at Atria in New York, who convinced me to go ahead and write it—and I'm so glad they did. We put in a lot of work on this thing—and I couldn't be more proud of the result. Sarah got me thinking in so many directions, my head was spinning by the end of the editing process. This was my last book with Sarah—we had ten together—and now I'm working with another very cool editor, Rakesh Satyal, on the next novel, and he's got me thinking in all those same directions too. Judith Curr, David Brown, Lisa Keim, Emily Bestler, Haley Weaver, Hillary Tisman, Loan Le, and all the others—thank you once again for giving my books a home.

Let me sign off once again by thanking you, the reader. You guys have been brilliant. You guys are the reason I like to make bad things happen . . .

Paul Cleave
March 2017
Christchurch, New Zealand